RELAY PUBLISHING EDITION,
NOVEMBER 2019
Copyright © 2019 Relay Publishing Ltd.

Jo Crow is a pen name created by Relay Publishing for co-authored Psychological Thriller projects. Relay Publishing works with incredible teams of writers and editors to collaboratively create the very best stories for our readers.

www.relaypub.com

A MOTHER'S SINS

A NOVEL

JO CROW

BLURB

Burying the past only delays the inevitable.

Sarah Cartwright is on the cusp of having it all—a new baby, a devoted partner, and a great job as a political campaign director. However, Sarah's return to the office after maternity leave finds her powerful position assigned to someone else, and Sarah didn't work hard for years just so she could observe from the sidelines.

As her dreams threaten to crash and burn around her, the lies she's built her life upon are exposed. Smears that put her entire career on the brink are splashed across news headlines, and caught between a new boss, backstabbing co-workers, and a wary partner, Sarah can't be certain who to trust.

When bodies start to drop and the police show up on her doorstep, the past can no longer stay hidden.

All sins are punished one day.

CONTENTS

PROLOGUE

The woman felt as if her body had been run over, violently gutted. She'd pictured this moment, imagined how it should have felt to finally be able to move past this trial, to go through the pain and then move forward with the rest of her life, but lying there under the florescent hospital lights, she felt so much emptier than she'd anticipated. Ten hours of labor, vomiting from the medicine, trying to find the strength to not give up – and she'd have lived through it all again if it meant she could make a different choice. She wanted to rewind. Rewind everything. She'd do the labor again, the prodding doctor and the needles. The months of doctor's visits and the morning sickness.

She'd do it all again if she could just find some way to avoid what she had to do next.

Behind the curtain, the doctor was taking measurements of a wriggling newborn. Her baby.

I want her, she thought.

She'd asked and asked for the baby, but the staff seemed deaf to her.

The nurses didn't understand. To them, this was a job. There were a dozen other newborns waiting for them in other rooms. They were coolly removed from the process, eyes flat and feet moving and tapping across the floor. She knew there were other babies to attend to, some of them who needed more care than others. But this one was hers, a perfect and healthy baby.

"We're just cleaning her up," a nurse snapped dismissively at her from behind the curtain. The woman, alone, wondered whether the nurses treated every mother this way, or whether she may somehow be projecting her guilt, imagining them judging her without knowing the whole story. None of them would look her in the eye.

"Can I hold her?" Tears pricked the woman's eyes, blurring her vision. "Can I please hold her?"

One of the three nurses, stout and gray-haired, finally took pity.

She stepped over from behind the curtain where the baby was shrieking and placed a hand on the woman's naked shoulder. Her hospital gown was raised to just below her swollen breasts, the sleeves slouched down to her upper arms.

"Are you sure that's what you want?" The nurse, wisdom in the wrinkled flesh around her eyes, was searching the mother's face. "That can be difficult. To see her and hold her, before you ..."

"Please," the woman answered, reaching out her arms. "Let me hold her."

The mother felt her resolve melting, so she forced herself to recount the reasons why she couldn't take her baby home. *I can't possibly bring her home. There's no nursery, no crib, no father. I can't do this alone and she doesn't deserve the kind of life I can give her: the child of a struggling single mother.*

For the thousandth time, she silently cursed the man who put her there. The man who was nowhere to be seen. The man who was too afraid of the "implications" or of what it would cost him to embrace, or even acknowledge, his own daughter. He was never afraid of those implications before, when the woman first caught his eye, or later when they were lovers. He'd sworn he'd never in his life felt like this; he'd promised he was going to change everything to be with her. Well, everything had changed. He left her. He left her to make a choice, alone, and she had. Her daughter would have everything that the woman couldn't give her.

"Ma'am?" The one kind nurse was asking the woman about the very thing she'd never want to talk about again.

"I just need the father's name." She whispered it, as if to shield the lonely mother from embarrassment, even though her legs were still splayed apart and her heart was smashed to pieces. Still, the woman hesitated.

"It's just part of the paperwork," the nurse prompted.

But she'd never utter his name.

"I'm ..." The woman embraced the role the medical team had assigned her, that of a woman who'd clearly made one poor decision after another. "I don't know, to be honest. I can't say for sure ... who the father is."

The nurse pursed her lips and scribbled something on the paper in front of her, a birth certificate. The line for the name stayed empty. Behind her, another nurse was finally emerging from the curtain, a wrapped infant in her arms. The woman's vision closed in to the bundle coming closer, instantly forgetting all else. Then she felt the baby's weight, welcome and reassuring, in the crook of her arm.

Her tiny red face. Lips in a perfect pout. Eyes slick from medicine, but awake and aware. The baby girl craned her neck to see her mother looking down at her. The mother fell in love, in a single heartbeat.

"You did a good job," a voice, the nurse, said softly. "She's in great shape, an even nine pounds."

In silence, the woman loosened the blanket that had the baby pinned in position. She wanted to see her precious hands and fingers. She suddenly wanted to inspect every part of her, record it in her memory. The infant daughter reached out to her mother's index finger, holding on tight. *She wants me, too*, the mother thought. *You'll never know it, but I love you. I love you with all my being.*

"Ma'am, can you –"

"Not yet," the mother interrupted the nurse, thinking there was no way she could let go. "Not yet."

The nurse cleared her throat.

The woman wished with all her heart that she could just give her something, some tie to connect her to her real family.

"I want to give her her name." She looked, pleading, to the nurse with the clipboard. "I can't give her a father, but I can at least give her a name."

The nurse waivered.

"Please," she whispered. "Please let me do this one thing."

The nurse, thinking it was harmless, shrugged and smiled with a touch of compassion. She clicked her pen, ready. "Go ahead, then. I can't promise the new parents won't change it, but go ahead."

The woman studied the baby's contented expression. She could see her own mother in the infant's brow, her wide-set eyes.

"Her name is Sarah."

Sarah, I want to hold you for a lifetime, the mother almost whispered. *I want to give you everything.*

She kissed the little fingers. She kissed that beautiful, soft brow. She breathed in the warmth of her velvety baby skin.

And then came the moment she could never prepare herself for. It took all the nurses gathering around her bed to do it, to pull the baby away as the mother begged them not to, to please wait. *I've lost everything*, the mother thought, guilt closing in around her, suffocating. *No, I didn't lose everything. I gave it all up myself.*

1

NOW

A swirl of nerves have made my stomach queasy and my heart is fluttering like I'm headed into my first day of work, ever. I have to keep reminding myself I'm not. I've done this before. I know I can do it again. The oatmeal in my bowl, which seemed like a sensible idea when I was planning my smooth return to work, is unappetizing. I eat it anyway, if only to stick to my plan. Besides, I'll need my strength.

Cradled in the detachable car seat near my feet, Gracie's all ready to go to the babysitter. She hasn't picked up on my anxious energy as I force down another spoonful of maple-flavored oats.

"You added too much milk, sweetie." Brad glances at my bowl. "Want me to make you some eggs instead?"

"No thanks, babe." I empty the remaining half of my breakfast into the garbage. "I'm not that hungry."

"Nerves?" Brad tilts his head hopefully.

"Nope," I lie.

"You know," he ventures, "you really don't have to go back just yet. It's only been three months."

Precious Gracie chimes in with a happy gurgle at her father's voice. Daddy's girl.

I repress my frustration and try to stay cheerful, for both of them. Today is not the day to fight this battle yet again.

"Come on, Brad, we've been through this. At this point, I've already been out of the loop three months too many." I straighten the dark pantsuit I had to buy to accommodate my still-soft stomach. It's an in-between outfit.

"And there haven't been any disasters without you," Brad says, with an immediate gulp, and I know he's praying I won't take offense. "They need you, of course —"

"I can't do it from home," I object before he's had the chance to make the work-from-home suggestion for the umpteenth time. "I need to be boots-on-the-ground." I turn to Gracie to lighten the mood, maybe to avoid Brad's disappointed face. "I *want* to be here, with you two. My favorite people in the world. But Tennessee needs a new governor."

The state needs my guy in charge, and I've got to put him there. If I don't take this chance now, I may never get another opportunity to make an impact like this. This career step, a gubernatorial race, took years of work, building up from smaller races. I put in too much to get where I am to let it go to waste now. I left the job, temporarily, in the capable hands of my assistant, and mapped out my return for exactly three months after the baby. If I wait, stay a little longer with Gracie, it would leave room for someone else to step in as campaign manager until the race is over and my opportunity would be gone. No, we're so close. I'll be getting back for the critical final six weeks before the General Election. This is my window, my moment. Besides that, my paid leave is up. As much as I want to think I have a choice in the matter, sometimes practical considerations decide for you.

I slide a briefcase strap over one shoulder, grab the handle of Gracie's car seat with the opposite hand, and lean into Brad for a quick kiss. He tastes like coffee.

"Everything is going to work out just fine, babe," I say.

He stops me. I get one more coffee kiss, slower this time.

"I'm proud of you, Sarah," he says, and I let myself relax in the comfort of his affection, the reassuring glow in his blue-gray eyes that always gets to me. "You're amazing in every way. You've got this."

Fifteen minutes early, I pull up to the strip mall retrofitted for campaign headquarters, as noted by the giant "William A. Porter for Governor" banner covering two former storefront signs. The drive-up retail stores and offices that once flourished were shuttered a few years ago as McMinnville's housing developers built flashy new "walkable" retail connected to luxury residential developments for one of Nashville's hottest bedroom communities. To anybody who wasn't already rooting for the local guy, it was a bit of a selling point that William A. Porter, the city's best-known politician and former mayor, would choose to fill empty storefronts with a bustling campaign.

I've prepared myself in every possible way for this moment, down to the box of donut shop coffee I always bring to share, but I give one more glance in the rearview. My makeup has done a good job of masking my lack of sleep. I feel good physically. The Pilates has helped with my energy levels, and I'm working my way back to my pre-baby body. One more deep breath and then a swap to my lucky nude pumps to give me my final boost of confidence. I'm ready.

It's a quarter to nine and the office is already humming with activity. Phones are ringing. Volunteers are packing pin-on buttons and other Porter swag into boxes. A cluster of four or five cubicles run down both sides of the front room and a huge TV on the back wall is set to the local news station, there's an American flag hung on one side and Tennessee's three-starred flag on the other. Other young volunteers, ready to make Tennessee blue, are already making calls from their cubicles. A familiar face, our grandmotherly office manager, in a "Vote Porter" T-shirt, gives me a surprised smile.

"Well, now. Sarah Cartwright." She seems to recover and stands to give me a tight squeeze. "Nice to see you walk through the door today."

"You, too, Mary Beth." I move to put my box of coffee on a table behind her desk, but see someone's already stocked up.

"What brings you in today? You look great, by the way."

Before I can answer, I hear Bill shout my name from his open office door in the back. He moves quickly toward me, holding out a coffee mug cautiously as he gives me a half hug with his other shoulder. Then he looks around me, slightly confused.

"Where's the baby?"

"Gracie?" I realize how silly it sounds. What other baby could he mean? "Yeah. She's with the sitter."

"Oh." Bill makes the expression I've warned him not to, the one he makes when he's a little unsure how to start a difficult response. But he shakes it off. "Well, we're glad to see you."

"I called." I grip my briefcase closer to my body. "I left a few messages to remind you that I'd be in today, as scheduled."

"Oh ... yeah." Bill waves me back toward his office. "I thought you meant you'd be bringing the little one in. You look fantastic. Doesn't seem like you've been gone too long. What? A couple months?"

"Three."

"Ah. Maternity leave." Bill holds his door for me. "Should be longer. Places that are more progressive offer six months. I'd like to see legislation that makes it easier for families to be families. Better maternity leave."

"Paternity leave, too," I offer.

"Certainly." Bill takes the seat behind a long maple desk, the nicest in the office. He glances toward me expectantly, so I take advantage of the moment and start right in.

"I've been thinking, it's so easy for us to get caught in Nashville's growing pains and getting people here excited. Our ads lately are focused on taking advantage of that and making sure the surrounding rural communities benefit, too. But Nashville and the immediate countryside only get us so far. I know we're strong when it comes to addressing rural poverty, but I still think we can do better with that out east. If we could make a serious impact with leaders in those counties, really hit Gatlinburg and Knoxville strong. I mean, there are a lot of working families out there, a lot of young people especially, who are more open to policies that provide more opportunities. I think we're misguided to write those off as im –"

"Did you see the first debate?" Bill cocks one eyebrow and heaves a deep breath into his barrel chest.

"I did," I answer, a hint of irritation making my words sharper than I mean them. "You came off as compassionate … but firm on change. Burtner was less likeable, I thought. But he did touch on –"

"We talked about revitalization efforts for Memphis. Jobs."

"I know. I think you're preaching to the choir there, though. We won't have a problem with Memphis, or Nashville. I want to make sure we're not assuming we haven't got a shot, at least among younger voters, in our eastern counties. I'd asked Helene to spearhead that when I was leaving. How's she doing?"

"Helene?" Bill thinks for a second and then remembers. "Oh yeah. Gone."

"What?"

"Listen, she had big shoes to fill."

"No patronizing, please." *I knew I should have stayed more closely connected.* "What happened?"

"Just didn't think she could do it without you." Bill shrugged. "I thought she gave you a call about that. She quit. More than a month ago, I think."

"No one told me anything."

"We had to move forward. We had no choice."

"Wait. What?" I can feel my cool slipping away. "What did you do?"

"Well." Bill leans back and crosses his arms. "We had to hire someone."

"As my assistant?" It was all I could do to stay seated. "Without asking me what I thought, you hired a new assistant campaign manager?"

"Not exactly." Bill clears his throat and gives me his politician's grin. "I want you to meet someone."

I wait and try to stop the spinning in my head as Bill steps out of his office. *I've been here ten minutes and it's a train wreck. I can't be a train wreck, too. I can fix this, whatever it is.*

"Sarah, I'd like you to meet Janette Freeman ..." Bill returns, holding the door open behind him. "Our new campaign manager."

My head cocks automatically. "My new *assistant* campaign manager?"

Bill shakes his head. "Nope," he says, firmly. "We've brought her on to – to run our campaign."

I'm stunned, but I find my way to my feet and force a smile. *Hello, Janette, who took my job without anyone asking me. Nice of Bill to not have the guts to tell me before he throws me in front of you. He seemed squirrely. And I've got to seem like I've got myself together.*

"Nice to meet you, Janette," I hear myself say.

She had to know this was a surprise, unless Bill had played it all off like I knew. Even if she thought I already knew about her, she could have reserved some of her enthusiasm. She grabbed my outstretched hand with both of hers and clasped it, a smile of delight that she couldn't seem to tame.

"Oh my god." She's still holding my hand. "Sarah, I can't tell you how much I've been looking forward to meeting you." Finally, she lets go. "I've heard so many amazing things about you. And the work you've done to get this campaign off the ground! I mean, there's no way we'd be where we are without your work. Did you see the latest poll?" She doesn't wait for an answer. "Of course you did. You're Sarah Cartwright. You don't miss a thing."

I'm still numb from surprise, but I make my best attempt at a smile and resist the urge to fall back into my chair. My replacement is standing in front of me. My worst fear about having a child is coming true, immediately. This woman even looks like me in a generic way, even down to the navy suit. Maybe a couple of years older, and right now looking a whole lot happier than I feel. And I'm supposed to look her in the eye and be friendly? Instead, I glower at Bill, still standing next to her like he's got something to show off.

To her credit, Janette notices either the silence or my dagger eyes and politely excuses herself.

"I – I've got to check on that press release we talked about." She touches Bill's shoulder and lets her hand linger an instant too long. There's some message she's trying to get across to him with her gaze, and I suddenly feel like a third wheel. I'm not sure what's going on between them, but her gesture feels a little overboard.

"Check back with you soon. Sarah." Janette turns to me suddenly and smiles. "Welcome back to the front lines."

I look immediately to Bill for an explanation, but see he's watching every step of Janette's slow exit until the door clicks closed.

"What the hell is this? What's going on? Why hasn't anyone talked to me? Who is this woman?"

Bill is shaking his head. "Sit down."

"No. You made this woman campaign manager. You gave her my job. And now I'm back – and somehow she's keeping my job?"

He shrugs like there's nothing he can do.

"You can't just do this."

"We didn't *just* do it," he says, resolute now when he tells me to sit. "We didn't want to replace you. No one can do that."

"Except you did." I cross my arms over my chest, still standing.

"We had no other option. Helene left. You were ..." he gestures vaguely toward my stomach. "Busy. And I understand. Family first. But, for us, we have to put the campaign first. We were without a manager for the final stretch of the campaign. I didn't want to bother you and we couldn't afford to wait."

"You should have called me."

"Listen, I don't love this situation, but it was something that had to be done." Bill took his seat at the desk. "I know how much you care. But we needed someone fast. Someone who could be here, on the ground, finishing the good work you started. It's no more complicated than that."

"What are her qualifications?" I don't want to pace, but I am. I dig in my purse for a mint, wishing I could have had even five minutes to prepare myself for this.

"Impressive," Bill answers, a little smug. "She's not you, Sarah, but she's done a really good job with what you left behind."

Left behind? My head is spinning again. This is the worst possible return I could have imagined. No job. Maybe no career. My thoughts are spiraling to the worst, to years ahead, as a woman – a mother – in a dead-end job that has nothing to do with change-making or campaign-leading. The worst part is that I *knew* this would happen. I knew it from the moment I found out I was pregnant. I knew it when Brad was encouraging me to keep "our baby," when everyone close to me was promising they'd be supportive.

Bill clears his throat impatiently.

"There's still plenty of work to do, though, Sarah. I know this is a shock to you, and I'm sorry for that. We should have let you know about the change."

"Yes." I glower. "Yes, you should have! You definitely should have told me you were going to freaking fire me."

"I didn't say we are firing you," Bill answers swiftly. "What I'm trying to say is I hope you'll stick with it."

"If this is some pep talk, I don't need it."

"I don't do pep talks. This is a job offer. The assistant campaign manager position is still open. We still want you here. No one else knows this like you do."

"Well, why not just bring me back as planned, then?" I wait for him to answer, but he doesn't. "Have you talked to HR about this? Is it even fair, or legal, to replace someone on maternity leave?"

Bill looks like he'd been expecting that question: "You were not replaced *because* you were on maternity leave. We were forced to do some restructuring at a critical time in the campaign. We certainly aren't leaving you without options. We want you here."

"Then why not bring me back as campaign manager and make Janelle the assistant?"

"It's Janette. And it's too late in the game to be making those kinds of changes," Bill answers, curt. "I won't do that to her."

But you had no problem doing it to me.

"Hours would be easier. The pay is a little bit of a drop, but nothing drastic. You'll keep your benefits and have more flexibility. I just think it would work better with ... where you are right now."

Backed into a corner is where I am right now. At this second, I'd like nothing more than to storm out of here and never think of the William A. Porter for Governor campaign again, ever. But I know I couldn't do that if I tried. This was supposed to be my moment. I've worked for years to get to where I am, or where I was before having Gracie. If I left the campaign right now, I'd be the mom who couldn't stand to leave her baby, the woman who backed out for "other priorities." If I'd just had time to prepare for this, I'd know what to do.

But there's no more time. Bill is out of patience. He's tapping one fancy leather shoe against the carpet. He doesn't have to say *take it or leave it*. I can read it on his face.

"Okay."

"Okay, you'll do it?" Bill looks a little surprised. Had he not expected a yes?

I nod.

"There we go," he says. One quick phone call, and Janette is standing before me again, beaming the way she did the first time. The woman cannot stop smiling. *I could use a little bit of whatever she's on.*

"Janette, I'd like you to meet your new assistant campaign manager."

Janette gasps and presses a hand over her chest.

I grin half-heartedly and muster up the best response I can at that moment: "I'm looking forward to working with you."

"I just can't believe I'm going to get to work with you," Janette says, and she actually hugs me, not losing a drop of enthusiasm when I stay stiff under her grasp. "This is such an honor. I can't tell you how much I hoped this would happen."

"Ready to get to work," I say, starting to regain my composure. It may not be the back-to-work day I'd imagined, but at least it's not a completely closed door. I'll just have to work twice as hard as before. And I worked damn hard then.

2

THEN

Mommy's still not home.

I've been watching the door for the past hour. Gram said it would be soon, that I would see her and Daddy, and the baby that was in Mommy's tummy.

"How much longer?"

My grandmother huffs.

"It should be any minute. Are you sure you don't want to come and watch a movie while you wait?"

"Yup." I'm already in my favorite pajamas with the yellow duckies. I hope he'll like them.

"Gram?"

"Yes, Sarah?" Gram doesn't move from her chair.

"Does he like duckies?"

"Who?"

I go over to sit on her lap.

"My new brother."

"Well … he might like them, someday. You have to understand he's not as old as you."

"I'm six already!" I say it the way my mommy does when she's bragging about how I'm growing so fast. I've been watching her belly grow round. I'm getting a brother. And I can't wait.

"Why do I have to wait so long? Mommy's been gone since …" I twirl my hair around my finger, thinking.

"It's only been a week, sweetie," Gram fills in for me.

"Why couldn't I go see him in the hospital, like you did?"

Gram doesn't answer. I ask again. She just sighs real heavy.

"You got to go. I wanted to go. Why couldn't I?"

She still doesn't answer me.

"Why, Gram? Why?"

Suddenly, I hear the garage door cranking open.

"They're here!" I bound out of my gram's lap and meet my parents at our car. My mommy looks sleepy when they walk around the side to bring him out. I try to move in the space between my mommy and the door, but she moves in front of me. I haven't seen him yet.

"Just stand back." Mommy *sounds* sleepy, too. And crabby. "Get back for a second."

I walk over to hold my father's hand, but he doesn't hold mine tight. I have to hang on to him. Finally, Mommy brings over my new brother, but I can't see him. Not really. He's all wrapped in blankets.

I tug on Mommy's dress because I want her to bring him down, closer to me so I can see him, so I can kiss him and hold him the way I do with my dolls. But Mommy jumps back. I think maybe I hurt her.

"Not here. Let's go inside."

Inside, Daddy pats the space on the couch next to him for me, and Mommy asks Gram to move so she can sit in the comfy chair. It all takes too long. They're being soooo slow. I want to see him now! Finally, she's sitting down and then she pulls back the blankets. His face is the tiniest one I've ever seen! He's still wearing his hat and a bracelet with his name on it. It's so cute. They make him look like just like my Newborn doll, squishy face and everything. He's just like my plastic baby, only more beautiful.

"Can I hold him?" I try to stand up, but I feel Daddy pull my arm back. He tells me to sit back down. He says it like I'm in trouble. I don't know what he's so mad about.

Then Mommy pulls the blankets back up. I can hardly see him anymore.

"Mommy?" I don't know why they'd need to cover him in his blanket again, unless it's his bedtime, too. "Can I please hold him?"

I sit up nice and wait, but my mommy just looks at Daddy sitting next to me. He wraps an arm around me and makes a sound in his throat before he talks.

"So, the baby – your brother – is small, and he's breakable," Daddy says, talking slow. "I know you're excited, but we have to be so careful."

"I will be so careful!" I promise, and I mean it.

"He's just … too small right now."

But I've waited so long.

"When can I hold him?"

"Maybe on another day. Your mother and I are tired. The baby is too."

"Just for a minute?" I tilt my head and plead. I make the face that usually gets me one extra storybook at night. "Pleeeease?"

I'm so sure this will work that I'm already walking over to Mommy.

But Mommy stands up fast, and she holds the baby close against her so that I can't see his face at all.

It's been two more weeks, and Mommy is still doing it. Every time I try to get close to him, she picks him up. If she's holding him and I come up to her, she moves away from me. I promised to be careful. I just want to play with him. He looks just like my doll, except he cries a lot, but that's okay because I love him.

Daddy hasn't read me one storybook since he came home, and that's okay too. I know the baby needs a lot of attention right now. They keep telling me that, in those words. And that he's breakable and I can't touch him.

But they can't see me right now. Mommy and Daddy are sleeping, and I think the baby is too. I won't hurt him. I promised them that, over and over, and I mean it. I just want to see if he feels the same as my Newborn doll. I won't even move him. I can touch him right through the crib. I can see his eyes closed because there's a little cloud night-light in here. He looks happy, and soft.

He *is* soft. His cheeks feel like marshmallows.

"Hi, brother," I whisper. "I wanted to hold you. I can't wait until you can play with me. I hope you like ducks. My blanket has ducks, and so do my favorite pajamas. I like the lambs on your blanket. I'm six already."

Baby Brody's face moves just a little, but his eyes are still closed.

"I love your face."

Then his face squeezes together, lips curling down, and the buttons on his pajamas jump up. Once, twice. I hear him start to whimper.

"No, baby. It's okay. It's just me. I'm your sister."

But his mouth is open, and he's screaming so loud and I think I should run but when I turn around Mommy is there. And she's so mad.

"You woke the baby!" She just keeps yelling that. She won't even look at me.

"I just wanted to meet him," I say, squeezing the bottom of my pink pajama shirt.

Daddy's here too now. Mommy gives him the baby and grabs my arm, hard. She doesn't let go until we're back in my room. She doesn't tuck me in.

She just points at my bed. All she says is: "Don't ever, ever, ever do that again."

I wait until everything is quiet to look at him again. I won't wake him up this time. I can just watch him, without saying a word. I watch him for a long time, so long I think I might accidentally go to sleep. When I go over to him to say goodnight again, I hear Mommy's voice. She still sounds mad. But it's not about the baby. She's mad about that baby squirrel, the one that stopped moving because I squeezed it too hard. I told her it was an accident. I told her a bunch of times.

"She's just a kid, Diane."

"Bob. It was dead in her hands, and she was still carrying it around."

"She didn't know."

"I know … But still, I can't stop thinking about it. We have more to worry about now."

"But we can't just keep her away from him forever."

Mommy is quiet for a second.

"I've been thinking, we don't know that much about where Sarah came from. I never thought about it much before, but now the idea bothers me."

I don't know what they mean. Didn't I come from Mommy's belly too?

Like my brother did? I don't get what they're talking about, but I really think they wish I weren't here. I don't even worry about being caught as I walk back to my room. As long as I don't "wake the baby" it doesn't matter to them. Under my blankie, I keep wondering why the squirrel made them so mad. I wish I'd never picked it up off the ground. Maybe they would still want me if I had never touched it. Or maybe they'd still hate me. All they care about is the baby now. I'm not as cute as him, or as small as he is. I'm six already. Maybe my mommy only wants little babies. I wonder if six is too old to cry.

3

NOW

For a day that started with a gut-punch, I feel like I'm doing pretty well. As much as I hate surprises, I bounced back as much as I could from Bill's bombshell. I set myself up in my new, smaller office, put up a little frame of Brad holding Gracie, and went straight in to meet with Janette so I could pitch my plan for the new demographic. Not the way I'd planned for this to happen, but I rolled with it.

Bill was right about one thing. Janette is not me.

She's spent most of her career doing corporate public relations, for starters. She gets the image side of what we're trying to do with the campaign, but I'm not sure she understands strategy. She took the report I'd had printed and bound over the weekend and promised to look at it as soon as she could. She was busy with a press release about a ribbon-cutting next week at a manufacturing plant. We'll see. If she doesn't take action on the targeted ads I suggested, or at least present them at one of our briefings, I can always pitch it to Bill myself. Like I would have been doing before all this happened. I had taken the liberty of doing a little extra digging on my own, gathered a few quotes for billboard space in and around Knoxville. I took care of a lot of busy-work this morning, too, like an agonizing call with HR to discuss my new job title and benefits, but I've made it through.

Now, to regroup, hopefully with my best girlfriend, Enid. It's what I need most right now. I'd sent Brad a "rough day" text and promised to explain when I got home.

Enid's the kind of gal you can call in a pinch. When I was overwhelmed at the beginning of this campaign, she'd come over after work – after she'd spent a solid ten hours wrangling campaign volunteers – to help me brainstorm. She's been in on this since the beginning, as soon as Bill, McMinnville's former mayor, announced he was aiming for the state capitol. Bill knew her from her work in high-profile nonprofits. Both of them were frequent flyers at press conferences, and so he thought she'd be a great local face for the campaign. The assistant volunteer manager post was open, and Enid jumped right in, like she usually does. She was actually one of the people who recommended me to Bill when I told her I was hoping to add a gubernatorial campaign to my list of successes: a mayoral election in Chattanooga and an unusually nasty city counselor race.

Even better than her efficiency at work, Enid manages her friendships even better. She's never been overly warm, but you can count on her. She always shows up when you need her – and boy, do I need her right now. I should've asked her to visit when I was home with Gracie, but I know she's got so much going on. Today was a whirlwind and I've only seen her a couple times in passing. Now, finally, we'll get our chance to catch up. I'm sipping a gin and tonic with some serious kick, a luxury I didn't realize I'd missed so much until this moment, waiting for Enid at McMinnville's homegrown version of Applebee's. Casey's is a lunchtime hotspot that simmers down to a less-populated, more relaxing place for weekday dinner, or in this case, a spot for a back-to-work mom to unwind after a tumultuous day.

When Enid strolls in twenty minutes later, she's still on her phone, giving instructions for an event tomorrow, it sounds like. She gives me a wave and tosses her handbag into her side of our booth before she plops down. She's talking and huffing into the phone for another five minutes before she can finally unhook. Enid stopped by right after

Gracie was born, but things were such a blur in those first few days. We haven't had a real chance to talk, face-to-face, in months.

"I missed you." I stand up to hug her now that she can talk to me instead of her phone.

Enid meets me there but doesn't seem to have much energy.

"Long day?" I ask, as we both slide back into our seats.

"Always." Enid's chestnut bob has fallen as flat as her spirits.

"I know what can help with that."

Our favorite waiter appears with the drink I'd ordered for Enid – her own gin and tonic, no lime.

Her face brightens just a little.

"Thanks," she says, taking a sip. "I missed you, too. Things have been a little hairy. How's Gracie doing?"

"Ah, she's great. Starting to sleep more than five hours a night, which was a win for us. The colic made things tough for a while, but I think we're turning a corner. Brad has been absolutely amazing."

She nods briskly and takes another sip. "Well, it'll be good to have your help back at work."

"Seriously. It felt good to be out of the house a little bit, you know?" I say, but her face tells me she doesn't know. "I mean, having Gracie was amazing, but I don't know if it could be the only amazing thing about me, or that I'd want my life to end up being that way."

Enid's expression is still blank, so I veer us closer to what I really want to hear about.

"What's the office been like? What's your take on Janette? Does anybody actually like her?"

She shrugs at me from across the table.

"She's alright. Still kind of figuring her out. Hasn't been as bad as you'd think while you were away."

I try not to feel stung.

"What about Denise and Jim? Did they finally come right out with their relationship? What else is happening, girl? I feel like I've been away for a lifetime, buried in dirty dishes and dirty diapers."

Enid grimaces at that thought, and I can't say I blame her. Not a great visual.

"We're all plugging along pretty well. Nothing wild to report, and I think Denise and Jim are on the fritz, to be honest."

"Why?"

"Just, everything's been pretty quiet." Enid glances over the menu, though we've been here so many times, I could order her turkey club for her. I get the feeling she's avoiding my eyes.

"Well, what have you been up to? How's the volunteer scene? Picking up?" I hope asking her about work will break the ice. I don't know what has her so steamed that she won't open up, even to me.

"A whole lot, but I guess that's what you'd expect for this late in the campaign." Enid makes eye contact, finally. "I'm doing okay, too. Tired most days, but we're getting close to the end here and our volunteers are working tirelessly themselves. I was actually ..." She pauses for just a second, hurt flashing across her face. "I was really hoping to get to move around a little bit in the campaign. I wanted to get some experience outside of coordinating volunteers, though I know how much difference they make."

"Moving around?"

She nods but purses her lips, not giving anything away.

"You'd be great in any position." I think I see my opportunity to cheer her. "Let me help out. I'd recommend you. You're the hardest worker I know. What position were you thinking of?"

24

"Well ..." Enid hesitates and looks down at the table.

"Where?" I prod. "I'm serious, you'd be so good anywhere. What you lack in experience you make up for in enthusiasm. I feel like maybe I've got enough sway with Janette, and Bill sort of owes me a favor right now, after what I found out today."

"That's the thing," she says, staring at her hands now.

"What is it? You're driving me crazy. Just say it."

She breathes out deep and confesses: "I actually was hoping I might be considered for assistant campaign manager. I put my formal application in a week ago." She searches my face. I can't tell whether she's hoping she hasn't upset me by saying she wants the job I now have – or whether she's hoping I can help. She almost looks ready to cry.

At least her mood makes a little more sense. I'm relieved there's a reason she's acting so cool toward me. It's not that she hates me. It's that I took the job she wants.

"I'm sorry, Enid," I stammer, unsure how to react. "I didn't know."

"It's okay," she answers, but I can tell it's not. She blinks hard a few times.

"Listen, I didn't know any of what was going on inside the office. I didn't know I was being replaced. I didn't know you'd want Helene's old job. I didn't even know she left."

"Yeah. I get it," Enid answers, the thumbnail she's biting muffling her words. "And you're right, I guess, about the 'lack of experience.'"

I'd just said that off the cuff. That must have stung. I can tell from her crushed look that she desperately wanted the job.

"I didn't mean –"

"Don't apologize," she snaps.

"Enid, I'm sorry. You ... would have been a great assistant campaign manager."

Enid sucks in a deep breath like she's forcing away her disappointment.

"I get it," she says. "You didn't have much choice. That will happen when you're away, which isn't really fair, either. None of this feels fair."

"Man, you could have been my assistant. We'd have been a dream team."

Enid doesn't reply, and I wonder whether she's come here to see if I'd somehow back out of the job I've just accepted today, my consolation prize. She wouldn't really want me to do that, would she? Not when she knows I don't have other options right now, other than staying home. Of course, I'd love to help her, but she has to know that even if I gave up my new position, there's no way to know for sure that Enid would land the job. There's no one in the office I care about more, but I just can't give up the final tie to my dream of getting a governor elected. I can't change all of that because Enid had her eye on what became my only opportunity to salvage things. I don't want to hurt her, but I didn't ask for this, either. And I need the job.

The silence between us grows, and I wish I'd never brought up work, even though that's what I came here to vent about.

"I totally get your frustration," I say, finally. "Just a few more months until we make Bill governor and then, when I head to another campaign, why don't you come along?"

My suggestion doesn't seem to brighten her mood. Enid makes a small, irritated-sounding chuckle and a forced smile, then checks her phone and says she has to run.

"Alright," I answer. "But let's try this again soon, okay?"

"Yup." She gives me a rushed embrace and leaves her half-finished drink at our table. I guess everyone's out of sorts today.

4

NOW

The Buck's Auto Repair van is parked outside, so I know Brad has beaten me home. When you manage fifteen stores, you get to delegate evening work. It was one of the other reasons I thought it made sense for me to go back to work after three months: Brad's work is flexible enough that he can work from home sometimes, and he can call off when the baby's sick without a campaign event going haywire and without returning to an office in chaos. He must have switched out with the sitter who said she was going to drop off Gracie. I can picture my two loves waiting inside and I have to say I can't wait to go in and hold both of them.

My phone beeps and I know I can't miss a single thing from work. Not anymore. Just one more second. I dig it out from the bottom of my briefcase and glance at the screen. It's not work.

It's something worse.

I knew this day was coming.

My phone calendar notifies me that I have an "important appointment" coming up next week. I don't need it to remind me of the day I lost my mother ... but a therapist years ago suggested I give myself a little extra space for reflection around this time of year. I've written the note myself, but it still reads like a stranger has typed the memo into my phone: "MOM. Coming up soon." It's probably time for me to erase the recurring message. It hurts too much.

As much as I prepare for everything else in my life, I'd never have been able to get ready for this. The therapist didn't help. The calendar reminder doesn't help. Nothing makes this easier. It will be eighteen years in just a couple of weeks. I can't help but imagine what my mother would look like now, how she'd feel about her very first grandchild. I'd pictured her with me in the delivery room and saw the smile she'd wear the first time she picked up little Gracie. She was always beautiful when she smiled; I wish it had happened more often.

Just go inside, ignore/delete the message and hug your baby. Call it a day.

I try to push my mother from my mind, or at least to the back of my mind, for now.

"Well, it sounds like you handled it like a champ." Brad, always even keel, kisses my cheek again and goes back to a searing pan of onions, mushrooms, and green peppers that smell like heaven.

"Can you believe it, though?" It feels good to have my pumps off for the day, and that I've made it back in time to give Gracie her evening bottle. Maybe it wasn't so bad that Enid left so abruptly. And Brad is doing his best to make me feel better about what happened at work.

"Well, it's not fair. That's for sure." Brad's still facing the stovetop. "But I know you'll make the best of things. You're a trooper that way."

Gracie's gulping down her dinner eagerly, which makes me happy, and I can't wait for my own. I'm too distracted at first to catch where Brad was headed with the "trooper" talk.

"You don't always have to be so tough though, you know."

"What do you mean? Do I come on too strong or something? After today, it's clear they're not afraid of pissing me off."

"Oh," Brad turns to me. "I don't mean at work. I meant … you know."

"What?"

"The time of year, sweetie. I know it's not easy for you."

I can't help but suck in a breath. My chest tightens.

"It's really okay." Brad reaches an arm behind me and squeezes me and Gracie in one move. I don't wriggle away, but part of me wants to. "You can talk to me about it. I want to be here for you."

"Thanks, babe. But I don't really want to. My brain is all over the place today. I just want to … not think. Not think about that, at least."

Brad bristles but I just really can't handle it today. I need him to give it up and go back to the food. It could be my growling stomach, but I'd really like to just sit down to dinner and have a quiet night. It seems that Brad's got other plans.

He opens the fridge, cracks open a beer and settles back into a countertop corner. He gives me that good old Southern charm that I used to love – that I still love, actually – but I'm just not up for guessing games.

"What is it, babe?" I ask.

He rubs the scar over his left eyebrow, fidgeting the way he does when he's working himself up to something.

"I was just thinking of how hard you're working to make this all happen," he says, reaching out his arms toward me and Gracie. "Mom. Campaign genius."

I smile, ready to demure when he lays down the big question. And I do mean *the* question.

"What if we add wife to the list?" He grins. "Think you can pull that off, too? I'd be willing to lend a hand."

My mouth drops open. I can't believe he's asking me this right now.

"Are you, um …" It's a little difficult for me to shape a response on my feet. I start to take Gracie over to her bouncy chair to stall, but he stops me.

"Yes, I am." Brad's got both hands on my hips now, pulling me close even though Gracie's between us. She coos happily. "I am proposing, in fact."

I don't back away from him, but I avoid his kiss.

"This feels a little out of nowhere, don't you think?" I try to make a sweet smile, try to soften the blow.

"Baby. Sweetheart. We've talked about this before. I thought you were thinking about it. Thought maybe now that you've seen you can work and raise Gracie, we could make it all work. I know today wasn't perfect, but you made it work. We can make it work. Together. A real family."

"It's only been one day back," I stammer. "And it didn't go well. And we are a real family. We don't need someone else to approve it for us. You know the whole idea of marriage bothers me a little, more about ownership –"

"I know all that, baby. I just want us to be able to do –" He smiles and pulls up close again. "I want … to do forever with you."

The thing is, I want to believe him. I want to think that he's in this forever, but marriage sometimes changes things. People change. In ten years or fifteen years, it could be more a trap than a promise. A baby is a commitment, but there are mothers and fathers who raise their children just fine without a marriage. What if we did marry and it fell apart *after* I built my life, and Gracie's life, around this marriage? He could just walk right out the door one day and I'd have been living in this false sense of security. It's hard for me to think in forever terms when it comes to men. He's a good man; I know that in my head. He's a great father, and I know that part in my heart. The rest just might take a while.

I don't want to wipe the hope right off his face, so I kiss him and then back away without an outright refusal, the same tactic I used the other half dozen or so times he's done this since we found out I was going to have a baby. Actually, it was earlier than that. When I first moved in, a couple years ago. I hate rejecting him … or avoiding giving him an answer. I just don't know that I can say yes right now.

I notice that Gracie's fallen asleep in my arms; I get a brief reprieve. I come back to a set table with two juicy, open-faced burgers and a smiling would-be husband, lighting a candle.

"A romantic dinner." I move in close to hold him, without the baby between us. I can just make out the sporty cologne I bought him behind all the onions and peppers, and I want more of both those scents. Dinner first.

"Just for you." He pulls out my chair like the gentleman he is and, thankfully, doesn't immediately bring up marriage again. I devour my food within a few minutes, and he reaches for my hand across the table.

"Have I told you that I'm proud of you?"

I pretend to think really hard.

"Not since this morning." I smile at him.

He winks at me, smiling and squeezing my hand. He's been joking lately about him packing on a few sympathy pounds while I was pregnant and how he needs to get back his pre-baby bod, so I know he could use a little affirmation. He needs to know I still want him, especially when I'm avoiding tying the knot. I do still want him. I'm just so tired right now.

"Glass of wine?"

I actually think that might do the trick. After we've eaten, I curl up next to him on the couch with a half-finished glass of pinot nearby, I'm ready to feel his kiss. My body responds to the heat of his hands down my back, around my waist and my hips. I lean into him, feel the weight of his mouth on mine and then his soft kiss moving down the curve of my neck. I try not to think about the pouch on my belly that I was inspecting this morning, or the way my breasts haven't recovered from my six-week attempt at breastfeeding. Maybe they never will. *He doesn't care. He loves me.* I think I'm ready for this.

And then a wail pierces the silence and pulls me back to reality.

"Shit." Brad sighs, but he doesn't sound overly frustrated. "My turn?"

"Hmm," I answer, an idea shaping. "Why don't you go ahead. Maybe she just needs to burp and then go right back to sleep. I might just head to our room and get ready."

"For a visit from a mysterious stranger?" A flash of mischief flickers in his blue eyes.

I laugh and squeeze him around the neck.

"It'll give me a chance to," I say, pulling out my handy air quotes, "'slip into something more comfortable' ... and maybe also something with a little coverage."

I laugh at my joke, but he doesn't. He just smiles.

"Not needed – but whatever you want, baby." He kisses me one more time. "Meet you there."

5

THEN

very other kids' parents were there today. Tiff's parents got her a new outfit, head-to-toe, just to wear for the graduation ceremony, and they're stingy as hell. I guess moving from eighth grade to high school is a big deal. Just no one told my mom that. Or she doesn't give a shit. And I wouldn't accept a thousand-dollar outfit from the guy who tries to pretend he's my dad. Not in a million years. It wouldn't come free, I can tell you that. He'd want something disgusting from me in exchange.

I bet when Brody goes into high school, Mom will be there. She'll probably have a party after, too. Cake. Balloons. A fucking car with a ribbon on the top. She's such a sucker for him. I get that he's cute. But he's annoying too. Annoying as all hell. I can't stand him anymore. He's always in my way.

In fact, right now, he's really in my way.

I found my "dad's" keys to the filing cabinet. Yeah. They're so sneaky and weird they keep everything locked up in the bedroom Mom made into her office. I know they've got something to hide. I've made it back, all the way up the creaky stairs without making a sound that might cause alarm, and guess who's here? Yeah. Fucking Brody.

It couldn't be worse.

Well, it could be if it were my dad, looking for me at night again. I hate when he comes in my room. I hate when he touches me. I *hate* everything about him. I hate him so much, I could kill him.

Second worse option: it's Brody on the steps.

His eyes are open, but they're glazed over. He's moving purposefully, but hitting walls on the way. He's actually not so far from falling down the steps. I'm surprised Mom hasn't put up a gate to keep him safe now that his sleepwalking's gotten really bad. I watch him bump into another wall, then turn toward the top of the steps. His toes are just inches from the edge ...

There's no landing. It would be a serious fall.

I don't think he's seen me here, on the third-from-the-top step. One more errant move and he might just tumble right down on his own. I hold my breath and don't move a muscle. I can't wake him up and stop him anyway. Then he'd want to know what I'm doing awake and I know he'd go running to Mom downstairs. He's irritating that way. No, saving his ass would cost mine, and I ain't doing that.

He's turned again now, heading into the bathroom. Guess he'll wake up in the tub again. He's safe for tonight, and so am I.

I'm like a real-life detective, nabbing the key and unlocking the cabinet to do a little research. I'm going to find out what they're hiding, just as soon as I can sort through this rat's nest my mom has made of her office files. The woman is a completely disorganized disaster. Who keeps old parking violations? It takes some digging, but finally I spot it. It *would* be shoved to the very back, way behind all those kindergarten papers where Brody has written the letter 't' over and over for four lines straight. What talent! Behind every little thing they've saved from him is a slim file, marked "Sarah" in sloppy cursive. There I am, a footnote. They've never acted like they cared about me – all they care about is Brody – so I'm not surprised there's not much here. I feel like I don't even exist in this house, or like they wish I didn't. I'm not like Brody. It's like they are a big happy family without me, like I've always been the one who doesn't belong. Now I'll finally know for sure. Let's see. A few printouts of shot records. One piece of paper from my kindergarten year, a paper I made about baby Brody, with his picture pasted at the center of a blue ribbon I drew and colored in. Last of all is what I came to find. My hands shake, and I don't know why. This is not a big deal.

I want to know, but I don't want to know.

For one tiny flash of a second, I think about not looking.

But it's too late. The answer is in my hands. I breathe in deeply and take a look.

I knew it. I freaking knew it.

I expected it … but it still feels like a slap across the face. Here, in my hands, is my birth certificate. Except my mother isn't listed as Diane Morton, aka the mom who doesn't give a shit. She's never acted like my mom and there's a reason why. She ain't.

I knew it.

I *don't* belong here. I'm not who my parents have made me out to be. They're not even my parents. They're not my family. The thoughts hit me all at once. Who I am. Who I'm not. Where I am. Where I should be. A dozen other questions, so overwhelming that all I want to do is find someone to ask, someone to talk to … but I'm all alone.

I have to sit down.

I force myself to breathe.

Somewhere out there, I have a real mother. Her name is Rebecca Cartwright. I try to picture her, us living together, a loving family, whatever that might feel like. I don't even know what that looks like. But I'm going to find out, I hope. I could meet my real mother. I try to picture it, but my brain is working like an out-of-focus camera. I can't see anything concrete. Finding her is the only thing I can think of that would start making sense of the swirling questions. Why wouldn't she want me?

Why wouldn't my real mother want me?

Why?

Maybe there's a whole story I just don't know yet. There has to be a reason, a good reason. Maybe it was a mistake. If I could just find her …

I fold the piece of paper and hold it over my chest. *Breathe.* Next step, pack. I rise to my feet silently and close and re-lock the filing cabinet. No need to give anyone a clue that might give them a head start. Not that they'd come looking anyway. I pad down the hallway. It'll be best if I sneak out without a fuss.

I've got half my ripped purple backpack filled – jeans, cigarettes, underwear, and a couple of tees – before I come to my senses. Who am I kidding? I don't actually know where I'm going. All I know is I want to go find her. But I can't drive. If I steal my mom's car – excuse me, Diane's car – I'll be way too easy to trace. You can go to jail for that, and she'd be all too happy to send me there. I wouldn't hold my breath for visitors, either, and it's a lot easier to find people when you're not incarcerated. I'll have to be a lot more careful than that.

I collapse onto my single bed and try to think this through. I could hitchhike. I'm not so far from I-65 if I go through a patch of pines behind our neighborhood. I'd emerge just outside the guardrails. Plenty of trucks coming down this way. Then I picture what it might actually be like, sitting in the cab of an eighteen-wheeler with a bearded stranger, spitting snuff every so often and eyeing me up the whole way to the next town, or the next truck stop. Too dangerous. They'd probably find my body, or my skeleton, someday in the next patch of pines down the road.

This might be more complicated than I thought. It's going to take planning. I'm going to have to wait even though that's the last thing I want

36

to do. I try to calm myself and consider the situation, but I just get more pissed off. Now I know I have a mother. I know why my family doesn't give a shit if I live or die. But I can't do jack shit about it.

I realize I'm crying, which almost never happens anymore. But I'm so frustrated. I've finally found out what the problem has been these last fifteen years – and I'm stuck, stuck as I was before. I shove my half-filled backpack off the side of the bed. It's 2:30 a.m. and I really don't want to have to face either one of my fake parents right now. I freeze in the dark and listen. No one makes a sound. Brody's probably still passed out in the bath. I make myself breathe again. At least I know. Now that I know, I can make a plan. I can stomach this place for a couple more years while I figure out how to find her, Rebecca, my real mother.

After digging to the bottom of my backpack for what I need, I tiptoe over to the window, where the streetlight casts a glow through the blinds. I unfold the paper. The truth. I'm not Sarah Morton, child of Diane and Robert. I am the daughter of Rebecca Cartwright. My name is Sarah Cartwright. I repeat it over and over in my head, like a promise. *Sarah Cartwright. Sarah Cartwright.*

6

NOW

Despite the circumstances – working in Helene's cramped office, which ended up becoming storage space for extra campaign freebies – I'm thankful I'm not at home right now; a quiet morning with Gracie would give me too much space to think about *her*. I know what my mind does in the fall. I don't want to remember, like I do every year, the last few days I spent with her, not knowing they would be the last. I don't want to agonize over every word she spoke to me or the way she looked the last time I saw her. No. I need things to fill the space in my head so I can't roam too far, especially not now, so close to the day she died. Regret and sorrow will swallow me whole if I let them.

Thankfully, there's enough here to keep me busy. The ads I suggested when I came back to work last week were deemed out of budget, but I put together a Plan B. Time to find out whether it worked.

The TV is on in the back room where campaign officials meet for our daily briefings, the ones I used to lead every morning. Today, Janette beat me here and must have switched on the news. The new poll numbers should be announced soon, and I've got my fingers crossed.

But the newscasters are still talking about the morning's top story, a triple-fatal crash at a nasty intersection, and promising an interview after the break with a transportation department official. Janette turns down the volume as the rest of the team leaders, and Bill, filter into the room. Enid is the last to join us.

To her credit, Janette did read the report I wrote. She'd presented it to the team and to Bill immediately and mentioned that it was my research. The finance manager wouldn't okay the ad investment, but I didn't give up at that. Instead, I suggested a field trip out east for Bill. Janette and I scrambled to help our press team arrange appearances for him at two fledging startup tech companies (where I'd hoped we'd catch some younger demographics), and we sat down together to prepare talking points that will matter most to Tennesseans in their twenties and thirties.

Once everyone is settled, Janette rises. She's as polished as the first day I met her, dark hair flat-ironed sleek and straight over her shoulders, her suit perfectly tailored, deep red lipstick lined impeccably. She looks more enthusiastic than the rest of the group, exhausted from a long week on the campaign trail. Bill had a radio interview already this morning and Janette and I did a three-hour evening coaching session with him last night, gearing up for the next debate. Almost half our team traveled with him to his appearances in Knoxville this week, myself, unfortunately, not included. Bill said he wouldn't want to take me away from the baby that long. Janette seems to be bouncing with energy, but the rest of the team look like they could use some more coffee. Thank goodness it's Friday, as they say, although some solid poll number gains might perk everyone up too.

"We're hoping today's numbers show at least a three-point pickup, which would put us at a comfortable distance from the Burtner campaign," Janette says, "and if my hunch is right, we'll have Sarah's insight to thank."

I smile when she nods at me, though, I'm a little unsure how to take her praise. There's a glint in her eyes that makes me wonder what she's really up to.

Don't get me wrong. Janette's been nothing but sugar sweet to me so far, but her shout-out, in front of everybody, still takes me by surprise. If I were her, a usurper, I'd be making sure to keep the spotlight on myself. That's the smarter way to go, especially if the person you hip checked out of the way is still waiting in the wings. Maybe she's underestimating me.

That's perfect, actually. Unless she's up to something else. It could be nothing; I just don't have a good feel for her yet. I can't work her out. The way she acts around me is … almost too eager. I can't tell what, or who, she is working so hard to win over.

Then comes the good news, and I think it might be my chance to emphasize my worth.

When the a.m. briefing closes with a climactic round of celebratory fist pumps at the new poll numbers – up not three, but four points in Bill's favor – I make a beeline for his office. I know he's exhausted, but he welcomes me in.

"Oh hey, Sarah, take a seat." He smiles and waves me over. "You're really coming back."

That feels good.

"Thanks, I'm thrilled at the numbers. We're going to head into November really strong."

"That, too." He leans back, and I'm not sure what he means by that. What else is he talking about? "It's really good to have you back, I have to say."

"Thank –"

"A lot of women can't pull it off." He sets his gaze on me, appreciatively. "I mean, you walk in here, three months after having a baby and … you look fantastic. I mean, really."

Then I realize *what* he's appreciating. I struggle to find the right response, to brush off the comments like I have before, but he doesn't wait for me to answer him.

40

"After my wife started having kids, she never really got back to the way she was before – as far as her shape, I mean. Great mother. Great wife. Just couldn't ever shake off those last, you know, five – or forty-five – pounds." He chuckles a little at his own joke and then says I could make a "killing" if I sold my secrets to getting back in shape.

"It's really nice to see a woman who cares about her body," he adds, as an afterthought. "You look amazing."

And you're getting really annoying.

"The polls are what looked amazing," I say, regrouping. "I've only been back a few days and we've got an expanded strategy and today … well, the results are in the numbers. And I think we can top that."

"That would be great. Make sure there's no room for Burtner to pull any last-minute stunts."

I breathe out a sigh of relief; Bill is successfully refocused.

I clear my throat.

"You know, I think Janette worked well as an in-between, while I … couldn't be here," I venture, "and she is great as part of the team. Shares the credit, good team player. I think people respect her." I watch his face and he seems to be following along. "But I don't know that a few years in PR have really equipped her to understand the nuances of political strategy."

Bill doesn't answer, but he looks like he's thinking. I just hope it's about my words.

"I mean, that's *my* strength. The strategy."

"You don't think you and Janette can work well together? I'd hoped you could both blend your strengths, pull together as a team."

"That's not what I'm saying. I think we do work well together, actually, but I'm not sure she has the background to lead us to the finish line, at least not in the way you and I had envisioned when we kicked off the –"

"She's had more than a few years in PR. If you'd taken the time to look into her a little, given her a chance, you might have found that she's got a wealth of experience."

"Like what?" I'd known only that Janette happened to attend my alma mater – I assume it was a few years ahead of me – and that she came from PR.

"Remember the Miller campaign?"

"Alabama?" Of course I remember. Miller's team got him, a Democrat, all the way to a recount. The recount didn't tip the scales for him, but it was a shocker all the same. Alabama never leans that way.

Wow. Okay, so she's nearly won an impossible battle before...

"Well," I search his face to figure out how much ground I may have lost, "Tennessee is not Alabama."

"Lucky for us."

"Yes, but what I'm saying is that if we want to make sure we win here —"

"Of course we want to win," Bill interrupts with an irritated huff. "What you're saying is you don't think she's the right person for the job. I understand where you're coming from, and I get the position you're in." He raises his hands in a gesture of helplessness. "But it's not the time to make this kind of change now. You're doing a great job where you are. Just look at how well things went this week with you and Janette working together."

I hope my face doesn't wince with my internal pang of disappointment. A twist in the gut.

"Janette appreciates you, too. Let's try to see this as a true team. More than that, we're a family. Let's not lose sight of the big picture. Like you said, we are so close now. We've had a good week. We're all tired. You stayed late last night. Why don't you head home? You've been working so hard and I know your husband – or boyfriend – is going to be glad to see you walk through the door. Lucky guy."

Thankfully, a whirl of commotion outside stops Bill from going any farther with that idea.

Janette pops her head in, looking a little blanched.

"We've got a problem."

"What is it?" Bill rises from behind his desk.

"You need to see this." Then she notices me and heaves a sigh. "You too, Sarah."

The news is still up in the back meeting room – though I can hear it cranked up in the front office, too, an echo of whatever story has everyone's attention. The voice I hear makes my stomach curdle. It's that bastard Charles Devante, the other side's favorite attack dog to send out when poll numbers are making them uncomfortable. He's always been my least favorite behind-the-scenes character in Tennessee politics and he's made it pretty clear that the feeling is mutual. I've never once seen him at an event when he didn't have a snide remark waiting to launch at me. More than a few times, I've had a reporter tell me that he makes derogatory comments about me constantly. Even before the gubernatorial race – way back when we were both plugging for opposing mayoral candidates five years ago – we didn't get along. I wedge in among the crowd with their eyes glued to the TV in the meeting room. I see that today, Charles is not working in the background, planting seeds. He's right out in front of the camera. His hair's greased back, bringing out the dramatic point of his widow's peak, and whatever he's saying has him so excited he's nearly spitting into the three microphones shoved in front of his face.

"Obviously, I think voters should take this seriously." He licks his lips a few times for a dramatic pause. "I don't want to jump to conclusions, but it clearly shows Democratic gubernatorial candidate William Porter, who purports to be an ethical family man, in what appears to be a very intimate interlude with one of his staff members. Certainly raises concerns. And questions"

I gasp audibly and glance around the room. I know from experience that Bill's a flirt ... but who would really get themselves into that kind of a mess? Denise from the press team? Not Mary Beth. Janette? Oh ... that would make a whole heck of a lot of sense. The screen goes back to a slim brunette reporter who looks about seventeen, analyzing the story.

"Brian, can we show the graphic again?"

Here it comes.

On a blue background, underneath the text, "Porter's New Problem," is a photograph of my boss, looking a little too hands-on with a member of his staff. I blink hard, like I can wish it away, and all the blood rushes out of my head. But when I open my eyes, it's still there. It's a snapshot of Bill, in a car ... *with me*. He has his hand on my knee and his head cocked toward my ear.

Shit.

Space forms around me, people edging away to glare at me in shock. I want to curl up under my desk.

But the TV is still going. The story is hot, and it's rolling right along. I can't force my eyes away.

The screen goes back to Charles Devante doing his impromptu press conference on a busy Nashville street with at least three other TV reporters there. Behind him, I see a print reporter I recognize. By tomorrow, it will be splashed across every newspaper in Tennessee, following hours of rehash on TV.

"I also know, from my sources, that Sarah Cartwright has just had a child," Charles says pointedly, shaking his head in shame. "It raises a lot of questions. We have evidence that *something* must have been going on at some point. Sarah, who I've known through the political scene for years, suddenly goes silent. This photo surfaces. And now we hear she's had a child." He shrugs. "I hate to say it, but it really makes you wonder about the timing, you know? I've always said she has questionable judgment."

Every reporter I can see on the scene nods their head, eating up every word, and I feel panic pulsing through my veins.

Shit.

Shit. Shit. Shit.

So much for salvaging my career.

7

NOW

H ere we are, back in the conference room where we were
exuberant just minutes ago, all fist pumps and pats on the back.
Now, it's a shitstorm. A complete shitstorm. The entire ten-person
press team is crowded around the table. Enid's in here too, smashed
against a wall near the back door, and I'm trying desperately to catch
her eye – but the cacophony, added to the mad swirl of thoughts in my
head, is making it hard to make sense of anything, let alone catch
someone's attention. The press crew is launching questions my way
and all I can do is shake my head. The chairs around the table are
empty and pressed up against the table. The back conference has
become a standing-room only show.

The TV is still on, blaring out. Reporters are doing what they do,
rehashing the big story over and over. No more mention of Bill's gains
in the polls, other than to set the scene for the new top story: *Is gubernatorial candidate William Porter a philanderer? Is he having an
affair with his recently demoted campaign manager Sarah Cartwright?
Did he father a child with her?* They've already promised to bring an
analyst in for their noon show to discuss how this might impact the
next poll numbers.

It all makes me sick. And the sound bites with slick-haired Charles

Devante are a nightmare that won't go away. This whole thing is a nightmare. A sick, disgusting nightmare. Somewhere behind the press crew, Bill is avoiding the hot seat, pacing behind them. They ought to be asking him all the questions right now. His flirtatious gestures were an annoyance before. Now they could be his doom. And mine.

One of the press team slaps a printout from a local TV station's website on the middle of the table. It's the image of Bill, touching my knee in a car, the door open. Out of context, it looks like a romantic gesture.

"When was this taken?"

I rack my brain to try to come up with a response. Certainly, when I was still campaign manager, there would have been plenty of opportunities for someone to snap a photo of Bill and I headed to a fundraiser. I try to make out the street behind us, but it's such a tight crop. I can't get a feel for where it is, much less when it was taken. I recognize my dress – a favorite – but one I'd worn dozens of times.

"Had to be sometime early in the campaign," I stammer. The more I stare, the more I wonder how this could be blown into such wild proportions. Still, here we are. It feels like the entire room is screaming at me, hurling questions faster than I can answer them.

In my peripheral vision, I see Bill slide right out of the room. Weasel. He's happy to let me take the heat alone. Of course, so is everyone else.

"Alright." The press team leader, gray-haired PR pro Dick Murray, grabs the photo off the table and slips it into a folder. "We need to figure out a concrete plan for damage control."

The room erupts again. Everyone is talking over each other, drowning out the TV and Janette's voice in the background, telling everyone to calm down.

"Stop. Let's –" she clears her throat loud and whacks a folder hard against the table. It shocks everyone, and the voices drop into silence.

"Thank you. Now, we have to take this one step at a time." Janette has officially taken the reigns. "Dick, I want you and your team to prepare a PR plan to mitigate the damage, see whether we can shore up his reputation. If that means finding people who will go on record to defend his honor, then do that. If it means lining up interviews with his loving wife or getting b-roll of him at home with his family, then do that. I want a plan completely mapped out and ready to launch ASAP."

Dick harrumphs.

"I don't see how we can make a plan to mitigate the damage when we still don't know what we're going to do about this, internally."

"What we're going to do," Janette makes her voice slow and clear, "is handle this situation and clear Bill's name."

There's so little space in this room, but Dick has managed to clear a circle around him. He crosses his arms and shoots a look in my direction.

"What I'm saying is I don't know that I can have my team build a plan before we know what we're going to do ... about her." He glowers at me. "Is she staying? Going? What do I have to work with here?"

"Well ..." Janette swallows. "Let's at least hear what Sarah has to say. Obviously, this photo, emerging right now, is too convenient. We all realize there's no substance to it and, as a team, we should have her back. And Bill's back. But when it comes to appearances ... Sarah, I'd like to know first how you think this might affect the campaign."

I can feel people pushing up against my back and my arms. Their body heat is stifling. I try to clear my thoughts the best I can, on the spot.

Janette's asking for my professional opinion, which is a little hard to separate from my personal outrage. "As much as you'd like to think people aren't gullible enough to believe there's a whole story to this single photograph – an affair –"

"A child." A woman's voice, muffled, interrupts me from somewhere along the back wall. I can't place it at the moment, but the suggestion sends a new wave of rage through my veins.

"That's enough." Janette slaps her folder against the table again. "I want to hear from Sarah. Let her speak."

"It creates a really difficult situation for us, for Bill's chances," I start in again. "At this stage in the process – weeks away from the election – we're going to need to take action."

Janette nods her head.

"So, is your thought that you should … stay on the campaign team? We'll need your help now, more than ever, but I want to know whether you think it's going to reinforce what this photo, and the media, and this Charles guy from the other side are all suggesting. What do you think is the right move here?"

I try to crop out the hoard of people watching me expectantly and focus on Janette's face. She holds up both hands to quiet the rest of the room again and she gives me a compassionate go-ahead nod.

I take in a deep breath and keep eye contact with Janette.

"I know the knee-jerk reaction is that I should resign," I say. "But the truth is – and I'm really trying to speak objectively here – that even if I leave, it won't make the story go away. In fact, it might add fuel to the fire. If I step out of the picture immediately, it creates suspicion. For some people, it will confirm the story completely. A photograph shows up, people are suggesting it means that Bill and I had or are having an affair – and then I'm suddenly dismissed … it may add more problems than it solves."

That's not to mention the problems this may create for me, at home. Poor Brad. *Shit.* He could be watching this right now. If he's not, his sister has probably called him to fill him in herself. I don't need to give him any other reason to wonder why I avoided giving him an answer about marriage again.

Janette absorbs my response, nodding slowly.

"And so, if you stay?" she prompts me.

"Well … that's not easy either," I answer, truthfully, even though the

49

thought of what I'm about to say makes me sick. "If I'm even in the room at a press appearance, a debate, a meet-the-candidate night – the focus will immediately shift from Bill to me and Bill."

"Even when you aren't there," Dick says, his face hardening, "the focus of anything Bill does in the next few weeks is going to shift from him and his platform to you and him."

I immediately wish that I hadn't suggested that Bill pick one of the most aggressive PR managers in the region. But I also know he's right. Every reporter is going to want a chance to get an inside scoop. If he agrees to do an interview about anything, it's going to lead straight to asking him about me. Can you address the rumors that you had an affair with your campaign manager? How do you think the photograph is going to affect how voters see you? Did you have a baby out of wedlock with Sarah Cartwright?

"Dick." An authoritative voice breaks the silence. It's Bill, back in the room and the conversation. "Your first action item is to prepare a statement, denying any inappropriate behavior and making it clear that I stand for families and family values. It needs to be ready and sent to the media before the TV stations air their noon shows. We don't want utter silence on our end while Charles Devante and a crew of eager analysts are wagging their tongues all over the place."

Dick shakes his head helplessly.

"I'll do what I can," he says, shrugging. "Give me twenty minutes to get it ready."

"Janette, Sarah." Bill looks at me for the first time since the disaster. "Let's figure this out."

"Thanks for stepping in there," I say, closing Bill's office door behind me.

"We need to take action, not stand around and argue," he answers, with a heavy sigh. "The two of you know that. Dick can just be, well, a dick sometimes. No question this is bad, but we need to wrap our heads around the things that we can control."

"Right." Janette jumps in. Always eager. Maybe always plotting, too.

Bill shoots her a glance. "What do you think we need to do?"

Janette turns to me.

"Sarah knows strategy. She's probably got the best feel for what should happen next and the fallout we should expect. The campaign has a lot at stake. So does she. I think it's only fair we get her thoughts first."

I stop pacing the carpet and breathe in deeply.

"Thanks, Janette. I really hate the idea of this – but we need to do something to counteract the whole story." I cringe internally at what I'm about to say. I can't believe I'm in this position. "I should probably have a paternity test done on Gracie."

Janette shakes her head in disbelief.

"No, really. It's probably for the best. We'll have statements denying the rumors. Maybe we can get a trusted reporter to interview Bill at home, with his wife, who of course stands beside him and doesn't believe the rumors. In a week, we could have the paternity test results back, showing that Brad, of course, is the father. Then, hopefully, we can return to focusing on issues that affect the voters."

"As far as your position?" Janette prompts.

"Well, it probably makes most sense for me to distance myself from Bill within the campaign, take a position that moves me farther from the core of the campaign. I would think it's a safer move than having me resign."

"Agreed," Janette answers with reluctance and a glance at me that I can't quite read. "I hate to see it happen, but I think you're right. That adds another problem. If we have you working elsewhere, who will we move to assistant campaign manager?"

"Someone who's been here a while, preferably since the beginning," I say. "We don't want to be starting over. Too bad Helene's already relocated."

A silence settles over the room. I hate that I'm being replaced again, but I can't think of another way. And then the answer comes to me. I might be able to help out my friend after all.

"Enid told me a week ago that she was hoping to fill the assistant campaign manager spot."

Bill's face brightens.

"That's right," he says. "She already put in her resume for this. She *has* been here since the beginning."

"There we go." Janette grins so wide I can see all her teeth. "Smart idea. Should be a smooth transition."

At least it works out for Enid. A train wreck for me, but Enid will get what she wants. Maybe it will bring us closer again. I miss feeling like I have a friend here, like I'm not completely surrounded by people whose motivations I have to second-guess.

"Have we talked about who could have planted the photo?" Bill asks, interrupting my thoughts.

Janette spins in my direction. "Is there anybody who would benefit from you getting axed from the campaign? Can you think of anyone who'd want to hurt you?"

"The Burtner campaign manager," I answer, thinking aloud. "Charles Devante and I – we've butted heads before.

"And Charles happened to have the morning off to give all his opinions on the photo," Bill points out. "I guess we can assume he's our troublemaker."

The room falls silent and, in my mind, I try to isolate who else could have been around at that time. There are so many people working the campaign now, but we'd started out much smaller.

"I want to pin it totally on Charles," I answer, trying to push away a dark thought that's just dawned on me. *God. Enid.* I wish she wouldn't have told me she wanted the job. I'd never have suspected her otherwise, but she was acting so weird when I saw her. *She wouldn't have, right?* A move like this would be damaging to the entire campaign, though. She'd be stepping into a disaster. She couldn't have. "I want to say it's Charles, but to be honest –" I try to refocus. "I don't know how he would have been close enough to us to snap a photo like that. I think I'd have remembered him standing outside the car door. Unless someone else gave him the photo and he leaked it to the press."

"That's probably more likely," Janette offers. "Had to have been someone who was around early in the campaign, though. I hate to say it, but I think it's most likely that it came from … inside."

"I don't know who here would do that to Bill … or to me," I answer, quietly, trying to stop thinking about how Enid had sulked over her lost job opportunity when she met me for drinks last week. I shake away the idea. *Enid would never do this to me. Never.*

8

NOW

The last time I had a gin and tonic, I was waiting for Enid in a booth at Casey's Grill.

This time, I'm sitting bar-side at the Red Rooster Saloon, wondering whether my closest girlfriend might have been plotting to stab me in the back when she met me for drinks. To say she was acting unusual would be an understatement. Enid was silent, shut down. And she had wanted my job. Still, what kind of friend would splash my picture across the news? *She couldn't have. She wouldn't do that to me ... or to Brad. They've been friends forever, long before I knew him.*

It doesn't help, though, that she avoided me altogether today, the worst day of my career. Now, instead of being here with Enid to sort through my thoughts, I'm with Janette. I didn't see this coming, any of it.

"So, back to the original question," Janette says, stopping to swig her beer, "if it was an inside job, who would have been around at that point in the campaign?"

"A ton of volunteers. Mary Beth. Dick," I tick off the names, trying to avoid Enid's.

"Any of them ever act like they wanted you out of the picture?"

I cringe at her choice of words, but she seems oblivious to what she just said. *I sure as hell would have liked to be out of that picture.*

"I can't imagine," I say. "I helped Bill bring Dick into the campaign. He's tough, but that's why we hired him. He's just doing his job. Mary Beth loves what she does, loves all of us. I can't imagine her making such a destructive move. She's never been anything but kind to me."

"Who would do this to Bill, and to you?" Janette grips her beer, leaning in closer to me so I can hear her above the booming honky-tonk music. "And why now?"

I squeeze my glass in my hands, wondering whether I should trust Janette. I don't want to, but she's given me no real reason not to. In fact, as much as I hate to admit it, we've made a decent team over the past week. I don't like her because she was brought in to replace me. But that's not her fault. It wasn't her doing.

I let out a sigh, conflicted.

"You know, I hesitate to even say this ..."

"What is it?' Her eyes light up. "You can tell me."

"Enid and I have been friends a long time." I hate that I'm even thinking this way, but maybe just saying it will get it out of my mind. "The last time I met with her, a week or so ago, she ... she told me she had really been hoping to move up in the campaign. She wanted the assistant campaign manager job. I mean, *really* wanted it. Pretty upset that she didn't get it."

Janette sits back in her chair and scrunches her face together. I can't entirely make out her expression under the neon lights.

"Well, I guess she got it now." Janette moves closer to me again. "I can't imagine this is *how* she'd want it to happen. It's a disaster for the campaign."

"And for me. You don't think she would –" The words stick in my throat the same way the picture and Charles Devante's twisted delight stick in my mind. "She's been my friend for a long time."

"How long?"

"Years. I convinced Bill to bring her into the campaign in the first place. I knew her from her nonprofit work, but also ... she's been friends with Brad since they were kids."

"Brad?"

"My boyfriend."

"Gracie's father. That's right," Janette says. "There's no way she would do that to you, right?"

"I sure hope not."

Catching the muscle-bound bartender's attention with a flirty wave, Janette orders me a second drink.

"Well," she says. "I'll keep my ear to the ground. She'll be out of a job immediately if I find something – I mean anything at all – to link her to the pictures or rumors. I'd insist on it."

"But you don't think she really would have leaked the picture?" I realize it's a silly question. Janette doesn't really know Enid – or me, for that matter.

"I don't know," Janette answers. "I haven't spent much time with her, so I can't say that I'd rule it out entirely. In this business, you can never be too careful though. There's too much at stake. Everybody plays dirty."

I nod. The sinking feeling in my gut tells me I was wrong. Bringing up Enid didn't make me feel any better.

"Speaking of which," Janette goes on, "because it's clear our opposition is going to go to any lengths and we know this story is going to be scrutinized from every direction ..."

Please don't go there. I wish immediately that I hadn't agreed to go out for drinks. I'd already told Janette what I think about how we should react. I don't think we can fight back dirty. Bill wouldn't agree to that.

It's not his style, or mine. I didn't agree to come here so we could talk about the campaign. I just needed to try to recover before I go home. I'm not sure how Brad is going to handle all of this. He wouldn't buy into the story – at least I don't think he would – but he has to be worried.

"Is there anything else I should know about?" Janette asks, digging for more. "I'm not trying to pry, really, but I need to know if there's anything else we should be prepared for."

I automatically recoil. "What are you saying?" I can feel the heat rising in my cheeks.

Janette sighs heavily, chewing over her choice of words reluctantly: "This is hard. I'm just asking whether there's any substance to the rumors – and whatever you say will stay just between you and me, I promise. You can tell me anything. I just need to know."

"Me and Bill?" My stomach turns at the idea. "You're asking whether there's any substance to the suggestion that Bill and I were – had an intimate relationship?"

She doesn't answer. She stares at me blank-faced, just waits for me to continue.

"God, no. Hell no." I stand up and push the chair out behind me with a loud screech. This is crazy. I shouldn't even be here. I knew I should have stuck with keeping Janette at arm's length. "Is that why you asked me to come? To accuse me of sleeping with my boss?"

"I'm sorry." Her expression softens. "Listen, I'm not saying that I believe that anything happened. I just … I would need to know, if it had. I know. This is all horrible. I'm not accusing you. You know that if we swapped places, you'd have to ask me the same thing."

I try to calm myself and see things from Janette's perspective. She's right, unfortunately. In her position, which used to be mine, I might have needed to have the same awkward conversation. I look her right in the eye and tell her the truth.

"Of course there's nothing to the rumors. Nothing has ever happened between Bill and me. Ever."

"Good enough for me." She smacks her hand against the bar-top emphatically. "And thank you. I didn't mean to be insulting. I can tell you're smarter than that. I'm sorry I had to ask." Janette puts a hand on my arm. "I really am."

I simmer back down and take my seat again.

"Outside of that," she starts again, "anything else I should know about? Old lovers? Secrets? Anything?"

Jesus. What's with this woman? I shake my head in disbelief, trying not to let my rising anger get the best of me.

"Seriously, if this is why you asked me here, I'd rather just head home."

"I asked you here because it's been a rough day … and I'm worried about you," Janette answers. "I'd be lying if I said I wasn't also worried about the campaign. Knowing what we have to work with is part of my job, as you know. And everyone's got a skeleton or two in their closet."

"Not me," I answer, a little too quickly.

She chuckles to herself.

"It's nothing to be ashamed of. I'm not judging you now, and I wouldn't judge you no matter what you say. I just would need you to tell me."

"Sorry to let you down," I snap. "I've got nothing to hide."

"Honey," she says, "we all do. It's okay."

Thing is, I know she's right. If there's something else to dig up, she'd need to know now. The other side has shown they're willing to stoop and, if these affair rumors keep getting traction, they'll only be emboldened to keep at it. It's only going to get worse if I stick around. I hadn't been looking for a reason to stay home with Gracie, but maybe it would be for the best, at least for a little while. There will be other campaigns. It would be a setback for my career, but I could manage. I could be home to watch Gracie grow. That's worthwhile. Plenty of women do it, and I'd never hold it against them. And who would want to walk back into a shitstorm every single day, knowing they are the cause of it? Well, technically, whoever leaked the photo is the cause. But I'm the face of the problem. Just me being there is going to be a mess.

When the bartender asks us if we want another round, I decline.

"Time to get home to the baby?"

"Yeah. Might be where I belong."

"Just for tonight, you mean?" Janette watches my face. "I hope that's what you mean. You're not going to let all this change your mind."

I answer as honestly as I can. "I'm just not sure."

"Listen, you need to make the decision that's best for you, but I hope you won't let this ... *situation* make the decision for you. If you give in, you let them win. I don't mean the race, though it might reinforce the rumors, as you said yourself. But you can't let them win over *you* this way. You've been through tough times before. This is politics after all. Sometimes, it's not fair. A lot of the time it's not."

But if they keep digging ... A dull pressure is pulling tighter and tighter around my head. The room feels hotter than it was just a second ago. I should've stopped at just one drink. Or maybe I should have been watching over my shoulder better at work. I hate being unprepared. If I'd just known this was coming, I'd be in better shape now. And I can't spend the next few months waiting for some new dirt to pop up. I suddenly feel like I'm in the wrong place. Like I should be at home, figuring this out, not sitting with a woman I barely know. I've taken too many chances already.

"You know what," Janette says, kindness in her tone, "I really want you to just take some time to think about this, about what you want. If you want to stay with the campaign, which also happens to be what I want, I've got your back, one hundred percent. If they come up with some new story, we can handle it. We can refocus the narrative, we just have to use my PR brain to spin it the right way. Promise me you'll think about it, okay? Don't make any decisions right now."

I consider what she's saying, wavering. The exhaustion of the roller-coaster day suddenly hits me hard. My head is throbbing so hard it feels like it might burst. Her goodbye embrace catches me off guard, but it's a comfort.

A short-lived one.

The whole way home, my mind is searching for all the ways this could go wrong. I strain to remember who knows what, trying to identify the weak spots I must be missing. I squeeze my hands around the steering wheel like it's a stress ball, but it doesn't give. *I can think my way out of this. I've done it before.* I should have known a bigger campaign would mean bigger risks and more crafty opponents. I need to be more careful. I have to … or I'll lose so much more than just my job. Gracie's innocent face flashes across my mind and panic grips my chest so tightly it's hard to breathe.

9

THEN

You'd think I'd be good at this gig, parking along the side of the road, hiding out. I should be the queen of invisibility. My family – and I use the term loosely – has done such a good job of pretending I don't exist that they don't seem to have noticed that I'm gone. I stopped at a pay phone an hour ago to check with Tiff. No one has called her house looking for me and that would be the first place to check when I didn't come back "home" last night. The school would have called today, too, to tell my parents I didn't attend. If they got the message, they ignored it.

So what.

It's not my home.

Not my family.

Here, in front of me, this little split level, is where I belong. I just have to work up the guts to go up there. You'd think, after two years of planning this out – digging up hospital records and dozens of phone calls pretending to be a bill collector looking for Ms. Rebecca Cartwright – that this final step wouldn't make me queasy. But I hadn't thought out what this would feel like. I planned my runaway, stowed away bits of cash I found around the house, and took that stupid fast-food job so I could pay for a car, all so I could get here. I was always focused on the A-to-B part. I'd never thought out what it would feel like to walk up and knock on her door.

Dumbass.

I'd imagined her, the frazzled, sleepless woman who's waited for years to be reunited with her child. I hope she'll recognize me. In my hunt, I'd dug up her old high school yearbook, happy to see my face in hers. I've pictured her first glance, kind, and then the longer look, realization dawning.

Just go up there. Quit stalling.

What if she doesn't like me? What if she's mad that I found her? I'll tell her I forgive her, that I know there has to be some explanation for her giving me away as an infant. But what if she doesn't like who I am now? It's easy to love a baby or a little girl in pigtails. It's harder to love a teen who can't seem to get along with anybody. But that's because I haven't been where I belong.

Just walk up there. This is what you've been waiting for.

I think of us embracing, and how she'll cry. Maybe I will, too. Two broken pieces. Finally whole. We can finally be together. Everything else will work itself out. Life is going to be different now. That's if I can ever get out of this car.

My heart feels like it's going to beat right out of my chest.

I glance a couple more times in the rearview, nervous. But then I realize I don't have to be worried at all. Tiff said no one had called her house. Not my parents. Not the cops. No one is looking for me.

Except her.

I hope.

I look at the number on the mailbox again, 417. 417 Redbird Drive,

Scottsboro, AL. I've looked at that address a thousand times. There are no flowers planted around the front, the paint is peeling, and the grass is parched to all hell. This has to be it; it has the look of a place where things have never been quite right. Besides, I feel her in my bones. I know she's close. I just hope she needs me as much as I need her. Two of a kind.

But I still feel frozen. If this goes wrong, everything that was my reason to keep going … it's all gone. *Just go.* I exhale, long and slow, and pull down the mirror for one more look. Ugh. I add a slide of cheap lipstick to look less tired, less like a scared rabbit. *Okay. It's time.*

I look at the door one more time. *Here I go.*

But then it opens.

My breath catches in my throat.

My mother. My mom.

Her hair is a contrast of high, curled bangs against two columns of straight blonde locks cascading down both sides of her face. Her features are a blur from here, but I can tell she's smiling, and she hasn't even seen me yet. Today is our day.

Wait.

She's turning behind her. She's not alone.

I slink back into my chair, my wrist slumping away from the door handle, my mind trying to register what I'm seeing.

Behind her, a girl walks out into a bare patch of red dirt between what's alive of the grass. Her top is trendy and so are her clunky shoes and bootleg jeans over rail thin legs. I'd put her around thirteen years old or so, a little spoiled and snotty. When she smiles back at my mother, I can see her mouth is full of braces.

Then there's someone else bringing up the rear. A man, maybe mid-thirties, pulls the door shut behind him and rushes up to open the car door for my mother, who leans in for a quick kiss before she steps inside. The girl waits behind them, crossing her arms a minute before losing her patience at their show of affection and moving around the car to the other rear door. The guy, a real looker, doesn't glance in my direction, or anywhere, before he jumps in the car. They're all too wrapped up in their little world to notice me.

I don't know why I expected anything else.

I'm invisible anywhere I go.

In a belated flash of courage, I think maybe I can catch them. I could still step out of the car right now and wave them down before they pull out ... but what good would it do? I didn't ever picture my mother as someone ... happy. I thought she'd be looking for me. I thought she'd be alone. I thought she'd want me, but it looks like she's managing just fine without me.

I came for you. Why didn't you come for me?

For the past two years, I'd imagined her just showing up at my door. I've watched for her face everywhere, just in case she might be the one to find me first. I was convinced that every moment I was looking for her, she was doing the same thing. I thought for sure that she had to be searching for me this whole time. Now I know why she wasn't look-ing, why she never showed up. She moved on with her life. She's got another daughter, one she wanted to keep. The car's gone and so is my opportunity, for now. The windows are starting to fog on my cheap-ass car. I hate that I'm bawling. I hate that I've just seen my replacement, the girl living the life I should have had. I hate that my mom has found a way to not be a complete, miserable wreck – just like me.

I grip the wheel and wish I knew what to do, wish I had someone to tell me what I *should* do. But it's just me.

Alone. Like always.

My throat aches from trying and failing to hold back the tears. I'm tired from driving all night, sleeping in the car. My brain is swirling from shock. What now? What the fuck am I supposed to do now? I came all this way. I can't go back where I came from. I just can't do it. I want to beat the shit out of this fucking stupid car with a baseball bat. I want to beat the shit out of those two assholes with my mother too. *Stop. Think. Don't be a dumbass, Sarah.*

Time to take matters into my own hands. Again.

10

NOW

By Monday morning, I've made up my mind.

I just don't think I can go back.

Gracie's taking her bottle, and her face is so content, her eyes shut as she sucks, looking like a chubby little angel. Her sticky fingers have got hold of a strand of my hair, pulling me down toward her. I kiss the tip of her nose and smell baby. This quiet, beautiful life is what so many women want. I should be grateful. I hold her tiny body closer to me like she's all I've got left.

Then I think about what the office will be like. Just an hour or so until they notice I've not shown up. There might be a few phone calls to check on me, a little bit of a fuss, but that will all blow over quickly. They'll manage. I can prepare something for our press team, a statement that says I've decided to put motherhood first, for now. "My most important role" or something along those lines. I mull over what will satisfy and silence everyone, which is, of course, impossible. This story will be a dark cloud over my head for a long time. And Enid and Janette will have their hands full working with Dick to smooth things over. I've thought about it. I don't wish them ill; I just wish I could erase the way this all went down. I wish Enid had never told me she wanted the job in the first place. Then I wouldn't have to wonder whether she's the one who's pushed me into a corner like this.

"You okay, sweetie?" Brad's in the kitchen, making breakfast for two, turning around to study my face periodically. He's been doing that all weekend. I know he's just trying to help, but I wish he'd give it a rest.

"I'll be fine."

"We'll be fine," he says, correcting me. "We will get through this. Maybe it's all for the best anyway. You'll see."

"I know." I watch Gracie give her typical response to Daddy's voice. Her eyes flash open, suddenly wide with delight, and her body freezes, waiting for more.

"I know it's not how you wanted things to happen." Brad's turned his back away from me again to pay attention to the eggs sizzling over the stove. "I'd never have wanted this. You didn't deserve it, and we will figure this all out. You know my mom and sister. If there's any way to find out who might have done this to you, they'll hear about it first. They know everybody."

I squeeze Gracie a little tighter. I know he's trying to help – and he's so protective – but I'm exhausted from thinking and worrying, and I really don't need anyone else digging around, especially not the two he just mentioned. If I know Brad's sister, she's probably already leapt to ugly conclusions. She'd be all too happy to make me out to be a cheater. I just want to be left alone. I glance at the microwave. A few minutes to eight. Brad will be leaving soon, and I'll have the house to myself.

I'm so busy wishing the minutes away, I nearly jump out of my seat when I hear a knock at the door.

Brad looks to me.

"Who could that be this early? You expecting somebody?"

I shake my head and put Gracie over my shoulder, my hand behind her protectively.

67

"It's okay. Stay there." Brad switches the stove eye off. He's hurrying to put my plate on the table when the follow-up knocks start.

"Be right there," he yells.

I push the plate back and listen in as he answers the door.

"Can I help you?"

"Looking for Sarah." The voice is chipper, and familiar.

Janette?

I hear her introduce herself to Brad as "one of Sarah's friends from the campaign" and then see her step around him, a huge coffee in each hand. *What's she doing here? She thinks we're friends?*

"Hey, Janette. What are you up to?" I try not to sound as shocked as I feel.

"Thought we could use a little boost this morning." She eyes my sweatpants and oversized T-shirt suspiciously and then smiles at Gracie, who's lifted her head upright to inspect our visitor. "Oh, hi, little one. Oh my word. Isn't she darling!"

"Thanks." I gesture toward an empty seat, but Janette shakes her head.

"No. We'd better get moving. Just thought you could use a pick-me-up. Want me to hold Gracie for a minute while you um … finish getting ready?"

I see Brad gathering his lunch for work from the fridge in the background and glancing at me, brows raised, with a question in his eyes.

"Actually …" I sigh. "I mean, I've thought a lot about going back, or not going back, to be honest."

"Oh, no. Don't say it. You're not giving in, are you?"

I don't have to look directly at Brad to sense that he's boring holes in the back of Janette's head with his glare. I see his mouth make the silent question: *Who is this?*

68

"Well, I've got plenty of reasons to stay at home." I try to make my voice sound more resolute than I feel.

"I know you do," Janette answers, crossing her arms. "Of course you do. But you're not giving up those reasons by deciding to stick it out with the campaign. It doesn't have to be an either-or decision."

"I think the media has now made it easier to make a choice, maybe one I should have made in the first place." Brad should appreciate that comment. He comes to stand behind me, offering his physical presence as moral support when what I really want is a quiet, empty house. I could really just use a few minutes alone, and I was minutes away from that.

"It's okay, babe." I turn to him. "I don't want you to be late for work. I'll be just fine."

His shoulders fall almost imperceptibly, and he nods and steps away. I'll make it up to him later.

"Sarah –" Janette jumps back in.

"I just don't want to."

"If I believed you, that would be fine," Janette says. "But I know where your heart is. I know it's hard. But we still need you. Bill wants you there. We need your guidance. We can figure out a way to make this work and keep you protected and out of the spotlight, and then keep the campaign moving in a positive direction, the way it has been."

I keep quiet. Either Janette's a fabulous actress, or she actually cares that I don't give up my career.

"You didn't get all the way to running a gubernatorial race without a few bumps along the way, right? I mean, it's politics. People sling mud. It can be vicious. You know all that. You can't let them win. You can't let something like this stop you. That's not you. It's not who you are."

I want to believe her. I want to think it's not me. I know Janette doesn't realize the extent of things I'm worried about. I can't believe I'm thinking this ... but she seems sincere. She must have checked in with Bill before stopping by my house, and he obviously told her he wants me to come back to the campaign or she wouldn't be here now, prodding me. Brad won't be thrilled if I go back, though he'd never say that outright. I know he'll support me either way. It's one of his amazing qualities. I turn to see him walking down the stairs and hustle to meet him at the front door, the one he painted red just to make me happy. I need him to be alright with this; he'd been so cautiously excited about the idea of having me staying home. I know it's what he wants most, if it really came down to it.

I give him a quick kiss and try to read his expression.

"What do you think, babe?" I whisper, hoping I'm out of earshot. I don't need Janette to assume that I only do what my boyfriend wants.

He sighs and seems to weigh what he'll say.

"I think," he pauses a beat to cup my face in his palms and kiss my forehead, "you should do what you feel like you need to do."

God, I love him. I really do. In that moment, I wish I could be everything he needs me to be.

"I told you, we're going to make it work, either way," he adds. "I want you to be happy. I don't want you ever to feel like you missed an opportunity."

"Thank you, babe." I kiss him one more time. "Thank you so much."

He knows what I'm going to decide – and he loves me, even if it hurts.

"Up to you. Just let me know if you need me to have my mom watch Gracie," he says, turning to leave. "Your call."

When I walk back down the hall, I find Janette studying my gallery wall of framed movie posters from cinema's glamorous golden era. It's a silly thing to collect, but old movies have always been my escape. Everything was less complicated then, or at least that's how it looks. No reality TV or high-def images to make things look grittier or too real.

"Gilda's one of my absolute favorites," Janette says, facing the poster of Rita Hayworth smoking coolly in a slinky gown. "You know it was a sort of copycat of Casablanca. Little less squeaky-clean."

"And a little more twisted," I answer with enthusiasm I can never contain when it comes to old Hollywood. "Producers wanted another Casablanca-style hit. They got close ... but no cigar."

"I think the trouble was less about the lack of cigars and more about the lack of Humphrey Bogart." She snickers and stoops to inspect a poster of Gene Kelly, Debbie Reynolds and Donald O'Connor dancing in rain slickers. A real gem.

Funny. I hadn't really pictured Janette as a kindred spirit. A few of the women from the neighborhood who've stopped by have asked where I get my "vintage art," not realizing Rita was once bigger than the Kardashian sisters and Gene was the most charming man who ever walked the planet.

"So," Janette whirls around to me, "back to business. Or, back to work, I hope."

She gives me another moment to consider.

I take a deep breath and make my decision.

"Well, if you and Bill feel good about it, then maybe I will."

"No." She crosses her arms and presses her lips together. "It's about whether *you* feel good about it. I just would hate to see you give up something you want because you think other people want you gone, especially when it's not true at all. Bill and I want you there, and I don't want you to give up something you've worked so hard for, if you're making that decision for the wrong reasons."

"You're right."

"So ... that means you'll come to work today?"

"Yes, I think I will."

She gives a warm smile.

"I knew you wouldn't let them get to you. That makes me happy. We'll do whatever it takes to make this work."

I think about Brad, always giving and always being supportive of me, no matter what. And Janette took the time to make sure I was okay. Maybe Bill was right to bring her in … and maybe I should give her a chance. Sweet Gracie in my arms fingers my collarbone tenderly. For just a second, I relax. Maybe everything will work itself out.

"I'll leave this here with you." Janette slides the coffee toward my plate of uneaten eggs. "I'll let everybody know not to worry. You just got a little tied up this morning. See you in a little bit?"

"Yup," I answer. "And thanks for this."

"No prob."

"Oh, Janette." I catch her at the door. "Curious how you found my house?"

"Can't pull any fast ones on you, honey." She laughs and shoots me a playful wink. "On your resume."

"Oh, yeah." I set Gracie in her swing and shuffle to meet Janette at the door and give her a hug. "Well, I'm glad you found me." I mean that. "Thanks again, for everything. I'll see you soon."

11

NOW

B oots on the ground.

Literally.

The rain is pouring down, but my spirits are high, or as high as they can be under the circumstances. I know exactly how to step up, or down, to the role of volunteer manager; it's where I started out and it's a great way to feel like you're really doing something that matters. Canvasing neighborhoods, talking to people face-to-face, getting real-time feedback. It's as grassroots as you can get. I've packed my galoshes and I'm ready to meet the team. I've already been replaced, had my name dragged through the mud – potentially by my closest friend – so I can't imagine what could stop me now.

Besides, our hardworking volunteers deserve an enthusiastic leader. I'm not going to let them down.

Mary Beth gives me an uncomfortable smile when I step through the front door, but I don't let it get to me. I ignore the whispers I can hear arising from the cubicles I walk past and the surprised looks. *Yes, I came back after all.* I make it to the rear conference room just in time for the last ten minutes of the morning briefing. Janette beams at me as if my arrival were a personal victory for her, some unspoken accomplishment for the two of us.

"There she is," she says. "Glad you made it. I can't believe your sitter bailed on you like that. Can't depend on anybody anymore."

Dick scowls, and every eye in the room is on me, suspicious.

"All taken care of now." I give my most confident greeting and apologize to have missed most of the meeting.

"No, no. You're just in time," Janette says. "Everyone, I'd like to give a quick update on Sarah. After brainstorming about the best way to handle Friday's *incident*, we've decided Sarah is too valuable to lose and that her dismissal could raise even more questions. Instead, she'll be mobilizing the troops as our volunteer manager." She shoots Dick a satisfied glare. "As we noted in our last statement to the press, Sarah of course denies the rumors outright and has agreed to a paternity test."

I feel heat rising in my cheeks and try to will it away. I need to remember to schedule that. There's something I never would have thought I'd be doing.

Thankfully, there are no follow-ups from the press team and Janette sends all of us out to get started on a busy week. I've only been back at my desk for a few minutes when I notice a visitor lurking in the doorway, waiting for me to notice.

It's Enid.

How long has she been standing there? Was she watching me?

She's looking polished, looking like a sharp assistant campaign manager.

I don't know what to say at first. All I can think is *you didn't, did you?*

I don't need to come up with a line though, as she speaks first. Her hands fall to her sides like she just can't keep inside whatever she wants to say.

"Sarah, I can't tell you how sorry I am about what's happened to you," she says, her eyes scanning the floor around my feet.

I don't move toward her. I don't know what to do or think. I want to believe her, but I don't know whether I should. Brad had said, emphatically, there was no way Enid would hurt us like this. I want to think he's right.

Enid finally looks up and breaks the silence.

"It's so unfair," she says in a way I can tell she's practiced. "This whole thing. First, you coming back to … what you came back to after you had the baby. Then the picture and the stories. I spent the whole weekend worrying about you."

"I thought you might call."

"I wanted to. I just – I had a lot to take care of. And I thought you'd need some time and space to regroup. You and Brad and Gracie. I didn't want to interfere."

"You wouldn't have been interfering. It would have been nice to hear from you actually."

Enid falls silent again and wrings her hands. I don't think I've ever seen her nails polished and manicured. Come to think of it, I haven't seen her in heels since she was running around press conferences when she was working the nonprofit circuit.

"I know. I'm sorry. I just – I guess I didn't know what to say." Her voice is quiet. I don't know if she's ashamed or if she wants to make sure no one else can hear her.

"Well," I search for how I should respond, "I guess congratulations are in order."

I don't mean to sound cold toward Enid. I just don't know for sure that I can trust her anymore.

She lets out a long, shaking breath.

"You know this isn't how I would have wanted this." She watches my face, trying to convince me. "I never would have wanted it to happen this way. I'd never want you to be hurt like this."

She looks upset, her forehead wrinkled in concern – and yet, she doesn't look quite as upset as the day she told me she wanted to be assistant campaign manager. She's not on the verge of tears. She looks more afraid than anything else.

"That means a lot," I answer coolly, grabbing my cell phone, if only to have somewhere else to look. "Thank you."

"Sure thing," she answers.

I wait for her to get the hint and leave, but she stands there a few moments too long. Finally, she gives in.

"If you have any questions or need any introductions, or anything at all, let me know," she offers. "I want to help out any way I can. I think you'll find we have a pretty great crew of volunteers."

"Thanks for the advice. I'd better get to work. Rain's not going to let up, and the sooner we get started, the better." I know how fabricated that excuse sounds. I can feel my enthusiasm for the day's work slipping away as Enid steps out of the room. I try to push the thought from my head, but it's too heavy. *Who else could have done it? Who else would have been around long enough to snap a photo like that?* Enid had the access, she wanted my job in the worst way ... and she was more than ready to make a leap for my position when it suddenly became open.

I can't let my mind spiral like this. On to the volunteers, and the front lines. They need a strong, confident leader.

We're only on our second working-class neighborhood when my phone dings the first time. A text from Enid. Now she wants to go out for drinks. I don't know why she's so interested in being friends now.

Huddled under a stranger's front porch awning, I type out a polite response. Erase it. Then I type out what I really want to ask: "Why would I go for drinks with a backstabber?" I erase that rapidly. I can picture her watching the text message bubbles show up and disappear. Maybe I should just ask her outright. But what if she didn't do it? What kind of friend does that make me?

"Sarah?"

It's Elaine, pretty much the carbon copy of our front desk manager Mary Beth, only she's sopping wet. She's got a Porter campaign poncho – it's been a seriously rainy fall – but the hood is, inexplicably, back from her head. Dripping, dark curls are smashed against her plump cheeks, and she's asking me again how many times we should knock before we head to the next house in the cul-de-sac.

My phone dings again. Enid.

"We didn't really get to catch up last time. I feel bad. Want to see you. Hope everything's okay between us."

What do you feel so bad about, Enid?

"Sarah?" Elaine is persistent.

I huff and put my phone in my pocket. It dings again. *Hold on, Enid. Jeez.*

"Think we should move ahead now, Sarah?"

My phone buzzes once again, and my patience cracks.

"Elaine, does it seem like no one is home?"

"I've knocked three times," she answers, shocked at my tone.

"Then, obviously no one is coming to the door. Obviously, no one is going to answer, so yes, I would think we are safe to go ahead and move on to the next house."

I watch her face change in shades – from stunned to crushed to indignant – as she absorbs my response. I instantly want to backtrack. *Damn it, Enid.*

77

"I'm sorry. We're all tired," I stammer. "My daughter hasn't been sleeping well. I haven't had much rest over the past week. She's sick and my boyfriend won't stop messaging me about her."

That doesn't soften her icy glare. *Great, I've made an enemy.* I can actually picture her telling her family around dinner about how her ass of new manager completely snapped ... and then telling them the back story. The rumors. How I was quietly moved around, probably how everybody in the office wonders whether I really did sleep with the boss. How some people are saying it's how I got the campaign manager job in the first place. *It might not even be her husband's baby! And he's not even her husband. She isn't married at all.*

"I am sorry, Elaine." I try again. "I didn't mean to snap at you. Let's go ahead and leave the door hanger."

She won't look at me, but she hangs the paper with Bill's picture on it and the bulleted talking points I helped him write on the back. I pull out my phone and type a curt message to Enid:

"Sorry. Busy. Can't do tonight. Too much to take care of. Brad waiting for me after work."

That's more than enough explanation. I tuck my phone away and ignore the text message alerts that follow, almost nonstop. In my pocket, I feel for the silencer button and switch the sound to *off*.

Four neighborhoods later and Elaine is still sullen. By now, I know she's relayed the incident – my nasty response – to the rest of the crew. Few of them will make eye contact. We're soaked to the bone. We're supposed to hit two more neighborhoods, but we've only got an hour left on the clock. I try to remind myself that these folks are here on their own time. They have generous spirits. They care about the cause. But everyone is chilly toward me; I feel like hanging up my poncho for the day and wonder whether it wouldn't be a welcome announcement. Dashing from porch to porch in this weather is a serious drag. Doing it when you know everyone thinks you're a sham, or some kind of slut, is even worse.

When a woman in a turtleneck and tiny glasses answers her door and tells Elaine that she'll never vote for a philanderer and slams the door in our face, Elaine gives me the smuggest of shrugs, a satisfied smirk on her face. I know I've made the right move avoiding Enid. I couldn't keep my cool if I saw her face right now. And I thought she was *my person*, my confidant at work. *What a friend.*

At least there's Janette. I'm here, doing what I believe in – even though it's hard – because she insisted. She wanted me here, wouldn't let me give up. For now, that's enough to keep me going to the last door. At least I know someone's got my back.

When my phone starts vibrating in my pocket again, I'm ready to tell Enid what I really think of her sudden interest in maintaining our friendship – but then I see she wasn't the one trying to get in touch with me. It's Brad.

"Please call.

"Sarah?

"You okay?

"I need to talk to you.

"Where are you?"

He's been texting me the entire afternoon, and I've been ignoring my phone. I think of him at his office, trying to check on me – and getting nothing, for hours. He's probably worried sick.

I sneak back to one of the volunteer vans for a quiet moment. The driver, a guy around Bill's age, wearing a baseball cap, is pretending not to listen as he eats a bag of greasy potato chips. He's a terrible actor.

"Babe?" I whisper. "What is it?"

"Are you hiding somewhere?"

"No, why?"

"Your voice sounds muffled."

"In the volunteer van. Not alone."

"Why'd it take you so long to call?"

"Sorry. Just, we're running around. It's a total mess. I've been ignoring my phone. Thought it was someone else."

"Who?"

"I'll tell you later."

"I hope so." He sounds irritated, which is out of character. Maybe just worried.

"What's wrong?"

"Not great news."

"What's happened? You okay, babe? Gracie okay?"

"We're fine. I just want you to know that you should probably come around to the back door when you get home."

"Why?"

"There are –" he pauses to count aloud. "Two, three, four. Four TV news vans out front. A couple other cars too."

"Ugh. Babe. Seriously?"

"Yup."

12

NOW

Brad's never talked to me like that. He hardly ever calls me at work. He's never suspicious. He's never not warm to me. Replaying his conversation in my mind has my stomach in tight knots. Somebody must have gotten to him. If I'd just looked at my phone once, I might have averted this whole thing. Maybe it was just pent-up frustration.

But my gut tells me it's something worse. I know the man's moods entirely. Almost every one of them is on the optimistic, empathetic, supportive side of the personality spectrum. Nothing gets him down, or at least nothing we've been through together so far. I don't really want to think of him any other way. It wouldn't be Brad.

My windshield wipers are cranked up to full blast when I pull into our development, tidy new houses that contrast with the haphazard look of the older neighborhoods I spent the day trudging through. I'm sure our neighbors would be secretly thrilled to watch from their windows to take in the scene Brad was describing on the phone. More gossip fodder for the wine-cooler club at the next backyard barbecue.

Damn.

Brad wasn't exaggerating. I cruise past the front of the house and, sure enough, at least five news crews are now parked outside. Thanks to the downpour, there aren't reporters standing on the lawn. I'm sure they're all crouched in their vans, cameras ready to go the moment I pull up. An ambush. *Sorry, guys. Not today.*

I keep moving without attracting attention and pull around to the road behind our house, parking on the street. I squish through the mud to our back porch and rap softly on the door. A single blind cracks open – and then Brad appears. I want to collapse into his arms, but he's holding Gracie. His mouth is set in a hard line, and I wonder whether he's regretting being so supportive of my second return to work. Something's eating at him. Maybe it's the makeshift newsroom out in our front yard.

"Hi babe." I keep my voice low.

"You made it."

"Undercover, yes." Inside, I hurry to lock the door behind me.

"They sure are a pain in the ass, aren't they?" He grumbles. "I was kind a hoping this would all blow over."

"Not how it usually works, unfortunately." I leave my soaking wet boots next to the back door and reach for the baby. "Momma missed you."

She reaches her arms out to me and gives me the most beautiful gummy smile, the one that literally stole my breath the first time I saw it, just a month ago. When things were quieter. When things were more sane. More in control. I'd called Brad on video chat the second I recovered, both of us euphoric. A depth of love I never knew I could experience. Fierce love for my baby girl. A bright light in my life, and a reason to keep fighting.

Now, the rooms are dim, lights off except in the kitchen and every blind on the first floor drawn tightly closed.

"Babe, thank you. I'm so sorry about all this. I know it affects you too."

He's silent for a moment, looks directly at me. Not angry. Forlorn. I want to beg him to tell me what's wrong – but part of me is afraid to ask. I don't want to have to answer his questions. I don't want to cause any more trouble or take any more risks. When he sits at the dining room table, I get the feeling that I'm being brought in for questioning, or at least invited to confess. Brad would never be able to pull off the bad cop role, not my Brad. He's just hurt. And I don't know why.

"My sister is all kinds of worried," he says, finally.

She's never liked me. Who knows what she's said to him.

"What does she think?"

"They called her too," he avoids the question, nodding toward the front yard.

"She didn't talk to them?" A fresh burst of panic spreads in my chest. I hadn't thought about that. Tracie would enjoy hurting me, or at least distancing me from her brother, but I can't imagine she'd want this for Brad.

"No." His dark hair, just starting to thin a little on top, is more tousled than typical. I can picture him raking his fingers through it. This might be worse than I thought. What nasty idea did his sister plant?

"What is it, babe?"

Gracie's bouncing happily in my arms, batting at my shoulders and my bottom lip. She wants to play. I kiss her fingers absentmindedly.

"I just – I think we should talk."

My heart sinks to my stomach. *What has he been told? What did they find out? What does he want to know?*

"Now?" I stall. "Want to get something to eat first?"

He doesn't answer and doesn't look at me when he moves to the sofa, as if he's trying to get away from something by moving from room to room. But he can't shake whatever's bothering him.

83

In the dark living room, I can't read his face. I move closer to him, and Gracie reaches out and grabs a fist of his shirt sleeve. He kisses the top of her head and I inhale the smell of him. Sporty cologne and shampoo. I want to just forget today and sink into his embrace, but he seems far away from me. I want the Brad I had this morning. Eight hours ago, he was still himself – the man I love. The man who's always got my back.

"You know I love you, Sarah."

"And I love you, babe." I can't help but sound desperate. It's the first time I've ever felt like I can't read him.

"I love you so much I want to marry you," he keeps going, "and even if you decide marriage is not for you, I want to be with you. I want us to be a family. I'd never want to pressure you, and I understand why you worry. Marriage is a huge step."

You don't really understand. You can't possibly. Like so many other times, I think of telling him everything, sharing all of me. I do care about him. I love him. I want to believe he'll love me no matter what. But I can't bring myself to take that risk. I hold my breath, waiting for him to tell me the rest of whatever's on his mind, afraid to give away too much before I know what he's really asking.

"With all this going on, I just hope you know you could tell me anything."

I wish I could, babe. I want to hold him close to me. I want to tell him I love him over and over – because it's the one thing I know is the absolute truth.

He repeats, "I hope you know that you can tell me anything. And I hope you would."

I nod, but don't offer anything else. It seems like the right response. If I had something to hide, I'd be rambling. Right?

"So … is there anything you want to tell me?" He isn't letting it go. He clears his throat and stands up, waiting and shifting his weight nervously. "When it comes to the rumors … I mean, I trust you completely, but if there were something going on before – I'd understand that you wouldn't want to tell me. But I'd want to know, if anything ever had happened, if something were going on. Something I should know about. You know I don't want to ask it, but … is there any truth to what they're saying?"

Relief floods over me. Why didn't he just say that?

"Bill? Bill and me?" I jump up and wrap my free arm around his neck, press my cheek into his stubble. "Baby, never."

He watches me, wanting to believe me.

"Baby, I would never do that to you," I urge. "Listen, unfortunately this kind of thing sometimes comes with the job. I hate Charles for doing this to us."

"You think he gave the TV stations the picture?"

"It's my best guess," I answer honestly. "He's hated me forever."

"He does what you do?"

"The same thing. He runs campaigns, only for the wrong team." I dare a small smile at Brad, relieved that he's at least talking. These are questions I *can* answer.

Brad gives in. He sighs like a weight's been lifted from his shoulders and wraps both of his arm around me – the embrace I'd been waiting for – and buries his head in the crook of my neck. Gracie squeals with joy, her hand flexing open and closed on her daddy's shoulder.

I don't deserve a man this loving.

"I love you so much. I'm sorry to ask that at all," he whispers, staying near my ear. "I just never want there to be secrets between us. No matter how hard. I'd rather at least know."

I'm glad we're still in the dark so I don't have to worry about my expression. What I'm telling him is true. Bill and I have never been romantic in any way, other than me maneuvering around his occasional flirtatious gestures, which gross me out, to be honest. I've no interest in him whatsoever, other than in making him governor. My endeavors at work are completely focused on furthering my career and following my passion. And look at my life! Aside from the past few weeks, I've got things held together pretty well. The love of my life. Our precious baby girl. A nice house, nice car, promising career prospects. Everything looks just right. I'd never cheat on Brad, but the trouble is ... there *are* things he doesn't know. And I'd be letting him down if he ever found out the truth.

But isn't that true of everyone? Even Janette said it: *Everyone has a skeleton or two in their closet.* Mine just happens to be more devastating than I imagine everyone else's to be. But maybe that's all in my mind. Maybe Brad would still want me ...

"I think they've given up." Brad is peeking through the blinds. "We're in the clear again."

"Thank goodness for that." I look down and notice that Gracie's resting her cheek over my heart, starting to get sleepy. A few circles on her back and her eyelids are getting heavy, lashes fluttering. She smiles, half awake, when I kiss her soft brow. *My love.* Behind me, I feel Brad encircling both of us in his arms.

"Five minutes, babe," I promise him. "Meet you in our room?"

In her nursery, painted in soft teal and so pretty it could have come straight out of a magazine, I rock her until she's motionless, fists curled, and breathing deeply, warm against my chest. When I lay her in her crib, she doesn't stir at all. She's angelic in the soft glow of her night light. Life is so perfect the way it is right now, too perfect to let go of. The truth is too much to risk.

13

THEN

F*ind a way.*

That's become my motto.

The turn-of-the-century house severed into four rundown units came at the right price – two-hundred dollars a month, per unit – but it happened to not have any vacancies. A stinking dead rodent or two solved that problem. I knew the little old lady would be the first to crack. I watched her grown daughters load her belongings into a van just a week after I planted the rats on her back porch. The landlady was surprised that I wouldn't want to wait for the exterminator, but I said I would just let him come in and do his thing whenever he could. No need to hold off. My old lease was up, and I was in a hurry – that's what I'd said. What I really meant was that I was sick of sleeping in the backseat of my car and a little worried that the man of the family, the man hanging around my mother day and night, might one day wonder why the same beat-up Ford was always parked within viewing distance of his house.

I've finally got my own place and it offers the perfect view: right into Rebecca Cartwright's yard. When they have the blinds open to let the sunshine in, I can see directly into her kitchen. I make a point to eat my breakfast when she and her other daughter do, a morning ritual. Mom's usually got her hair wrapped in a towel piled on her head as she eats what I assume is cereal. I do the same, propping my feet up on the cheap outdoor furniture I got for a steal, quite literally, from a general store in town. My job sucks, but that's to be expected. I went from greasy fast food to greasy spoon. I've become a pro at dodging men who can't seem to keep their hands to themselves. I can spot them the second they walk in the door. If the hostess gives them one of my tables, I've got my steaming hot pot of coffee ready to go. I'll tell you, it can cause a nasty burn for anyone dumb enough to try slipping a hand up the bottom of the circle skirts that O'Dell's makes every waitress wear, the kind that drive old men crazy. Luckily, I'm here to teach them all a lesson.

When a portly gentleman with a mouthful of snuff steps through the doors this morning and I see the hostess nod in my direction, I've got a fresh pot of joe to grab before I escort him to his table.

"Right this way, sir."

His smile shows off a mouthful of rotten teeth.

I run a quick calculation: It's been two weeks since I accidentally poured hot coffee into the last groping customer's lap. It might raise suspicion if I do it again this morning. Besides, I don't want any trouble today. It's Tuesday, grocery night. We – meaning my mother, my sister, and I – typically stop to load up on frozen dinners tonight. At least, that's been their routine for the past month. They don't know, yet, that I join them. I'm planning to introduce myself when the time is right. I think tonight might be my chance. I'm going to say hi to the girl, if nothing else. I don't want any work drama to hold me up and Bubba here's got drama written all over him. I'll have to manage this one without causing a scene.

"Coffee?" He doesn't know how lucky he is. I know exactly where I'd like to pour it.

"Sure thing, sweetheart." He edges the cup toward me, his eyes at the buttons straining to keep the top of my dress together. The boss who couldn't keep his eyes off my low-cut top during my job interview had insisted on having the head waitress give me a size smaller than I should be wearing. I'm surrounded by creeps.

I ignore his term of endearment and take his order, making sure to keep my distance as much as I can manage. Lucky for both of us, he doesn't try anything and the morning and afternoon pass without incident. In the kitchen, one of the other girls, a teen mom, catches me shoving packets of soup crackers into my purse. She raises an eyebrow at me and I think she's going to rat me out ... then she grabs a plastic bag and leads me to the back where there are boxes of day-old pastries and rolls that are marked with the name of a local food shelter.

"If you want, just take a bag and leave out the front door at the top of the hour. Maggie always goes out back for her smoke break at exactly the top of the hour. Gives you about a five-minute window."

"Thanks, Jess." I like her over-the-top eyeliner and consider asking her where she gets it, but I've got places to be. No time for chitchat. And I don't need anyone prying into my business. I've got enough plans to keep me busy for a long time. That means there's no room for friends.

"Hey, girl's gotta eat, right?" She smiles at me like we're in this life of struggle together. She's wrong. She can't even imagine.

"You got it," I answer, faking enthusiasm. "Thanks again." I toss a few bear claws and a row of dinner rolls into the plastic bag she's handed me and hurry out the front door. A nice gesture. I file the information away in case I need to point the blame elsewhere down the road. That dark eyeliner makes her look guilty as sin. I, on the other hand, have been perfecting the art of looking like the sweetest, most squeaky-clean seventeen-year-old you ever ran into in the cereal aisle.

My mom must have had a rough day of work at the gas station. Today was a scorcher and the last time I meandered into the rear of the store with my sunglasses down, the foreign guy who owns the station clearly hadn't bothered to upgrade the air conditioner. I had to keep pretending to look at sodas to keep the doors open on the refrigerator section.

My mother and my sister are a half hour later than usual when they come in through the front doors in matching pink flip-flops. Mom's hair is wilted, mascara melted into smudges around the edges of her eyes from the way she rubs them when she needs more coffee. They head straight to the frozen food section, as usual. Next will be the snack aisle and then milk and cereal.

I watch them, deciding whether to pick the frozen pizza brand that's on sale or to splurge on something fancier. I finger the wad of one-dollar bills in my pocket, wondering whether there's a way for me to help them out without outing my identity. But I'll need to save most of my tip money to make my rent this month. Then I hear the girl ask my mother about cereal. Mom sighs, rubs her eyes again, and says she's in a hurry. That's fine. The girl can go grab what they need and meet her mom at the front. The lines are really long today anyway.

This is perfect.

My heart is beating so hard I can hear it thumping in my ears. I don't want to wait any longer to at least make contact, but it takes everything I've got to calmly head over to Aisle 3 instead of just giving up and going back to my car and my crummy apartment and my own stupid sad life like I always do. *Grow a set,* I tell myself. *She's just a little girl.*

Not like *little*, little. I'm really only a few years older than her, though my life's much more complex. Naturally, she's a little more innocent. She's unsuspecting, standing there in front of the sugary cereal brands, tapping painted toes. An image of my mother and her lounging around her bedroom – I'm sure it's all done up in girly colors to match the white lace curtains I've seen – painting their toes together sends a stab of jealous rage through my stomach. But I compose myself, again, and walk right up to her.

Her silky ponytail swings when she turns my way.

"Excuse me." I smile politely and reach for a giant bag of generic cereal, Toasty-Os, at her feet. I see her toes are not just painted hot pink but also coated in a layer of glitter.

"Cute polish," I say, pointing at her feet.

"What?" She giggles, bashful. "Thanks."

"You do them yourself?"

"Oh, no. From a sleepover last weekend."

That explains why I hadn't seen her all day Saturday.

"Sounds like fun."

The moment is getting a little awkward when I'm saved by the girl's klutziness. Too adorable. And it worked out perfectly. She went to put one of the two boxes of cereal she was holding back on the shelf and knocked four others onto the floor. I bend down to lend a hand.

"Thanks." She laughs, a little embarrassed. "My mom likes this kind, but it's really not my favorite."

"Ha. I understand that. Moms are always trying to steer you toward the healthy variety."

"Yeah, but it tastes like tree bark."

Out of nowhere, I have an urge to protect, or at least guide her. If things were the way they were meant to be, I'd be her wise older sister, trying to keep her out of trouble. I'd never pictured myself that way, as a loving sibling, but standing here with her I can imagine what it might be like. Makeup tutorials. Talking about boys and telling her the type to stay away from. Helping her with algebra and bitchy friends. I don't dislike the feeling.

"I hate to say it ... but sometimes moms know best." Suddenly, I really want her to like me. I want to be part of her life, too, not just my mother's.

She shrugs at me, losing interest.

"Yeah. My mom's pretty cool usually."

"Not everybody can say that." I tell her, hoping it doesn't sound preachy. I want her to think I'm cool. I hadn't expected to like her this much, but her patch of freckles combined with the braces and the swishy ponytail is pure innocence, with just a dash of budding teen to make her feisty and unpredictable. I could picture us having a mani-pedi night and watching some cheesy soaps.

"If you've got a mom and dad who love you, you're pretty well off." Now I do sound preachy, but I have to say it.

She cringes at that and I wish I could take it back. Maybe I'm giving too much away.

"Well, I've got a mom who loves me. That's true. Don't know much about my dad."

That explains her reaction. No dad. We're the same that way.

"Oh." *So the guy hanging around is just a boyfriend.* "I'm sorry to hear that."

"It's okay. It's been that way my whole life." She fidgets, and I know she's thinking it's about time to go meet our mom in the checkout line. Instead, she opens up just a little. "Mom's got a nicer boyfriend now, though. I didn't like the last guy. I don't love this one, either –"

"Why not?" I jump in.

"It's just that he's a little too … open sometimes."

What kind of open? I don't want her to be going through what I went through with my adopted father, that asshole who felt free to sneak into my bed at night.

"What do you mean?" I ask her, feeling another unexpected surge of protectiveness.

"Makes out with her right in front of me. He just lets his hands go anywhere. Makes me feel really creeped out."

Searching her face, the way she won't look at my eyes right now, I know there's more that she's not telling me. I know what it's like to live with a sicko, someone who lets his hands go wherever they please.

"He doesn't ever make you feel weird otherwise, right?" I have to ask it outright. I'm her sister. It's my job to take care of her.

She squirms, uncomfortable.

"No, not really. He's just kinda gross."

"What do you mean?" I wish she knew she could talk to me, that she could tell me anything. I can tell I'm prying too much, but I can't help it. All I can think about is the disgusting things my adoptive father did to me.

She pulls her box of breakfast tighter against her chest and avoids my eyes. "Anyway, nice to meet you. Thanks for the help."

By the time she's rounding the corner, I'm stuffing the giant bag of generic cereal back alongside the others. I don't really feel hungry now and I need to save my cash for rent. All I can think of is the man hanging around my family, the sensation of him shoving his tongue down one of their throats. I know all about gross men in the house, and I want to keep all of them the hell away from my little sister.

I wait until dark to make my next move.

When I was packing up from the house where I used to live with my adoptive parents, I'd grabbed a few things I didn't think would be missed. Some spare soap from the closet. Boxes of mac 'n cheese from the pantry. An unopened tire changing tool set from the garage. At the time, I thought the kit's lug wrench could make a decent weapon against an attacker. It's heavy enough to knock someone out cold and, as a bonus, it doesn't look out of place in the backseat of my car.

I spend the next hour or so staked out a few houses down the street, thinking about how far I've come. When I started, I only had this beater. Now I've got my own place and a job that, I guess, is as good as any. The first time I saw her, I was parked near here, just like this. Of course, that was the first time I saw my little sister too – and him. I hated her at first, but I've come to see she's not the main problem. It's that guy. I knew there was something about him I didn't like. Old men who frequent diners and harass waitresses aren't the only kind who can be creepy. He's handsome, but he had that look to him. The look of a guy who just grabs what he wants. Asshole.

Not anymore.

I'd watched them eat dinner, presumably frozen pizza, from my balcony. For a while after, the TV made sporadic flashes of light through the living room curtains. Then I saw the girl's light switch on for a little while. Now all the rooms are dark. I'm just giving it a few more minutes to be safe. Luckily, there's a row of young pine trees that grant some privacy around the side of the house. They block out nosy neighbors to the left, right around where this boyfriend likes to park his truck. When I think I've given it enough time, I reach for my weapon.

The lug wrench weighs heavy in my hands as I step onto the street. My sneakers don't make noise on the pavement, and I'm hoping the grass crunching under my feet is drowned out by the air conditioner units whirring in the windows of my mother's house. When I'm hidden behind the truck and the row of trees, I pause to make sure I don't hear talking and the image my sister described today – the two of them making out – makes my blood boil. *He can keep his hands off both of them.*

The air conditioners are the only sound I can make out, so I've got the green light. Time to put on my gloves and get to work. I've got to make this quick.

The next day, I call off sick and spend the morning enjoying the view from my balcony. Everything looks pretty normal. Jackass climbs in his truck with a coffee in one hand. He doesn't notice a thing. He'll probably drive right past the dense woods where I tossed the lug wrench last night. I'll have to remember to pick up a new one the next time I'm at the general store.

I'm on to my second pot of coffee by the time I see police cruisers pull up across the street. Took them long enough. I can't see what's happening from my vantage point, but I can hear my mother let out a piercing wail and it makes me wince. Somehow, I hadn't prepared for that kind of reaction. I'd never have wanted to hear her hurt like that. I guess she's just shocked.

When it stops, I feel a burst of relief. I remind myself that this was the way it had to be. For a fleeting moment, I wonder whether I should go to her now. Not to tell her what I know, but to comfort her, to tell her how much better off she is with that jackass out of the picture for good. But it's not the right time, of course. My moment with my mother needs to be joyous. A reunion. A hundred questions answered. Today will be too hard for her. I'll let her work through this, come back to herself – and then I'll finally get to meet her. I hope she likes me. Maybe she'll be proud of the independent woman I've become. Yes, we've both been through difficult times, but we both bounce right back. We can take care of ourselves, no need for some guy hanging around. It's the Cartwright way.

The police seem to linger a little longer than I'd like. I wish my mother would have drawn the living room curtains. I'd be able to see if they were comforting her, or questioning her. *If I have to come up with a Plan B ... maybe that girl from work could end up with the tire tool somewhere.* Except there'd obviously have to be some connection between her and the guy whose guts are being peeled off the highway right now. Shoot. I should have thought that part through better. Lesson learned. Oh well, though. If there's a problem, I'll be here to fix it.

I smile and think of my sister safe in her bed tonight. *I'll always be here to watch over you.*

14

NOW

Brad's been trying not to ask about my mother, but I know he's worried. He keeps asking if I'm really okay, outside of the crap with my old enemy Charles Devante and the photo. After our chat the other night – and the intimacy that followed – I know he's been waiting for me to open up in some way. I just can't bring myself to talk about her and, truthfully, I'm a little afraid I'll say the wrong thing. Brad pays attention to detail; right now is not the time to raise any suspicion with him whatsoever. With this whirlwind at work, I haven't been able to take time for myself the way I normally do this time of year, but I can still feel the day, the anniversary of her death, approaching like a distant, dark cloud. Every time I look in the mirror, I see parts of her.

When he was getting ready for work this morning and I was still in bed, he seemed to read my thoughts, which is endearing, and also dangerous.

"You haven't talked about her as much this year." He'd curled up behind me, completely dressed for work except for his shoes. "I don't know whether that's good or bad, but I want you to be okay. You've been so strong through so much lately and the way you've been with Gracie is just amazing. You're an incredible mother, just like she was."

Instead of giving a response, I'd pulled his arms tight around me. He held on until his phone beeped. Early morning at the office, training two new managers. He had to leave by six-thirty to get everything ready. He's been working so hard to make sure our little family is all taken care of. I need to do my part, but there's a small broken part of me that wants to just hide under the covers, maybe indefinitely.

Gracie's whimper pulls me back from the edge.

My baby needs me.

I find her doing a tiny pushup. It's wobbly, but she can raise her head and chest now when she's on her belly – and she's always rolling over to her belly in her sleep. The changes are happening so fast already.

"You're so strong, baby girl," I coo.

But she's not having it.

Her face is red from strain, lashes wet. *How long has she been crying?* The second she hears me, her chest falls back to the mattress and she starts a long, piercing wail. I berate myself for waiting too long, though I came the second I heard her. I shouldn't have stayed in bed this morning. Sleeping in never helps.

She screams all through her diaper change, but in the rocking chair, I make it up to her. Her bottle soothes her, though every little jump of her chest as she calms back down from sobbing breaks my heart a little bit. *I never want you to hurt or be sad or wonder where I am. Never.* With my index finger, I trace the curves of her face. Blue eyes like her daddy's stare at me, intense, unmoving, full of need. *I'm going to be here for you, Gracie.* I have an hour left before it's time to meet Brad's sister, Tracie, and I spend every minute of it with my sweet baby girl, setting her on her tummy on my bed while I dress so she can show off her new trick.

This time, she giggles outright when I tell her she's so strong. Too precious. I pause to record the moment and text it to Brad to brighten his morning. "Your girls are missing you. XOXO." I think I'll hear right back, but he must be busy.

Tracie's place is a good twenty-five minutes away, so I have plenty of time to wonder how she'll react to me. I haven't talked to her since the photo of Bill and I was leaked, though Brad's interaction with her was troublesome enough to spark his heart-to-heart with me the other night. I'm sure she's just concerned about him; he's her baby brother, no matter how old he gets.

It worked out really well that Tracie had the day off today so she could watch Gracie. Brad's mom had an appointment and I can't afford to miss a day of work. I know Janette's on my side, but she might be the only one, especially after my outburst in front of the volunteers. When I pull up to the side door – marked with a "Trims by Tracie" sign and a scissors silhouette on the window – she's already waiting for us. In her knee-high boots and slouchy dress, Tracie's completely rocking the Southern belle look, autumn style. Her auburn hair is blown out as big as those country music stars whose hair she's dying to get her hands on. So far, she's got one reality show hairstyling gig under her belt, working her way up to bigger and better things. In the meantime, she's dressing for the job she wants: hairdresser to the stars.

"Where's my little Gracie girl?" She's at the door, gushing in full-on Reba McEntire twang, the second I put my car in park. "There's my baby girl. My little pumpkin. Aunt Tracie's been missing you like crazy."

Hi, Tracie.

She doesn't acknowledge me at all – but Gracie *is* an adorable distraction. She's all coos and questions for Gracie, who she pulls out of the car seat herself. I circle around with her diaper bag and thank her for stepping in to watch her.

"Of course, Sarah. Anytime you need anything. You know all you have to do is call. We'd love to hear more from you guys." She turns her attention back to the baby. "We're going to have a girls' day, aren't we? Just the two of us."

I ignore the remark – Tracie and her mother can never seem to get enough of Brad and the baby, which is understandable – and kiss my baby girl goodbye, happy to see her smiling.

"Hope you have a good day at work."

Ouch.

I can tell from her tone that Tracie's parting remark is a throwaway comment, just to be polite; she's not even looking at me when she says it. But I have to work hard not to believe there's no sting of sarcasm hidden there. She's the type of Southern belle who can be all "honey, darling" to your face while they poke right at whatever hurts the most. Brad got all the same charm, without the venom. *Let it go.* I have no real reason not to trust her and, right now, I need her help.

———

From the look on everyone's faces, you'd think I was wearing a mourning veil. Surprise – then silence and stares. Word must have gotten around about my rough day on the campaign trail. Elaine probably relayed her story in vivid detail to every single person in the office. It's probably morphed into a whole new strain of terrible by now.

Except it's not just me that's causing everyone to go close-lipped. I realize the whole place seems quieter than usual. The TV is on mute. There are voices talking into phones, but it's like they're working hard to keep it down. Everyone is talking in whispers. *What's the big secret?*

I walk into the conference room in the back and think, at first, that the morning briefing hasn't started yet. It's remarkably empty. Janette's at the head of the long table, arms crossed firm and her entire face a frown as she engages with someone sitting with his back to me. He's leaning back with comfortable ease, feet crossed in the space he's made in front of him on the floor. I recognize him just from the sheen of his slicked hair.

Oh. Shit.

Charles Devante.

What the fuck is he doing here?

I freeze at the doorway, sickened by his presence. My enemy, my territory. No warning.

He turns to me slowly, as if he were expecting exactly this scene, something he'd played out in his mind. I want to slap the satisfied smirk right off his face.

"The woman of the hour." Charles brings his hand up to rest his chin over bony knuckles. "Nice of you to finally drop by."

"What are you doing here?"

"He says he's come to meet with Bill," Janette snaps at him. "But he won't share what this meeting is about. As campaign manager, I can't just allow this to happen, without an appointment, without an explanation. Bill is a busy man."

"As I've told your pal Janette here," Charles drawls, "I've got some material I think he'd be interested in seeing. In private. Before everyone else does. And I do mean *everyone* else."

A knot tightens in my throat and flashes of heat pulse into my cheeks. *What else could he possibly have on us? What does he know? Why would he come here?*

"Just tell us what you've got, Charles." Janette's trying her best to pull off a cut-the-crap tone, but Charles is unmoved. Whatever he's brought here to unveil has to be a complete fucking disaster for him to be this cocky in our campaign office. He's acting like he's one hundred percent certain he has the upper hand. Janette and I both glare at him, in standoff mode, but he pretends to be particularly taken with the buttons on his shirt sleeves.

He's going to wait this out. My brain is spinning in so many directions – from my past, to Enid's every word over the last week, to the picture splashed across every news station in town – that I actually feel like I might fall over. My entire body is trembling, and I hope it doesn't show.

Bill's voice booms into the room.

"What is this bullshit about?"

Charles stands to attention, still with the grin on his face. He reaches out a hand to shake, but Bill lets it hang in the air.

"Why are you here?" he challenges.

"Nice to see you too, candidate," Charles says. "I'm just here to be helpful."

"You'd better get to the point quick."

"Oh, I won't waste a minute of your time, sir. I'd like to meet with you in private. Janette here doesn't think you've got the time to meet with me, even though I'm really just trying to help you out."

"Whatever you've got to say, you can say it right here, right now." Bill plants two hands on the tabletop opposite Charles. If Charles were game and not a total wimp, I'd say it looks like the beginning of a brawl. But I know that's not how Charles fights. I've known him long enough to know that he only goes for cheap shots. Instead, he reaches down into a weathered leather briefcase and pulls out a crisp white folder.

"I guess you can suit yourself. Might be good for Sarah to have a gander at these anyway." He fidgets through the folder, dragging out the seconds as terror races through my veins. *Fucking bastard.* I should have confronted him years ago. The knot in my throat is so thick I can't swallow. I search Janette's face for any clues, but her eyes are wild with worry. She has no idea what to expect, either.

Finally, he slaps the first piece of paper down on the table. A photograph, blown up and printed on a letter-sized sheet. I have to squint to make it out. It's a long hallway punctuated with terrible hotel art, giant abstract florals. One door in the hallway is half-open.

He slaps another down. It's closer, more focused.

I can see exactly who it is now. He's now the youngest Chattanooga mayor in recent history.

The handsome Tripp Payne, leaving a hotel room.

And, behind him, me.

When Charles slaps a third image, I recoil.

Both my hands are over my mouth, covering a laugh. Tripp is reaching behind me and *I* know it's just to pull the door closed, but it looks a hell of a lot like someone's snapped and recorded the instant just before he pins me against the wall for a passionate kiss. *Fuck.* This is worse than I could have expected.

I half expect Charles to just keep punching these out, but of course there's no follow-up. There's no photo of us kissing, because it doesn't exist, but this is enough to suggest the worst. It looks like the two of us sneaking out of a hotel room, like two people who can't keep their hands to themselves. Janette is as white as the folder. Bill still has both hands on the table – but it looks more like he's propping himself up than threatening an intruder. Charles is wearing his gotcha grin and waiting for me to say something.

Bill clears his throat. I pray he's about to tell Charles to get the fuck out.

"Care to explain, Sarah?"

"What?" I'm momentarily stunned. Bill is buying this completely, or at least acting like he is. How could he? He knows the last photograph splashed across the news was a complete lie. Now, he's going to shame me right in front of Charles Devante? Does he not know that Charles will be describing this scene, word-for-word, for salivating news crews before the day is up? I can see his mouth making the words in front of eager camera crews: "Even the candidate himself doesn't believe her.

He wanted her to explain but, unfortunately, she didn't have anything to say for herself."

"What is all this?" He's looking at me, not Charles, when he knows damn well that these are photos meant to insinuate something that's a total lie.

"It's me and Tripp leaving his hotel room, during a campaign five years ago. We were there for a meeting before a critical fundraiser."

"Why were you in a hotel with him?"

"Because his house was being fumigated."

"Fumigated? From what?" Bill is almost spitting. I can't believe I'm under attack like this, from all sides. "Forget that." He stops me from answering. "That doesn't matter. Why weren't you in an office? Why would you ever be in a hotel room with your candidate, a married man?"

"We had put every penny we raised into the campaign itself – very little overhead. We had no office. I – I worked from home or at coffee shops or at his house." That part doesn't help. Nothing does. I feel like everything I say is burying me deeper. I know I need to give a clear answer here, but I am so unprepared for this. Even Janette is looking at me in total disbelief. I try again. "His house was being fumigated. We needed to go over his speech and had run out of time. I was working with him in his hotel room. His wife was there, too."

"I don't see her in any of my pictures," Charles has the nerve to say.

"Your pictures? Where did you get these?" I can't hold it in any longer. All I can see is red. "Who gave these to you? Who gave you the one of me and Bill?"

"Hey now." He throws up his hands defensively. "I'm only the messenger here. These were emailed to me this morning by one of my friends at the TV station, asking whether I knew anything more about this."

"You're lying," I say through gritted teeth.

He shrugs, nonchalant, and I can feel the hair prickle on the back of my neck, the blood rushing to my head. I can't keep it all inside any longer.

"You're a fucking liar." I lunge toward him and he jumps back, surprised but amused. Definitely not scared of me.

"Sarah, come on now," he says. "Let's keep this civil. You've known me for years."

"And maybe it's time for me to tell you exactly what I think of you."

Janette steps in between us.

"Okay, Sarah," she pleads with me. "Let's keep it together here. We can handle this."

I step back, trying to catch my breath, feeling like the room is closing in on me.

Charles is completely composed as he delivers his final message.

"I just thought I'd give you all a heads-up, as a courtesy." He turns to Bill as he packs the empty folder back into his briefcase, leaving the photographs sprawled out. "However, should you decide you've got some family concern or health issue that will force your hand here – meaning if you decide it's better for you to step away from politics for now – rest assured that David Burtner will send his best wishes. This can all be handled as gentlemen. We wouldn't, at this point, harp on any of your personal weaknesses ... or your staff's personal problems. You could step out of the race and be free to pursue another elected position down the road. Entirely your call. Just thought you'd want to know."

Charles turns his gaze to me and wears a twisted grin I know I'll never be able to wash from my mind as he walks slowly out of the room, leaving the three of us in stunned silence. I'm the first to break it.

"I can prepare a statement explaining why Tripp was in a hotel room that day and also –"

"I don't think the question is why he was in a hotel room," Bill interrupts. "It's why *you* were in a hotel room with him. Nobody's going to give a rat's ass about his house being fumigated."

"So, let's consider how we can best handle this." I try to keep my voice steady. "Maybe we should have Dick weigh in."

"It's not for you to consider right now, Sarah." Bill's face is solemn, resigned. "Janette and I will work on our next course of action."

"What?"

"I'm going to meet with my campaign manager to decide the best way to handle this," he says, unflinchingly.

My face is burning with rage. Janette's staring at the floor, avoiding my eyes. From his hardened expression, I know Bill means what he's saying, and I can't even believe that he would treat me like this. Actually, I can't even believe any of it. *Don't let them see you cry.* I let the door slam behind me, holding back a flood of angry tears and the urge to punch something. I could kick a hole through the wall right now. All I want to do is make Charles Devante sorry he ever stepped foot inside this building. *Fucking asshole.*

15

NOW

"**Y**ou are a complete fucking asshole."

There, I said it.

To his face.

Outside the glass doors of headquarters, Charles is trying to slink to his vehicle – just slip out the door without anyone noticing. Not on my watch, buddy. He turns to me and puts one hand over his heart in mock shock.

"Now, Sarah. This isn't like you," he taunts. "I've never seen you break down like this. I've always thought you were coolheaded."

"Not today." I ought to slug him; he's begging for it. *Keep calm. Keep it together. He wants to get under your skin.* But everything in my body wants to stop him in his tracks. This man is ruining my life, outright. And it's a game to him. *Don't give him anything else to work with. I don't need more trouble.*

"I didn't mean to stir up problems for you." He dares to step closer to me, his head cocked like he's talking to a child. "This is about what the voters need to know … about the candidate. Part of that is who he chooses as his team. It's not personal, of course. Just a matter of public concern."

My ass it's not personal. My career, my family, my entire life is on the line.

"It's mudslinging and it's lies and it's cruel and – "

"Not personal," he repeats. "You'll bounce back just fine, if I know you at all."

"You've known me for eight years. Either you've been so obsessed you're snapping photos left and right without my knowledge – or you're having me followed. Tell me who. Tell me who you got to do your dirty work for you."

Charles clutches his briefcase in front of his body with both hands, a sly grin on his face.

"I am not having you followed, I can assure you of that," he says, patting the front of his briefcase. "But if I were … well, I never tell my secrets. And I always cover my tracks. I'm a little more careful than it seems like you've been lately. Well, maybe longer than that, now that we know about Tripp. No need for you to see what else I have." He chuckles under his breath.

If that's a challenge, I'm game.

I lunge for his briefcase, but he leaps out of the way. I've managed to grab the strap, though, and I yank it so hard, it rips right off.

"You bitch." His voice goes high in surprise.

"What?" I feel like I'm a guy in a bar who's had one too many drinks, testosterone raging through my system. I can't control it. "What did you call me?"

"I called you a bitch, but that was wrong." Charles is starting to recover, patting down his shirt, grabbing the leather strap I'd tossed onto the sidewalk. "What I should have called you is a whore. Catches up to you sooner or later, huh?"

That's it.

I reach for his briefcase again. It's coming with me. He pulls it back in a ridiculous tug of war, until he stumbles over the curb behind him and falls to his knees.

"Fucking slut! Get away from me. I'll call the police."

"No, you won't," someone behind us scolds. "It's time to let go and be on your way."

I spin around.

It's Enid, standing there. My cheeks are burning with shame and I wonder how much she's seen. Her eyes are glued to Charles, watching him threateningly until he shuffles back to his feet, grabbing his brief-case. He slams himself inside his Cadillac and peels out of the parking lot like someone's hot on his tail.

We stand there in silence for a moment. My heart is still racing, fists clenched. I can't believe any of this is happening. I can't believe this is what my life has become. I've really let him get to me.

"You okay?" Enid ventures. I don't know whether she really cares or whether she's just giving the response she thinks she's obligated to. *How long had she been watching me? Why did she follow me out here?*

"To be honest, I'm not okay. Not really." I've got questions I'd like to ask Enid … but I may have picked enough fights for one day. I'd really just like to know she didn't do it, that she'd never do that to me, so I could just feel one little piece of normal again. I'd feel so much better if I thought I were standing here with someone who cares about me.

"I'm sorry about Charles," Enid says, watching me process my feel-ings. I can't tell what judgments she might be making from what she's just seen. "I can't believe they even let him in the front door."

"Everybody's busy. And he knows how to be sneaky. Not your fault." *I hope it's not your fault.*

"I know, but it still sucks." Enid gestures toward the headquarters door.

"Maybe after work we can finally grab a drink again. I'm sure you could use one."

"I'd like to hear how things are going," I answer politely.

"You mean with the assistant campaign manager job?" she asks, her voice perking.

"Sure," I say.

"Oh my god, I love it," Enid can't contain her excitement. "Janette has really helped me out a lot and I think I've got the hang of it. Bill's nailing that demographic you suggested we focus on and I've been able to help him build it out to a whole other level. I can't wait to see the numbers. Absolutely can't wait."

I pause. I'd really meant more that I'd like to hear how she's doing in general. I wasn't prepared for an automatic response about how she's become an immediate all-star in her new job – my old job. It hurt more than I would have thought. I want her to be happy ... but she'd have to know that was my exact pain point, if she cared about my feelings. Wouldn't she? That doesn't require a ton of emotional intelligence. If you take your friend's job, maybe don't rub it in her face.

"I mean, I feel like this is what I was meant to be doing all along," Enid goes on, oblivious. I can't get a read for whether she's intentionally digging in harder, or genuinely so giddy she's lost all self-awareness.

"Glad you're finding your calling," I answer flatly. "Just be careful how you act around the candidate. Never know who's watching, or who might want your job next."

I can't help it. I lost my cool once today and it's hard to get it back.

Enid stops dead in her tracks and glares at me, her lips curled inward like she's chewing over how to take this.

"What's that supposed to mean?"

"Nothing … I'm just spent, is all," I backtrack. "I'm sorry. This whole Charles thing has me –"

"How about trying not to go after the people who are still on your side." She stops at the door. "Though, from what I just saw, you don't seem to have any problem attacking people whatsoever."

The door closes hard behind her.

Maybe she's right. Maybe this whole scenario has me spinning into becoming someone I don't want to be. I've always been able to manage what other people think of me before, but then again, I've never had the floor yanked out from right under my feet like this. I have to figure out a better way. If I could just think. The air outside is unseasonably warm and sticky, the way it gets just before it rains. A few minutes alone at my desk will do me good. I can think my way out of this.

But Janette's waiting for me in my office – and she looks like she has more bad news.

"What's happened now?" I'm afraid to ask it, but I do.

"Are you okay?" she asks

I stiffen.

"I will be."

She nods, tentatively, waiting for me to share more. Knowing Enid, Janette's probably already heard about the scuffle.

"This has been a difficult day," she says soothingly.

"Understatement." I sigh and sink into my chair.

"I think … maybe it would be better if you call it a day."

"What?"

"Pick up Gracie early. Or spend some quiet time at home. Refocus. Re-center. Get yourself back together."

I close my eyes for a second, embarrassed as a chided schoolgirl. I hope my face isn't as red as it feels.

"I'm okay," I say, taking in a deep breath. "I'll be fine. Tell me what you and Bill are thinking. He's not dropping out, is he?"

She pauses and then leans against my desk, looking at a framed photo of my family.

"Well, we're still deciding," Janette answers, finally. "It really puts us in a difficult position."

"I know. I feel horrible about all of this."

"I know you do. And you can't blame yourself. Mudslinging is part of what we have to deal with, but it's really unfair to you. Dredging up your past –"

"It's not even true. None of it. Nothing ever happened with me and Bill. Nothing ever happened with me and Tripp."

"Yeah. Someone's really got it in for you." She stands, as if her time is up. "I told Bill the same thing. This isn't your fault."

"How's he holding up?"

Janette chews over her answer. "Eh, he's got a lot to deal with, a lot to think about."

"You think he needs me to step down?" I'm afraid to ask it.

"I'm working on him. I don't know what the right move is yet. We'll have to see how this plays out in the news today. I'll let you know."

I cringe at the thought. Charles will have plenty to say in his interviews.

"Whatever happens, don't be so hard on yourself. I'll help you out in any way I can. On the campaign trail, or off, okay?"

I mumble my thanks. Maybe she's right. Maybe going home for the rest of the day – or at least getting the hell out of this office – isn't such a bad idea after all.

16

B y the time I get home, it's dark.

Brad meets me at the door, Gracie happy in his arms. He kisses me in an automatic way, but then he steps back and watches me with uncertainty. I can't tell whether he's waiting for me to tell him something or whether he has something he needs to unload on me. We exchange questioning glances, both trying to read the other, until Brad gives in.

"Long day?"

I breathe out my frustration.

"The worst."

"It's almost nine o'clock, babe. You have to set boundaries."

"It wasn't that," I answer, walking with my two loves to the living room and collapsing on the couch. I reach out to hold Gracie. Her tiny hands are hot against both my cheeks when I kiss her. Her head feels a little warm to me, too, but she's not fussing.

"What do you mean it wasn't that?" Brad settles in next to us and wraps an arm around me protectively.

"I mean, work was … hell this morning."

"This morning?"

"I actually left early."

"It's almost nine o'clock." He repeats his observation and I try to suppress all I'm feeling. I don't want to be the kind of person who comes home treating everyone they love like they're the problem when it's really got nothing to do with them. My day has been awful, but it's really almost too much to talk about, to think about. Besides, that's all I've been doing all day long.

"I know what time it is, babe. I just … needed time, that's all," I answer quietly. "I needed time alone."

"Where did you go for the rest of the day?"

I avoid his eyes and don't answer.

Finally, I feel his body relax. "Thinking about your mom?"

"What?" It hits me like a bowling ball in the chest. He usually tiptoes around it. Right now, it feels like he's slapped me in the face. I almost snap into two pieces. "That's not it. It was just a hard day, alright."

Now Brad looks like the one who's been slapped. A rush of guilt hits me.

He's just trying to help. He's just trying to love me.

"I'm sorry. This whole situation at work, Charles Devante. He showed up at the office today. It wasn't good. He has more pictures, from five fucking years ago." I feel myself unraveling. "God. The pictures. The stories. It's endless. It's a disaster and every day reminds me of how far I've fallen, to be honest. I try not to let it get to me, but I'm surrounded by it every single day. I just needed some space to be away from it, to think."

I'm not intentionally keeping mum about the situation with Charles in the parking lot. I just can't, right at this second, relive it out loud. I've been replaying it in my mind the whole damn day and wondering just how much Enid saw of me acting like an out-of-control maniac. I can't bring myself to talk about it. I'll tell him later. It might make more sense later. Right now, all I want to do is be close to them, to hold my baby, to pretend my life is not unraveling inch by inch until there's nothing left but fragments of who I used to be, who everyone believed I was, who I thought I was.

"Okay, baby." Brad whispers.

I feel the weight of his hands on my shoulders and sense him moving in closer.

"We missed you," he says. "A lot."

I lean into his chest like it's a pillow. He holds me there, giving me the silence I need so desperately, until I can hear the soothing rhythm of his heartbeat. Even Gracie's wriggling has slowed, and she leans in too. This is the greatest gift Brad gives me, a safe space. He trusts me, believes in me even when I don't or can't believe in myself. When he's not pushing me to decide something or promise more than I can, when he's not asking questions, I'm safe from everything else. From the world that feels like it's closing in on me. That's what I need most right now.

After I put the baby to bed and eat the plate of leftovers Brad warmed for me, he stands behind me, reaching down to kiss my cheek. I don't have the energy to respond the way I'd like to tonight, but I squeeze the hands he's put on my shoulders and press my cheek against them. I hope he knows how much I appreciate him.

The tension twisted into hard knots starts to loosen as his strong hands press and squeeze. Goosebumps raise on my arm when he slides down from the base of my head to my shoulders.

"Move to the couch?" he suggests.

I take him up on the offer, curling my feet underneath me and leaning my side against the cushions as he works his way over my shoulders and the spot where he knows my muscles pinch, just under my shoulder blades. When my body is finally sinking into relaxation, I hear him clearing his throat.

Please not the marriage thing again. Not tonight. I love you – but I can't tonight. Please don't go there.

I can sense him rubbing his temples, the scar on his face, and I know he's working up to something.

"Baby?"

I'm afraid to answer. Also afraid not to answer. Maybe I can steer this, if I handle myself the right way.

"I'm okay, sweetheart. Thank you. Thank you for all you do. I'm just readjusting to going back to work. And, to be honest, it's been a hundred times worse than I could have ever imagined. But it's still the work I feel like I'm supposed to be doing. We're going to be alright. The three of us. Once this election is over, I'll be able to find something else, maybe something better."

I turn around to hold him, but his face is tentative. There's a spark of hope that I don't want to crush … but I also don't know what could be causing it.

"I wanted to talk to you about that, actually." He rests two hands back on my shoulders, but facing me this time. "I want to help you find something better, and I think we might have the right opportunity."

Not sure how to interpret what he's telling me. I watch for more. He's chewing his bottom lip, eyes bright with excitement.

Please don't propose again. Not right now. How can you not love a man who can be as happy as a seven-year-old on Christmas morning when he's thinking about you? It was something beautiful about him, a treasure, but I just can't take another push to get married right at this second. Really, I just don't want to disappoint him again, I can't bear to let him down again. Inside me, I'm afraid if he asks me right now, I might leap in – if only to not hurt him. That's the wrong reason. You shouldn't get married just because you don't want to disappoint someone.

"I have some news that might be really good for us," he says, finally.

I exhale. This is something else. I reach out and squeeze him tight around the neck.

"Sweetheart! Why didn't you say that? What is it? I will take any bit of good news."

"Well." He releases me and looks into my eyes to prepare me again. "It might mean a little bit of change. But it could be good for us. I really think it could."

"Enough with the suspense," I say, with a giggle, "just *tell* me."

"The boss had scheduled a call with me for today. I didn't know what it was about and he wouldn't say. I was kind of nervous about it, I wanted to tell you but didn't want to add to your stress or give you too much to think about when I know you have a lot on your plate already. Anyway, so … I guess, long story short is that they're offering me a promotion, a district manager position."

"Sweetheart, that's amazing." I kiss him full and fast on the mouth. "That's wonderful news."

"Thank you, baby."

"So, you have fifteen stores here under your watch as regional manager … how many would you have as a district manager?"

"Forty." He says, a flash of pride in his smile. That BA in business management – and he'd worked so hard to do that while he was a mechanic working full time – is really paying off.

"Are there even forty Buck's Auto Repairs in the state of Tennessee?" I laugh, so proud and so happy for good news. "Holy shit, you are moving up. Did you say yes?"

"Well, that's the thing I wanted to talk to you about," he says, worry clouding his expression. "It would be actually multiple states."

"Wow. A lot of travel?"

"Um, some. But the thing is, we'd have to, probably, relocate. Not probably. We would definitely have to move."

There it is. The bit that would make this hard. The part that made him do all the rest of this song and dance.

"To somewhere nearby?" I ask, hopeful, trying not to instantly smash his dreams.

"Well, no. Buck's is really growing out West. It's an important area for them."

I feel my own dreams being smashed to pieces. Unless – and I try to look for the bright spot – if it's a blue state, that might be my ticket. Start over somewhere else, walk in with good references and great experience and maybe leave all this behind. That might be perfect after all.

"Where, sweetie?"

"Salt Lake City."

Of course. GOP all the way.

That part of my brain that can put a positive spin on things, or at least try to for Brad's sake, is silent. It would be starting over, in the worst possible place for my career. Actually, there would be no starting over there, not doing what I do. It would be giving in, or giving up, for good.

"Oh. It's great they thought of you." It's all I can muster.

"It would be more pay, thirty-five percent increase." He holds my hands in his like he's waiting for an answer.

"I don't know. I mean, I'm happy for you –"

"It could be good for us, not just me."

"I know. I know. It's just … it would mean not just walking away from my job, but my career. I've been working here in Tennessee for ten years to get to where I am. Before the story and photo of me with Bill broke, people knew my name and associated it with something meaningful. I was a changemaker. I loved doing that." I felt the swell of tears I'd been holding back all day start to hit me. I hate being forced into decisions, but maybe this is right. My name, at least recently, wasn't being associated with positive change or grassroots activism. I've become the face of scandal.

"I know how hard this is for you, baby." Brad wraps both arms around me. "This whole thing. You've been treated so unfairly. I just want to make a better way for us. This is an option for us to think about. I never, ever want to make you feel like I'm taking anything away from you. Or trapping you. I just want you to think about what it could be like. Even if you stay home for a little while with Gracie, we have time. You have time to figure things out. I'm going to be here for you, and maybe this is the right opportunity for us to just regroup and for you to decide what you want to do."

For just a moment, in Brad's arms, I let myself imagine staying home every day with Gracie, at least while she's little – seeing every little change happen instead of letting someone else tell me about it. There are so many women who would love to be in this position. It doesn't have to mean giving up. It might be the best thing for us, especially considering the current circumstances. I just hate to walk away from everything I've built. But Brad's right; it's at least an option.

"Let's talk about it, sweetheart." I speak into the warmth of his chest. "I'm happy for you, and happy for us. Maybe we try to figure out how to make it work. Let's talk about it a little more tomorrow, okay?"

He presses a kiss to the top of my forehead.

"I want it to work for you, baby. Thank you."

Brad is satisfied, content to have me close to him and open to him. I've come back down from the disaster of a morning, made it through the rest of the day fighting my darkest thoughts, and Brad's right – the job offer is simply another option on the table. It's good to have those. I let it be another level of potential stability in the whirlwind that has become my life. We don't have to decide right now. I grab the glass of wine I've been thinking about all day and a beer for Brad and turn on the television for the ten o'clock news. Maybe the cycle will have moved to something more pedestrian.

A Buck's Auto commercial pops up and I picture Brad inside the office there, working hard every day to make a better life for us. Then there's a teaser for the upcoming news, a city street scene with flashing police lights and a couple fire engines in the foreground. Behind it, a row of smashed cars and a close-up still photograph of a mangled silver Cadillac. The text under the video is scrolling: Fatal four-vehicle crash on Knight Street ... multiple injuries ... coroner on the scene ... full report coming up.

The emergency sirens startle me. I turn the volume down a couple ticks, a sinking feeling in my stomach. Brad doesn't say anything as the next couple commercials pass. My brain is running in circles, trying to remember why the car looks familiar to me, running through the list of people I care about and their vehicles. I can't think of anyone who drives a car like that, but the sight of a car crash always makes me uneasy. It's part of the string of dark events I never want to relive, the one thing that led to another that eventually led to me losing her. My mother.

When the salt-and-pepper haired news anchor and his bodacious co-anchor appear for the top of the news cycle, they're both wearing sober expressions.

"Some sad news tonight as we wrap up our coverage today," the woman says, staring into the camera.

"We've just been updated from our reporter in the field," the man in his 60s announces from behind the desk. "The victim in the fatal crash we told you about earlier today has been identified. He's well-known in the political arena –"

Panic floods my veins as I watch in disbelief. A picture of the victim, a portrait I've seen used over and over to accompany his quotes for newspaper stories, flashes onto the screen.

"– and well-respected for his contributions to Tennessee's GOP over the past fifteen years. Forty-nine-year-old Charles Devante was killed in a tragic accident on Knight Street this afternoon. Our reporter, Allison Ross, has been on the scene all day, talking to police. We'll hear more from her in just a minute. We've also got a statement from GOP gubernatorial candidate David Burtner on the impact Charles had and how much he's going to be missed."

The anchorwoman breaks in with her condolences: "Shocking. A truly tragic story."

17

NOW

I haven't been able to get him out of my head all morning.

Even with the pain he's caused me, I can't take pleasure in Charles Devante's death. Charles was a scoundrel, a sneak, a cheater at this game. He deserved a lot of things, some retribution, but he didn't deserve to die. Be hurt, maybe, or at least put in his place, but not dead. When someone dies suddenly, even someone you don't like, you can't help but think about how many hours ago it was that you were with that person … you can't help but sit the strange ideas side by side in your head. Alive before. Dead now.

Twenty-four hours ago, he was alive, arguing with me in the parking lot. Calling me a slut, taunting me that he had something else to hurt me with in his briefcase, looking shocked when he found himself on the ground. Enid was probably watching most, if not all, of it. I still don't know how long she was watching me.

Fast-forward just a day, and Charles doesn't even exist anymore. His family is shattered and probably busy at this very second making arrangements. Tearful, stunned meetings with funeral directors explaining options for a situation that have never crossed their minds before. He was forty-nine. Healthy. Mean as a snake, but healthy.

The contrast will make you crazy. I know. I've been around surprise deaths enough times to know exactly what it's like to chew over the difference a day can make. Alive. Then dead. With them. Then gone from them, forever. The people close to you are hardest, of course. Those you never get over. But even people you've just met; when you hear they're dead the next day, you can't help but be shaken by the difference a day can make. Alive. Then dead. I know all about it, unfortunately.

This is where my mind goes, staring at the expanse of cluttered desktop, while I wait for Bill in his office. He's called me here for a "brainstorm" but hasn't told me what it's about. I've been waiting fifteen minutes, getting more antsy by the second. My teams are supposed to load up in the van again today, within the hour, and I've spent the morning psyching myself up for a good day at the office. I'm way overdue for that. Maybe – if there's anything good to come from Charles' death – it at least takes the spotlight off the supposed affair. I know I shouldn't think that; it's not fair and I know what his family has to be feeling. But news crews will be talking about him, eulogizing him through the mouths of anybody they can round up to say a good word about him, for days. I wonder whether it's wrong to hope that the extra images he was trying to blackmail us with, the ones he'd taken with him in his briefcase, will just slip into the ether with him ...

Yes, it's wrong. I shouldn't think that either.

But there's no reason for his last sneaky act to make it out into the open, right?

When Bill steps in, finally, I'm relieved and hoping we can move this along quickly. I've got work to do.

I can feel the smile fade from my face when he greets me like he'd forgotten I was waiting. Maybe he had. He looked like he'd sneaked into his office for a moment of quiet and then found an unwelcome visitor.

"You said you needed to meet with me?" I remind him.

He nods, resigned, and motions for me to sit back down as he takes his place behind his desk, immediately turning the side of his body toward me rather than looking me in the eye. Whatever is coming will not be pleasant; he's uncomfortable already.

"What's this about? Things are going alright with the volunteers. I'm doing the best I can." I hate that I'm automatically defensive. But I've a feeling that if this were really a routine brainstorming meeting, I wouldn't have received this kind of greeting.

Bill pinches his eyebrows together and turns to lean over his hands, deep in thought.

"I'm worried about how the media is going to spin this fatal crash." He looks up from his folded hands to gauge my reaction.

I snap back at him, frustrated that he's wasted my time on something we can't fix or change.

"I don't know what you mean," I answer. "It's terrible, but I don't see what we can do about it." And it's true. I don't know why he'd call me in here to talk about a situation that we can't control. The media will make him out to be a hero, as they always do when someone dies, but there's no way we can manage that story. It would be gauche for us to try to sling mud on a dead man, wouldn't it? I wouldn't do that. I can't imagine that Bill would either. So what's he suggesting?

Bill clears his throat and shoots me another prodding stare.

What's he trying to get out of me?

"I don't think there's anything we can do, if you're worried this will somehow win sympathy votes for the other side," I say, with the distinct feeling I'm spinning my wheels. "People will say nice things about Charles, that he was dedicated or whatever they want to say instead of 'ruthless' and that's alright. Nothing we can do about that. In fact, I agree with Dick that we should be sending a statement with our condolences. Take the high road and be civil about everything, the best we can."

"That's not at all what I mean," Bill answers, his voice a rumble.

"Then, please, fill me in." I don't mean to sound short, but I've already lost precious minutes just waiting to hear what this is about.

"Don't you think, Sarah –" He takes a fatherly tone that I can't stand. "– that this could shed us in an incredibly negative light? A real problem. For you, in particular?"

"What?" My brain can hardly process what he's suggesting. "Are you saying you're worried that I will somehow be tied into this? It was a terrible accident. But that's what it was, an accident. There's no way anyone could blame me for this. None."

"Sarah. Think about what happened. Yesterday, when Charles Devante was very much alive, he was in our office. He had images that made you look like you were hanging out in hotel rooms with the mayor you worked for, that furthered the story that you're getting way too cozy with your employers." He shifted uncomfortably and rubbed a palm over his face, exasperated. "Then he walks out of here and you storm out after him."

I wonder what he's been told, what the story inside the office has become. *Sarah knocked him to the ground. Sarah punched him. I heard she spat at him.*

"I'm just saying there are ways it could be … misconstrued," Bill continues. "You two get into it, your career is on the line – and then, hours later, he's dead."

The thoughts are swirling around in my head like a swarm of bees, pissed off bees. It was hard enough for me to think about Charles alive-then-dead, but now my own boss – the man whose candidacy I forged for him – is suggesting that not only am I perhaps guilty of sleeping with the mayor I got elected, but that I also may be capable of arranging a four-car crash that killed Charles and left three others in the hospital. It's absurd. Crazy as it gets.

Have I not accepted enough garbage, complete and utter shit, from the people at this office, the people I've invested my time and effort into helping? What else do they want from me? I can feel myself snapping, but it's too late for me to stop now. I'm cornered, and I won't be trampled all over.

"First, I come back from maternity leave to find that I've been replaced. I don't even, to be honest, know how that's legal. But you did it. And I didn't give you problems over it. I accepted where we were, and I was going to do absolutely everything in my power to make sure we made you governor. Even if it meant a demotion for me. Even if it meant sucking up my pride and working alongside the woman who replaced me."

Bill is calm, nodding and letting me spill my guts. There's a lot more where that came from.

"And then, when I become the target of a grimy PR stunt aimed at you, I don't attack. I didn't say, 'Bill, how did this ever happen – and also why the fuck did you have your hand on my knee?' And you don't even stand up for me. You just let me take all the heat, in here and out in public. Just as if you weren't even in the car. This is all about me; some slut."

Bill's raising his hands defensively, trying to bring me back to level ground, but I just can't keep it all inside now.

"I didn't attack or blame you in any way. In fact, I took *another* demotion. And I was trying to do my best there, because I care about this campaign. But then, when Charles is here, in our office – and everybody knows he's hated me for a long time and all of this is utter bullshit – instead of sticking up for me and defending me when he's wagging these new pictures in our faces, you're acting like I need to explain myself. And now, when there's an accident – a terrible accident but an *accident* nonetheless – you're calling me into your office to explain myself again? How can you even be trying to pin this on me? I am not the problem."

But I realize, standing here exploding in the middle of Bill's office, I look exactly like the problem. I probably look exactly like the kind of problem Enid must have described to everyone after I left yesterday. I could tell by the way Janette was talking to me, as if I were emotionally fragile and needed some cooldown time. I can tell by the way Bill is now waving his hand downward toward the floor, staying in silence to give me space to cool down. I look like a hothead. Like a mishmash of poor life decisions: sleeping her way to the top and exploding on anyone who gets in her way.

How did I get here?

With pseudo-compassion, Bill asks me to sit down.

"I know this has been a difficult transition for you, coming back to work and to this kind of mudslinging. I'm not blaming you. I'm certainly not trying to say you had anything to do with the death of one of our most vicious opponents. It's not your fault he picked you to target." He eyes me cautiously. "But you ended up in the bulls-eye. I'm just saying the media is going to be looking for any way to stretch the story out. Charles is killed in a crash. First, they'll keep collecting quotes of people saying what a gem this guy was. When they run out of that, they'll be at the police station, making a huge story out of whatever report police prepare, looking for any angles to blow this up into more than what it is. You know how all of this goes."

The thing is, he's right. He's absolutely right. Even if police have nothing to offer, the reporters will be poking around anyone who had any connection with Charles, good or bad. They'll be looking for any way to make a hot story hotter.

If anyone gabs about what happened in our office yesterday – and it's pretty clear someone already has – then it could put me in worse trouble. *Shit, I wonder whether there's surveillance outside ... and who's got access to that tape if there is?* I don't risk asking that. I don't want to give Bill any more rope to hang me with.

Bill's not the enemy.

I breathe and try to collect my spinning thoughts.

"Okay. I'm sorry for exploding. There's just so much pressure."

"Hey," he says, catching my eye. "I get it. I'm not here to add to that. I just want us to have a plan."

"Thank you."

Bill's not the enemy ... but someone else is. I decide there are way too many coincidences and I need to devote more time to protecting myself, separating friend from foe. I wince, thinking about Enid, the way she's been lurking around and showing up in all the wrong places. The betrayal I felt before – thinking she may have tried to get me out of a job – hurt. Now, if she's out to make me look like a murderer by spreading everything she saw of our fight yesterday ... I can't even go there. Right now, I need to work with Bill to handle this smartly.

"So what do you think we should do? I can't believe I'm asking this for the second time in a span of two weeks, but ... would it be better for all of us if I resign?"

Bill leans back in his chair, arms folded over his barrel chest. He heaves out a big breath.

"No. I think we're past a point where this all could be swept under the rug with you stepping down. Before, maybe there would have been some people who would buy a story about you deciding you wanted to stay home and be a mom. Now ... too much has happened. It's a little too late for that to unfold neatly or solve any problems at all. Might create more."

"I see your point." I fidget with my hands. "Then what is there that we can do?"

Bill shakes his head and sighs.

"I'm really not sure. I just need you to assure me that if there are any questions over this ..."

He eyes me, choosing his words carefully, then continues: "If the media approach you, obviously, you refer them to Dick. Act like you're shocked and sad, which I know you are, but don't say anything else. Nothing at all."

"Of course." I try to keep a lid on my anger. This isn't my first day on the job.

"If the police talk to you, well that's a different matter."

I can't keep my mouth from dropping wide open. We're back to square one. *Bill thinks I had something to do with this. What did Enid say to him?*

"I need you to promise that you'll be completely open with them, cooperate in every way."

"Why wouldn't I be?"

Bill makes the hand gesture – calm down – that I'm sure as hell sick of seeing.

"I had nothing to do with this," I answer, standing to leave.

"I believe you. Make sure they do too."

The shock is almost too much for me to handle. I swallow down the rest of what I want to say; I've already let loose one tirade. I'm done talking. *Thanks, Bill. Glad to see you've got my back.*

Today is feeling more and more like a repeat of yesterday. I was supposed to leave with my volunteer teams, but I was so steamed after my meeting with Bill that I told them I'd meet them out there. I can see questions in every look, or at least from anyone brave enough to look me in the eye. People in the office are talking about me. Everyone is. I hear their chatter break to surprise or drop down to a whisper when I walk into a room, like I've interrupted their conversation. Maybe they heard me yelling in Bill's office. Maybe they picked up on some of the other rumors that I'm certain are floating around. Maybe they heard how I snapped at that campaign volunteer last week. Maybe they're worried I arranged for someone's commute to turn deadly.

I'm sure not making any friends here.

I want to call it a day again. I've only been here two hours, but it's clear I'm not accomplishing anything. In fact, my presence here at all is clouding the entire mission to get our guy elected.

Janette is the only person to speak to me today other than Bill.

"I just wanted to make sure you're holding up okay," she says, setting down a fresh cup of coffee.

When I look up at her, I feel like I could burst into tears. Maybe it's just part of her job to make sure the team doesn't fall to pieces, but I appreciate the gesture. She's the only person who dared to come close to me today. Of course, I haven't seen a glimpse of Enid.

"Thanks," I answer, biting my lips to keep back the floodgate of tears. "It's been rough."

"I can imagine," she says. "Just hang on. One day, this will all be over. I'm not sure we'll laugh about it, even then, but we'll be past it. Two more weeks, and this election will be behind us. Something better will come."

I try to clear the lump out of my throat.

"I hope you're right."

"If you need to regroup again, it's okay. I can have someone else take care of the troops out there. We'll be just fine for today. I need you to put yourself first so you can come back to focusing on our mission here. We're so close. We still need you."

I really want to believe her, but all I know for sure is that I need to get out of this place. My nerves are bound in a tight coil. I can't stop counting all the ways everything has gotten worse than I could imagine. My boss is suspicious of me. Everyone here thinks I'm a hothead. Enid – who was supposed to be my friend – is obviously spreading nasty rumors, taking what she saw completely out of proportion. I exploded on Charles in the parking lot. I needed to get out of the hot seat before anyone looked too closely – and now I've made my situation unspeakably worse.

Everything's ready to unravel. I need space to think, to make sure I've patched up any of the holes in my story; too much depends on me keeping it together. I can't let my life, or my family, be ripped to pieces.

18

THEN

I'm feeling better about this life every day. It has a nice rhythm to it.

I wake up and start the coffee and grab a bagel, both of which come compliments of the job. I deal with their crap; they can fill my pantry in return, even if the boss knows nothing about it. I shower and spend a good half hour taking in the view from my porch, which is right into the kitchen window of my family. Every day, I can feel myself inching closer and closer. One day, I'll be there with them – with my mother and sister – eating cereal or bagels, all of us warming up for our days together. I'll get to watch my sister with her backpack running out to catch the bus from our front steps, instead of from up here. Heck, I'd even give her a ride maybe, on my way to work.

She'd think I'm the cool older sis. She'd want me to drop her off.

Soon, I'll work up the courage I need. If I can pour scalding coffee in a perv's lap, you'd think I could just walk right over there. But there are different kinds of bravery. It all depends on the risk you're taking. I don't care if the perv never speaks to me again (in fact, that's the point), but I can't blow my first chance at meeting my mother. When it comes to that, I'm chickenshit.

This morning, I slide the door open, a towel wrapped around my head, a steaming fresh cup of coffee in one hand. But when I see what's happening, the cup shatters against the concrete of the porch floor.

There's an ambulance.

Two police cruisers.

No lights whirling. No sirens wailing. It's a silent terror.

It almost makes me more angry. If I'd heard something, if I'd known something was wrong, I would have been there in a heartbeat. I should be there.

I have to be there.

I toss the wet towel on the only chair in my living room and pull on my sneakers as fast as I can. I don't even think I shut the door behind me. My mother needs me. Something's wrong.

But everyone's in my way. I'm not the only one who's noticed the commotion. Three women, their hair in rollers, are standing right on the small paved pathway to the front door. I sneak around to the grass and try to see what's happening. The door is open, but I can't see a soul. The drapes are drawn tight over the picture window to the living room. Four or five other neighbors are standing around on the grass, too, their hands in their pockets. Helpless. Curious.

"What happened?" I try to get something from the women in curlers.

"Honey, I don't know much."

I know she's lying. She's got sharp eyes that see and watch everything. I want to scream at her that this is my family and she'd better tell me everything her beady eyes have seen and everything she picked up on the round of phone calls I know she's made from the moment she noticed a commotion.

"Who are you?" She takes me in. Sopping wet hair. Sweatpants.

"I'm … a friend. A neighbor."

"I've not seen you around." Her face says she's trying to call my bluff.

I want to strangle her, but there are too many others crowded around. "I'm Mildred."

"I'm Sarah." I give her my real name because I don't have the energy to think of something else. It's common enough not to cause trouble. "Do you know when they got here? Anything? Is everybody okay?"

Mildred points her beak of a nose at the ambulance waiting at the curb.

I wonder what would happen if I go inside. How bad could it be? So what if the cops throw me out. I could always explain later. What if this is my only chance? *Go, chickenshit. Go to your mother.*

What if it's the girl? My sister?

If anyone hurt them ...

One of Mildred's posse, a lady shifting nervously in her mint-green nightgown, chimes in.

"I heard it's the Cartwright woman."

"Obviously." Mildred snaps. "We're at her front steps."

"I mean, I heard she did herself in."

Oh my god. Please no.

"Always had trouble." Mildred decides to give her take.

Shut up. Whores. I hate all of you. Please, let this not be real. Please. No, no, no, no, no. I see everything I've worked for, the pain I lived through with my first family and my one window – my one shot at happiness – shatter like glass. I see the picture of my mother, my dream of her love for me, break into a thousand tiny pieces. It can't be true. I was this close. I was feet away from her ... and I may have lost her. Forever. I'll never get my chance.

It's one of those moments where everything around you fades into nonsense. The old crows gossiping. The other, younger neighbors watching from further back on the lawn. The police, irritated, making broad waves with their arm and shoeing us out like we were all nosy neighbors. I'm not. I'm not a friend or a neighbor. I'm family. But my mouth wouldn't make the words. My entire body fell numb. I don't remember walking away, but I must have moved back at the cops' angry shouts. I could have fallen over, for all I know.

All I can picture is my mother, her heartbreak over the missing piece of her – me – and me missing my chance to make it better. For her. For me. I ruined it. I could have had her. We could be together right now, at the breakfast table, like normal people. We could have been a real family and I did everything to get this damn close and now I will never get to hear her say she missed me, that she wanted me, that she's proud of me, that she loves me. Never. I'm a complete screw-up. I probably deserve this.

I stand there, next to the bushes, like some asshole. Frozen. I can't move when they wheel out the gurney, a body draped in white. There is no urgency to their movements. She's already gone. There's no one to save.

And then she wanders out, as dazed as I am.

There is one person left to save.

It takes all I have to muster a sound from my throat, but I call out to her. She turns to me, a tear-streaked face, her mouth trying to make words but not able to do anything. She looks ready to collapse.

Go to her. Go to your sister.

I'm finally doing it. My feet are walking, running, to the girl. My only family left. This is all wrong, so wrong, but she needs me. I need her too. I reach out my arms to hug her. She's confused and lost and broken. I know that look by heart.

But stupid fucking Mildred and her crew cut me off, Mildred shooting me a distrustful look.

"Sweetheart." Mildred gives the hug I was aching to share. She rocks the girl, whose sobs are muffled into the old woman's shoulder, and the woman rocks her back and forth. "I'm so so so sorry, baby girl. There's nothing I can say to ever make this less of a heartbreak. Let's get you out of here."

An engine growls to life on the curb. The ambulance crew is buckled in in the front. My mother's body has been loaded into the back. Mildred walks away with my sister. The ambulance crews, in the most casual way possible, drive away with my mother. I stand there watching my last chance at love cruise right out of sight. I never even got to say goodbye.

Or hello.

Or I missed you.

Or I love you.

I whisper it now. I don't give a fuck who hears me, but my throat is so tight I can't do anything louder than whisper:

"I love you, Mom."

The crowd has dissipated. The police are wrapping up. One of the officers eyes me warily, heading out of the house, talking into a mobile phone. He covers the receiver.

"Who are you?" he asks. Not angry, but eager to wrap up loose ends and get out of this place.

I swallow, hard. It feels like shards of glass in my throat.

"Nobody."

My feet start to carry me home, but I don't even know where home is. The piece of shit apartment – that was just a perch, a hideout, a place to get closer to her. But I screwed that one up. I find myself aimless, walking the neighborhood like a stray cat. The next street down, I find Mildred's place. The house is built like my mother's, with a big picture window to the living room, except Mildred has planted huge rose bushes to mostly obstruct the view.

But I still see her. My sister is there, wrapped in a white quilt. It's not cold now, but she's quivering. She's in shock, poor baby. Her eyes are puffy, her lips still curled and trembling in a stifled sob, when she meets my frozen gaze from the sidewalk. *Our mother is gone.*

What are we supposed to do now? It's hard to fathom that you can't live without a person you never really had in the first place – but somehow that makes it so much worse. Never had and, now, never will.

19

NOW

I t's not like I didn't know this day was coming.

I did.

I'd set my phone reminder like my therapist told me to.

I'd told myself to take it a little easier, to leave some brain space to think.

With the train wreck that was work, I've never in my life wanted so badly to lean into someone who loves me. The real me. The only person who could have done that is the woman who left me eighteen years ago. My body senses there's something wrong before my brain registers why. I wake up with a heavy weight on my chest. It's so thick, so suffocating, I feel like I might drown in it, this feeling, this endless sadness and darkness she left me with. I hate her for it.

And I love her. So much.

And she's gone. She'll never see Gracie's sweet face or stop by to fuss over her – or spoil her when she's older. She'll never pick up the phone to comfort me or to give me advice if Brad and I are fighting. I'll never be able to run over to her house to crash when I'm upset.

I've never felt so alone. I don't move at all while I watch Brad getting ready for work. I just want him to leave. He knows. I know he does.

"Love you, babe." He kisses me, soft, on the cheek. I don't stir. "Let me know how you're doing, okay? Call me?"

The worry in his voice hurts me. I can't keep cutting him out. I can't keep him locked out forever. For the first time in a long time, fear of being left alone, feeling like this forever, grips me. I want to show him all of me, but I know I can't.

"I will. Thank you, sweetheart."

This year, being a mother myself, it's a fresh wound. I've held my baby girl in my arms, felt a love I could never have comprehended before. I knew the second I held Gracie that I'd do anything in this world to protect her, to make sure she never hurts and never – not even for one day – feels alone.

How could you do this to me, Mom?

What could ever be so bottomless that you couldn't find your way back to me? How could you lose your will to fight to be with me?

This year, holding my precious child in my arms, I know this time is different. This time, I'm not just sad broken. I'm angry broken. Gracie's eyes are a well of sweetness, of innocence, as she watches me and takes her bottle. I sit with her in her rocking chair in the perfect light through her window and hold her close to me, letting the gentle back and forth motion soothe both of us. *At least I have you, my love. I'm never giving you up. I'll never leave you.*

I'm so lost in my thoughts I almost jump when I look up to see Brad.

"You're still here. You gave me a little scare."

He's leaning into the doorframe, a coffee mug in hand. His work shirt is unbuttoned.

"I called in and said I'd be late today," he answers, taking a sip from the steaming mug. "Made us some coffee. Thought maybe we could spend some time together this morning ... only if you want. I just want to be here for you, if you need me. It's my Saturday to work, but I figure they can manage a little while without me."

"Thank you, sweetheart, but you really didn't have to do that."

He moves in closer, tucks a stray lock of hair behind my ear. I really don't deserve this man. He's trying so hard ... but I want this day alone, or just with Gracie. I don't want it; I need it. I can't spend the anniversary of the day I lost my mother forever worrying about Brad's feelings – I have too many of my own to sort through.

I grab his hand and press it to my cheek, trying to remind myself he's only trying to help.

"You know what?" My mind is working this out. "I was thinking a run might do me good. I might drive over to the trail."

He perks at the idea, encouraged. I can tell he thinks it's a healthy outlet. It's also a perfect cover.

"Think Gracie will be satisfied with me for a few minutes?" His smirk tells me he knows the answer.

She's delighted to have daddy hold her. He swaps places with me and grabs my hand.

We're going to get through all of this, baby," he tells me. "I want you to know, I'm here for you no matter what."

The image of him in the soft morning light, holding our Gracie to his chest in the most nurturing way – all of his daddy love showered down on her and all of his love for me shining in the deep blue of his eyes – sticks with me as I drive through town.

Not to the trail.

To the storage unit where I keep my secrets.

The storage unit smells of dust and mildew. This is what's left of my life, packed away in a room in a row of rooms full of other people's forgotten things.

I haven't forgotten you, Mom. Never.

I haven't been here since last year. Every year, on the day she died, I think I'll work up the courage to open this box, this final piece left of who she was. I know, if I were brave enough to open this, I'd find the necklace she wore almost every single day. There will be other things, too, meant to make me feel close to her. Somehow, it's always been the last place I can go. As long as I don't open this, there's some part left of my mother still to discover.

I move past the other boxes and sit right on the filthy concrete floor and wipe the top of the box of its dust.

It's the final missing piece of me, the piece I need to make me brave enough to become not just the woman I want to be, but the woman I really am. Even if today was not the anniversary of her death, it's time. More than ever before in my life, I need to step up. Brad, the love of my life, needs me to figure out who I am and what I want. The disaster at work is turning up the pressure, forcing me to figure out what matters most to me. But I can't deal with any of that until I face what I've been avoiding all these years. If I could open this, maybe I could handle my own truth. And maybe I'd be brave enough to tell Brad. He might leave me … but at least he would know. At least there would be someone else in the world who knows.

Mom, if you ever for a moment thought you didn't matter, you should see the size of the hole you left behind. I clutch the old banker's box to my chest, trying to imagine the way it might feel to bury my face in her frizzy curls, to breathe in her smell, to have someone to talk to when I don't know what to do. *Right now. I need you so much right now, Mom.*

When I've had a good, long cry with my mother, I put the box back where I found it.

Not this year. I just can't.

Too many other things to take care of. If I could just clear some of those away ...

There's always an excuse. There will always be a reason.

I hesitate, try to work up one more ounce of willpower ... but it's impossible, the willpower doesn't exist. It's too heavy a burden. I need sanity. I need stability right now, not an upheaval of all Gracie and I have left, now that my career is crumbling to bits. I wipe the tears away and put the box back on the plastic tub of old photographs. *Next year.*

I rush back in the house, apologizing profusely for taking too long.

"Don't worry, baby." Brad is grinning, apparently mistaking my red face for the exhilarating flush of a good run. "You didn't have to hurry back. I texted you. I called off for today. I decided this is where I should be."

He's looking at Gracie when he says the last bit. They exchange smiles like it's a secret code. My heart sinks down low, my expectations for a day of solitude swept away in a swell of Brad's good intentions.

"Oh," I try to recover. "Well, I guess it's a Saturday at home then."

"One of the perks of the job," he answers. "The higher up you get, the more you get to call the shots."

I know he's hinting at the job offer that we haven't quite come back around to talking about ... but I just can't jump into that discussion today.

"I'm sorry, sweetheart. I'm just ... trying to deal today."

He sets Gracie in her playpen. She protests for an instant but then is immediately dazzled by the elephant rattle he picks up and shakes before her. Her face lights with joy and she grabs it in one swipe.

When he turns to me, I can't bear to tell him I don't really want to be touched right now. I feel so guilty cringing when he holds me, but all I want to do is wriggle free of his grasp and head to the shower for a moment of peace. A place where I can cry without dodging sympathy.

He doesn't even know why. He doesn't really understand. He doesn't know the weight I carry, but he could. I could tell him now.

I shake the thought away, not realizing at first that I'm physically shaking off Brad's loving grasp.

"Baby," he says, a prick of hurt in his tone, "I want to be here for you."

"I get that. And I love you and I appreciate that, but I …" I hesitate. This is the moment I could tell him. "I just sort of want some space today, to think." I avoid it altogether. Again.

He nods, soaking it in, weighing the idea – and then decides it's fair.

"I can understand that. I wish I could take the hurt away. But I want you to have what you need. If it's space, you get space."

"Thank you, sweetheart. You don't know how much it means to me to have you."

I look at his face and realize it's true. He doesn't know. I wish I could explain the depth of it. I squeeze both his hands in mine, wishing I could just make all of this right. But there's so much to unravel, and so much to risk. It's even hard now to separate the version of myself I've given him for so long with whatever used to be real. I can't go there right now. I'm about to head to the shower when there's a knock at the door.

"I'll get it, baby. You go on up."

"Janet?" I hear him ask.

"Janette." My friend corrects, but gently. "Good to see you again, Brad."

"From the campaign office, right?" Brad's polite but I can tell from his voice he's about to send her away. I freeze in place, weighing whether it would be best to slip upstairs ... or whether a friendly face might do me some good. At least a distraction. Unless she's come with bad news, which would make things worse.

"Actually," Brad is saying, "I don't know if today's a good day."

Sweet, protective Brad.

"It's okay, sweetheart," I shout out. "I have a few minutes to spare."

When they walk in together, I can see the pain on Brad's face. Rejection in his eyes, a droop in his shoulders. I know what he's thinking: I don't want *him* in my space, but I'm okay with a work friend. I wish I could explain too, or take a minute to smooth things over. I can tell he's done dancing around my feelings for the day and I decide not to push it. He says he's going to stop over at his sister's and I don't protest. I wish I could catch his eyes to make sure he's okay, to gauge how upset he is, but he's avoiding mine.

She doesn't, at first, disturb the quiet Brad left behind. Glances pass between us, and I think I see understanding.

"You doing alright?" she finally asks, curling her legs up underneath her in a side chair.

I sigh. It would be so nice to be ... myself with someone. To not have to cover up all the time.

"I guess as good as I can be," I answer. "Actually, no. Not so hot."

"You really can't let the work situation get to you. I know it's terrible. I can't imagine how I'd react. But you have to know, it doesn't represent everything about you. Sometimes when one area of your life is going to shit, you start to feel like it's everything, like it's a reflection of everything about you. It isn't. You're more than your job."

Sound advice, if my job were the only real problem. She doesn't know the rest of the story – about how Brad thinks I'm someone I'm not, about how so much of my life is only a reflection of who I pretend to be.

"Well, all of that, at the office, has been hell." I squeeze my hands together in my lap, considering how much I should tell this woman. How much do I really know her? Or does that make it easier to talk to her? If I tell Brad, I'm shattering what he's believed about me since he met me. I could lose the man I love. If I tell Janette, I guess it could change the way she sees me, which I wouldn't like. But I can't picture her using it to stir up trouble at work. Besides, what could compare to the trouble already brewing? It can't possibly get worse.

I breathe out my indecision.

"The truth is that today is actually a hard day for me, no matter what's going on in my life."

Janette cocks her head, waiting for more.

"This day, every year." I hear the hitch in my voice. "My mother died. Eighteen years ago. Today."

I swallow but it doesn't dissolve the hard knot in my throat.

"Oh, honey. I'm so sorry. I didn't know."

"Of course you didn't," I answer. "It's alright."

"Brad said it was a bad time … maybe, if you need a quiet day, I won't bother you." She shuffles, watching me to see what I'll say next. It feels really good to not feel pressured into talking about it.

"It's okay." I'm surprised at my answer. I want her to stay. I don't want to be alone. I want to talk.

"What happened to her … if you don't mind me asking."

But I still don't want to tell the truth, not even to Janette. Not now.

"Pancreatic cancer." I tell her what I've always told Brad.

"Oh, no. That's terrible. You would have been … just a kid, right?"

I nod, staring at the floor, watching Gracie in my peripheral vision and listening to her shaking that rattle as excitedly as she did the first time she saw it.

"Honey, that's terrible." She pauses, lowering her voice. "I can't imagine what it would be like, to lose your mother."

"I always thought that as I got older, I'd be better at handling it."

"That kind of pain doesn't go away. You can't be expected to just forget about it. This day will always be harder than the others. I'm sure."

A comfortable kind of silence settles between us, one where I'm not expected to fill in the gaps. Gracie's on her back in the playpen, reaching for her toes, blissfully unaware of my hurt.

"Well," Janette says, finally, "you know how to find me if you ever want to talk. If there's ever anything you need, even if it's to be near someone when you're feeling low, please promise you'll let me know."

"I appreciate that."

She gets up to leave but then pauses, her handbag already draped around her shoulder.

"Brad okay? He seemed to leave in a hurry. Did I interrupt something? I don't mean to be a bother."

"You're not at all. I'm really glad you came over," I answer. "He's alright. We've just had a lot to deal with lately, as you can imagine."

"I was wondering how this whole thing was sitting with him. Poor guy. He knows you didn't do anything, right?"

"That I didn't have an affair with Bill?"

"Yeah."

"He does. He trusts me. It's still been a lot of pressure," I say, pausing to pick up Gracie, who's suddenly realized that no one is holding her. "He actually got a job offer. That's part of what we're dealing with, or thinking about."

"Well, that's good news, right?"

"Sort of. I mean, it's good that they've offered it to him. He worked like crazy to get his degree. School full time and work full time. And it's really paid off. He's got fifteen stores under him now. In the new job he'd be overseeing forty."

"Wow," Janette beams. "That's wonderful. So what's the catch? That should be alleviating some of the stress. I assume he'd get a nice jump in pay. That never hurts."

"He would." I bounce Gracie in my arms. "But we'd have to move."

"Oh." She crosses her arms. It's sinking in. "Would the move be somewhere close?"

"Nope. Salt Lake City."

"Well," Janette considers it. "It's an option. Geez, though. Not much promise for your career. He couldn't have picked a redder state."

"He didn't pick it, to be fair, but you're right. My career prospects would be … all losing. Not that I'm exactly winning at work right now anyway."

"Sarah."

"No, it's true. This whole debacle, maybe it's my sign. Maybe I should hang it up. Brad would be happier. Maybe … you get to a place where you stop fighting whatever the universe is trying to tell you."

"Getting kind of existential on me now," she teases.

I laugh, grateful for a little lift in the mood.

"Maybe. He'd really like to get married. I've been avoiding making a decision."

"How do you feel about him?"

I search my heart for the answer.

"I love him, and I've always known it," I answer, truthfully. "If I felt like it wouldn't ruin things, I'd be walking down the aisle immediately."

"How would it ruin things?"

"Ah, my mother didn't do so well in the marriage, or boyfriend, or man-in-general department. I know I need to get over that, or work through that. It's not about Brad at all. It's my own hang-ups I need to deal with."

Janette reaches out to give me a quick embrace.

"Well, you've got a lot on your mind right this second. And I'm no help there. I've never dated a guy longer than a couple months. They just seem to get in the way, to be flat-out honest about it. There's too much I want to do, for myself."

Another knock at the door.

Brad would've walked right in. I don't know who else would be stopping by today ... I shrug and hand Gracie to Janette, feeling grimy and wishing I'd gone through with my quick shower. I'll make sure to freshen up as soon as I take care of whoever this is. Maybe just a package delivery.

But when I open the door, I feel my jaw drop.

It's men in uniform, but not someone delivering a package.

It's the police.

"Mrs. Cartwright?" the shorter of the pair, a doughy fellow, asks me, his brows pinched together.

Heart and mind racing, I struggle to respond intelligently.

"I'm Officer Martinez with the Metropolitan Nashville Police Department. Are you Mrs. Cartwright?"

"Miss."

"Yes, I'm sorry. Miss Cartwright, do you mind if my partner and I come in for a few minutes? We have a few questions to ask you."

20

NOW

I motion for them to come inside, my mind pinging around to a hundred different places to try to figure out how my life could possibly have come to this. Police are here. They have questions for me. I watch them eye my wall of old movie memorabilia, scanning every inch of space as if they're looking for clues.

You're supposed to let them in, right? Can't show you're nervous. Cooperate. Be nice.

But tell me, how can anyone *not* be a wreck when the police show up at your door?

Janette's looking at me, shock written all over her face. Gracie's squeezing at the long pieces of her flat-ironed locks, grinning happily until she sees me and realizes I'm not holding her. I reach for her, stunned, as the officers gather in my dining room, standing up rigid and impatient. The taller one, who's identified himself as Officer Adams, gives Janette a questioning stare.

"I was just heading out." She nods toward them and then eyes me.

"I'll be okay. I'm not sure what this is about, but I'll be fine."

The officers don't shed any light, not with Janette present. As soon as she's gone, I turn to them, feigning politeness.

"Can I get either of you something to drink?" Stupid question. I just don't know how to react.

They decline, and both take a seat. Solemn.

"Miss Cartwright," Officer Martinez starts out, "do you know why we're here?"

I search my mind for the right answer.

"No." I grip Gracie closer to me. "Is everything okay? I – I'm happy to help with whatever it is that you need."

"That's good to hear. I think you can help my partner and me out." He thrums his fingers against the tabletop, mindlessly, then leans forward. "Can you tell us where you were on Thursday evening?"

Outside, I can see the morning has evolved into a bright, invigorating fall day. I wish I had actually gone for that run and that I'd actually showered afterwards. I wouldn't look like such a bumbling, hot mess.

"Thursday?" *God, I'm coming off as evasive.*

Officer Adams crosses, then uncrosses, one long leg over the other. His face is pockmarked, and his eyes are kind, watching me with some kind of pity. I straighten and focus.

"Thursday, I was at work. I'm the volunteer manager for the Democratic gubernatorial campaign."

"Okay." Martinez is leaning onto his elbows on the table, eyeing me skeptically. "Did you work the evening shift then?"

"What?" I shake my head. "No."

"I asked what you were doing Thursday evening. Approximately what time did you leave work that day?"

Thursday. The day I left work early … and didn't come home until late. How will I answer for that? I shift on my feet and then move to sit at the table with them, Gracie still in my arms.

"I left in the afternoon."

"Earlier than normal?"

"Yes," I answer, trying to gauge what they already must know.

"And what time did you come home?"

In my head, I hear Brad repeating the time. *It's nine o'clock.* I wish he were here with me right now, or maybe I don't. He'd just think worse of me.

"Sometime in the evening," I answer.

"Do you have any better feel for exact times? When you left your office? When you came home?"

I press my lips together. I can't believe they're here. I cannot believe I'm sitting with two cops at my kitchen table grilling me on what I was doing that day.

"It might have been around one or two when I left," I answer. "I'm less sure about when I came home. Maybe seven? Eight?"

"And where were you between those two points in time?"

"Um, I – I just went for a walk."

"For several hours?"

"Yes. It's been a rough few weeks getting back to work. I'm sure you know about the stories of ... the candidate and the photo of the two of us. It's really created a lot of problems for me, professionally and personally, and I'm getting just back to work after having a baby."

"We just want to stick with what happened on Thursday." Martinez cuts me off.

I suck in a breath.

"Well, I went to the park. I walked around until I'd calmed down some …"

"Riverfront?"

"Yes. The trails."

"For about how long?"

Shit. I don't know the right answer.

"I don't know. Until it was dark."

"Must have been pretty upset."

"I was." My voice catches. *You can't let them get to you.* "Like I said, it's been hard."

"And you didn't want to just come home after that hard day?" His patronizing tone makes me want to stand up and march away. But I don't.

"I just needed some space to think."

"Hmm." Martinez and his partner exchange glances and Martinez clasps his fingers together. Here it comes. "Miss Cartwright, we are looking into the death of Charles Devante. I'm certain you've heard he was killed in a tragic collision on Thursday evening." Eyeing me, he adds: "Three others are still in the hospital."

My heart slams in my chest. To this point, against all logical odds, I'd hoped that maybe, somehow, this was about something other than the crash. But how could they have found any reason to tie Charles' death to me? There's no way. It was an accident, a four-car pileup.

And yet, they're here. Martinez' eyes are scanning everything in sight, as if he's watching for something out of place. Adams is watching me, making a smile at the baby in my lap. I bounce her, without thinking much about it. It's just a reason to do something with the nervous energy taking hold of my body.

Martinez zeroes in.

"There were some unusual circumstances surrounding the crash," he tells me, with a piercing gaze. "The officers who responded have turned it over to us to pursue any potential criminal implications."

I can't hide my surprise. *Seriously?*

"It was a four-car pileup," I answer. "Horrible, but I don't see how it's anything other than … a tragic accident. I don't know why you're here, asking me about it."

A smirk slides across his face. A gotcha grin.

"We just have to look into every angle, Miss Cartwright. You'd understand why we would have to look into a suspicious car crash, wouldn't you?"

Suspicious?

That's where he really got me. A hint that he knows more of my story than what they've obviously gathered from my coworkers, who I'm sure were delighted to share all they know, or think they know. When that chump my mother was dating died in a car crash, police wanted to know anything and everything. That has to be what they're hinting at – but how would they know? How much do they know about me? This is feeling more and more like the morning Mom's boyfriend died.

They can't possibly think I did this, unless … Enid must have told them about the argument in the parking lot …

I swallow, hoping the sound isn't as loud as it is in my head.

"Listen, I'm sure you've heard that Charles and I weren't the best of pals –"

"Actually, we heard there was a fight."

Fucking Enid.

Martinez continues: "If my sources are accurate, the fight happened just hours before Charles lost a wheel on his car going sixty-five miles per hour on Knight Street and lost control of his vehicle."

Lost a wheel? Tell me his lug nuts weren't loosened too.

I swallow down the fear, try to stare Martinez down. I have to take this head-on.

"What exactly are you asking me?"

"Is it true?"

"That we had a fight?" Gracie seems to sense my emotions getting the best of me. Her low whimper gives me reason to pause, and I comfort her against my chest. "Yes, he was in our office, making accusations, and then in the parking lot, I told him what I thought of him trying to ruin my life, and my family's life. He was threatening to release new photos."

"You really didn't like him very much, did you?"

"What are you asking me? What kind of interrogation is this?"

"It's not an interrogation, ma'am." Martinez lifts his hands off the table, defensively. "No charges *at this point.*" He gives a dramatic pause to let that veiled threat simmer. "We're just asking a few questions, tying up a few loose ends. The trouble is, reports from the scene show that Mr. Devante's lug nuts were all loosened. Only one wheel came off entirely, but the rest were ready to give too. Would you call that a coincidence?"

Shit.

How is that even possible? Of course his lug nuts were loose. Of course it would happen just the way it happened before. My curse. Yes, somebody wanted to kill him, but it sure as hell wasn't me.

"I don't know what you mean by *coincidence.* I'd call the accident horrific, and I'm glad you're looking into why his lug nuts were loose. But I still have no idea why you're here."

Martinez doesn't answer, so I come right out and say it: "I didn't loosen Charles's lug nuts, if that's what you're accusing me of."

"You just acknowledged that you didn't like him very much, though, right?"

"I didn't like him. But I also wouldn't hurt him."

"That doesn't quite line up with what we gathered from your office when you were out yesterday afternoon, unfortunately."

Damn it.

"Okay. Well, I couldn't tell you the first thing about fixing cars, changing tires or lug nuts," I answer, trying to keep the panic out of my voice. Gracie reaches up a hand to my lips. I hold onto her tiny fingers.

"Your husband works at an auto shop, though, right?"

Oh my god. Brad does not deserve this shit. These two need to get out of here, right now.

I pull my baby close to me and try to paint on a poker face.

"He does. Not a mechanic. A manager. What does that have to do with any of this?"

"Just checking, ma'am. Just covering all our bases. But it would be helpful if you could tell us where you were between the hours of 2 p.m. and 8 p.m. on Thursday."

"I already told you. Riverfront Park." I stand up, hoping they'll get the hint.

To my surprise, they do.

"Can you tell us whether there's anybody who might have seen you? Someone who could confirm that that's where you spent the afternoon?"

"There were people there, of course," I answer, my words clipped.

"No one you knew?"

I shake my head.

"Alright." Martinez sighs. "We'll try to canvas the park, see if we can find anyone who might have seen you there. You tell anyone where you were going?"

Shoot. I hadn't even told Brad. My own boyfriend couldn't confirm my story.

"No." I admit it.

"Okay, ma'am. Thank you for your help. We'll be on our way." He reaches into his pocket and pulls out a card. "Please, if anything comes to you, I'd like for you to let us know. The sooner we can find some answers, the sooner we can all hopefully put this behind us."

I nod and lead them toward the door, but Martinez has one more thing he needs to tell me: "Just, to be on the safe side here, I think it would be best if you avoid heading out of town. Just until we get this all straightened out."

"Thank you. I'll take that advice."

"Thank you," Adams speaks. "Sorry for all the trouble. Hoping we can get this ironed out quickly."

I try to look both of them in the eye and smile as they go. They're just doing their job.

And I'm in deep shit.

Not because I killed Charles. I didn't. But if they decide to keep digging around … they'll find more coincidences that I can't explain.

Like I said, I'm in deep. But I've dug myself out before. And I have so much more to lose than ever before. Gracie reaches her tiny fingers to my face, like she knows I'm thinking of her. I have to protect her.

I can dig myself out again. I will. I just have to be smart about it.

21

THEN

F unny. I never pictured myself as the nurturing type.

But with her, my sister, it's different.

For the last few years, I've watched her and watched out for her. I'm still holding down my job at the diner – plenty of others, less dedicated or maybe moving on to something different, have come in and then out. I've kept to my pattern, even with my mother gone, built some sort of life for myself here.

But I can feel change stirring. I've been able to scrape together some money. This dump doesn't cost much. I don't spend much and most of my food comes right from work. My sister's getting older. She doesn't take the bus anymore from that neighbor's house who took her in after Mom died four years ago. She has her own junker. Sometimes I follow, a few cars behind, to make sure she gets there.

There are times when I really wish I could step in, tell her who to look out for. I don't like that one guy she was hanging around for a while. I've seen her sneak out, too, at night. I don't want to be a drag, I know I'm not her mother, but I worry about her.

Seems like she's mostly okay with Mildred. But who wants to live with an old lady? I'm sure the whole house stinks of cheap hand cream. I want better for my sister, for both of us. A couple weeks ago, I followed her to the mall. Her one bratty friend, the kind who's always got the best of everything, was tagging along and talking a million miles a second, so I knew my sister wouldn't have a spare moment of space to notice me, trailing behind.

They were in and out of the kind of standalone stores teens love, the ones with the punk clothes and the other with the surfer cool rags. The bratty friend got something at every store. My sister was empty-handed. When they went into the big department store, I watched from the aisle full of towels as they poked around the trendy tulle and silk in the junior's dresses section.

Bratty bitch picked out something she liked, in fuchsia, immediately. My sister, more thoughtful, took her time until one dress jumped out at her. I watched her handle the turquoise fabric, run her fingers around the sweetheart neckline, feel the bones of the bustier. It was lovely. She might look too sexy in that, but I could tell she thought it was the most beautiful thing she'd ever seen. Brat was in the dressing room, or probably ringing up purchases. I could almost read my sister's mind. Where would she ever find the money for that?

I wanted to walk up to her then. Tell her to go try it on anyway, see how beautiful she is. There's no way she knows what an amazing young woman she's becoming ... and her big graduation party is coming up soon. For once, I'd like to see her as well-dressed as her friends who still have parents around to care for them, not some old hag.

But I don't walk up to her like I want to, not now. *See the pattern?* I want to, but something stops me every time. I missed all those opportunities to meet my mother because ... I guess because I was afraid I would be less than she thought. But with my sister, it's different. I don't constantly picture a happy reunion. She could never answer the questions my mother could have. She probably doesn't even know that I exist, that she has a sister.

I thought, at first, that one day I would go up to her, but I could never imagine what it would feel like for her or for me. What's better, I think at least for now, is that she has a guardian angel. Someone who'll slide a twenty-dollar bill in her window when it's cracked to make sure she has enough lunch money. Someone to make sure nobody's giving her trouble at home or at school. Someone to put that perfect trendy turquoise dress, size extra-small, in a little gift bag sitting on the back of her car when she heads out to school the next day.

I've learned to live with being invisible. I don't need to take credit for the things I do for her or the things I give up to be close to her.

It's enough just to know that I'm someone's angel.

When I saw the brat's black Jeep pull up to the curb around 11 p.m. on graduation night, I knew there'd be trouble. That bitch is bad news. I can't get a good gander from my patio anymore, so I slide on a pair of flip-flops and pad down the road, always staying in the shadow, out of the streetlights.

Sure enough, there's my sister. She's changed out of the turquoise dress she wore to graduation tonight and has on a low top with tight jeans. She's tiny enough to contort her way right through what has to be a six-inch gap between the window and the windowsill of her back bedroom. Brat's waiting for her there, but I can see the Jeep is already full. At least six other kids, probably already drunk, are piled into a backseat made for three people. I don't like the look of this, but I don't have much choice. I'll have to hurry. I run back to my car, glad I hadn't changed into my pajamas yet or washed my makeup off from my day spent hanging around the back of a high school graduation ceremony. I make it out of my parking lot just in time to see the Jeep spin, way too fast, around a corner.

I've got a feeling I know where they're heading – and I'm right. Besides bratty bitch's Jeep, there are at least two dozen other vehicles out in Middle of Nowhere, Alabama. Just a few miles outside town, but it's got that deserted feeling that attracts delinquents. I've seen enough drunk teens at 1 a.m. at the diner to know this is where the craziest parties happen: the quarry.

Neighbors won't be around to call the cops. The cliffs around the edge of the gouged-out pit are at least a thirty-foot drop. Kids dare each other to get close to the edge. Great fun. Also a great place to get smashed. If I'd had a normal life or had the chance to complete my junior or senior years instead of picking up a GED, I'm sure I'd have been one of the troublemakers to party at the quarry myself.

I pull down the mirror for a second and think I can pass as a high schooler. I'm not much older than them in years. In shitty life experiences, I could be their grandmother. One swipe of lipstick, quick brush of my hair, and I'm all set. I should blend into the background just fine. It's all I ever do.

Ahead, I can see the fire pit roaring in a bare patch between the pine trees.

I can hear their god-awful pop music up loud too. I scan the silhouettes for my sister and creep a little closer. God, everyone's got a can of beer. Cheap beer, too.

Honey, we've got to get out of this dead-end town.

I freeze when I hear rustling just a few feet away. I need to pay better attention. I tiptoe closer. Guy and a girl, making out. She's already got her top off and he's yanking clumsily at the back of her bra. *Yuck.*

I tiptoe past them, knowing they don't give a shit that I'm here anyway. Around the edges of the party, I find the host, one of the cool kid crowd I recognize from my sister's school drop-offs in the morning. His parents own some big company. Maybe it's even the quarry itself. Taylor. I think that's his name.

I give him a sexy smile and reach for a beer. It'll give me something to do while I keep an eye out. He tries to ask me a couple questions, but I pretend to be already a little tipsy and disconnected from my girlfriends. I wriggle out of that one and try to keep to the edges of bare patch around the big fire pit. Then I spot her, lit up in a warm orange glow of the fire, she's hanging on to some guy's arm while he roasts a couple marshmallows on what appears to be an outstretched hanger wire. They catch on fire and become torches and my sister's lovely laugh floats out over the sound of shitty pop music.

I already don't like whoever this marshmallow-toasting loser is. Hat on backwards, jeans hanging down too low, preppy collared shirt. He's a mish-mash of everything that's wrong with backwoods kids who don't have much to look forward to other than high school.

"Mark, you ruined them." I hear her laughing. She's got a beer in her hand too.

Just be careful, honey.

It seems pretty harmless for a while. By the time my sister's on to her third beer, she's cozied up to him, wrapped up in a blanket while most of the crowd watches a rousing game of beer pong set up under a pavilion nearby. I know what that asshole has on his mind. He's got her just far enough away from the crowd to not raise any attention. I watch him move in close behind her, wrap his legs around her and start planting kisses on her neck. I squint to see my sister's reaction.

She grimaces and moves away from him. When he does it a second time, I'm ready to step in.

But, maybe not.

It looks she's got things under control. She gets to her feet immediately. When he jumps up too and grabs her around the waist, shoving himself up against her, she punches him, straight in the face. I make a tiny fist pump myself. *Nice going.* Not sure I could have done better myself.

The guy is totally stunned. He's holding his nose like a third grader on the playground as my sister marches off, and then he goes to whine to his buddies. I watch the group gathered around the beer coolers try to console him. I step up a little closer to refill my own supply and see him unroll a long stretch of paper towels to dab two teeny drops of blood from underneath his nose.

"Man, you gotta get better at this," one dude tells him, in earshot of me. "Either she needs more drinks or you need to come off smoother."

Maybe she just doesn't want you.

But I don't say that. I grip my beer and pretend to sway a little to the boy band pop song playing in the background.

"Girls are too much fucking work, man."

"For you."

The whole gang shares a good laugh.

"Hey," Mark says, letting the jab roll off his shoulders. "Hand me one of those nasty ass wine coolers, will you? Actually, give me two."

The tallest in the group complies and I watch Mark twist off the top of one of the bottles and slip something from his pocket in the glass mouth.

"Going to go give her another whirl around the Mark-mobile."

They all crack up.

"Better luck this time, Romeo."

I make a beeline for the last place I'd seen my sister. She's not there, by the beer pong tournament, but I see that Mark, the punkass, is still there. From his slight stagger, I know this one will be easy. His eyes are scanning the crowd. I tug my top down by three or four inches and lean against a pine tree, like I'm tipsy enough to need support. Little girl, all alone, nursing a beer.

Works like a charm. He notices me, and I tilt my head and smile. I set down my half-empty can and reach out for what he's holding. He hands me the drugged drink and then opens his own, watching me as he takes a sip.

I giggle like I'm drunk when he makes a stupid-ass joke. Then I grab his elbow, not wanting to waste any more time. He follows me behind a row of trees. Like luring a little kid with candy.

"Who're you?" He stops his sloppy kissing for one second. "I've never seen you here before."

"I've been hanging around." I answer, reaching for his pants. I can feel him harden underneath my hand.

That stops every question. I feel him eying my breasts while I fuss with the buttons on his jeans. He's shaking with anticipation. Right in the palm of my hands. That's where I have him. I kneel down, stopping to look at his face. His head is titled back, eyes closed in ecstasy. He's moaning while I stroke him with my right hand. With my left, I swap our drinks.

By the time it's over, he's collapsed on the ground, breathing hard, thanking me. I pick up my wine cooler and motion for him to do the same.

"Cheers."

The glasses clink and he sucks his down, thirsty.

I guess I could have just left it at that. But I don't leave unfinished business.

Mark's eyelids are drooping as I lead him down the path, further away from the group and deep into the woods – all the way to that steep cliff edge. Time for a friendly dare. Maybe a little shove too.

The night of his life.

He'll never bother my baby sister again.

22

NOW

I had my reservations about meeting Enid, but I'm not sure I've ever needed a friend so badly. Most of all, I wish there were some way for me to know that she still is my friend, that she would never shove me right out of a job, or shove me right into the heart of a potential homicide investigation by playing up what she saw of my fight with Charles. *Please say it's not true, Enid.* Brad had dismissed Enid's involvement in the police investigation as quickly as he had said she wouldn't have given the news the photo of me and Bill. He said he knows her and knows she'd never do anything like that, that she'd never hurt me, or him. I hope he's right. I hope to god he's right about her.

I've been short with Enid, avoiding her texts to meet up, but she's persisted. I finally gave in. Maybe if I see her, talk to her face-to-face, I'll know for sure.

Through the gilded doors I go.

The location is Enid's suggestion. My favorite Thai restaurant, Lemongrass.

We used to come here all the time. The hostess tells me my party's already here, right as I spot her over in a nook by a window, waving at me with one hand, clutching a stack of papers in the other. Working dinner. She's really embracing her new role.

"Hey, you." She hugs me tight. "I'm so glad you said yes. I know it's been busy, but ..."

"Just a lot going on." I fill in for her.

"I'll say."

My feet are aching when I climb into my side of the booth. I've been working the neighborhoods in the south side of the city for six hours straight. What I could really use is a stiff drink.

"How were the troops today?" Enid's in a sharply pressed blouse, her hair pulled up in a stylish messy bun. I glance at the stack she's just set on the table, printouts of the latest stories about the governor's race. Thankfully, this time, none of the headlines I spot includes the phrase "scandal-ridden." Small victory, but I'll take it.

"Oh, it's not too bad. Nobody seems to be losing steam. I think your strategy for swapping out crews every few days is smart. It'd be hard for them to be out there day after day after day."

"Except that's what you are expected to do."

"Seriously," I answer. "You and I both know it's a tough job."

She nods emphatically.

"But rewarding," I add, quickly.

An awkward silence passes between us. I look away and peer over the menu, not reading, wondering how to broach the subject of *how* I ended up in this job and whether she might have had something to do with it. I think back to how she'd told me days ago that she feels like she's found her calling. I can't bear to listen to her gush about her new job, my old job. I steer the conversation to something slightly safer.

"Brad's having a hard time with my hours, says I come home exhausted every day," I mention, glancing at the menu for the fifth time.

"Yeah. Staying on your feet all day can be a bear. But I'm sure it's nice to come home to a whole, happy family." She smiles at me. I can't help but wonder whether it's genuine. It's the kind of smile you give to someone to force them to smile back. "Aside from what's been happening at work, look at how your life has come together."

"That's true." I wait a moment for the waiter filling our glasses to step away. "It's just, a lot of pressure, to keep everything together ... Brad keeps wanting to get married."

"And?" Enid looks at me in surprise and then lights up like any good girlfriend would at the prospect, but it looks a little put on, to be honest. "How do you feel?"

"I can't tell," I answer. "I have a hard time with the whole idea."

"Sarah," Enid clicks her tongue reproachfully. "I never tagged you as one to be worried about commitment. You've got a great guy, a darling baby girl. He's got a solid job and wants to tie the knot ... so then what's the catch? Do you know how many women would love to be in your position?" From the emphasis on her last question, I think maybe she wouldn't mind being in my position. Relationship-wise, of course. She already has my job.

"I know. I know," I say, trying to push away my resentment and my suspicion. "I'm grateful. I just never liked feeling cornered. I don't respond well. It hurts his feelings. Then I try to overcompensate, but I don't want to make the wrong decision just because I feel bad."

"There's not some other reason you wouldn't want to marry Brad, is there?"

Her face says the question is innocent concern, but panic flashes through my chest. *What does she know? What is she asking?*

"No," I answer. "He's great. I just don't know how I feel about marriage in general."

"I get you." She nods slowly, a little uncertain. "It's a big decision. Don't add any more pressure to what you're already feeling. I've always thought a lot of Brad, but I don't want you to feel pushed. There's a lot happening in your life right now. You've got time to think about the rest of it."

"Yeah. Having the police interviewing everyone we know isn't helping things one bit, I can tell you that."

I wait a moment to see whether her expression gives anything away, whether she might mention that she spoke to police. But she seems suddenly interested in the silken table runner. I'm about to say something else about the investigation when we're interrupted.

The waiter brings our noodles out, fragrant spices making my mouth water. I've ordered Brad's favorite, drunken noodles. And they are delicious. After a few minutes, I work up the courage to ask Enid what I really want to know.

"You don't really think I had anything to do with Charles' death, right?"

She sets her chopsticks down immediately.

"Oh, Sarah." She looks at me with a pained expression. "This *is* all really getting to you, isn't it? I'd never think that of you. Not ever."

"Thank you."

"I mean it," she says. "I've known you for years. I've known Brad even longer. I know you're good people. I consider you one of my closest friends."

I have to swallow back the lump in my throat. I want so much to believe her. I want so much to know that she's a real friend.

"Sarah, I mean it. You're a bright, beautiful person. I know none of this represents who you are. You're just … pushed into a corner. It's really not fair. I'm sorry. I'm sorry for all of it. I care about you. I've been so worried." She pauses a second and sucks in a deep breath, as if this is what she came here to say: "I really don't want this situation to come between us. Our friendship is more important to me than any of this."

My gut tells me to believe her, but my brain tells me to be skeptical. So much has happened. There are so many ways someone has been trying to hurt me – hideous ways – and I still don't know who. But it can't be Enid. I hope.

"I appreciate you saying that." I push my plate away, suddenly full. "I really do. I can't wait until all this is behind us."

She grins.

"Just a couple more weeks to go. We're almost down to days now until the election is over."

"I know. Oh, I wanted to ask you about the one lead volunteer." I stop to remember her name. "Maddie."

"Oh yeah. She's got a way with people, when she's energized. I have to start her out with donuts to get her going. Actually, that's been my secret all along."

I laugh out loud.

"*That's* what I've been doing wrong."

By the time the waiter is boxing our leftover dinners, Enid has given me a few good insights on who shouldn't be mixed with whom on the campaign trail and who to keep an eye on. It's helpful, but I'm beginning to see a pattern. She's not asking me much about the specifics of my job, meaning she's taken right to it. And she would. She has the right temperament, the right gritty kind of drive. Work – my work, not hers – is a neutral topic, so we stay there, but it doesn't make me feel any better. I make a trip to the ladies' room, if only for a second of quiet.

In the mirror, I see an exhausted woman. My hair is flat, makeup washed away from a day spent sweating it out in the trenches, worry lines carved into my brow. *Who have you become?* I've assumed my closest friend is out to get me. I'm avoiding the man I love. I can't even face the box my mother left behind, and I've waited eighteen years to do it. I need to make a change, maybe a lot of them.

Brad *is* worth hanging onto. He's struggled so much lately, trying to help me through my lowest moments. And I know it bothers him that I won't jump right into the life he wants to make for us.

Maybe being married wouldn't be so bad. Spending more time with Gracie would be incredible. On its face, Salt Lake City sounds like a terrible move, but a fresh start isn't. Not with everything that's happened with the campaign. Oh god, or the police investigation.

Guess we'd have to wait until that wraps up.

I splash a bit of water on my face.

I hate feeling like I can't figure out what I want. I'm a grown woman, smart enough to get all the way to running a governor's race, despite where I came from. I can make a new way, in a new place. And it will make Brad so happy. I owe him that. I'll tell him tonight.

I don't remember until I pull up to the house and see the van missing from the driveway: Brad *had* told me he'd be home late.

Even better. It will give me a few hours to get cozy with Gracie and then get cleaned up. Brad has been so loving, so patient, he could use at least one "yes" from me. I stash my leftover drunken noodles in the fridge in a hurry to get back to Gracie, who hasn't stopped fussing since I picked her up from Tracie's. She doesn't seem to want her bottle, either. The only time she stops crying is when I'm standing up and moving, patting her back and bouncing her just a little.

Sweet girl. I'm right here, baby. Momma's here.

When the phone rings from my handbag on the kitchen table, I think maybe I've run out of time to get ready for Brad. I'd really wanted a hot shower and just a few minutes to regroup. Gracie had other plans. Of all the nights for her to get fussy, tonight's a bad one. I had a picture of how I wanted it all to happen, and it wasn't this. It takes me so long to dig my phone from the bottom of my bag with Gracie kicking in my arms, I think I might miss it.

It isn't Brad calling.

"Sarah, I thought you weren't gonna pick up."

"Hey, Janette." Gracie wails in the background. No further explanation needed.

"Aw."

"Yeah. Poor babe. I think she must have napped all day." I imagine Tracie just letting her snooze away for hours, knowing it would make grief for us later, enjoying the idea.

"Well, I'm on my way to your place. Was hoping we could grab a drink or something."

My whole body's bouncing, trying hard to soothe Gracie.

"Um, I don't know that it's a good night."

"I could hang out there, if that's easier than going out."

Gracie huffs in a deep, labored breath, starting to simmer down. *Sweet love. It's okay. Mommy's right here.*

"I'd like to get together, but I think Gracie needs some mom time. She won't let me put her down, not even for a second."

The other line is quiet for a moment.

"I'm almost there already, but I can turn around I guess. To be honest, it's been really hard with Enid. I was hoping we could talk a little about the campaign. Think you could spare just a few minutes?"

So maybe things aren't going as well as Enid let on. Maybe my old job is harder than she thought it would be.

"Well …" I chew over it. Brad won't be home for a little while. I'm clearly not going to get the chance to fix myself up for him anyway, or make a nice dinner.

"How about this?" Janette's voice is chipper. "Let's get you out of the house for a couple hours. Bring Gracie along. We'll get a chance to chat. Maybe you can offer some guidance on how to deal with Enid. It'll get your mind off the police investigation. What you do think?"

"It's Gracie's bedtime, though."

"I know. Maybe a car ride would put her to sleep," Janette offers. "I'm sorry. I just was really hoping we could talk. Enid is making me batty."

"I'd love to help you, but I wanted to get some quiet time with Brad tonight too. I've been thinking about his job offer."

"Then you definitely need a few minutes to clear your head. Besides, I'm here now."

That was fast. I dance on my toes a little bit, deciding. But my friend's at the door already, and maybe she's right. Besides, she lifted my spirits the other day ... before the cops came and added a whole new layer of crap to my worries. I might owe her one. Maybe Enid's not doing as well in her new job as she let on with me earlier.

I answer the door, and Janette's still holding her phone.

"Hooray! You're giving in to the dark side."

It feels good to laugh a little after all the tension of my dinner with Enid. I'm still not sure whether I can trust her, even though I want to. How can you patch up a friendship before you even know where the holes are? Something doesn't add up. Not yet. It hurts me to think that way, but I still can't set it all right in my head.

I'm shocked when Gracie leans out to Janette's outstretched arms.

"She really likes you, Janette."

"We girls are going to have fun tonight, aren't we?" She's cooing into Gracie's face, and my baby is loving it, though her chest is still shaking occasionally from letting it all out before.

"Actually, maybe we could just hang out here." I'm wavering again.

"I've got a bottle of wine. And I had really wanted to make something good for Brad for dinner."

Janette's nose wrinkles.

"It's seven now, though."

"He's coming home late, so … late dinner I guess. I know he's been feeling a little disconnected lately. I just wanted a nice evening with him."

"When he gets around to coming home."

"Hey, now."

"I'm sorry. Kidding. How about …" She whirls Gracie around and my sweet girl bursts out with laughter. "How about we head out for a little bit and pick up something he likes. You can have your makeup sesh later, as planned. And I can pick your brain about Enid."

She *is* good. Maybe it's because Gracie's stopped crying, but I've got a little burst of energy. Just being around Janette makes me feel more hopeful. She's helped pull me out of my slump a couple times now with my career being smashed to pieces. That's what a real friend does. I think of Enid, how she asked that this not come between us. But she hasn't come over here once, not since days after the baby was born. It would have done me good to have someone here, just to talk to every once in a while. Maybe I need to be better about choosing my friends. Start with people who care enough to spend time with me.

"You know what?" I say to Janette, who is half listening to me and half making Gracie squeal with joy. "I already have Brad's favorite Thai food in the fridge. Plenty leftover. We should be good. I'll just write him a note and change quick."

"Yay! Mommy said yes!" Janette taps her index finger on Gracie's tiny button nose and it makes her giggle.

I pull one of the Buck's Auto sticky notes and a pen from the kitchen's junk drawer.

Hi Baby.

Missing you a lot today. Dinner in the fridge for you. Ran out for a little bit. Gracie and I will be home soon.

XOXOXOXO

I tack it onto the fridge under a magnet, hoping he'll read it the right way. I've been so withdrawn, and he's been standing by, waiting and loving the whole time. I'd been so hopeful about tonight, and I want to be warm to him, but staring at my X's and O's makes me wonder whether it doesn't look like I'm trying too hard, or that there's reason to be suspicious.

Why can't a working woman head out with her girlfriend every once in a while? I'm overthinking this.

"Okay, girls," I say to the pair of them as I head upstairs to change, "be right back."

23

NOW

C asey's is busier than usual tonight and the waiter recognizes me instantly, but then looks around me, presumably for Enid. I just smile and ask for a table for two. He sits us at the exact same booth as when Enid and I were here after my disastrous first day back at work. This time, he scoots over an upside-down high chair so I can set Gracie's carrier right next to us. Janette was right; the car ride put her right to sleep. She's was out like a light and is still sleeping soundly.

I'm not hungry, but a Merlot sounds nice.

After the waiter has taken Janette's order and left us, she leans in closer to me across the table.

"She's driving me crazy," she whispers.

"Oh, Enid's not that bad. She's smart. She's a worker bee."

Janette rolls her eyes dramatically and gives an exaggerated sigh.

"Yeah, she works hard – but only if I tell her exactly what I need her to do."

I bite my bottom lip. Nothing would feel as good as railing on Enid the way I feel right now … but even after what I think she may have done to me, it just doesn't feel right. I don't want to be that kind of person.

"Well, she is new to the job. It's a little different from the volunteer manager. I came up through the same trek. You can't expect her to be an instant pro at running a campaign."

Janette smirks, incredulous.

"Bet you were, though."

At the bar a few feet away, the crowd roars. The Titans have just made a touchdown, from the sounds of it and from what I can make out on the television set up behind the bar. I'd forgotten it was a football night. Brad might have been glued to the TV anyway if we'd had our night at home. It makes me think of him, though, and wish we were cuddled up together on the couch.

Gracie whimpers and stirs at the ruckus, but miraculously stays asleep. For now, anyway.

"It's almost like …" Janette is pinching her lips together, thinking and watching me from across the table. "It's almost like she wanted to *be* you. I mean, she's got your old job now, and you're busy, out doing her job, but she can't stop talking about you."

"Nah." It's a weird idea.

"I mean it. It's always, 'Sarah would do this,' or 'Sarah would do that.'" Janette huffs. "She can't seem to think on her own."

"Maybe just a confidence thing." I stop to dig in my purse for my phone. Brad hasn't called. "Maybe once she feels like she has a better handle on what her responsibilities are and where she needs to take initiative without guidance, she'll step right up. I know she's got the drive."

"I'm not sure what the problem is … but it sure as hell is making my job a lot harder."

The waiter interrupts with Janette's burger and my glass of wine, but she doesn't seem interested in it. She moves the plate away from her.

"I know you've seen how hard Enid can work as the volunteer manager, but I have to say I'm frustrated."

"Fair," I answer. "But have you tried talking to her about it? Maybe she doesn't want to step on your toes or something. I'm sure she's still just figuring out where she fits, and she doesn't feel comfortable stepping up the way you'd want her to. Maybe she's looking for your permission. I know she's capable."

Janette just rolls her eyes.

"You know her outside of work?" she asks. "Personally?"

I nod and take a sip of my wine, part of me still wishing I'd stayed home.

"How long have you been friends? Are you close?"

I shrug and try to remember, actually, when we became good friends. She was one of Brad's friends, but I'd known her first from her work at nonprofits when the organizations she was working with had some connection to one of my candidates. Always upbeat. *Always* moving. I admired her get-shit-done attitude and was happy to spend some time around that kind of energy. When Bill brought her on to his campaign at my request, we finally had the chance to work together. Things were great ... before the baby. We'd joked that we were a "work couple," connected at the hip. Then it seemed like I slipped her mind when I was home with Gracie. Obviously, there was a lot brewing behind the scenes at the office, too. I had no idea until recently that she wanted to be assistant campaign manager. Come to think of it, she was remarkably silent while I was away on maternity leave. Hell, she didn't even send a text when my assistant quit.

The thought hit me hard. Another strike against her. Janette is suggesting that she has some kind of obsession with me, but it feels a lot more like she couldn't care less. Except, she *had* kept asking why I didn't want to marry Brad – like maybe she was worried he wasn't good to me, or he was holding me back. Now, thanks to Janette's two cents, I'm analyzing every word she said earlier.

Janette finally takes a few bites of her burger, glancing over at the football game on the screen.

"Well," she says, stopping to chew, "I'll tell you one thing. You and I would have made a killer team. It's such a shame that it didn't work out for you to come back as the assistant campaign manager. If only Charles – God rest his soul – hadn't screwed everything up."

And there's another person I could go without thinking about or talking about. I try to redirect the conversation.

"There will be other campaigns, I guess." When I realize what I've said, and remember the position I'm in, I rephrase. "Maybe there will be other campaigns with candidates ballsy enough to take a scandal-on-wheels as one-half of their campaign manager team."

Janette throws her head back and laughs.

That's the sound that wakes the baby, not the howling over the football game, go figure. Maybe Gracie's used to her dad's hoots and hollers over every play.

"Oh shit," Janette puts a hand up over her mouth. "I'm sorry."

I go to pick her up, but Janette beats me to it. "I'm sorry, Gracie. Silly Auntie Janette didn't mean to be so loud. Forgive me?" She leans into Gracie's face, shaking her head and smiling. "Forgive your crazy Auntie Janette?" Janette's hair grazes Gracie's cheeks – and she stops fussing and flashes a big, toothless grin.

"Anyway," Janette turns her attention back to me. "There *will* definitely be other campaigns. I'd love to get to work with you."

"Well, I'd like that too," I say, smiling at the idea, "but I'm not sure there will be anyone willing to take the risk, after all of this. The pictures, Charles' death, a police investigation –"

"Yeah, what happened the other day after the police showed up?"

Janette interrupts me. "I felt bad to leave. I wasn't sure what I should do."

I sigh.

"It's okay," Janette doesn't make me go into it. "They talked to all of us. I'm *sure* it is just routine and will work out just fine." Her tone becomes motherly, reassuring, like she's decades older than me rather than just three or four years. "It's politics. People know campaigns get ugly and sometimes there are innocent victims. I'm the PR pro. We can make you out to be whoever we decide."

I chuckle at that. "All the same," I say, watching Gracie in her arms, "I think it might just be time."

"For what, exactly?"

"I mean ... the right time for me to take a break. Let everything simmer down. Spend a few years with Gracie –"

"Years?"

I take a deep breath in and try to decide whether I feel like arguing about this. I get the feeling Janette's going to push me toward staying in politics, no matter what. She's a cheerleader that way. It's sweet of her, but I'm not sure that's what I want right now.

"Yeah. Brad wants to get married."

"But you'd have to move." Janette shakes her head adamantly.

"I know. And I'm coming to terms with that. It might be good for all of us."

"You mean *good for Brad.*"

"Well, yes, I guess," I answer, a touch defensively. "But good for me and Gracie too."

Janette searches my face and stays quiet for a lingering second.

"Well, I want you to have what you want." She stops to take a breath. "But I want you to be sure that's what you want. I'm not letting you get away that easily. I want you to spend enough time thinking about it. Make the decision that's best for *you*. I don't want you giving into pressure to be a wife now that you're a mom, unless that's what you really, really want. I don't want you giving up on your career because you think you have to. This garbage with Bill and with Charles will blow over. You'll see. You just have to give it time."

I try not to squirm.

I just don't know for sure what I want. I don't think I've given Brad enough of a chance. My automatic response has been to keep things the way they are between the two of us – we already have a baby together – but I know he wants to make everything official. He wants to be a whole family, wedding bands and all. That's because he loves me.

I breathe in deep and stand to stretch. I need to get back to Brad; he's waited long enough.

Janette smiles at Gracie and buckles her back into her car seat. We drive in comfortable silence back to the house. The lights are on. Brad's here.

"I'm really glad you came out tonight," Janette gets out of the car quickly. "See you soon, Sarah."

I watch her drive away and give myself a few seconds to rehearse what I want to say to Brad before I get out of the car myself. I think of all the ways he's encouraged me over the past few months and how excited he'll be when I finally say "yes." Yes, let's take that promotion and the move to Salt Lake. Yes, let's get hitched, baby.

He's going to be so happy.

I expect to hear the football game blaring inside, but it's deadly quiet. So I tiptoe the best I can while lugging Gracie's bulky car seat. Around the corner to the kitchen. The notes gone, but Brad's not here … Maybe upstairs.

When I turn to look around the divider between the kitchen and living room, I freeze, almost dropping Gracie's carrier at the sight … a body on the carpet.

It's him.

No. Baby, no.

"Brad!" I scream, and Gracie does too.

He's on the floor, eyes shut, mouth open.

He looks dead.

"Brad!"

I put Gracie down, still buckled in, and fall over Brad's body. His skin is warm but sticky, sweat slicked over his brow. He's breathing. I shake him.

Nothing.

I grab both his shoulders and try to wake him. He doesn't flinch, but his head lops to the other side.

"Baby, baby. Wake up."

Please wake up.

Gracie's scream is piercing but all I can think is that Brad won't wake up.

What happened? What's wrong? How long have you been here?

I fumble for my handbag and dig around and then dump everything on the floor beside us in a panic. Finally, I find my phone. My eyes move around the scene to half-eaten noodles spilled across the floor, but I don't have time to process what that could mean.

Shaking, I dial 9-1-1.

A man picks up on the first ring.

"911. What's your emergency?"

24

NOW

How can nine minutes feel like two hours?

Why aren't they here yet?

The 911 operator is still on the line with me. I've told him everything I can about how I found him ... just lying here. I'm holding Gracie now and bent over on my knees, squeezing Brad's hand. I'd give anything in the world to feel him squeeze back.

But he doesn't move.

It's long minutes of agony before the operator on the line tells me the crews have arrived. I drop the phone and rush to the door to let them in. The sirens are squealing and the van jerks to a stop in the driveway. Two EMTs leap from their seats and I stand back, praying. One rushes past me. The other opens the van's back doors and pulls out a folded gurney.

Let him be okay.

Please let Brad be alright.

In a daze, I watch them working over his body, moving fast, calling out measurements and numbers to each other and into their radios. The world is spinning in circles around me as I watch them one-two-three lift and shift his lifeless body onto the gurney.

"Are you riding with us?"

I don't even register what the guy is saying.

"Is he going to be okay?" I ask the question in my heart instead of giving him an answer.

"I don't know, ma'am. We're taking him to Saint Thomas right now. You can sit –" He stops and sees Gracie sucking her thumb against my chest, disoriented and needing comfort.

I breathe in, trying to clear my head.

Oh god, they're wheeling Brad away from me.

"I'll be there as soon as I can."

Before the ambulance has left the house, I have Tracie on the line.

"Brad's hurt." I breathe into the phone. Every part of my body is trembling.

"I don't know. I don't know," I'm almost yelling. I don't need her questions right now. I just need her help. Brad and I need her help. "I need you to meet me at the hospital to take care of Gracie."

I'm coming, Brad.

All the way there, I can't stop thinking of all the things I should have done tonight. I should have stayed home. I should have listened to my gut. I should have been there when he got back … I should have called. Maybe he would have said he hadn't been feeling well. Maybe something was wrong all day and I had no idea.

I couldn't even answer whether he had been complaining of feeling sick when the 911 operator asked me.

When was the last time I even spoke to him for more than two seconds?

When was the last time I hugged him tight? Or really kissed him?

What if I never get to tell him everything I wanted to tell him tonight? What if I never get to tell him I love him again?

Oh my god, Brad. I'm so sorry.

I've deteriorated into a complete self-loathing disaster, a sniffling mess of hot tears, by the time I've met Tracie in the parking lot and made it to the ER intake desk. A heavyset woman looks me over from behind a wall of glass and sighs like she detests every part of her job, especially this one.

She slides back a small square of glass.

"Who are you here for?"

"Brad – Bradley – Carlson." I swallow and try to still the sobs still shaking my chest.

She spends an agonizing minute, head tilted, looking at her chart.

"He's here –"

"Is he okay?"

She puts up one hand to quiet me.

"Your name?"

"Sarah Cartwright."

"You a family member?"

"Girlfriend."

"Oh." She frowns and looks down at her paperwork. "I'll let the doctor know you're here."

"Is he okay?" I want to pound the glass.

She doesn't look up again. "I'll let the doctor know you're here. You can have a seat."

In the hard plastic chairs, I'm racking my brain, trying to think of what could have happened. He was okay this morning … but then again, I didn't pay him much attention at all. Maybe he hadn't been okay. Maybe he's been sick but didn't want to tell me. Maybe he thought I wouldn't care, even if he was.

An ancient man hacks so violently next to me that the entire row of chairs, connected by armrests, shakes like it might give way. On his other side, a gray-haired woman in tight curlers rubs his back as his cough goes on and on and on. I watch her knotted, wrinkled hand move in circles over his bony back as his body shakes.

Brad's all alone.

Where's the doctor?

I'm about to go back up to the grouch behind the intake desk when a man in a white coat emerges behind her. Through the glass, I see her point me out to him and whisper something. He nods and opens a door.

"Miss Cartwright?"

I'm already on my feet, headed toward him. *Brad, I'm coming.*

But the doctor's in my way. And he's not moving.

"Is he okay?"

"Bradley is in stable condition right now. He'll need to stay, of course, while we work on figuring out just what happened and make sure that he is improving."

"What happened to him?"

"We are working on finding that out now."

"Is he awake?"

The doctor nods his head and I exhale.

"I need to see him."

"I'm afraid that's not a good idea right now." The doctor avoids direct eye contact with me. "Also, we can only allow family members in the ER."

"What? I'm his fiancée." I stretch the truth. It could have been true.

"Even so, ma'am, I'm afraid it's not allowed. Perhaps when we've moved him to inpatient, during visiting hours. We're past that for tonight though."

"What?" I can't wrap my head around what he's saying. They won't let me see Brad. He's right here. He's awake. Surely he's asked to see me?

"Who are you?" I'm trying not to get pissed, but it's Brad we're talking about and he'll hardly tell me anything.

"Dr. Ingalls."

"I mean … why can't I go to him?" My heart feels like it's in my throat. I can't even swallow. I'm here, and they won't let me see him.

"I'm not leaving." I announce. I don't know what else to say. I can't believe Brad is right here. He's awake. I could be holding him. I could see him again. I want to tell him everything – and they won't let me close. A fucking technicality. I am his family. I am the mother of his child.

"You can stay," the doctor says, turning to leave, "but I'm afraid that it'll have to be in the waiting room."

The door closes behind him … and I'm so stunned I just stand there. I don't know what to say, think, or do. How can this be happening? If he asks for me, do they have to let me in? I consider rapping on the glass, but I know that woman won't help. I try to think of who I can call as I take my seat next to the elderly couple.

Helpless, I text Tracie: *Doc says Brad is stable.*

Her reply: *What happened???*

My thumbs hover over the keys … trying to think of what I can say. I don't know what happened. I don't know why they won't let me close to him. I don't know anything except that I wish I could start today over – maybe start the year over. I would do so many things differently.

Finally, I answer: *They aren't sure yet.*

I can't stomach telling her that I've been barred from Brad's side. Maybe – because she is a family member – Tracie could get us in. She could come back, maybe just bring Gracie along. But what if the doctor still wouldn't let me in, outside visiting hours?

That's what I really want, to see him. I need to see him myself.

I try to sit still and think of a way to try again with the woman at the front desk. Maybe I could prove to her that … God, I don't know. All I know is Brad needs me in there, and I'm out here. It's insane, but I actually think of sneaking through with the older couple when the doctor is distracted. But the door's not that wide and they'd probably stop me before I found Brad's room. I'd be kicked out altogether then. I need a different plan.

When I realize my restless legs are shaking an entire row of chairs – the woman in curlers cleared her throat obnoxiously until I noticed her glowering at me – I stand to my feet. I can't be still any longer. I pace the hallway, arms crossed over my chest, eyes glued on the vinyl floor panels as I march up and down.

What happened, baby? Brad, I'm so sorry.

Then something knocks the wind out of me.

I've run into someone.

Disoriented, I look up, the apology on my lips automatic.

"I'm sorry."

Oh shit.

I'm staring directly into the face of Officer Martinez. I hadn't realized he was so short. I've got at least two inches on him and I've never been considered tall. But, wait. Why is he here?

"No problem, Miss Cartwright."

"What are you doing here?" Behind him, Officer Adams is towering over both of us, his arms crossed as if he has bad news to deliver.

Martinez pauses before he speaks.

"We need to talk to you again. We have some questions."

"I told you everything I could about Charles. I'm really sorry it happened. I hope you were able to find what –"

"This isn't about his case."

What? What the hell else could this be about? And why are they bothering me at the hospital?

"I don't know what you mean," I stammer. "I told you, I was at the park the day the accident happened. I want to be helpful, but right now is a really bad time. If there's something else you need to know about Charles, I'm fine with –"

"This isn't about the collision that killed Charles Devante."

I feel the heat rising in my cheeks, rage curling up in my chest. Why would they be here, at a time like this? This is no place to harass me. I narrow my focus to just Martinez' cool gaze, try to stare right through his attempts at intimidation.

"What *is* this about, then?"

Martinez locks eyes with me, his own gaze unwavering. I sense Officer Adams moving in closer.

"We need to speak to you about your boyfriend." Martinez enunciates every word.

"What? Why? He's hurt right now." None of this makes sense. I want to run in the other direction, but just from their posture, I know I won't make it two steps.

"Actually," Martinez tilts his head and holds his stare, "he didn't *get hurt*. From the doctor's assessment of his symptoms, it appears that Bradley Carlson overdosed."

"What?" I scream.

"We'll have to wait for the toxicology reports, but the doctor says the symptoms line up with a toxic ingestion of some kind of prescription sedative, probably Valium."

I shake my head, my world spinning around me.

"Either your boyfriend has a problem with drugs that aren't prescribed to him – or else someone tried to poison him."

"How?" I can't shape a clear thought. I think of his blue lips, the beads of perspiration on cold skin. *My Brad.*

"Well, either he's lying to the doctor about not taking enough Valium to kill a man ... or someone else was dead set on killing him." Martinez tilts closer to me. "Who's telling the lie?"

25

THEN

For a while, I thought chasing my sister around was going to be a drag.

But it's actually better than I thought. I'm not sure I would have had the guts to try to get into college if I'd had an excuse to avoid it. Not that I think I'm stupid. Just … what's the point? Now that I've been here a couple years, I see the point. No more O'Dells Diner. A lot more opportunity. Thanks to my low-income status, I've only had to take out a small student loan. And the best part is I can actually blend right in. Among a few thousand college students, all of them vaguely familiar, my sister's never given me a suspicious glance. A lot easier than trying to keep an eye on her in a one-stoplight redneck town in Alabama.

Besides, we're going places.

We've both been working hard in political science classes, public relations, communications. I try to keep to myself in my dorm room so my bunkmates don't get too nosy. I've never said yes to one of their party invites and they mostly ignore me. When it's just me in my room, I daydream sometimes that my sister and I one day will run our own PR firm. We'll have fabulous clothes, make more money than we know what to do with, and spend all our time coming up with campaigns for big, flashy brands. Maybe it'll happen in a big city. New York. Chicago. LA. We're blowing the south altogether one day, I hope. It's been nothing but misery for me. There *has* to be a better world out there.

For now, I'm still anonymous in her life. But I'm proud of her. One day I'll tell her how much. She works hard, stays mostly out of trouble. No punk has tried to pin her down to any long-term relationship that I know of, though there's something I'm not really feeling about the bro in white-guy dreads I've seen trying to get her attention. I'll have to watch out for him. I heard her saying to her girlfriends in the caf today that she was going to the Sig Ep party tonight. I don't mind her having fun, but I know what those parties are like. Mr. Dreads might be there looking for his opportunity. He doesn't know what he's up against.

I can't let my baby sis get hurt or risk everything she's worked so hard to earn. I haven't forgotten the incident in the woods – the asshole who tried to drug her drink. I'm sure his family hasn't forgotten it either. I'm not expecting trouble, but I'll go just in case.

Besides, I'm feeling good about how close we've become, my sister and I. She doesn't know it yet, but I think she senses it. I was standing in line at the coffee shop last week, my sister a couple people behind me. When I turned around and smiled at her, she said hi. If you didn't know better, you might have thought she was just being polite, but I think it's more. I was so surprised that she acknowledged me that I didn't react quite the way I would have liked. But I know in my heart that the time is almost right. Maybe tonight at the party we can at least talk. I might not tell her I'm her sister or that I've been watching her for years; that'd be a lot to take in, and I'd want her to be sober when it happens. And a frat party isn't the place for that kind of heart-to-heart talk. No, it has to be more special than that, and more natural too.

Friends first.

That might happen tonight. I pull on my University of Georgia sweat-shirt and jeans and start the walk to the other side of campus, the row of frat houses where keg parties are all already started. One after another after another. Looks like the whole school is here tonight. People are everywhere, already shouting and whistling, rowdy as a close championship football game. The music thumps out from every window and door. I spot a kid behind a row bushes, barfing his guts out. It's not even nine o'clock yet. Couches may be lit on fire before the night is over. No place for my sister to be all alone, but it's the perfect place for her to meet her new best friend.

Tonight's going to be big. I can feel it.

I just hope she likes me. After all this – and everything I've done for her – she'd better.

It takes a while for me to spot her in the Sig Ep house. She's not wearing her own red-and-black sweatshirt like she usually does when she heads somewhere at night. Her eye makeup is outrageously dark, her breasts pushed up high in a dangerously low-cut top. I seriously hope she's not strutting for that asshole. God, she needs my help so bad.

You know, when she looked at me in the coffee shop, I think something flashed between us. She didn't say *I know you from somewhere*, but something inside her had to recognize me. From that first time in the grocery store, years ago, when I helped her pick up the cereal she'd dropped, there was something special between us. Then there are all the ways I've looked out for her, everything we've been through together. There has to be some kind of special sister wavelength that she senses. Even if she doesn't know what the feeling is, she has to know it's there. I know she does. I saw it flash in her eyes when she whirled around to smile at me.

Here, at the party, the regular lights are out and strobe lights are on. But I see her face, lit up in flashes. I can feel her mood is different tonight. She's not with the nerd girl crowd. She's looking for something new. I lose the sweatshirt so I look less frumpy. My shirt's not flashy or anything, but it's tight enough to show off the girls a bit. If my sister wants to get a little wild, I'm down. I just want to be around to make sure she doesn't hurt herself. I recognize one of the popular girls, lips slick with shiny gloss, hair pulled up tight in a high, smooth ponytail like a cheerleader. She's wearing an impossibly short skirt – I'm sure you can see her ass cheeks when she bends over – and now she's whispering in my sister's ear. Moments later, they leave the room, arm in arm.

I brush off some loser dude trying to talk to me and make a beeline for the door I saw them leave through. *You're not shaking me now, sis.* I follow a hallway to the end, past the couple humping disgustingly near the bathroom door, and find the back room where they've all headed. It's dark, aside from the glow of a computer screen set to psychedelic. There's a coffee table somebody's bent over. It takes a moment for my eyes to adjust. I recognize the ponytail shape moving across the table.

Blow.

My sister's in a room where they're doing cocaine. I look around for her and spot her on the bottom level of a bunk bed, legs crossed underneath her.

"Hey, baby."

Someone's talking to me. Another loser. God, they're everywhere.

But I can't exactly blow him off; I need to stay in this room.

"What you looking for?" He's eying me up, appreciating my top. I let him look and give him half a smile.

"I left something here, I think."

"You look around, baby girl. Maybe you decide you want to stay a while." I look down to where his eyes are directing me … down, down … to his pocket, a little plastic bag he's showing me.

"Maybe I will." I wink and then make my way toward the beds in the back, where my sister is sitting. We're so close. I wonder whether she senses it, that her guardian angel is here. But I look up and she seems dazed. She's sort of staring out into space until she notices me looking at her.

"Hey," she says. "Do I know you?"

My moment.

"I'm not sure. I think I've seen you around." I try to act cool, be natural.

"Hmm." She smiles. "I haven't been to one of these parties before."

I know. This is our first time here together, silly girl.

Loser Number Two, who's really starting to get on my nerves, walks up and hooks an arm around my waist, pressing himself into the back of me. I shake him loose without doing what I really want, which is to give him a solid jab in the stomach with my elbow or maybe a knee to the groin. He backs up and asks whether I found what I'd lost.

My sister's sweet voice chimes in.

"What did you lose?"

What's the right answer here?

"Oh," I shake my head. "Nothing real important. I had a set of earrings."

"Bummer. Maybe we could ask them to switch on the lights."

"Nah." I plop down beside her and brush my hands over the comforter like I might come up with something. "They were just a pair of cheap hoops."

"Sucks, though."

"Baby, we got you all set up." Loser boy is back. Not getting the hint. "Lines all set up, just for you. Here you go."

He hands me a dollar bill rolled up tight. My little sister giggles ... and I walk over to the table. I've only seen this done in movies. *Shit, I have no idea how to do this.* I shove one end of the makeshift straw in my right nostril, cover the left and suck through my nose.

Ouch.

That's all I have to say. This shit hurts. Like getting water up your nose in the pool. My body recoils and … I don't think I've done it right. Nothing seems to happen. There's a pair of dudes next to me having some weird conversation about mushrooms and watching the damn computer lock screen's wiggling lines. But I'm not hip to it. In my head, everything feels the same. The guy who set up the drugs for me slaps me hard on the back.

"You good, girl?"

"Yeah, yeah." I nod. "Thanks, man."

"You know where to find me." A stupid thing to say. I have no idea where to find him, nor do I ever want to. I look back and see, though, that my sister is gone. *Damn it.*

Frantic, I check every other room and finally I find her around the Ping-Pong table, waiting for her turn to toss balls into red cups of beer.

"Hey, there you are." She smiles at me. "You find those earrings?"

"Not yet."

"But you're wearing them." She laughs and it's so beautiful every guy nearby turns his head. She doesn't notice that, though.

I put my hands up to my ears and realize I am wearing big hoops. Dumbass move. But I laugh it off.

"What happens in the back room …" she says, waiting for me to fill in.

"Stays in the back room." We both start cracking up, and then she's overwhelmed with the idea, laughing so hard she has to wipe back tears.

"I don't know why that's so funny," she says, "but it is."

When she's got control of herself again, waving both hands over her eyes, she turns to me.

"By the way, I didn't ask your name yet."

I smile and extend my hand for a handshake like a total goofball. What

I really want to do is hug her tight. This is my sister, the girl I've watched grow since I ran away from my adoptive parents. She's the only person in the world I care about. I don't just care about her; I love her. I know she'll love me too. We are the same.

"I'm Sarah." I tell her, tingling with excitement as I wait for her reaction. If she only knew the real story. She'd be blown away. The truth is, we don't just happen to have the same name. It's way more than that. We have the *same mother* who gave us both the *same name*. For a split second, I picture sitting down with her one day, hoping she will take it okay when I have to tell her the truth: Our mother felt such a deep loss after she gave me up that she named her second daughter the same as her first. Two baby Sarahs.

Now we're two grown-up Sarahs, finally meeting.

My sister's jaw drops, and she laughs that good laugh again.

"Well, guess what?" She pauses. "I happen to be Sarah, too."

"With an 'h'?" I ask, though I know the answer. Two baby Sarahs. Sisters. Soon we'll be best friends, too.

"Yup." She smiles and loops one arm through mine. "We're like twins."

I knew it. A deep sense of euphoria unfolds around me, an invigorating kind. I want to walk her right out of here and talk about everything. Tell her every little way I was the guardian angel looking out for her for so long. Older sister Sarah watching out for younger sister Sarah. She'd see everything in a whole new light, her whole past, our whole future.

I look at her. She's staring at nothing, the drinking game in full swing in front of her. But she's not watching that. She's feeling the connection. Sisters. Together. Finally together.

She doesn't know it, but I've been waiting for this moment for years. I didn't picture us at a frat party, didn't think we'd both be high, I didn't

194

think we'd be surrounded by losers trying to get laid – but I don't even care. The point is that our new life together is starting.

I try to think of what to ask her first. There are so many things.

"What are you studying?" She'll think we're even more like twins when I tell her that I'm enrolled in almost the exact same courses as she is.

"Hmm?" She turns to me. "Oh, political science and communications. Double major."

I grin and get ready to tell her that's a crazy coincidence … but someone cuts me off.

"Look who's all of a sudden chatty and chummy with everybody." Dreads. He's here and brought a posse with him, I see. He doesn't acknowledge me in the slightest. He walks his stupid tough cool guy carriage right up to my sister's body and takes her face in his hands to lay a disgusting kiss on her mouth. Right in front of me. He has no idea what I do to guys who fuck with my sister. Mark, that asshole who walked off a cliff with a little help from me, might be able to tell him. Oh yeah, he's dead. That bastard hanging around my mom and touching my sister would warn him, too, if he didn't happen to die in a freak car accident … one that I orchestrated myself.

My sister lets go of my arm instantly. I think it's so she can push him away from her. But she doesn't. She reaches up around his neck and giggles.

Sis, no. Seriously? Can you not see what an asshat this guy is? We can do way, way better.

I turn my head as they nuzzle, sick at the idea but not wanting to cause a scene.

Finally, when Dreads comes up for air, I expect my sister to introduce me and let this loser know that she's talking to someone and busy for a while. *Buzz off, buddy.*

But that's not what happens at all.

195

I'm watching. Waiting for her to tell him to take a hike so we can pick up where we left off ... I was just about to tell her that I'm a comms major and poly sci minor ... but she never looks at me again. Not one fucking time. I call out her name a few times but all she does is stick her hands in my direction, palms out. As in telling me to stop, to go away, like I'm the one who should get out of here. She's pushing me away from her.

I can't even believe it. After everything I've done for her, she picks *him*. She lets that guy run his sick roaming paws all over her body and then take her away instead of staying where she belongs.

With me.

She should be with me.

I'm the one who loves her. I'm the one who's looked out for her. I sacrificed so much just to be close to her.

And she blew me off.

She doesn't want me.

I'm there alone, in the spinning room, drinking games and writhing bodies all around me. The music is thumping so loud and hard, the lights flashing, and I can't even fathom what's just happened. We finally spoke. We connected. She felt it. I know she had to feel it. We were finally together – years of work and years of me helping her in every way I can. The entire reason I'm here right now is her, my sister, Sarah.

I want to sit down, want to throw up. I have to do something, but I don't know what. My heart is racing, wild, in my chest, adrenaline fueling through my veins. I have the energy and the rage to run up to Dreads and beat the living shit out of him ... and I really feel like I could do it right now. I'm strong enough. I'm pissed enough.

But some part of me wants to just sit down and weep, all at the same time.

It's too much to think about. I need a plan. I need ... a life.

I can't believe I wasted so much of my life chasing my sister around. For this? For her to turn on me this way? Like I'm completely disposable. That's how I feel. Like she could not care less that I've given up so much for her, that I spent my gas money on those bags of clothes I'd leave for her and hitchhike a ride to the diner to work, that I spent weeks at a dumbass community college taking classes to get me ready for the SATs so I could apply to the same college as her, that I decided not to study music – which is what I'd actually fucking want if I were acting like a selfish fucking bitch like she is – because I wanted to be close to her.

And then she dumps me for some trash with dreadlocks. He doesn't give two shits about her. He wouldn't do one-tenth of what I've done for her. He doesn't know anything about her. I know everything. Everything.

Now, trashy dude is bringing her around trashy people and dragging her into his trashy problems. And me too, by proxy. I snorted coke so I could share an experience with her. She doesn't know what she's getting into. She doesn't know who she crossed, who she just dumped in the garbage.

I try to breathe in and out.

I can't hurt her. She's the only person I have.

But she doesn't want me. Nobody does.

What's wrong with me? Why didn't my mother want me? Why doesn't my sister want me?

How could she possibly not know she is everything to me?

A wave of nausea hits me in the gut and I bowl over, hands on my knees, sucking in deep breaths and waiting. Nothing comes. I'd feel so much better if I threw up, but I can't. I'd feel so much better if I could just break down crying, but I can't. I can't do anything. I have to leave, now. Someone has to teach them both a lesson.

Ten minutes later, after I make my anonymous phone call, I watch the bust happen from across the street.

Five cop cars come swirling in, sirens screaming, and the buildings start puking people out. People running out the back, jumping out of first-story windows. Dozens and dozens of dumbasses running for their lives across the lawns and back to the more sober side of campus. I try to watch all the ones who get away. None of them are her. My sister's still inside. Armed officers rush in to stop the outward flow.

"Police!" I hear them shout, repeatedly. "Everybody stay where you are."

People are still sneaking out the back. None of them look like her. So far, so good.

It takes a few minutes, but the ten or twelve officers emerge. In between them, a row of people with hands behind their backs.

There she is.

I watch as an officer places a hand on the top of her head to help her into the back of his cruiser. The silver of the handcuffs on her wrists glints in the streetlamp and then they close the door. She's not even looking out of the window for me, she's just staring into space.

I don't like it any better than you do, Sarah.

Well, maybe just a little.

Some lessons are harder to learn than others, I guess. She'll be a better person for it.

Always looking out for you, sister. Always.

26

NOW

The word *poisoned* hangs heavy as a millstone around my neck. I can't believe what I've just heard, I can't process it at all.

My body recoils away from Martinez, my back slamming into a hard wall of tile behind me. Who would want to hurt Brad? I know someone's after me, but Brad doesn't have an enemy in the world. It doesn't make any sense. I think of him, motionless, on the floor, the noodles spilled next to him. It was surreal. More like an idea of a crime scene than the real thing … but I'd felt him, shaken him, done everything in my power to wake him. He hadn't responded. He was breathing, but lifeless, his skin a sickening gray.

Someone *had* tried to kill him. He *was* poisoned.

I look up at Martinez, his eyes cool and discerning, taking in every layer of my reaction. I swallow and try to speak, but nothing comes out of my throat. *Who would do this to Brad? Who would ever want to hurt him?*

Adams eyes are blank, not cruel but not giving away anything.

They think I did this. Martinez does, for sure.

Never. I'd never hurt Brad. I love him. I wanted to tell him so. I wanted us to reconnect tonight. I wanted to be closer to him than we have ever been before. Everything is so fucked up. I suck in a quick breath and have the urge to tell them both that I love this man more than anyone else in the world, that I was going to go along with the job he wanted, even though it meant a ruined career for me, that I was even thinking of marrying him … and that I wasn't even there when it happened. I'd never hurt him.

He's the father of my child, for godsake.

I try to speak again. But nothing comes out when I open my mouth.

"I need you to understand, Miss Cartwright, that you have not been charged at this point," Martinez says, watching me tremble, "but we do have some questions for you."

My throat has dried up into such a hard, angry knot that it pains me to swallow, but I do. I try to breathe, try to make sense of what's happening around me. I have to get a handle on this situation, or the police are going to make it into anything they'd like. From the way they've acted, I'm sure what they'd really like is to hang everything on me.

"Of course," I mutter. "Of course. Anything you need."

"We appreciate that, ma'am," Martinez says, his shoulders relaxing downward by an inch. "Your cooperation makes all the difference."

I let the cold hospital corridor wall hold me upright and half listen as he speaks. My mind is re-examining every exchange I've had in the past day, week, month – with anyone. Janette. Tracie. Enid.

Jesus, not her. Please.

Why would she want him dead?

"Miss Cartwright?"

I snap back to right now, standing in the empty hallway with two police detectives. "Yes, I'm sorry. I just can't believe it. I can't believe someone would try to hurt Brad. It doesn't make any sense to me, at all."

It was barely perceptible, but Martinez actually let his eyes roll. I wanted to shake him. I don't even have a moment to absorb the fact that someone has tried to kill the man I love – and I'm being interrogated. How am I supposed to act normal? They expect me to just pull my shit together and tell them everything I know before I can even sort through what I know and don't myself.

"I was saying," he cocks his head condescendingly, "that we're going to need you to come with us to the police station."

"Of course," I answer. My thoughts are swirling like mad. "I can do that. My daughter ... she's with my sister-in-law right now –"

"Perfect. We'll walk you out."

You mean escort me out. I'm leaving the hospital with two police detectives who think I tried to kill my boyfriend.

I'm not being arrested. I'm not cuffed and put into the back of a police cruiser this time. I'm driving my own car to the station. I'll answer anything I can ... maybe they'll even help me to figure out who actually did this. That's their job, right?

But my hands are shaking as I take the wheel.

Maybe I need a lawyer.

I didn't do this. I'm innocent. But I don't want to dig myself into something worse. What if they have questions I can't answer? What if I give the wrong answers?

The real problem isn't about Brad. I *want* to find out who did this to him. I *need* to. But I can't have them digging around my entire life, my history. I suck in and out, trying to calm myself. My heart is racing out of control. My hands are trembling. I don't know if I'm doing the right thing. I see the police cruiser pull up behind me. They're waiting for me to leave, keeping a close eye on me.

I drive, but my mind isn't on the road.

All I can think about is the pile of noodles on the floor and the only person who would have had access to what Brad ate before he collapsed.

There's only one person. The person who was with me at the Thai restaurant.

Enid.

She would have had access to my food while I was in the bathroom. Did she expect me to eat it? Or did she know I'd be sharing with Brad? Then I remember; it comes back to me crystal clear:

I'd told her it was Brad's favorite when I ordered it …

I think back to everything she said to me when we were eating. She was asking about Brad, wondering whether he was holding me back. Or, was it that she wanted to make sure she kept my job? Maybe she knew Janette wasn't happy with how she's handling things. She couldn't have me stepping back in to take the job back. Did she try to frame me? Would she go that far to get me out of the way? Or was she actually obsessed with me?

Why, Enid?

Why would she try to hurt him? To kill him? If she were the one who planted the photos to steal my job, she's already done that. She has my job. Why hurt Brad? Even if she were trying to make it look like I did it … was there really any reason to knock me down lower? To take not just my job but my family? Will she not be happy until I'm locked away in jail? No, no. She can't be a monster. I can't see it. I shake away the idea. I'm not thinking clearly. I'm so desperate to find some kind of an answer that I'm twisting things all around in my head.

I think about her expression, the sorrow in her eyes. She had seemed genuine today. She wanted to be close again. She didn't want this work situation to come between us, she'd said. She pestered me about going to dinner for days so that she could make that apology.

But Janette said Enid had seemed *obsessed* with me and I can't get it out of my head.

When Enid and I were together, what was I talking about? I was just venting. I'd said Brad and I were struggling and that I was thinking of telling him to take the job to smooth things over with him. I hadn't hinted that Brad was hurting *me* in any way, had I?

I try to remember, but nothing makes sense right now. Enid is the only person who would have had the opportunity to do this … It makes me sick. I need to know that Brad's okay. I need to know he's going to make it. I should be at the hospital, by his side. Instead, I'm parked in a visitor space in front of the police department. Martinez and Adams are waiting for me to get out of my car, both with their hands folded over their crotch. Not patient. I feel like I'm volunteering for my own execution.

I'd imagined the questioning would happen in some gray box of a room, probably with a two-way mirror and a heavy door that would shut hard behind us. Instead, Adams and Martinez walk me past the front desk and empty chairs to a small room with a conference table.

Adams gestures for me to take a seat.

Here I go. I still have no idea what I'm going to say or how I'm going to keep myself from digging a bigger hole.

Martinez's chair is loud as he scoots himself in across the table from me.

"Now, again, Miss Cartwright, we are not filing charges. This is not an interview. We just want to ask you a few questions to see whether we can narrow down the list of people who might have the means and or the motive to hurt Bradley."

I look up and notice Adams has left the room. I wish he hadn't. Clearly, Martinez was the talker, the one in charge, but Adams' sudden departure leaves me wondering what kind of game they are working. Maybe there *is* a two-way mirror ... my eyes dart around the room and Martinez makes an irritated huff.

"So, tell me, is there anyone you can think of who would have something against your boyfriend?"

I shake my head vehemently. "Everyone likes Brad."

"Not everyone. Obviously, someone wanted him dead today." He leans back and crosses his arms, as if to say this could last all night.

I press my lips together, thinking. There's no way around this. I don't want to believe Enid would take things this far. But there's no one else. I look Martinez right in the eyes, try to still my shaking voice, and I tell him what I think, that the only person who would have reason to do this is our friend Enid, and I talk him through our dinner at Lemongrass.

Martinez reaches for a notepad and pen that I hadn't noticed on the table. He scribbles as I spell her name.

"You say she knows Brad as well?"

I nod, heartsick over the whole idea. Wanting to erase this entire day.

"How long?"

"Since they were in grade school," I answer.

"And you think she has some kind of obsession with you? Or with him? I'm not clear on the connection."

I should have thought this through better, but to be honest, I'm not one hundred percent sure either.

"Listen, all I really know is someone gave the media photographs of me that caused a huge problem and I had to step down from my position –"

"I thought it was the man killed in a crash who you believe planted the photographs?" He interrupts me. Adams appears again and, without a word, takes a seat on Martinez' side of the table.

"Yes, I assume he must have. But he wouldn't have been able to snap that photograph in the first place. It had to be someone close to me, someone within the campaign. That's the best I can figure. And the only person who benefitted from the scandal … it would have been Enid, who got the job she really wanted, which was my job."

I could see from his face that my story wasn't lining up well.

"Okay, so … then how do you make the leap from your friend plotting to get your job, which she now has and has had for the past few weeks, to your friend now trying to kill your boyfriend?"

A glance passes between Adams and Martinez.

They don't believe me at all. I can hardly believe it myself, but I have no other choice. Nothing else makes sense.

"Well, what I've heard around the office is that Enid is obsessed with me in everything she does in my position. And, lately … she'd been really trying hard to make it up to me. Trying too hard, maybe. She convinced me to go out for dinner with her today. I told her Brad and I have been struggling lately with everything happening at my job –"

"Had you two been fighting?" Martinez picks up his pen.

"No. No. He's been amazing." I say it emphatically because it's true, not because I'm trying to fool them. I hate that this is all coming out so garbled. "He's been supportive in every way."

"So? Were you telling Enid something different, though? You just said you told her the two of you were struggling."

"No. Just venting with a friend … someone I thought was a friend. The thing is, Brad has a job offer, but it's in another state, heavily Republican, where I will probably never be able to pick up the pieces of my career. That's been a strain on us. No fighting. No arguments …" My voice trails off. I think of Brad, alone, in a hospital bed. I swallow and keep going. "I actually wanted to tell Brad tonight that he should take the job, that I wanted to marry him and we could start our family in Salt Lake City."

Brows pinched, Martinez is scribbling notes.

"Okay. Okay. We will look into all of that while we wait to hear more from the hospital."

He looks over at Adams again. There's something else coming ...

I cross and uncross my legs, trying hard not to fidget, not to squirm in my seat like I know Martinez wants to see me do. They've already decided that I tried to kill my boyfriend and, probably, that I arranged for Charles Devante to be killed in an unfortunate 'accident'. They haven't mentioned a thing about that case. Maybe that's what's about to happen.

Finally, Adams clears his throat. I wonder about the switch. Why is he suddenly the one taking the reins?

"Here's our problem, Miss Cartwright." He looks to me, worry lines wrinkling across his forehead. "We did some checking into your background."

Shit. My heart feels like it sinks to the pit of my stomach. *They know. That means Brad will know ... and he'll find out from someone else besides me.* I feel all the blood rushing from my face. I wish I could melt into the seat, or evaporate, or just disappear. This is what I was afraid of for so long, all unfolding right before my eyes. Everyone will know that I'm the woman who can't seem to get away from death. My mom's boyfriend died. My mother didn't die from cancer; she killed herself. That kid Mark died, the same night I was with him. The rest will unravel too. I wasn't a star college student. I got into trouble ... I dated a drug dealer.

I'm so fucked I can't wrap my brain around it. I can hardly breathe. My throat feels like sandpaper when I try to swallow. I want to ask for water, but I can't make a sound.

Adams shakes his head regretfully.

"Your mother's boyfriend was also killed in a car crash, when you were around …"

"Fourteen." I answer, wishing I could disappear. "I was fourteen years old. My mother was crushed. It was eighteen years ago, almost exactly."

"Yes," he answers, "and we'll get to that."

You asshole. I hate this man. I loathe myself for giving him the benefit of the doubt. He's as much of an asshole as Martinez.

He clears his throat again. "So, your mother's boyfriend at the time was killed in a crash with some … some similarities to the collision that killed Charles Devante. In both cases, it appears someone loosened the lug nuts. And that wasn't long before your mother … took her own life."

He looks at me like I'm a cornered animal, expecting me to melt under his accusations. You killed your mother's boyfriend. *You caused your mother to kill herself.*

I don't say anything. Inside, I'm exploding with rage and guilt – so much I can't speak. I don't dare. I don't know what will come out of my mouth. I feel hot tears pricking at the edge of my vision.

"So you can understand the problem we're faced with." Martinez picks up the conversation. "It's a little hard for us to believe what you're telling us when … the circumstances are uncannily similar. And now, with your boyfriend in the shape he's in, our situation is even more difficult. Is there anything you're not telling us about that you'd want to share? Can you give us any insight into how there could have been two people with connections to you who happened to die from having their lug nuts loosened?"

I can't hold back the tears now. I feel them slide down both my cheeks. I know my face is flushed; it's burning hot, on fire hot. So is the rage inside me.

"Listen, I don't have an explanation for what you've found. I've had a really shitty life and have done everything I can to make it better. I'm not guilty of anything, other than being really, really fucking unlucky. I hated watching my mother deteriorate. I miss her every single day. I would *never* have wanted her to lose someone she loves..." I can't finish the rest of what I want to say: I would *never* have wanted to lose *her*. I miss her every single day.

Adams rises and hands me a box of tissues and Martinez waits for me to gather myself again.

"So, if you're not charging me, I hope you'll excuse me." I suck in one labored breath, knowing I have to find a way to get out of here. Now. I'm sure they brought up my mother just to rattle me – which is the cruelest thing I can think of – but I can hardly breathe right now, let alone think straight to answer their prodding questions. "My boyfriend is in critical condition and we have enough to deal with already. I'll help you in any way I can, but I'd like to be able to find out what I can about how Brad is doing, get my daughter, and go home."

Martinez shrugs like he's giving this up for tonight. I let my guard down just a hair, thinking I'll at least get to go home. They can't pin this on me now or they'd be making an arrest. Maybe I'll be holding Gracie soon. Maybe tomorrow this will all sort itself out. Brad will be okay. We can just start over.

"One last thing – and I appreciate your patience," Martinez says, standing up. "I'm afraid we're also going to need to search your home and your vehicle. Just make sure we've covered all of our bases for now."

What?

He searches my face, studies every measure of shock and disbelief. I can't even go home. What other choice do I have? I already look guilty as sin.

"I'm sure we'll have no problem getting the district judge to sign a warrant if we need to go that route ..."

208

"No need." I stand to my feet, finished with this place. "You can come with me right now."

In the parking lot, they find exactly what I thought they would: diapers, a pacifier stuck underneath the passenger seat, and a stash of makeup in the dashboard. Martinez looks a little disappointed as they let me get back in my own car.

He perks up slightly when I hand him my house key.

Go for it, asshole. You won't find a thing.

As soon as I'm back on the road, heading to a hotel, the first thing I do – even though it's one in the morning – is dial Janette.

"You okay?" She answers on the first ring.

"No. Not at all."

"What happened?"

"I'll tell you later," I glance in my rearview, nervous, and half expecting to see the police cruiser again behind me. "Right now, I need you to tell me if you know anything about where Enid was tonight."

I have to give police something more substantial. They have it out for *me* so I'll have to help them see it was someone else. I can't let this sort itself out. It won't. Now that everything – my entire history – is threating to emerge, I have to take control. I can't afford one more mistake. It's not just my career on the line anymore.

It's everyone I love.

27

NOW

G racie's crying. I need to go to her. She wants her mother. Her whimpering turns into a series of wails ... but I can't seem to find her anywhere. Panic floods my body, terror rising inside me. I can hear her, but I can't see her. I run to her nursery, but the crib is empty. I check her playpen. Only her toys. Helpless, I find her car carrier seat on the floor. She's not buckled in, not anywhere around.

Where's my baby?

When there's a knock at the door, I think maybe it's Brad, with Gracie. I run as fast as I can, but there's no one standing there. The doorway is completely empty. And yet, I can still hear her crying.

Not crying. Screaming. I run the other direction, searching the house again.

Where's my baby?

The knocking starts again and gets louder. Louder and louder and louder until it jolts me awake. Breathing hard and heavy, I glance around. I'm not in my bed. I'm not even in my own house. I'm in a hotel. Gracie crying was a dream. A nightmare.

Then I remember my real-life nightmare. I think of Brad, lying on the floor, not moving. All the images from last night flash through my mind again. The woman at the ER desk, the doctor, the police.

Then the knocking starts again, so hard I can feel the vibration. I stumble to the unfamiliar door. In the hotel hallway, Martinez and Adams look surprised when I actually answer.

Martinez stays silent, like he hasn't had enough coffee yet. I can't tell how early it is.

"Sorry to bother you at this hour, Miss Cartwright," Adams offers. "We wanted to update you on the situation. We began searching your house last night and are headed there again now. Also … it would be better if you don't leave town while the investigation is underway." He looks at me, and the confusion that has to be written across my face, and seems to soften just a touch. "I … hope you got some rest."

Not much. I've slept in the clothes I was wearing yesterday and I'm sure it shows. I stand back and sigh.

"That's fine."

"You still have my card?" Martinez says, handing me another, just in case.

"Thanks." I take it and wait for them to leave, to head straight back to my house.

Finally, thankfully, they leave it at that. I watch them head down the hallway and I close the door behind me, turning the lock on instinct. I'd prefer to make my next move, a call to Janette, without the cops listening in. And visiting hours at St. Thomas begin at 10 a.m.

Within ten minutes, I've changed my clothes and taken the opportunity to wash my face. I picture police, combing all of my possessions and rummaging through the kitchen. An unsettling thought. I do my best to ignore it, but then I think of Gracie's crib. It would be empty, other than her favorite elephant rattle. I remember my dream, the terrible fright of hearing her cry and not being able to pick up and soothe her, to let her know that I love her and hold her close to me.

I have to fix this, all of it. Thankfully, she's small enough, she'll never have to remember any of this, never have to relive it. If I can nail down the person who's trying to hurt Brad and show him how much I really do love him ... maybe we can still have the future he wanted for us. I want to be at the hospital the minute visiting hours are open again, to try to get through to Brad. Maybe I can still give my daughter a happy, whole life. I don't want her to have to live like I did.

Janette, God bless her, picks up right away.

"You okay? I still can't believe this is all happening to you."

I breathe in to try to steady my heart rate and glance up at the light. Still red. They won't even let me in to see Brad for another hour and a half, but I don't want to sit still. I can't afford to. And I sure as hell don't want to be at home, with officers second-guessing my every move and gesture. I need to give them another direction to search. That's where I'm hoping Janette will step in.

"I wouldn't say I'm okay." I try to hold myself together, but I feel like a dam is about to break. The dam that spills out everything I've tried to protect Brad from since ... I met him. I never told him about my mom's boyfriend or the guy, Mark, who died the night I was with him, or how much trouble I landed in when I was in college. He doesn't even know the real story about my mother.

"Okay," I admit. "I'm not really okay right now."

Janette makes a sympathetic sigh on the other end of the line.

"Sarah, if you're worried about what they'll say at work, I'll handle it."

"I've got way bigger problems than that right now." I almost don't care what happens with the campaign anymore. My whole career is wrapped up in it ... but it's the furthest thing from my mind. Someone is out to destroy my entire life, not just my career.

"I'm so sorry," Janette says. "Let me know what I can do to help. Anything."

"I'm on my way to the hospital now. Gracie's still with Brad's sister. I'm hoping they'll let me in early. In the meantime, I really have to figure out who did this."

"Enid didn't answer me until this morning. She sent a text back, apologizing, saying she'd gone to bed. I'll see her in the office soon. I'll think of some reason we need to spend some time together today. See what I can find out."

The hospital's towering brick rises up in the distance. I hope they're taking good care of my Brad. I want to destroy whoever did this to him.

"Let me know when you have Enid," I say. "I'd like to give her a piece of my mind. See what she has to say. Myself."

There's a pause on the other line.

"You sure that's a good idea?" Janette asks. "I could check her out first."

My mind goes back to the scenes it's replayed again and again over the past ten hours. I see her heartbroken expression when I told her I was thinking of giving in to Brad, telling him to take the job, telling him I'd go with him. Hours later, that option was almost eliminated. Brad almost died on our living room floor. Because of her.

"No, I want to see how she reacts myself. I have to find out who's got it out for us, and why. I need to do this." I throw the car into park resolutely. No one else is going to decide how my life is going to happen. If the cops want to try to destroy me ... well, I'm not going to just sit back and watch. This is my family.

"I'll send you a text. I'll try to get her in here for a sit-down, alone with me, before our press conference."

"When is that?"

"Noon."

Good. That will give me at least an hour to try to be with Brad. *If he still wants me.* I wonder again how he might have taken my note, my sudden fondness for X's and O's. Would he see that as out of character for me?

I'm relieved that someone else has taken over the shift at the front desk. It's a young woman, slim and upbeat in freshly applied makeup. She taps into her keyboard to look up where they've moved Brad to. I take a moment to look around the waiting room. All the chairs are empty. The elderly couple are gone of course ... I hope the bent over old man is okay this morning, with his loving wife beside him.

"Unfortunately, our visiting hours don't begin for another hour." The young woman is explaining what I already know. "Because you're not technically family – I'm so sorry, but you'll have to wait."

"I understand. Any update on his condition?"

She frowns.

"Unfortunately, I'm not allowed to discuss that either. And I really don't know." She stops to glance around her and then drops her voice to a whisper. "But I've heard he's awake and seems to be doing okay."

She winks at me and I want to give her a hug. Maybe everyone in the world is not a complete asshole. Maybe today is going to go my way, finally. I let myself collapse into a chair, trying not to think about the police tearing my house up right at this moment, eager to find any scrap of evidence. An hour is going to feel like a lifetime, I know, but it beats giving the police any extra opportunities to probe me about my past.

It was just days ago that I held the box, the box that's the last remaining link to my mother, my real story. I'd thought about telling Brad then, just letting it all out in the open. Why hadn't I? And why hadn't I seen how much my decisions were hurting him, holding our whole family back? I hug my arms to my chest. I want my life back. I want to do things differently. I want to hold Brad and tell him I've made my decision. I've chosen us – over everything else. I want him to know me, the real me, and I hope he'll still love me when he does.

I glance around the room for the tissue box.

I need to hold myself together, but it takes every ounce of energy I have. I give myself the luxury of a few tears, dotted away before they can leave the inner corners of my eyes. The woman at the desk isn't watching me – and if she is, that's okay.

I glance at my phone. Four minutes have passed and I'm already falling to pieces. Fifty-six minutes more to wait. I take a sec to send Tracie a text: Gracie okay? I'm at the hospital.

She doesn't immediately reply, but I know Gracie is in good hands. I can't wait until this is over. Please tell me it will be over soon. The phone in my hand dings. A new message.

But it's not from Tracie. It's Janette, letting me know that she's got Enid to agree to meet her at eleven. *Shit.* I type the campaign headquarters address into my maps app to check. Yup. It's twenty-eight minutes away. That only gives me a half hour with Brad.

But what I find out from Enid – that conniving, twisted bitch – might just save our family.

I let my head relax back and feel the weight of my eyelids. I couldn't have had more than a few hours of sleep last night and the idea of a nap is delicious. My body desperately wants to nod off while I wait, but I'm afraid I'll miss my opportunity. I'm afraid I won't get in to see Brad before police announce that I'm a suspect or officially file charges against me: attempted murder. *God, no. Please.* This has to happen now. I need to see him.

So I pace. I pace and pace until I feel like I might wear holes in the low-lying, industrial-grade carpet, and finally, a nurse emerges.

"Miss Cartwright?"

I've already got my bag over my shoulder, ready to go.

"Right this way."

We take an elevator to the sixth floor, to the inpatient rooms. With every level we rise, my anxiety goes up a notch. The nurse is silent, clutching a clipboard over the front of her scrubs. I can hear my heart thumping in my ears. My chest feels all fluttery, my stomach a whirl of nausea. I should have bothered to eat something, maybe my stomach wouldn't feel so seasick.

Ding.

We're on Floor Six. The nurse turns to me with a smile. "Right down the hall. Second door on your right. 611."

There's a different nurse at his side and an IV stuck in his bare arm. His face is the same gray color as when I saw him, but his eyes are open this time. He's awake. He's alive.

"Baby." I run to him, reach out to touch his arm.

He seems disoriented. He blinks hard and then examines me as if he's not sure who I am at first. It comes to him slowly, and then I register surprise on his face.

Not a happy surprise.

"What the fuck are you doing here?" He pulls away suddenly, recoiling at my touch, and the IV bag attached to his arm shakes.

"Mr. Carlson, your IV." The nurse turns from whatever paperwork she was working on.

"I'll pull it right out of my arm if I have to."

I wonder what kind of meds he's on. I've never, not one time, seen him angry. I've never seen him pull away from me, either. He's never not wanted me. He glares at the nurse and clears his throat. "Get her out of here."

She looks to me, questioning.

"I'm his girlfriend. I've been waiting to see him for an hour."

"You can wait for the rest of eternity, for all I care." He's angry, but I can see the swell of tears gathering in his beautiful blue-gray eyes. I see the hurt too, the betrayal. He thinks I did this to him. Brad thinks I tried to kill him.

"Baby, you don't think I did this?" I reach out toward him again, but he pulls his arm away so swiftly it almost knocks the IV stand over. The metal clatters against the side of the hospital bed.

"Who is it, Sarah? Is there someone else?" he asks, accusingly. "If you were that unhappy, you could have just told me so. You didn't have to try to kill me."

In my peripheral vision, I see the nurse headed toward me. I'm frozen in place, feeling my heart shatter into a thousand tiny pieces. I'm stunned into silence. I can't speak to the nurse when she asks me to leave. I watch over her shoulder, see Brad's face. There's no trace of mercy. No understanding. No tenderness. Just a man who's reached the end of what he can give. No turning back now. He's snapped. I know things will never, ever be the same. I should just walk away, but I can't. Maybe if I can prove that someone else did this …

I feel the nurse's hands around my elbow now, pulling me away. I look up, pleading, to Brad.

"Don't act like that." He's almost spitting. "You know what I think? If there's not someone else chasing after you, you just wanted an easy way out. You're a coward. And you're selfish. You're the most selfish person I've ever met in my life. We have a child together, Sarah. A beautiful baby girl. You were going to take her father away from her. You know what it's like to lose a parent … and you were going to do that to her?" I can see all of his teeth as he lays on his accusation, trying to pierce me in the place he knows hurts most.

"Brad, I would never – "

"Bullshit. Was this Bill's idea? The two of you arranging for him to become governor. You thought you'd rise right up with him. Maybe he was going to get his wife out of the picture too. Whatever. I'm done with you. If it's him, you deserve him. You deserve everything that's happened to you. I can't believe I let you walk all over me for this long. I wanted to give you everything, babe. But you wanted to throw everything away."

My heart lights with hope when I hear him call me babe. It slipped out unintentionally. I can read that it was a mistake on his face … but it was in his mind, his heart. He still thinks of me that way.

"I would never hurt you."

"Yeah right." He sits up as best he can on the bed in his hospital gown. "Fortunately for me, you'll never get another chance to. We're finished. For good."

"I'm sorry, Miss Cartwright." The nurse glances from him to me and back again. "You're disturbing the patient. I'm afraid you'll have to leave."

Hot tears are streaming down my cheeks. I can't believe it. I can't believe I've pushed Brad to this point, to a place where he could even conceive that I would try to hurt him. I want to beg him for another chance. Things could be different. I want to tell him what I was really hoping would happen last night. Everything inside me is dying for any sign of tenderness from him toward me, to know he can't possibly mean what he's said. But his eyes are determined. His stare tells me everything I need to know. If I can't prove, beyond a doubt, that someone else was behind this … Brad and I are done. Forever. A broken family for Gracie for the rest of her childhood. A broken heart for me.

I swallow back everything I want to say, all the apologies that will sound hollow to him. I have to leave. I have to fix this. In the elevator, I check my phone. Nothing new. I'll have plenty of time to be there when Janette pulls Enid into her office, now that Brad has kicked me out. I just have to do this right. Every part of the life I've built for myself, and my baby, depends on it.

Janette got Enid to agree to a coffee run earlier than eleven – but Tracie's not answering me.

I think back to my dream, the terror of hearing Gracie cry but not being able to find her. I can feel the edge of panic starting to creep into my body. What if something were wrong? What if I had that dream because some part of me connected to Gracie knew something was wrong? She needs me, and fucking Tracie won't at least pick up the line to tell me everything's okay. At least that would stop the downward spiral of thoughts. Come on, Tracie.

But she won't answer. I've called four times and sent at least a dozen texts messages, but I'm hearing nothing back. Enid's silver car is already here. She's inside the café, meeting with Janette. The answer to all of my problems, my family's problems, may be right inside – but I'm out here, waiting for just one word of confirmation that everything's okay with my baby girl. That's all I need. One word.

But I get zero. I get nothing.

Maybe she stopped by the house, saw the police. God, maybe she's talked to them, thrown me right under the bus. I can picture her there, the sweet, small-town Tennessee girl sticking up for her brother, holding Gracie in her arms and cooing in her Southern drawl that "Momma's not here right now."

I bet Tracie hopes I never will be. I shake away the thought.

I try one more time. It goes straight to voicemail. The phone is dead, or Tracie's outright ignoring me.

Both make me feel sick. *Why today, Tracie? Why would you pick today to start messing with me?* I've never felt like she's especially fond of me, but I always thought it was more that she was protecting her brother. Same thing with her mom. At least his dad likes me. Did like me, I should say. No telling what they all think now …

I pull in a deep breath, wondering whether I shouldn't just go to Tracie's first. There's no decision to be made. I can go to Gracie soon.

For now, I'm already here. Enid is inside, and she's going to have to answer for herself. I find her, hunched over a laptop next to Janette, in the café's more secluded back section. I march right up. No use pretending.

Enid jumps to her feet, surprised that I've showed up. Her mouth drops open and she fumbles around for something to say. "Sarah," she manages, "are you okay? How is Brad?"

I don't stop my swift steps. I walk right up to her, our faces close enough that you couldn't fit a hand between our noses. She recoils back.

"Surprised to see me?" I press her. "Thought I'd be locked up by now."

"What?"

"Is that what you were going for? You know, if you kill someone the police tend to start snooping around. They won't stop until someone's in jail. You can't just get rid of Brad and expect me to thank you for it." The words start to choke in my throat. The weight of what I've lost comes bearing down onto me like a waterfall. If I'm wrong about Enid, I'm acting like a maniac. But my gut tells me there's no other possible explanation. "You know he doesn't even want to see me. The love of my life. Is that what you wanted? For me to never get to see him again?"

Enid's pale face goes ten shades paler. She's backed up so far, her hands are pressing against the window behind her.

"Sarah, we don't want to cause a scene here. Let's just ask Enid a few questions."

Enid's head spins around to Janette, standing to my left.

"You were in on this? This – this assault?" Enid dares to look offended. "Is that why you asked me to meet you here?"

Her voice is raised, heads are turning, and I realize I'm going to have to find a way to avoid drawing too much attention to us. I have to get a handle on this whole thing. I can't risk letting Enid walk away from this. Not until I know the truth.

"You know what," I say, swallowing down my rage, "I'm sorry." I shake my head like I'm at wit's end, which is true. I dredge up all the hurt. I let myself cry. I hate all of this – everything that's happened, and especially the part where my closest friend betrayed me. Right now, I let her see what a mess I am. "I just don't know how much more I can take. I didn't mean to … attack you like this. I just don't know what else to do or what else to think."

All of that is the cold, hard truth. I let myself sink into an easy chair. My legs won't seem to hold me up any more. Enid's still acting like she's reeling from surprise, but she plays along, sits beside me, gives a moment of silence.

"How is Brad doing?" She looks into my face. Hers is scared, her lips trembling like she's the one who's been pigeonholed instead of me. "Is he going to be okay?"

An image of his dead-set expression, his eyes commanding me to get the hell out, flashes into my mind.

"He's recovering. I didn't get a chance to speak to the doctor yet today, but I saw Brad … for a little bit." I bite my lip. "He's stable. Neither of us can imagine who would do this, though."

Enid shakes her head and the hair tucked behind her ears shakes free with it.

"I can't believe it," she says. "I don't know who would do this to him. Something so extreme. I mean, *he could have died.*"

I examine her face, and I know she's hiding something. Part of me wishes I could believe her … but there's just no other answer at this point.

"Enid … I know you and I have been friends a long time – "

"I've been friends with Brad even longer," she answers, her voice quiet.

It hits me as a strange thing to say, as if she's trying to convince me that she cares about him. It's time to get down to business. I won't scream in her face, but I'm going to ask her. I squeeze my hands together in my lap.

Just ask her.

"The photograph." I swallow before I go on. "The one of me and Bill. I need you to tell me the truth. There's so much shit here to sort through ..." I watch the flush reach her cheeks as I speak. "You planted the photos, didn't you?"

Her mouth is agape. She doesn't say a word, just stays frozen in mock shock.

"I know you did it, Enid. Charles might have packaged them up and sent them to the media, but someone else – someone on the inside and someone close to me – had to have given him the picture first. There's no one else who could have managed to take that picture. No one, but you."

"Are you kidding me?" Her voice rises, and I can see heads turning from farther away in the café. "Are you actually saying this right now?"

"Enid, come on. You wanted my job."

"I don't have to listen to this bullshit. This is crazy. This is batshit crazy. I can't believe you'd think for a second that I had anything to do with this."

"Well then, tell me, how is it possible that when you saw me fighting with Charles somehow everybody in the office seemed to hear about it – and not just them. The police. They think I loosened Charles' lug nuts. They think I'm the reason he's dead right now. And *they* asked me about the fight. They knew about it. You were the only one who saw it."

"I can't lie to the police."

"Enid, you have no trouble lying," I snap. "The police suspect me of having Charles killed. Now they think I tried to kill my boyfriend. The only connection between all of those strange circumstances … is you."

Nostrils flared, Enid bites her bottom lip, hard. She glares at me like I'm her worst enemy.

"You know what. You're the most self-absorbed person I've ever met. I can't believe I once called you a friend. You don't know the meaning of the word." Enid rises and slams her laptop shut. "I'm finished with you. To think, after all I've done for you, you come in here and accuse me of making all the trouble you mixed yourself into. You brought all of it on yourself. Every single thing. And you are *not* dragging me down with you. You can stay the hell away from me, for the rest of your life."

"If you're so innocent, Enid, explain to me how Brad nearly died after he ate the leftovers I brought home from my dinner *with you*. After you'd insisted, over and over, that I meet with you?"

Enid was looking under the table, frantic, feeling her hand around the sides of the chairs set up around us.

"I asked you to dinner with me because I've been worried about you," she answers. "Because I care about you. But you wouldn't know anything about that."

"Yeah. You're a fantastic friend. Except that you did everything you could to ruin my career because you wanted it, including making me out to be behind Charles' death in a fatal car crash, and then you tried to poison my boyfriend."

"I had nothing to do with any of that!" Enid screams so loud it brings every note of chatter in the café to a complete halt. The only sound left is the surreal jazzy music of the coffeehouse, a complete contrast to the tension exploding in its back room. Janette clears her throat to get Enid's attention. She's standing a good ten feet away, Enid's handbag looped over one arm, her own cell phone in the other.

223

"Were you looking for this, Enid?" Janette's voice rings out, clear and firm.

Enid doesn't answer. She just starts moving toward Janette, but Janette backs away.

"I found the prescription bottle, looks like you had your Valium already crushed up and ready to go," she says. "I've called for help. Police say none of us are supposed to move until they get here."

Oh my god. She had the Valium ready. She insisted on meeting for dinner. She planned it, had it all mapped out. *Premeditated murder.*

Enid, why?

"You dirty bitch." Enid's words come out one at a time, hoarse-sounding. I watch for her feet to twitch, break into a dash. Lucky for me, there happens to be an audience of a dozen or so shocked coffeehouse patrons, their eyes glued on the three of us. Finally, at least I have an answer. It doesn't feel good to know who's done this to me and my family – not the way I thought it would – but it's one kind of relief. I wish it had been anyone else but a friend ... but at least it's an answer. At least I've uncovered the truth.

28

NOW

F ive minutes stretches out like it's an hour. The entire coffee shop is tense, the jazz a bizarre background filler to dead silence. Enid has the nerve to act like *she's* pissed, clutching her handbag against her body, shaking her head every time she looks at me. Janette stands coolly in front of the back door, her body saying nobody's going anywhere.

"How could you?" I can't help but repeat it every time Enid catches my eye. She has nothing to say for herself – no apologies for the state I'm in, out of a job and probably out of a relationship with the man I love. My entire world has been smashed to pieces … by someone I considered a dear friend. Maybe I should have known better. I study her small features, look for sign of a traitor that I'd somehow missed before. But all I see right now is frailty, and rage, the kind that simmers in a person who is pissed she got caught.

Thank god for Janette.

No one budges.

After our five-minute standoff, the police rush through the front door. Patrons jump up to get out of the way. I'm relieved that it's not the two investigators I'm all too familiar with by now – I think they suspected me from the start – but then I realize those two are probably still tied up at my house, snooping through my possessions, stirring up trouble.

Enid stays silent as they arrest her. No cuffs. She says she'll go peacefully, but a female officer is careful to separate Enid from her handbag with the prescription pill bottle inside. The evidence. I have the urge to take my last opportunity to confront her, to blurt something out, to try to prod some kind of answer from my friend, or my former friend, but I resist. It wouldn't do any good. I know who she really is now; I just can't believe I never saw it before.

I feel an arm wrap around my shoulder, a gentle hug from the side.

"Answers a lot of questions." Janette sighs heavily and searches my face.

I can't manage an answer. Now that Enid's out of my line of sight, I feel the hurt bubbling up. My eyes start to water, and I try to shake away the prick of tears.

"Hey," Janette says, "honey, it's going to be all right." She holds me tighter and I stop trying to hold back the tears. I just let the weight of it all bear down on me, sinking into the arms of the one person who's been there for me through the nightmare that has been the past few weeks.

"I just can't believe it." My voice is muffled.

"It's going to be okay," she says. "Everything will turn out alright. I'd rather us know than not know, even if it does hurt."

Janette lets me go and gives me a chin-up pat on the back. "Things are looking up. They'll start turning around. You're just overwhelmed. I understand that."

I nod and dig through my bag for a tissue.

"You know what?" Janette eyes me with concern. "I'll let Bill know I got tied up for a little bit. You want to head to my place. Regroup?"

I consider for a moment. It's sweet of her. But I have to go home, to my own home, sometime. And I really miss my baby girl. I feel like if I can just make one part of my life feel more whole, maybe everything else will start to pull back together again.

"I think I'm going to go get Gracie."

"Where is she again?"

"Tracie's." I try not to grimace when I say the name. Not really the person I want to see right now. "Brad's sister."

"Oh, yeah." Janette nods and thinks for a moment. "Well, if you want a ride, I'd be happy to take you over."

"I don't want to be trouble. I can drive."

"No, no, no." Janette shakes her head like she'll be hearing no more of that. "It's no trouble at all. Let's go get Gracie. You'll feel so much better."

Janette lets me cry in silence for the twenty minutes it takes us to get there. I love her even more for that, for not having to talk, to explain the stress of what happened to Brad, what it means to us, and how someone close to me could possibly hurt me this way. She just lets me feel it, without having to prod.

When I knock on the glass under the "Trims by Tracie" sign, no one answers. I peer in and see there's an older woman in a chair, but I can't make out her features under a black half sphere of a hair dryer. I turn the knob and let myself in. The old woman looks up at me and gives me a toothy grin. I ask where Tracie is, but she makes a face like she can't hear me. Then I hear Gracie cry, just the same as in my dream. My heart jumps instantly into mommy mode and I ascend the steps, two at a time, but when I get to the top step, Tracie fills the space with her body. She's low-key today, in sweats, but her hair is done in perfect waves. Her face is a hard-set frown.

"What's wrong?" I ask. "Is Gracie okay?"

"She's fine," Tracie answers, curt. "Her father's not, as you know – but she is safe and happy here."

But I can hear her piercing wail. A fresh burst of adrenaline makes me want to shove Tracie out of the way, but her body hovers over mine. I'm not in a good position here on the steps. In my mind, I try to cut through the confusion.

"I came to bring her home." I'm not sure why Tracie is looking at me as if I need to provide her with this explanation. She knows why I'm here.

She eyes me like I'm a bug she needs to shoe out of the house, or squash.

"Her home," she says, stretching out the words even longer than her typical Southern drawl pace, "is here for right now."

I couldn't have been more stunned if she had slapped my face.

"What?" I reel backwards automatically.

Tracie crosses her arms, doesn't answer. Her glare says everything. She wants me out. She thinks I tried to kill her brother. God – does she think I'd actually hurt my own baby? She thinks I'm a monster. A complete monster. She thinks I'm dangerous.

I fish around for the right answer, trying to swallow down my shock.

"I am taking Gracie home," I say, emphatically. "Right now." I move a few steps closer, my face perilously close to Tracie's knees. I hear a small click sound that doesn't immediately register.

"You're not," Tracie answers. "Not right now. At least not until every-thing is sorted out. We'll take good care of her. She's okay."

"What the –"

The door to the steps slams inches from my face. I pound as hard as I can, screaming, though it doesn't even sound like my own voice, so panic-stricken. I can still hear my baby girl, crying for her mother.

She's heard me. She wants me. I wrench the doorknob as hard as I can. Locked tight. Tracie had made sure to set the door to locked before she threw it shut. Stunned, I swirl around, race down the steps. The grandma getting her perm looks like she's just seen a demon. *Why is everyone scared of me?*

Outside, Janette's standing. I caught her mid-pace.

"What happened?"

"I can't even fucking believe this," I fume, making a beeline for the front door. Janette trails behind me. I yank open the glass screen door. The heavy wooden one behind it is locked, dead bolted I assume. A shadow emerges in the window to the living room, and the blinds go from half-open to drawn tight.

I slam my fists against the door, my heart feeling like it might explode out of my chest it's beating so hard. *What do I do?* It's faint, but I can still hear her. She needs me. *I need her.*

"She won't let me have her," I mutter, fumbling through my handbag for my purse. "What do I do?"

"Sarah, that's crazy." Janette answers, immediately moving around the side of the house like she's looking for another way in. She reappears a second later. "Back door is locked, too."

"She slammed the door in my face. I could *hear* her, Janette. Gracie's crying. Tracie won't even let me see her."

Hands shaking, I dial 9-1-1. I don't know what else to do. I can hear Janette banging on the front door again, trying to explain that someone else has been arrested for Brad's poisoning. But no one is listening. When emergency responders answer, I'm such a mess I don't even know what I'm saying. Kidnapping. My baby. The address. Police are on their way. I give myself a second of relief. This will all get sorted out. Maybe they can explain what's happened, that it wasn't me. I didn't poison Brad. I'd never hurt him.

But by the time I hear the sirens, I've spun back into a woman who's lost control. I knock with my fists until my palms ache. Nothing. I try again. Nothing. I slam the stupid glass screen door closed ... and it shatters. A thousand tiny shards on the concrete steps. *Shit.*

Two officers come running from their vehicle, eyeing me, then the glass on the ground.

"My sister-in-law has my daughter, my baby, inside," I explain, wondering how this must look. Why did I have to slam the door just now? "She was babysitting and – now she won't give her back."

The first officer, a man so young he looks like he could still be in high school, nods, taking in the scene but not asking any more questions before he steps gingerly over the glass on the ground. The other officer, a muscular middle-aged woman, stays back behind him.

"McMinnville Police." He gives three brisk raps, and then Tracie opens the door a crack.

"Thank goodness," she answers, sweet as can be. "I'm scared out of my mind."

What? You bitch.

"We're investigating a reported kidnapping." His statement sounds more like a question. Not a tough-guy cop yet.

I hear Tracie's fake gasp of surprise.

"Officer, I'm babysitting for my brother. That woman, the one who's just broken my front door to pieces, is suspected of poisoning him. We all thought it was best if I look after the baby for a while, until everything is all figured out. That's what my brother – Gracie's daddy – wants."

You fucking bitch.

I hear the female officer mutter something about "domestic altercation" to emergency services. I have to step in, even though I feel the pressure of Janette's hand on my arm, trying to hold me back.

I try to step in between them, my eyes focused on the gap in the door.

"Whoa." The officer turns to face me, blocking my way. "Ma'am, you need to just let us handle this."

"She won't let me have my baby."

"I understand. We're here to figure things out. Just stand back please."

I suck in a breath. He's right. I'm looking like the crazy one here.

"You just stay outside a moment with Officer Tovar here," he gestures behind him, "and give me a few moments. Okay?"

I feel the flow of tears slipping down my cheeks. I'm feet away from Gracie, but Tracie's in my way. So is the cop now. *Just calm down. Just let him do his job.* I fumble backwards a few steps.

"Thank you." He nods and steps inside.

The woman, the officer behind us, is a block of ice. She won't answer a single one of my questions, just keeps her mouth in a straight line, her eyes moving between me and the door. Why won't she say anything? When I glance at Janette, she lifts a finger to her lips. Cool it. Got it.

I've almost simmered down by the time the other cop emerges. But he's got bad news.

"I think, for now, we're going to have to ask you to leave the property." His words are firm, but his voice is timid.

"What? I'm not going anywhere. Gracie is inside. She's my daughter." My body lurches forward, toward the door, instinctively. Never mind the glass spread across the steps.

"Ma'am." The officer puffs up his chest and plants his feet so he's standing directly in the path between me and my daughter. "You are going to have to leave the property."

I falter. I can't believe this is happening. How can this possibly happen? I'm Gracie's mother. I am the mother. She's an aunt. I'm innocent. She's making me out to be guilty.

"I can't leave her here." My voice is small, weak.

"Your daughter is fine and she's safe. For right now, we're going to need you to leave. Head home." The cop is shoeing me away too.

"I won't." I bite my quivering bottom lip.

"Ma'am, I don't want to have to arrest you. Right now, you're in contempt." He glances at his backup for confidence. Her body stiffens, and she gives me a stern look.

Jesus. I don't think they can actually do this, but I don't know what other choice I have. I feel a tug on my arm. Janette. She whispers.

"It's okay, Sarah. This is all a mistake. It'll be okay, and Gracie is fine for now. She's safe and you don't have to worry. Once everything with Enid comes out, this will all be no problem. We can go over to my place for a little bit while we wait for everything to sort itself out."

In shock, I follow her to her car, trying to ignore the rookie cop's satisfied look. Not a job well done. He has no idea what he's doing. As we pull out of the driveway, I see Tracie pull down a stretch of blinds, eyeing us as we leave. The broken glass shimmers in the sunlight. I want my baby back. I want my life back.

29

NOW

The landscape outside is a blur as Janette speeds back into town. No matter how fast we go, it can never be fast enough. I can never seem to stay ahead of problems. Never. I can feel a tension headache wrapping itself around my head, pulling tighter and tighter into my skull.

I don't even realize I'm pressing against my temples until Janette interrupts my thoughts.

"Hey, there. You okay?"

I gulp, wondering whether to tell the truth. Or how much of the truth to tell. I don't know what I ever did to deserve the kind of life I've had.

"To be honest," I sigh, "not really."

"Girl, seriously." Janette takes on a tender tone. "Think about it. You trust Tracie any other time with Gracie. You might not like her, but you know Gracie's safe there. You will get Gracie back."

I peer out the window, trying to accept Janette's gesture of goodwill. As unimaginable as it is, my problems are bigger than today, bigger than being threatened by police and sent away without my baby girl.

Bigger, even, than my boyfriend being poisoned. I attract the worst. It's like I can't get away from it.

"You're right." I sniffle. "I know Gracie's okay."

"Then what is it? At least now we know … about Enid. Today was hard, but it will pass. Things will settle down. Things will work out for you."

Her kindness does the opposite of what I know she means to do. I wish I could curl into a corner alone; yet I don't want to be alone. I just want someone to tell me why. Why can't I ever catch a break? Why does shit like this always happen to me? I shake my head, trying to hold the tears back, but I just can't. A sob jumps up from my chest and I can't keep it down.

"Honey, talk to me," Janette pleads.

I pull out the ball of wrinkled tissue I'd used before. My nose is already raw from so much crying today.

"It's just … the amount of –"

"I know."

"You don't. You don't really know." I sniffle and catch my breath, afraid for a moment that I might have come off as rude. It's not Janette I'm mad at. "It's not just today."

"It's been a tough few weeks. Anyone would feel the way you do. I get it."

"No." I squeeze my fist around the tissue wad. "No. Not even that. That would be enough, but it's worse than that."

We're sitting at a red light, so Janette turns to me, her brows knit in confusion and concern.

"Worse than that?" She tilts her head, searching my face. "Tell me what's really wrong. Please."

A horn blares behind us. Janette mutters a curse word and hits the gas again.

I breathe out shakily.

"What's really wrong is that this whole … craziness – it's not even unbelievable. It should be, but it's not out of line with the bad luck I've had my entire, fucking life."

"What?" Janette sounds surprised but keeps her eyes on the road.

"I mean it." I'm trying so hard not to sulk. I hate self-pity, but this is all too much. Too heavy. And I've always borne it alone. "I attract bad luck. Crazy shit. I mean – how many other people do you know who've had three – no four, if you count Charles's car crash – people just drop dead around them."

First my mother's boyfriend. Then my own mother. Then Mark. Then Charles.

That's not even counting what almost happened to Brad.

Death, everywhere I go.

Janette stays quiet and I just let the stream of thoughts keep coming. It's cathartic to say it out loud. I almost want to scream it, to look up into the sky and demand an answer. *Why me?*

"I mean," I add, "I thought, I really thought I'd shaken it. The last few years had been okay. My life was … normal. Healthy. Good career. Good relationship. Now, a family of my own. You know, you won't even believe this, but before my mother died, her boyfriend was killed in a freak car crash. You know how? His lug nuts were loose. Exactly the same way Charles died. That's why police are at my house, or were. They thought it couldn't possibly be a coincidence. And you know what? That's what any reasonable person would think, right? No one is that fucking unlucky. No one."

I bite down hard on my bottom lip, letting the bitterness get the best of me.

Janette watches the road in silence, her own lips pressed together in a tight line while she listens and follows the familiar route to my home.

I can't stop now.

"In high school, someone I knew fell off a cliff at a party. I was there that night. I'd seen him. We were kind of ... *you know*. And, Jesus, I lost my own mother," I say, my voice cracking. "Isn't that enough death for one person's life? These are things that happen once in a lifetime to other people. Tragedies. They're shocked, and it's horrible, but they adjust. But then it doesn't just keep happening over and over and —"

Janette throws the car into park abruptly in my driveway. She stares at the wheel and pulls in a deep breath before she speaks.

"You know, losing your mother. That wasn't fair. There's no way anything can ever heal that." She studies her hands, folded in her lap. "The other stuff ... it's just life. It's the way things work."

"It doesn't seem to be the way other people's lives work," I muse. Half to myself, I mutter: "Some kind of shit life."

"Look." Janette touches my arm. "Outside of what happened with your mom – and that breaks my heart – at the end of the day, things have always worked out okay for you, haven't they?"

No. Not really.

She doesn't wait for me to answer.

"I mean, all of those things that happened, they were in your past."

"Not Charles. Not Brad."

She nods. "I know. I know. Right now is really hard. But all the other stuff, really think about it. Everything worked out alright. When you're in the middle of stuff, everything seems terrible, but you know things usually work out how they're supposed to. Maybe ..." I think I see a glint of tears in Janette's eyes as she searches for what she wants to say. Maybe there are parts of her past that hurt just as much as mine. "I mean, even with Brad," she watches me, warily, "I mean you two … things weren't exactly perfect. I mean, you're having all these struggles trying to get back on your feet at work, and his response is what? To just move away? How loving is that? Really? Would someone who really loves you want you to give up everything, just for him?"

I shake my head. Janette's not quite getting that part. I know she's just trying to help, but she's not.

"All I'm saying," she says, her words suddenly more clipped, "is that maybe it's all for the best. Things tend to work out the way they're supposed to."

"Maybe they do," I whisper, trying my best at a smile, hoping we can wrap up this discussion. "I'm just tired. This is all a lot to process."

She pats my hand in a motherly way and clears her throat. "We'll get through it."

I hope like hell she's right. I don't want to be insensitive to Janette or make it seem like I don't appreciate her attempt at a pep talk. Maybe one day she'll open up to me and I'll understand her a little better. Maybe she's right that all the trouble that's followed one step behind me is really just part of life. Maybe she's even had it harder than me. Who knows? But right now, in the middle of everything so wrong – the mess that my career has become, my own family falling apart, Brad recovering in a hospital *and* suspecting I tried to hurt him – I just can't find a reason to be upbeat.

I don't expect my upturned house to be any consolation whatsoever.

And it's not. The kitchen junk drawer has been emptied of its contents, a pile of flotsam laid out across the countertop. Food from the refrigerator is rotting beside it. They probably took freaking samples. I imagine the rest of the house is the same, evidence that it's been rifled through. They were thorough, and they had no inclination to clean up a single thing behind them. It was like they were trying to leave me a message. *We're onto you. If you've got something to hide, we'll find it.* But I'm not worried about that part at least. The only thing I really don't want anyone to see is locked away in a storage unit. Not even Brad knows about that.

Maybe he should.

I shudder, wishing I could shake the thought away. It's too late to turn back now, and too early to regret. Though the truth is that I've been living with regret my whole life. If I'd paid closer attention to my mother, if I'd been watching her more closely that day …

I sense my thoughts spiraling downward, darker and darker, and I know I can't go there. I instinctively start to clean off the countertops, Janette jumping right in to help, fishing around for the trash can.

"It's under the sink," I tell her. "Thanks."

We get the spoiled food out of the way, the counters wiped down – but I can't think of spending the rest of the day trying to put the house back in order. Janette seems to read my mind.

"You know what?" She puts her hands on her hips. "Fixing the house – it's not going to help anything. The mess isn't going anywhere and it's not hurting anything. And it's sure not going to make you feel better to see all of Gracie's stuff, or Brad's stuff. You need to let your feelings shake out a little bit, and you can't do that in the middle of everything that reminds you of what happened. Why don't you just grab a few things and come over to my place?"

The suggestion sounds good, but I'm not sure it's the right thing to do. I just don't know.

"You don't have to do that, really," I answer. "You've already missed another day of work, trying to help me."

"Sarah," she says, planting her hands on my shoulders. "It's fine. Really. I can't imagine what you're feeling. It's the least I can do."

"I don't want to be a pain."

"Oh my gosh, girl. It's no big deal."

I swallow. I really don't want to stick around here. Janette's right, just picturing Gracie's empty crib … it hurts to think about. I miss her so much. Every part of me wants to see her. I know in my head that she's alright, but I want to feel her, hold her against me, to know for sure that she's okay, that at least one part of my life is still intact.

"Are you positive it's not a problem?"

"Yes." Janette stretches out the word. "Of course I am. You stay with me as long as you like. I've had your back through this whole thing and it's not just because I admire the kind of work you do. I hope you know I'm someone you can count on, outside of work, as a friend." She pauses, thinking. "I know this sounds cheesy, but … I've felt like we were kindred spirits from the moment I met you. Connected. I haven't made much time in my life for friendships. It was always work, work, work. But I think that's wrong. I really hope this doesn't sound weird, but I think of you almost like family now. I don't want to see you hurt. I *want* to be able to be there for you."

"I guess there's no use staying here." I see Janette's shoulders drop, almost imperceptibly, at my resignation. Maybe I'm being rude. "And I really appreciate you," I add, emphatically. And I mean it. Janette's gone out of her way to help me, over and over.

She smiles wide and warm.

"I'm just doing what any real friend would do," she says. "Pack whatever you need. I mean it. You can stay as long as you like. We'll stop to get your car, maybe get a bite to eat. Things will look better after you get a good night's rest, too. You'll see."

30

NOW

I wake in the dark, too early, to an alarm tone that isn't my own. Then I realize I'm on a couch that's not mine. I peer around and see the outline of furniture that doesn't belong to me. *Where am I?*

Then I remember. Brad hurt. Enid arrested. Gracie alone, without her mother. The house was a wreck and so empty. I couldn't bear to stay at home last night.

Janette's bedroom light switches on and the door squeaks open. She's in a robe, sleepy looking, but smiling. My head is throbbing. There's no hint of light outside. I feel around for my phone to check the time, but don't find it.

"Time to get up, sleepyhead," Janette says, her voice too chipper. "I'd like to get a head start at the office today. Maybe we can start integrating you back where you belong, back into your old job."

My neck aches from sleeping on couch pillows. My tongue feels glued to the roof of my mouth. "I need coffee."

Janette laughs. "I thought you'd be a morning person."

"What time is it?"

"Almost six."

"Geez. Do we need to get that much of a head start?"

Janette ignores me and tinkers around in the kitchenette that faces the living room. Her place is tidy but tiny, not really what I'd expected. I guess I assumed that because she's so career-driven, and a few years older than me, she might have had her life set up a little better. Her home feels almost temporary, like a stopping place.

Soon, I hear coffee percolating. It doesn't do much to get me moving. I'm not that keen to get back into the office, not without fixing the Gracie situation. Or the Brad situation.

"The sooner we get you back to something that feels more normal, the better." Janette's handing out advice, pouring two mugs of coffee. "Getting back into a routine at work will help with that."

She nudges me aside so she can sit next to me, and hands me one of the steaming mugs. I feel hungover, but I don't remember drinking. Just picking up my car, stopping for dinner. I hadn't even eaten much. Hadn't felt like it. But Janette and I had stayed up late last night. I wonder what's the big hurry today, at least for me. She might have some catching up to do. If they bring me back on as assistant campaign manager, I will too. But there's no telling that will happen. I'd rather spend the day sorting out affairs, or at least getting a couple more hours of sleep so I can figure out what to do next.

A few sips down and I decide to tell Janette as much.

"Oh, I don't know," she says, "I thought we'd go in together. We can be ready for Bill when he gets there, meet with him before the morning meeting with everybody else. We can explain what happened with Enid … that we have identified the troublemaker, and the rest of the campaign should be smooth sailing. With you in your rightful place, he'll be back in business. He'll be happy to hear the news. He always liked you and the work you did."

"You could just tell him," I offer hopefully.

Janette wrinkles her nose at that.

"I don't want you to be here alone … worrying all day," she says, finally. "Not without me here to help out."

"I'm sorry. I'm just still, sort of, recovering, you know?" I answer. "I'd prefer to at least come in a little bit later. I've got a killer headache."

"I'll get you an aspirin, no problem," Janette says. "I'd really prefer we hit the road together. You'll feel better too, once things start to get back to normal. Work is part of that, getting back to the way things were."

Huffing, I clutch my coffee to my chest.

"I guess. If you think that's best, I'm okay with that. I'll get ready. Can we spare a half hour so I can get cleaned up?"

"Anything you need. If you need to borrow anything, I've got spares in the medicine cabinet. Toothbrush. Deodorant. Cute little travel sizes. What's mine is yours."

"Okay." I set my coffee down, forcing myself to my feet. "Half an hour."

"Take your time."

Except, when it's thirty-two minutes later, Janette's pacing the floor in an antsy shuffle. I hurry, not wanting to be rude, and my hair is still damp by the time I'm in my car. I watch her back out and then just sit there, waiting for me to pull out in front of her. *What's she being so weird about?*

Whatever. Might as well get this over with.

Janette stayed close the next few blocks, until I slipped through a yellow light. I've always been terrible at leading a line of vehicles. I forget that I need to hold off on yellow so the caravan doesn't get separated. Oops.

I was roused out of the bed and out of Janette's place so quickly I haven't even checked my phone this morning. Maybe there's news.

Something from Brad. A note from Tracie. At the next stop light, I reach into my handbag, irritated that it's become such a mess of papers. I always used to keep my bag organized. I fish around until the light turns green, but I still haven't found anything that feels like my phone. The familiar panic hits me. Is it buried in here, or did I leave it somewhere? Of all the times to lose track of my phone, this isn't a great one. At the next light, I get so frustrated I unload the entire bag onto the passenger's seat. A pile of junk – one not wildly different to the upturned drawer in my house – spreads out. I push around with my hands.

It's not there. Shit. Where did I leave it? Did I have it at my house? I think back, try to retrace my steps through the nightmare that was yesterday. I had it at my house; I remember that. Did I take it with me after?

Yes. I remember checking my email later at dinner. I'd done the same at night, at Janette's, when we were talking on the couch. I breathe a little easier. At least I've narrowed down the possibilities. A quick glance in my rearview and I see that Janette's nowhere to be found. I'll have to swing back by the house and then get over to work as quickly as I can. Maybe she forgot to lock the door. She'll be worried. I'll call her the second I find my phone.

Damn it.

Of course it's locked tight. Too bad I don't know how to unlock a door. Would have been a handy skill yesterday, too, except I'm sure Tracie would have had that naïve officer believing I was breaking and entering. God, I just want my baby back.

I tiptoe around the side of the house and then I spot my chance. The window that has to be Janette's bedroom window is cracked, ever so slightly. I'm in. I drag a cheap plastic chair off her back porch and within minutes, I'm crawling through like a bandit. Except with less grace. I land with a thump onto her dresser and spend the first few seconds putting the perfume bottles I'd knocked over back like I think they were when I passed them earlier this morning.

I head immediately to the couch and feel blindly around in every crevice, behind every cushion, but it's not there. Where did I have it last? It should be around the couch. Maybe when I was using the bath-room last night. I step back into Janette's room. Maybe I'd left it near the sink and she'd moved it. I feel a little sneaky poking around in here, but she wouldn't mind. I check the bedstand, her dresser top – any handy place where she might have set it and forgotten to tell me about it. It's nowhere obvious. So I look some more. Glance under the bed, pull open her closet drawers. I don't see it anywhere. Shit.

My eyes fall on a sleep T-shirt she'd tossed over the edge of her bedspread. Maybe underneath.

There it is. God. I'm at one percent. And I have, indeed, missed many calls. I plop down on her bed and reach for the charger hanging out of the wall nearby. It's plugged in and now I can play the voicemail from Brad's mother …

Sarah. Tracie told me about what happened today.

Her voice is a threat. Her words are carefully chosen, as if she were reading them from a script.

I'm calling to let you know that, first of all, Gracie is fine. We love her very much and want you to know that she is safe and cared for. Second of all …

I know what's coming. She doesn't even have to say it.

Until the police have finished their investigation and we all know what's going on, the whole family thinks it's better for Gracie if she stay with us for right now. All of us. I'm sure this is scary for you and I know you care about Gracie too …

Care about her? She's my child. I'd do anything for her. I don't *care for* her, I love her with all my heart.

But this is what we think is best now, and not just me and Tracie. It's

244

what Bradley has asked for at this time too. Thank you for your under-standing. We'll be in touch.

So formal. Almost like she was making a recording to share with a judge if she ever had to prove that they communicated clearly and effectively with me. Depressing. I click down. A message from Tracie. I'm sure it's a carbon copy. They're covering all their bases. I hit play and, sure enough, she started out exactly the same, condescending. Irritated, I look around at Janette's room and edge closer to her bed stand, where she's got an old scrapbook. The front is black leather, with antique typewriter keys that spell out the word "memories." Cute.

Through the phone, Tracie's voice grates on me. I need a distraction.

Mindlessly, I start turning pages, thinking I don't need to hear any more of Tracie. But I let her drone on. Maybe I should draft a reply of my own, if we're going to end up going tit for tat. An image of all of us at a mediation table, playing messages from our phones, plays through my mind. *Assholes. Trying to take my baby away from me, maybe for good.* I focus on the pages before me.

There's a picture of a little girl on the first page. She's sitting alone on a front porch swing. I recognize Janette's smile, but it's more toothy and less perfect than it is now. She was a cute little girl. I wonder whether she has any siblings; she's never mentioned any. The next few pages are all of the same little girl, mostly school pictures. Looks like it must have been just her, an only child. I can't even find any of her parents. She looks like any normal little girl, but she's smiling less in her pictures. Maybe she was embarrassed of those teeth.

Then the next page. Tracie's voice blends into the background, like everything else around me. The phone drops out of my hand and onto the floor.

What the fuck is this?

My brain can't register at first. I don't believe what I'm seeing.

I squint, move my face inches from the page.

This can't be. This cannot be real.

I'm looking at a picture of me. And not just me.

I'm a teenager, standing next to my mother, who's standing next to her boyfriend – the dead one – and his face is gouged out with a pen. Someone had pressed an 'x' over his face with such force, the photo paper is ripped straight through.

I don't know what to make of it. I don't know what to think. I can feel my heart racing in my chest, my wide open mouth sucking in gasps of dry air. What in the hell is this? Why the hell would Janette have had this photo? Where did she get it? We're standing in front of our home in Alabama. Was she there? Did she steal this from someone?

I look around the room and suddenly feel like it's closing in on me. Everything about it is sinister, suspect. I realize I know very little about this woman who's taken me in so willingly, who's worked so hard to get close to me. And why? Why would she? Why would she have pictures of me? Of my mother? To be honest, I'm terrified. I don't know what this could mean, or what else this could mean. What's been happening this entire time? Who is Janette? Who is she really?

Afraid of what I might see next, I turn the page.

Holy shit.

This one's not a photo. It's a page of newspaper clippings. The first is my mother's obituary. My mother's face, in black and white, smiles at me, her hair all done up for Sunday morning in the photo the funeral director had cropped for the newspaper's obituary page. The text next to it describes her in simple terms, staying away from the darkness she could never escape. A loving mother to her daughter. Survived by a daughter, Sarah.

Janette has saved this memento of her sudden death. I shudder. There is no explanation that could make this okay. None.

Next is my graduation announcement, a tiny paragraph clipped from a newspaper. There's a slightly longer clip of my first and only debate tournament win, with a photo of me and the others on our debate team. I can feel the hair standing straight up on my skin, goosepimples crawling up my arms. Why would she want any of this? Where did she find it? And why would she keep it?

The next pages are a shift. There's nothing about me or mom, thank goodness, but there are endless articles about my boss, gubernatorial candidate William Porter. Some are from much earlier than the governor's race. This is like a scrapbook of his entire career. What the hell?

There are photos, too, clearly clipped out of newspaper accounts.

Oh my god.

I look again at the image before me, in black and white. My mother, pale as a ghost.

My own mother. And Bill, next to her. A knowing smile between them. A caption describes something ridiculous about a loyal supporter – but I know instantly it's something so much more. It doesn't list her name. Maybe I'm imagining this. I blink, squeeze my eyes shut, hoping I'll see something different when I open them again.

No way.

It can't be.

But it is.

I'm staring at a newspaper photographer's snapshot of my mother, as a young woman, and freaking William Porter, a candidate for mayor. He's much older now, gray-haired and with decades of hard lines drawn into his face, but there's not a doubt in my mind that this is the same Bill Porter I know very well.

It's a young Bill Porter, in a celebratory moment, a moment of joy shared between two people. Him and my mother. They are both swooning. And it has nothing to do with whatever announcement they must have just heard. *Bill knew my mother.*

My heart is pounding so hard, I hear it hammering in my ears. The room swirls around me as the possibilities sink in. The questions too. I have no idea what this all means, but I know one thing: I have to get the hell out of here. I grab my phone off the floor, unplug it from the charger, and look around. The scrapbook is still open to the last page, the photo of my boss with Mom, standing a little too close to each other, smiling like they are hopelessly in love. I shake my head in shock, complete disbelief, and then pull the photo out, stuff it in my purse, and close the book. Back to the way it was.

But nothing will ever be back to the way it was. You don't recover from something like this. I know that, and I don't even know what kind of monster I'm up against. No wonder she didn't want me sticking around here without her. She was afraid I'd snoop, and she definitely had something to hide.

And what else do I not know about my own mother?

31

NOW

The office is far too busy for my liking, but we are just weeks away from the day everyone's been waiting for, the election. If the past few weeks had been different, I'd be brimming with the same kind of excitement, the same hustle going down the halls or urgency answering the phones.

But all I can feel now is dread. I'm hoping to avoid her, but I can't.

"What happened?" Janette eyes me nervously. "I lost you. Where've you been? I kept trying to call, but you wouldn't pick up. Everything okay?"

What now? I've at least thought this part through. I need to gather more information before I do anything about Janette. *Act like nothing has changed. Stick with the plan. Stay calm.*

"Sorry. Phone's been on silent." I force my voice into something that sounds like nonchalance. "Just stopped somewhere for more coffee. Line was crazy long. McMinnville's getting busy enough to have its own morning rush hour, almost as bad as Nashville."

"That's why I wanted us to get in *early*," Janette half scolds. "I didn't get a chance to talk with Bill yet. And I wanted us to do that together. I've been waiting for you."

I look around to see who else is in earshot. A few volunteers filter past us in the hallway, no one who seems particularly interested in the two of us.

"Yeah. I need to think about that, Janette. Is it okay if we hold off, at least this morning? I really want to think about what I want before we talk to Bill. It's important to me."

She looks disappointed, but agrees.

"Thanks for understanding." I watch her with a new wariness, second-guessing every movement, every twitch of her lips. Every blink. I don't know what to think. I thought I knew how to tell when someone is lying, in part because I had to learn to control those giveaways in my own behavior. But I don't know how to read her.

"Sure thing. I hope you don't mean you need to think about stepping back into the assistant campaign manager role?" She cocks her head at me.

"No. no. I'd like to be back closer to the core of the campaign, of course. The two of us would be working together," I add, carefully. "That is what I want. I'm just not ready to rehash the whole Enid thing with Bill right at this second. I don't want to have to relive it again, first thing today. Don't feel like talking about it."

"He might notice she's not at the morning meeting, though. He's going to find out. Better if we steer the conversation in our favor." Janette crosses her arms. I don't answer right away. "Well, I'm supposed to work with Dick for a few minutes on a release he's prepared," she adds. "Think about what you want to say, what you want to do. We can touch base in an hour or so?"

I nod, but don't speak. I don't want to blow my cool, or my cover. She walks away and leaves me standing there, stunned, wondering, letting my mind sink to the lowest possible places. *What the hell is she up to? What does she want? How do I protect myself, and my family, after*

I've let her in so close? I've got an hour to think about how to confront her.

I'll start with Bill.

No tact necessary. I've got the photo evidence in my handbag and I want answers. His office light is on. Now is my moment.

I knock but don't wait for invitation. Bill looks up from his desk, a flutter of surprise crossing his face.

"Sarah. Well, um – good to see you back." He rises from his chair to stretch out a hand like there's any relationship to be repaired here. He has no idea. He holds it out toward me for an awkward moment and then lets it fall back to his side.

"I'm so sorry to hear about Brad. Terrible. Truly terrible. I can't imagine what would cause a person to act that way. And she seemed so normal."

"You mean Enid?" I speak, finally.

"Yeah."

"So you know."

"Heard a little bit this morning. Nothing from the authorities yet. But, my goodness. Unbelievable. A real shame."

"It really is," I say flatly.

"I'm so sorry. You've been through a lot."

He's taken his seat again, expecting me to do the same. But I won't sit. I'm standing, arms crossed, near his desk, waiting for the right moment.

"I assume you think she's the one who gave Charles the photos." His mind can't help but go to how this affects him.

"Maybe." I haven't quite had the space to think back to how Enid might have actually played into this whole situation, in light of what I've discovered. Maybe she was in on it. Maybe she was only a pawn in Janette's twisted game ... there's still so much I don't know. I have to change that. "Someone definitely has been digging into my past. I had to do my own investigating, to protect myself. I actually found something interesting in all of this." I wait, and watch.

His eyebrows raise. He turns his head to examine me directly. "What have you found out? Something else I should know?"

"Not something I found *out*." I reach into my bag. "Something I found."

I lay the faded picture flat on his desk, in the middle of the calendar spread out across it. Seeing it again chills me. My boss. The candidate for governor. My mother. The suicidal, manic depressive. The woman who never got over some unspoken hurt.

In this picture, she looks happy. Happier than I remember ever seeing her.

That's the worst part. This man, a man I would have said I trusted, knew some part of my mother that I never got to know.

Bill squints over the photograph like it's a snapshot of two people he doesn't recognize.

"What is this?" He sounds like a bumbling fool. A pretender. "Where'd it come from?" He strains to read the text.

"I've had to do a lot of my own investigating lately," I say, making my voice as threatening as possible. "This is just one of the things I found." Let him believe I know more than I do. Make him talk. Give him enough rope to hang himself.

"When was this taken?" He picks it up, squinting like he expects it to change to something else, something less dangerous. He has to know. He must know he's looking at my mom. "Where did you find this?"

"Why don't you let me ask the questions. In case you don't know, this is my mother."

His jaw drops, his mouth a small, round circle.

"I didn't know. You – you're Rebecca's daughter?"

"Come on, Bill."

"Honest to god." His head is shaking. "I – I had no idea. I haven't heard anything from her in years." He looks almost nostalgic for a fleeting moment. "I always wanted to know how she made out. I never heard a word."

Wonder why, asshole.

I draw in a breath and let it go.

"What happened between the two of you?" I demand.

His mouth opens, and I can see a lie coming from a mile away. I stop him before he can pitch it out in my direction. "Don't make me do my own research. You won't want that."

"Calm down, Sarah. This is a crazy coincidence. This is unbelievable. I always wondered what happened to her."

Does he really not even know? Is this another lie?

"Were you two involved?" I let the question linger in the uncomfortable silence, setting my mouth hard, demanding my answers.

"Sarah," he finally says, "that was ages ago. Really. There's no use dredging all this up. I had no idea you were a relative –"

"Her daughter."

"Right. Jesus. I'm sorry."

The silence falls thick and heavy. Bill examines the photo again, this time with tenderness in his eyes.

"She was special. I couldn't help but fall in love with her. She had this light."

A light that someone crushed, blew out. And she never recovered.

"So you dated her?"

Bill looked down at his hands, shame written across his face.

"We were in love. I loved her."

I guess that's a yes. Bill and my mother. God. Bill had an affair with my mother. I know he and his wife were married his senior year of college. There's no way this was *not* an affair.

"But you were married at the time, right?" I ask anyway, already knowing the answer.

I hear him swallow.

"That's true. I was in love with her, but we couldn't be together."

"Because you were having an affair. You were running for – what was it then?"

"Mayor."

"Yeah. And you wanted to preserve your reputation."

"So much for that." He sighs and sets the picture down. "Is that why you came here? To ask me about this? I don't see how it matters now."

You wouldn't. You wouldn't give a fuck.

I nod, not satisfied in any way.

"Honestly, this was years and years ago, before you were born. This is old news. I hope you're not trying to take this out on me. I had nothing to do with what's happened to you, with Brad. We all know now. It's tragic. She was your friend, but obviously Enid was behind all this. The scandal – it hurt me. Why would I want to do that to you? To either one of us?"

Bill's still talking, but I can't respond because it feels like my heart has sunk down to my chest. I never knew my father. My mother wouldn't speak of him – except to say I was the most amazing gift anyone could have ever given her. That was on the good days. Jesus. I'm not standing next to … my own father? That would be more than I could process. I watch his face, still talking, still keeping the focus on how this could hurt his campaign, his political ambitions. Is that a family character trait? Did I get my ambition from him? Please, no.

But he said it himself: he knew my mother *before I was born. Years before I was born* is what he actually said. I have to hope that's the truth.

I snatch the picture off his desk.

I still don't know where Janette would have found this. And why the hell she would have kept it in her scrapbook filled with pictures of me and Mom. And she'd said Enid was the one who was obsessed.

32

NOW

I bump into the last person I'm ready to see. Literally. My feet are moving so fast, my mind such a mess that I'm not even watching where I'm going. I walk smack into Janette's back outside Bill's office door. I hadn't seen her leaning there against the wall, which is weird. But I don't have time to make sense of why she would be lurking around.

"Hey there."

I'm flustered, but I mutter a greeting.

"You alright?" she asks.

I shrug, trying to keep cool, trying to pull myself together. I still have to play everything off as normal in front of Janette, at least until I know more. "I'm managing. I just ... my mind's in a hundred different places right now." That's true. She doesn't need to know *why* but it isn't a stretch, considering the past few days.

"What were you doing in Bill's office?" she asks suspiciously. "I thought we were going to tell him together."

"Well, first off, he already heard about Enid. But I wasn't asking him about the job."

Janette waited, expectant.

I continued. "I went to ask Bill if it would be alright if I took a few days off. After all that's happened and everything. I just don't know that I'm ready for all this yet."

Janette looks disappointed in the idea. She doesn't answer at first. Her arms are still crossed and she's nodding her head like she's taking it all in.

I wonder whether I shouldn't just get it over with. Obviously, she knows something's up, something's wrong. I could go ahead and tell her what I know, what I found. I wasn't trying to snoop – but I'm not the one who needs to be explaining myself right now. It's her. I will confront her. But here, now, with the little information I have is not the right moment. I have to time this right.

And I need to know more. I'm going to have to do what I should have done years ago. The thought makes the knot in my stomach squeeze into a tight ball. I'll never be ready, but it's definitely time to face what I've been hiding from all these years.

"A few days off. Hm. That makes sense," she says, softly. "I can tell you're not yourself yet. I'm sure it's hard."

"I miss Gracie so much," I say. "I just can't help but worry about her every second."

"I'm sure." Janette says, finally looking like she believes me. "You have to be going crazy. You know she's okay, though."

"I do. It's just … I won't be okay myself until I see her. Not until I know that my daughter is safe and I won't be kept away from her."

Janette opens her mouth to speak, but no sound comes out. She tilts her head down, forcing away some other thought, some secret pain. She doesn't want me to leave. She's the one who's obsessed. I need to know why.

"You're a good mother, that's why," she says, finally. "I think you're on the right track to ask for time off." She breathes out a sigh. "Bill gave you the okay then?"

"Yeah."

"Alright. Not what I'd hoped we'd be talking to Bill about, but that's okay. I understand, about Gracie. I get what you're worrying about what right now. You have to know things will get better, but you need some recovery time. I think that's a smart move."

"Thanks." Relief I didn't know I was waiting for washes over me. I don't need permission from Janette to leave, to take care of my business, but I don't want to have to face her anymore. I'm not ready to tell her what I've learned. I pull my bag closer to my body, hoping we're done here.

"You sure you're alright?"

"I am, mostly. As alright as I can be." Especially for someone who's just discovered what I have: photos of my life, and my own mother, on a stranger's nightstand. She is a stranger now. I thought she was a friend, but she's someone I don't know at all.

Even though she sure seems to know me.

"Okay," Janette answers, biting her lip. "I can't sneak out again today. I'll have to stay here, and it might be an especially long day. Press conference late this afternoon. But when it's all said and done, I'll get back home as early as I can. I don't want you to feel alone in all of this."

Her offer of friendship sounds hollow, knowing what I know. And there's still everything I don't know. Maybe it's better than I'm thinking. More likely, it's worse.

"See you at home?" she asks, pulling me out of my thoughts. "You're welcome to stay over again. I told you, as long as you need it, my home is yours."

"Um, actually, I think I'm going to go see if there's anything I can do about Gracie."

"You know what the police said, Sarah. I don't want you getting yourself into a mess. More of a mess. You don't know what kind of picture they might paint to the police. Aren't you worried about how they might try to make this situation out to be? Tracie all but called you crazy to that cop yesterday. And he was on her side. She's convincing. I won't be around to corroborate. You need someone with you who's on your team. You don't want to go into something like that all alone."

"No – I mean, Brad's mom called me." That part isn't a lie. "She, um, just wanted to tell me she's sorry about all of this." That part is.

"Really?" Janette's face is shocked.

A volunteer, a young guy, walks past us, slowing down to eavesdrop. I wait a moment for him to pass farther down the hallway, and then lower my voice.

"Yeah. I think I'm going to go try to talk with her, see whether I might be able to get her to work with Tracie on this. Maybe I can get them to see things my way. Explain more about Enid. Get them to let me see Gracie again."

Janette looks unhappy with my decision, but she gives in with the kind of sigh that says she's tried to talk some sense into me, realized I'm not going to listen, and she's just going to let me fail to prove her point.

"Well, let me know how I can help." Her voice is flat, empty. "Let me know how you are. I'm going to get to work, I guess."

Fine.

I've got some major work of my own to do. Maybe the hardest thing I've ever done. I have to face the truth, no matter how much it hurts.

33

NOW

I stand here alone, trying to convince myself I'm ready to face
the box.

A box that may hold more secrets than I thought. Maybe, deep down,
I'd always worried about this, that I might find out things I'd never
want to know about my mother. Maybe that's why I've waited so long.

I squint, trying to spare my eyes from the burning reflection of mid-
morning sun beaming off the metal garage-door front of the storage
unit. No one else is around. It's just me, the abandoned gravel parking
lot, and a row of units, most likely full of junk. Junk someone just
couldn't let go of. So they parked it here, outside of town. They moved
it out of sight, people who don't know how to really let go.

With the key in my pocket, I hesitate.

Why? Why should this be so hard? I lived through the worst. The
morning it happened, the police, the old crows from around the neighborhood nosy in our front lawn, pretending to be there to comfort me.
The lonely teenage life I led, one without a mother to rebel against. No
one to talk back to. No one to try to keep me in line. No one to run to
when my heart ached and I just needed to be held.

I realize the secrets aren't even what I'm afraid of. I'm afraid, yes. I'm so terrified, my hands tremble, making it even harder to wriggle the key into place. It turns and clicks in my hands.

The truth is, I'm not even most afraid about what I might find. I'm afraid to lose some last piece of my mother. As long as the box stayed closed, I knew there would one more message from my mother, one more instant I could feel close to her again. It held a hope I'd never understood before now. I put my muscle into pulling the door up. It groans under my hands, reluctant to move. The mechanical sound whirs in my ears and I'm standing before a mostly empty room. Just a few mementos from my past. My graduation cap and gown wrapped in plastic and folded over itself. A box of my old stuffed animals. Another I know is full of our cheap kitchen dishware.

My eyes fall on the banker's box with my mother's name. The last thing the police gave me.

I wish, like anything, that it wouldn't have to happen this way.

It's all that's left of my mother, and I have to experience it out of desperation, not love.

But that's not true. It's a lie, a ridiculous one. Some, more sensible, part of me knows that. No one, no situation, no outside pressure can take away what I feel for her. I can open it, be with her, feel her because I want to. Because she is my mother. This is my moment.

No, it's ours.

I pick up the box, the one I'd dusted off just days ago, on the anniversary of her death.

I love you, Mom. I'm sorry you didn't feel the love you needed, or didn't feel it enough ... to stay. But I love you. So much.

Always.

I pull it against my chest, wishing it were her, in the flesh. Wishing for one more day. One more chance to tell her she is loved, that she meant the world to me. She still does.

Also, Momma ... I forgive you. If you're out there, it's okay. I love you anyway. Always have. Always will.

Fat tears roll down my cheek. I don't try to stop them. Still with the box in my arms, I squeeze and lean forward, imagining her embrace. Wishing she could tell *me* that everything's okay. Wishing I could feel her stroke my hair, hear her tell me again how much she loves me, how I'm the most precious part of her entire life.

I stand there until I can steady my breathing to an even rhythm. I'm ready.

This is it.

I curl my legs underneath me on the dusty concrete floor, still wishing this could happen some other way. After all this time, after waiting so long, it seems like I should be doing this somewhere else, not in an empty garage. But I don't have time to make it more perfect. The tape around the edges, more than fifteen years old, gives way with ease. The lid loosens. I lift it and set it beside me.

Someone organized this. Someone neatly and tidily put together what was left of my mother, in various plastic bags, the way police might do with evidence. On the right is a thick file folder. On top of a stack of clothes is a ziplock stuffed full of yellowed papers. I spot my mother's exaggeratedly curly handwriting, the kind I used to see on grocery store lists and school excuses. I touch it over the plastic, trying to reach through to her. I can't open this one, not yet, but I set it down on the floor, close to me.

Another deep breath.

Below that is her pajamas, a fleece top and bottom with a grinning, red-nosed Rudolph face repeated over and over in the print. She loved Christmas. Decorations went up the day after Thanksgiving, and she had no reservations about wearing holiday clothes year-round. These were her favorite. I can picture her laughing, cozy in her pajamas and watching TV with me. I can remember her wearing them on the bad days, too, still in her pajamas late into the afternoon, looking emptied of all life and joy on the couch. Unmovable.

She was still wearing them when she died.

I pick up the top and fold it against my cheek. I imagine I can smell her, the clean scent of soap, but in reality, it's musty. My mother's not here. Another plastic bag catches my eye. I see the glint of her jewelry, the tiny gold hoops she almost never took out, the chain with a small gold cross she wore around her neck. I let the necklace slide into the palm of my hand, wrap my fingers around it.

Why? Momma?

What could have been so wrong? What could have made you give up? Why did you leave me?

I don't want to think about him – Bill – or Janette in this moment. But I can't help it. I'm here to find out what really happened, her real story. My real story. If someone drove her to do this … I have no idea how I'll react. I have to stay focused. I clasp the necklace around my own neck and press the cross down against my skin. I'll take her with me, wherever I go. Wherever this hunt takes me, some part of her will be close to me.

All that's left are her slippers, simple pink satin, with a well-worn insole in each, a set of toe prints that belong to my mother. I remember her padding around the house in these. Cereal for breakfast. Hurrying to get ready, me taking every last possible second fixing my hair in the bathroom while she hovered outside the door, urging me to hurry so I wouldn't miss the bus.

I thought the worst that could happen then was a bad hair day. I once had normal people problems. I was just a teen like any other. Then everything changed.

I swallow, my throat a hard, painful knot, and reach for the bag of papers, sliding out the first one.

It's an envelope from my grandmother to my mom. Inside is a handwritten letter. Standard life updates, and one slightly cryptic note: *No matter how far off the path you think you are, Jesus still wants you back. I pray for you every day. We'd love to see you again.* My grandma was a church nut; my mother was not. I knew that was one of the reasons they'd clashed. Clearly, my grandmother was worried about my mom in some way. But that could be about anything from a lack of church attendance to some feeling my grandma had conjured during her prayers. I don't have reason to give it too much weight. At least not unless I find something else to piece it together with.

Below that are faded photographs, a few polaroids of my mom as a trendy seventies teen, short striped shorts, a tank top, and Farrah Fawcett hair. I'm positive Grandma would have scolded her about the amount of leg she's showing. A friend must have snapped this one. I smile and hold the picture up to the light. I love seeing her happy. This bag is a treasure, one I'll save for the right moment.

With both hands, I heave out the thick file folder wrapped in a giant rubber band. Inside is the pedestrian stuff of life, the things that were once monumentally important but now just take up space. Old tax returns. A stapled stack of life insurance policy documents. An entire page of a newspaper, folded in half. It's the birth announcement page. I feel the smile in my cheeks, imagining Mom at home with a baby like Gracie, proud to see a special name in the newspaper, her own daughter.

There's me, under the Memorial Hospital listings: Rebecca Cartwright, daughter Sarah Bethany Cartwright. No father listed, of course. I try to push the thought out of my head and turn back to the files. There's little else of interest.

Except ... wait. In a stack of receipts, I find one from a St. Thomas Hospital in Scottsboro, Alabama. The total, $1,899.35, is stamped PAID IN FULL. Too pricey to be anything other than inpatient. My mother's name is on here, a doctor's name is listed too. But the location doesn't jive.

Scottsboro? It's not where I grew up. I never knew she'd lived there.

Unless something had happened, some accident. Maybe it was something bad, something she never wanted to talk about. Maybe she'd been abused and she never wanted me to know. But I would have remembered. If I'd been anything older than a few years old, surely I'd have remembered a different house, or seeing my own mother hurt or sick.

I scan the page for the year. Up top, in the right-hand corner, is the date. The year was 1984, four years before I was born. I don't know what it means, but it's bizarre enough that I don't think I should ignore it. It may be my only clue to follow.

Scottsboro. I don't know anything about the town. I'd never been there, that I know of. I take one more look at the tax returns, digging back to the same year. The address it lists is 655 South Main Street, Apartment 4, Scottsboro, AL.

She *had* lived there. Why hadn't she ever mentioned it?

What the hell? The two years before that are from two different Tennessee towns. The knot that had been stuck in my throat sinks down low, into my gut. *No. No. No.* Bill's expression, guilty and evasive, pops into my head. He ran her off. Did he hurt her?

I didn't want things to line up this way. At least Bill was telling the truth about one thing. All of this is years before I was born. I load up the box, taking the plastic bag of personal notes, letters, and photographs – plus the old hospital receipt. Everything else goes back like it was.

Where do I go from here? I've only got one lead, and it's a real stab in the dark. But I can't think of any better course of action. The police had asked me not to leave town … but that was before Enid landed in the hot seat with the bottle of pills. Surely that directive from police wouldn't still stand? They'd only asked me, after all. No judge has said I'm not legally allowed to leave. For a half-second, I consider calling the police, just to be on the safe side. But I'm sure that would only raise suspicion. No. No one needs to know where I'm going. And if I hurry, maybe I can get there and back before anyone even notices I'm gone.

Besides, the way I see it, I don't have any other choice. I've looked in the last place I know of to find answers, and I've only found a few fragments, more missing pieces in a story that doesn't quite fit together.

I'll have to go south, to Scottsboro. Maybe my mother's real secrets are buried there.

34

NOW

M y hands are tight, white fists around the steering wheel.

I'm barely out of McMinnville and my imagination is getting the better of me. What if Bill hurt her? Physically? I've never thought of him as a violent person … but I know his ambition. He'd do anything to get ahead, to sweep away a problem. I wonder how far he'd go. Or maybe it was someone else. My mother never had much luck with men. *God, she deserved so much better than the life she lived.* I picture her leaving town, these same roads, turning onto I-24, wiping away the tears, leaving behind a life she might have loved. Was she on the run? Did someone chase her down? Did she get so ill she had to be hospitalized – and no one was around to take care of her?

The worst question, the anger I'm trying to diffuse, is why my mother would have kept this part of her life a secret from me. What would she have been afraid to tell me? What was she hiding from, or what was she shielding me from?

Boxed in between two mammoth trucks, I slam down hard on my horn in frustration. The truck beside me blares right back, probably three times louder. If we'd been anywhere close to an emergency pull-off I might have challenged him to a fistfight. I'm such a hot mess of anger, my mind in a whirl of dark thoughts. I can't imagine my mother holding her secrets inside, her hurt inside, from me. All those years.

The truck in front of me moves away and I press down hard on the gas. All I want to do is move, not think. But the gnawing idea won't go away. The prick of the reality that lies underneath the surface is that, of course, there's a parallel I can't ignore.

My mother and I weren't so different after all.

She had a secret life she kept hidden from the people she loved.

So do I. I bite my lip, wishing I could un-think it, just slip the thought back out to where it came from. But I know it's true. I ease up on the gas. The rage isn't going to get me anywhere. Today, I faced the box, my last piece of my mother. Now, I'm facing my own truth. Or, to be more frank, my own lies.

Everything Brad knows about my past is … fiction. I've always thought that he knows the real me, knows who I am now. That should be good enough. But I've always lived a lie, on some level. He thinks my mother died of cancer, that she was a model parent who helped guide me on the straight and narrow – through college, through the years of international travel and volunteer work I claimed to have enjoyed when the truth was … much uglier. I'd thought I could bury it, that it didn't matter. I've felt like I should tell Brad for a long time, but I didn't know how. I didn't want to see the disappointment on his face. I didn't want to watch him walk out the door the way so many men did to my mother, and to me. Especially not now, not with a baby and a family that was, until days ago, intact and mostly happy. My past doesn't match who I am now, that's true. But all of it – thinking about my mother's secret life and how she kept it from me – makes me wonder which version of ourselves is the real one.

Is my mother the manic depressive who can't bear to face her own life? Or is she the angel who helped instill in me my hard work ethic and drive to succeed, a woman taken from this earth too early, by cancer? Which story would *she* want?

Was I the troubled kid who couldn't seem to stay out of the principal's office, who no longer gave a fuck what happened to her? Or was I the ideal teenager whose only misstep was forgetting to get her homework finished one night of her senior year?

Was I the college kid who thought it would be exciting to date a guy who was dealing, the young woman who still didn't care how her life turned out? Or was I the studious college kid with her eyes trained steadfastly on a meaningful career?

Maybe everyone is a fraud on some level. We all have things we'd never like others to know about. What does the truth even mean, really, when we all tell the versions of our life? Maybe some people's versions are closer to reality than others, but looking back never tells the whole story. The dull stuff gets forgotten. The hard parts, unflattering parts get tucked away, shrouded by more attractive moments, the kind that make the best stories. Maybe I'm not so different from everyone else. But all of it has me wondering which me is the *real* me. Is it the version I lived, or the version I created? The stories we tell others or the stories we tell ourselves?

I go to pass another beast of a truck and when I turn to glance behind me, I catch a glimpse of the stump of Gracie's car seat, the plastic where her carrier should be. It's comforting, at least some tangible evidence of the life I have. A life that is real. I think of holding her, how I've missed her gentle baby smell, watching her fingers tangle into my hair, her gummy smile.

All the love I've felt, love I never understood before in all of my life, that's real. That's true.

And Brad. Despite how he treated me, despite what he thought and accused me of, I know he loves me. I think of our first few dates, his delight that I was willing to go and watch his old high school team play football. His pride at the life he'd lived, the victories he'd carried out right on that field. How could I tell him I had been, until the past few years, little more than one failure after another? I'd never want to take the sparkle out of those blue-gray eyes. I'd loved feeling like he was proud of me. I knew I wanted to be with him, from the moment I met him. I never wanted to take the chance of losing him over stupid mistakes that don't even represent who I am anymore.

And yet ... I know that I'll never be able to be close to him the way he's wanted when I don't know that he loves me. All of me. The mistakes. The pain. The heartbreak. He'll never know me until he knows those. I've had a chance at love ... and I may have lost it. I glance back one more time. The bottom of the car seat is still there, strapped in. Gracie's gone, separated from me.

I may have lost everything.

There's no way the St. Thomas has seen many updates since my mother was here. The décor is heavy on pinks and purples, light on subtlety. Oversized, cheap-looking prints of abstract flowers framed in white plastic line the hallways, coated in a threadbare layer of peach-tone discount carpet. In a triangular-shaped intake desk in front of a long row of windows, a heavyset woman is eating a late lunch, sneaking bites and tapping away at her computer, probably wishing away the hours. There aren't many others here. A glance at the signs behind her tell me which direction each of the departments lies. I don't know for sure what to ask for.

"Excuse me, ma'am."

She licks her lips and gives me the swiftest of glances to acknowledge my presence.

"You a visitor?" she asks, covering a mouthful of food with her hands. "Or you have an appointment?"

I shift on my feet, trying to shake some of the nervous energy away so my hands don't tremble and my voice doesn't betray me.

"Actually, I'm here because ... I need some records."

"Medical records?"

I nod, unsure of what other kind of records she'd be expecting me to ask about.

"Are they your own? We aren't permitted to release those without the right paperwork."

Not what I wanted to hear.

"They are my mother's." I clear my throat, rethinking. "They were my mothers. She died eighteen years ago."

The woman huffs as if to say this wasn't the kind of project she had the time to take care of today. She thinks a second, thrums her nails in a line on her desk. I pull the receipt out of my purse and lay it on the countertop. She looks at it, her brows knitted, a skeptical expression clouding her face.

"Give me her name and date of birth." She taps into her keyboard as I tell her. I can tell something's popped up on her screen. She's found something.

"Okay then. You have ID, right?"

"Driver's license okay?"

"Yes. You'll need that. I'll phone down to archives. It might take them a while. They have other things to take care of."

I take her irritation in my stride and move quietly down the hallway, following the directions she gave me, and soon I'm waiting in an uncomfortable chair while two women behind a half-wall of glass ignore me for a solid half hour. I thumb through my phone. Nothing new. No news.

I almost jump when the ringtone blares out while I'm holding it. One of the women behind the wall shoots me a dirty look like I'm disturbing her. I look at the number and try to think who it might be. It's a McMinnville number, but I don't recognize it. I almost let it go to voicemail, but then think better of it.

Big mistake.

"Miss Cartwright?"

I'd recognize that particular mix of condescension and disdain anywhere. Martinez.

Shit. I shouldn't have answered the phone at all.

"We're here at your office now, but we've been told you left work again today. Could you please let us know where you might have gone this time?"

"I did leave early. It's been a hard few days." Shit. Where do I tell him I am? Why would they be trying to reach me? "Is there something new? Is there something wrong?"

"Actually, the answer to both those questions is yes."

A twist of panic turns in my stomach.

"Brad is okay, right?" I ask, afraid of the answer.

"As far as we know. I haven't been told otherwise."

"Is this about the incident with my daughter yesterday?" My breath is short in my chest. I'm trying to keep it together, but his evasiveness isn't helping at all.

"What incident is that?" he asks, his voice rising in curiosity.

I am so botching this. Did someone tell them I was leaving town? I didn't tell anyone myself, unless someone saw me get onto the inter-state or, I guess, if I were being followed someone would know.

"Um, nothing. I tried to pick up my daughter yesterday, but my sister-in-law is pretty upset with me –"

"Hmm."

"– she didn't let me have Gracie. I didn't want to cause a scene." I try to stop the little white lie, but it's already come out of my mouth. "Anyway, I left her there, for now."

"And where did you go? Where are you now? I'm calling because we need to talk to you, in person. There's been a new development in the attempted murder case. It seems that Enid Forrest's fingerprints weren't on the pill bottle *supposedly* found in her bag when you called the police. They weren't on the takeout box we found at your home either."

I don't miss his emphasis on the word *supposedly*.

"What?" I try to figure out what he's trying to tell me. That was a problem I might have anticipated, but hadn't. Only a few passing thoughts of my friend who seems, more and more, to have been a victim of framing. Of course, that means the police are back to suspect No. 1. And I look like I'm on the run. How can I tell them where I really am? What I'm really doing?

"Unfortunately, this creates another problem for us ... and potentially for you," he says, breaking into my train of thought. "We'll need to speak with you again as soon as possible." He leaves a moment of silence, letting me squirm. I'm trying not to take the bait, trying to think on my feet.

"I understand," I answer quietly.

"So could you be here within the hour?" he says. "We could also meet you at your home."

"Um." I run the calculation in my head, with a glance over at the women moving around leisurely in the archive room. "I could be there by late afternoon, maybe early evening? I actually ... had to leave town." Shit. "Not far," I add, knowing my voice sounds more nervous than it should.

"Left town? You haven't left the state, have you, Miss Cartwright?" he asks, pointedly. "I thought we'd talked about that."

"No, no," I lie. "I just needed to spend some time alone. Away from the office. My house was such a mess, I can't bear to see it, to think about everything that's happened. Kind of just started driving and, well, now I'm walking around a park in Nashville. I needed space to think."

273

Without a hint of compassion, he answers: "Be here by seven, at the very latest." He hangs up before I can, and I let my head fall back against the blank wall behind me. Numbly, I stare at the shapes in the popcorn ceiling above, trying to think about who could possibly have put me in this position. I don't want to think it, but I've a feeling the police are right. It's not Enid. Right now, that leaves just one alternate possibility. There's another woman who, in retrospect, seemed all too willing to step into my life. Maybe someone who knows a lot more about me than she's letting on.

"Ma'am?" Then the sound comes louder. "Ma'am? Miss Cartwright?"

The woman's voice jolts me back to reality. I rise to my feet, more than a little disoriented.

"We've got your paperwork." She looks irritated, bending her head to face the slits in the vent that allows communication between outside and inside the archive office. I watch her slide a manila envelope in the letter-sized space under a small gap between the glass and a counter-top. I take in a shaky breath. I need to hurry. On top of everything else I have to figure out, the police are on my trail again. I glance at a clock on the back wall. It's almost five. To get to the station by seven and avoid raising Martinez' hackles even more, I only have two hours to get back into my car for the hour-and-forty-minute race back to McMinnville. I've already decided there's someone else I need to confront before I speak a word to police.

"We didn't have much in here," the lady announces, nonchalant, through the glass. "We checked as far back as we could. Only a couple hospitalizations."

I reach for the paperwork and give her a quizzical look. "Two hospital stays?"

"Well, three, I think. One was pneumonia, poor dear. Then, of course, the two births."

"What?" I must have heard her wrong. That or the depth of everything

I didn't know was far worse than I could have imagined. "I'm so sorry. Um, you said *two* births?"

35

NOW

The archive worker woman looks up at me, a little surprised, or maybe annoyed, at my reaction.

"Well, yes, ma'am. Just the births and the pneumonia."

Births.

Plural.

A sibling … I had a brother or sister. I reel backwards in shock, not picking up the paperwork.

"Are you alright?" I hear a voice call out. It sounds distant. The room is moving in waves around me. I've lost touch with where I am. "Ma'am, are you okay?" A pause. "Ma'am?"

I want to tell her *no, I'm not.* Not in any way am I alright. I didn't know my mother had a love affair with my current boss. I didn't know I had, or have, a sibling. I grew up an only child. That's who I am. That's who I thought I was. I reach out for the envelope, thank her with a head nod because I can't find a single word in my mouth, and step out into the hallway, panting, sweat beading at the nape of my neck, nausea spreading through the pit of my stomach.

I have to wait until I'm sitting down to look inside. I'm in my car, still feeling dizzy enough to almost vomit, afraid of what I'm about to see. I don't have time to waste. I need to be turning back onto the highway out of Scottsboro within minutes if I'm going to stick to the plan. I have just minutes to find out the truth and then somehow pull myself back together. I consider, for a split second, not opening it. Then I think of the box of my mother's belongings, the pain I created by waiting too long. By avoiding what I should have done long ago. I have to stop delaying.

I slide the papers out and spread them on my lap. The woman wasn't lying. Here, in front of me, side by side, are two birth records. Two healthy babies. Live birth records. Females. The one on the left, though, is from 1984. The same date as the receipt stamped PAID IN FULL.

I scan for details and find a name. I look twice. Three times.

It can't be. This can't be right. It can't be possible.

The girl, my mother's first daughter – a person I never knew existed until this moment – shares something with me, besides a birth mother.

What the fuck?

She has the exact same name as me.

Sarah Cartwright.

I blink hard. But when I look again, I know I'm seeing it right. It's true. It's right here in front of me, in black and white. My mother named her first daughter Sarah too. No middle name listed. On the right, there's me, four years later: Sarah Bethany Cartwright.

This is *crazy*. It's so beyond unbelievable I can't seem to wrap my brain around it.

Who does that? Who does any of this? First of all, have a child and never mention her? What even happened to her? Why would she give both of us the same first name?

I scan the page again. Later, the doctor's notes tell the rest of the story. This baby girl was given up for adoption. There's a case ID number and a phone number for an Alabama adoption agency that must have processed everything.

Not only am I not my mother's first daughter ... I'm not even the first Sarah Cartwright. My mother named me after her first child. Who would even think of doing something like this? How can this be real? I think of all the days my mother was heartsick, meandering around the house in her pajamas at four when I got off the school bus – or sometimes not even acknowledging me when I walked in. I remember wanting to shake answers out of her, to know why she was so sad, to know why I wasn't enough. All those years of counseling, starting when I was a preteen, I'd learned not to blame myself. But it *was* me. It was me after all, who broke her heart. Every time she looked at me, she must have seen Sarah. The other Sarah. The first one.

Oh my god.

I always wondered what made her so broken. That's why I freaked out about the Bill idea. I thought maybe she'd had her pushed away, crushed her dreams, rejected her love.

Yes, she was heartbroken.

But it wasn't over a man. It was a child she lost, a little girl she'd given up ... and then replaced. I look up at the row of pines in front of me, not seeing anything other than my mother in my mind. I'd witnessed her devastation, but I'd never understood why. I almost wish I didn't know now.

What was I to her? Did I remind her of the child she wished she still had? Was I a picture of some other, first daughter? I chew on my lip, feeling the sting of tears at the edges of my eyes. This is worse than I ever could have imagined. Earlier today, I'd thought facing the truth would feel liberating. This is a whole new burden of knowing, a kind of pain I never wanted to feel.

I rev the engine. The clock is ticking. I have to get back. I have to fix things. I'll have to fight for the life I created, no matter where I might have come from. I might not have a past – or my past might be one that even I don't recognize – but maybe if I can keep myself together, I might still have a shot at a future.

That's a big fat *if.*

I'm so pissed, so utterly turned inside out, that I make the hour-and-forty-minute drive a full twenty minutes early. I can hardly remember the drive. I need to get out of this car. I need to stop thinking. I need to find answers. And I can't go head-to-head with Martinez until I find them … or it's me they'll hang.

I glance at the clock. I have thirty-seven minutes before Martinez will be hunting me down. Time for another chat with Bill. He'd better be ready to talk, and fast. Beyond the shock of what I found out today, there's still the matter of the police, of clearing my name, of getting to be with Gracie again, of showing Brad I love him and telling him the truth.

I have to hurry.

If I don't get to the bottom of all of this now, I lose everything.

36

NOW

"**W**here is he?" I storm into the headquarters office with my mind on the mission.

Our office manager, Mary Beth, whirls her wide frame around from a box she's loading up, startled by the after-hours intrusion. To my relief, it looks like most everyone else has already cleared out for the day. I don't know how I'll respond if I run into Janette. I'm holding out hope that she's made good on her promise to rush home as soon as possible.

Mary Beth mumbles a question back to me, but I don't wait around. I make a beeline past her for the back office, steady strong strides directly to the candidate's door. The light's still on. I don't bother with knocking.

Bill's in a similar position as Mary Beth, his briefcase on his oversized leather office chair. He's sliding in a tablet and some paperwork when he turns around casually, probably expecting an evening sign-off from some member of his staff. He's got something entirely different coming.

"Sarah." His greeting is a question.

I don't beat around the bush.

"I know about the baby," I say, firm. What I don't know, for sure, is whether it was his baby, the girl my mother had in Scottsboro. But it's a fair guess.

"What?" The stack of papers in his hands drops to the desk. "Sarah, I think you've had a long day."

"Damn right I have." To hell and back, it feels like.

"What's this all about?" He puts his hands up, innocently. He tries for a note of compassion, a softer tone. "Is there some way I can help you?"

I won't be played that way.

"You can help me by telling me what you know about the baby. The daughter you and my mother had. The child born from your affair." I stress the last word. Not an accusation. A cold, hard fact.

He leans back on the balls of his feet, runs his hands through his hair, calculating what to say next, how much to give away. That's when I know it's true.

"I knew about the pregnancy," he says, with reluctance.

"You mean the baby." I give an icy stare. He doesn't melt beneath it.

"There was no baby." He matches me. Cool and calm. "She didn't go through with it."

"You're lying."

"Alright." He throws his hands out to his sides. "I'll bite. Exactly what is it that you know that I don't?" He glances at the clock. "You'd better make this fast, though. I have somewhere to be."

Perfect. Me too.

I step up to the desk and drop my bag on the scattered papers over the wide desktop. Inside, I pull out the manila envelope and slide out the paperwork I'd kept on top.

Irritated, he pulls out his glasses case from his own bag and slides the wire frames up the bridge of his nose. He snatches the papers from my hands and holds them up right in front of his eyes, as though to humor me, an unpleasant interruption.

But as he reads, his face changes. I watch him go from the text, up to the date, then back down to the notes again. Confusion clouds his expression.

"This is you?" he asks. "Sarah Cartwright?"

"It looks like that, but actually, no. It's from four years before I was born. It's from the years when you and my mother were … involved." I bite down hard on my bottom lip, daring him to try explaining this away. There's no way he can deny this.

"Well, there's no father listed." he says, at last, clearing his throat.

"Come on, Bill." I answer, clicking my tongue against the roof of my mouth. "You just admitted there was a pregnancy. You're right. There was. There was also a baby, a little girl."

He shakes his head and lets the papers drop, softer than his previous angry demonstration. He's taken aback a little bit, I can tell. He wasn't prepared for this realization.

"She – she, um, was pregnant, yes." he mutters, then pulls one hand up to his mouth to consider.

I let him mull it over. In the silence, I can almost imagine the wheels spinning in his mind. He knows. He has to know it's true.

"Where did you get these?" he asks, finally, still a note of denial in his mind. Not directly aimed at me.

"St. Thomas. Scottsboro."

"In person? They're real?"

"Yup. Picked them up today."

He breathes out a string of curses.

"Honestly, Sarah, I had no idea," he looks at me, solemn. "I knew

Rebecca was pregnant. She told me. I told her we couldn't have this child. It wouldn't be fair. Not to her. Not to the baby. Not to any of us."

I try not to roll my eyes at his show of magnanimous explanations. *As if he actually gave a shit about what happened to my mother. He ran her off. Swept her under the rug.*

He continues: "I – I told her I'd take care of the arrangements. When she left town – when I didn't hear from her again, I assumed she'd gone ahead with it. I thought she'd had an abortion. I was sad, of course. I cared for your mother, but I assumed she'd decided to move ahead with her own life. I had no idea, Sarah. Truly. I didn't know there was a baby. I never heard another word from her. She never asked for help, no support. There's no way I would have known." Another thought strikes him. He reaches for the paperwork, but I already have his answer.

"My mom gave the baby up for adoption. A healthy birth, a little girl, and then she went to the state. I haven't been able to track down, yet, where she might have gone from there." That's the explanation I give Bill. I don't know exactly where she went from there, but I may know where she ended up. I might have spent the night with her, my half-sister, last night.

"Adopted." Bill chews over the word for a moment and then lets out a long sigh. "Well, I guess I know now. A little late for me to do anything about it. She'd be, what? Mid-thirties by now." He shoves his hands in his pockets, something I've never seen him do before. Then looks up at me, still waiting.

"So … why now? Why burst in here and confront me with this? I can hardly see how I can do any good to drag this up. Unless you just needed to know. I could understand that." He looks like he's still taking it all in himself.

I move around the desk, closer to him, and cross my arms, holding them close to my chest protectively. "Here's the thing, Bill. We know this is not me. We also know someone's been after me and my family.

It wasn't Enid. I've talked to the police. It looks more and more like the poison was planted. Enid was framed."

His face wrinkles in confusion.

"Okay ... so?" He shrugs helplessly. "So what does any of that mean? What does that have to do with all this? Your past? Your mother's past?"

"So the person who wants to hurt me – and wants it so bad they'll hurt you in the process – is still out there, waiting for another opportunity."

He nods in reluctant, but helpless, agreement.

"Think about it, Bill."

A rap at the door makes us both jump. Mary Beth pops only her round head in, her cheeks flushed, brows knit in concern. "Everything okay?"

Bill's skin is a sick gray tone, his expression overcast.

"We're fine, Mary Beth," he says, curt. "You can go home."

She looks a little stung, but nods and closes the door again behind her.

"So?" I want to snap my fingers in front of his face. *Stay with me, Bill.*

"So ... " he fishes around, "obviously you think it's someone else. You think this sister you didn't know about is the one who's after you? Is that why you're here?"

I try to clear the frustration from my chest, ready to start in on what I'm really going for. What I have to know, right now.

"I'm here to ask you about Janette."

He arches a brow, listening.

"I stayed with her last night, ended up – I lost my phone and had to go looking for it. And I came across something ... unnerving."

"Okay ..."

"It was a scrapbook of hers. Except, instead of photos of her own past, it was photos of mine."

"Did you know her before?"

"No." I almost shout it. "I need you to follow me. I never saw her until the day I came back to work, after Gracie. But she's sure as hell seen me. Or been waiting to. She had pictures of me, pictures of my mother, newspaper clippings."

"The picture you brought in earlier today?" His jaw drops. "Was that where you found it?"

"Yeah. You and my mom, an old campaign rally of yours. And she had plenty of other clippings of your political career."

Bill steps back, away from me. Suddenly, it's become personal to him.

"Why in the world?" he says. "Why would she care? Why would she have those?"

"That's what I'm trying to figure out," I answer. "I was hoping you could tell me."

He shakes his head, helplessly.

"I don't know her either. Never, until we got into a pinch while you were away. She was just the best of the resume stack. Actually, the reason she caught my eye was because her credentials were similar to yours. I don't know any more than you do, right now."

"I think, for both of us, we need to figure it the hell out. Don't you?"

He turns, paces, absorbing, denying.

"You don't think ...."

"She's my sister?" I fill in for him. "Your daughter?"

The last question jabs him. He stops, dead, in his tracks. His head shakes vehemently. It's a thought he can't accept.

"No way." His voice is firm. "There's just no way."

"The dates match." I make my mouth into a hard line, watching his every move. "Did you run a background check?"

Bill is over his computer, firing it back up. He ticks away, his face a frown, and then looks up at me.

"We did," he says. "Standard background and credit check. No red flags. Nothing." He moves his fingers over the mousepad. "Hold on."

He turns the laptop toward me so I can see her resume, and then scrolls down.

"No AKA. Her name is Janette. The hospital records show the baby was named Sarah," he stops to consider. "That's a little weird, too. Maybe there's some mix-up. Maybe you've got this wrong somehow."

"I don't think so," I say, feeling the heavy weight of what it could mean. My mother had lived with regret, so much so that she tried a do-over. "It's all real. I picked it up from the hospital's archive myself. Two birth records. Mine and an earlier birth. Another Sarah. The first one."

"Who you now think is Janette."

"Who else could it be?" I answer, frustrated. "Why would she have photos of me and my mom? Of you?"

I swallow.

"I don't have any other explanation, as much as I don't like it," I say, softer.

Like Bill, I wish I could rationalize all this away as a mix-up or a misunderstanding. But we both know it's real. It has to be. If Enid wasn't the one on my trail … it leaves the only other person close to me, close enough to pose as a new friend, a long-lost sister. I think of the trail of bodies and misery … how much of that could have been her doing.

A shudder creeps up through my spine. I can't stand here, thinking about this, any longer.

Bill looks at me with fresh panic.

"What – so what are you going to do about all of this? How do we stop her, if it is her?"

"I'm still working on that." I gather the papers quickly, before Bill can decide to try to destroy the evidence. "I've promised the police I'll talk with them. And I have to. They think I tried to kill Brad, remember?"

"Do what you need to do, Sarah," he says. "I'm sorry about all this. I really am. Let me know if I can help in some way."

"I'm sorry too," I answer, honestly.

I'm nearly to the door when he stops me. He rushes over.

"Hey, I understand you'll have to work with the police on clearing your name," he pauses to press his fingers to his temples and then clears his throat. "But there's no reason to bring up … the past. Or at least my involvement in it. You can tell them what you discovered about a sister you never knew, who's now interfering in your life, but I can't see a reason to bring up –"

"The father?" I interject, pointedly.

His face goes ghost white.

"Right now, that's the least of my worries," I answer, shutting the door hard behind me. Even if he genuinely didn't know about his daughter, his selfish ways contributed to my mother's lifetime of pain. I know that for sure. He deserves whatever happens to him. Right now, I have to worry about me, my life, the man I love, our baby. I sprint to my car and check the time. I've got one more stop – one that will make or break my entire future – and the minutes are ticking down. Martinez will be waiting, itching to make an arrest.

When I get there, the lights are on. I don't have time to sit and think about how this will work. I can't waste a second. It's now or never.

37

NOW

My hands are trembling, palms and fingers so sweaty I can hardly navigate around my phone. I steady my breathing and make the call, watching a head-and-shoulders shadow wandering through the kitchen like a specter. The ghost of all my tragedies.

This is going to take some explaining.

Janette meets me at her door like a mother waiting up for her teenage daughter.

"I was so worried." Her voice sounds angry, but she wraps her arms around me and holds me in a tight embrace. I hug her just enough to not raise suspicion. Not yet.

"Thank you," I answer. "I'm okay."

"Where in the world have you been? Did you go see Gracie?"

I pull in a deep breath, trying to stay strong, doing everything I can to stick to the plan.

Janette doesn't wait for my answer before she peppers me with more questions. "Did you talk to Brad's mom? Have you heard anything about him? Is he really trying to keep you away from the baby?"

I nod, if only to buy myself a moment of peace as I make my way to the small plastic table in her kitchenette. I don't sit.

"Oh my god, Sarah," she says, chiding. "I knew it. He's bad news. Who would do that? He's keeping you away from your own child. He can't, surely, blame you? Not with what we know about Enid now."

Maybe that's my window.

"Actually," I say, setting my leather handbag into the chair she's pulled out in front of me, "Enid is no longer a suspect. The police called to tell me that today."

Her brows snap together and fear dances across her eyes at the word: police.

"Well, what – what did they say?" I watch her try to cool her reaction, pretend she's not as worried as she is. She forces her shoulders back into a posture that looks more relaxed.

"They said they confirmed, with multiple sources, Enid's alibi for the night," I answer, straightforward, watching her body for her next reaction. I see the breath rise tight in her chest.

"Where did she say she was? Who confirmed it?"

"I don't know, Janette. They only called to tell me that … and also that they need to speak with me again. With Enid out of the picture, I'm back to being, I guess, the prime suspect."

Her shoulders droop completely and she reaches out to hug me again. "I'm sorry. That's terrible. We will figure all of this out."

This time, I don't hug her back. I stay stiff – and she notices.

"What's wrong?" She steps back, both hands on my shoulders. I shrug them off, easing out of her grasp. Maybe the kitchenette isn't the right place for this. What if she snaps completely?

"We need to talk." I keep my eyes on her, watching for any sudden movement.

"What is it? Anything you need, Sarah, I'm here for you. I'll protect you. We can take care of all of this."

That's what I'm afraid of, Janette. You taking care of things for me.

I swallow back my frustration, my fear. I could be wrong still … but after my encounter with Bill, I know there's something to what I've uncovered. I have to keep pushing. I have to do this. Even if my suspicions are true, though, it would still make her … my sister. I'm in a difficult position, no matter how this pans out.

"You've been so good to me," I say, carefully choosing each word. "You've encouraged me, looked out for me, tried to help me every way you possibly can."

"It's because I care about you, Sarah."

I nod, slowly.

"You've been the sister I never knew I needed."

Janette's hands rise immediately to cover her mouth. A flicker of hope or fear – I can't tell which – makes her eyes wide, tears glistening and ready to fall. It's time. She needs to know what I've discovered.

I hand her the envelope and wait.

She turns it in her hands, uncertain. I don't answer her questions. When she slides the papers out, her expression sobers entirely. She leans sideways against the counter near her for support. She knows I know.

Her eyes lift from the paper, her birth records, to me, tentative. Her lips part, but no sound comes out.

"You are my older sister," I whisper. "I found out today."

Her eyes search me for how I'll take this, how I feel, what I think about her. I give her a smile and reach out my arms to her. Whatever else, whatever broken life she's lived, we share some of the same heartache. She collapses into me. I feel her body shake, her sobs releasing. I let her go, and she wipes her palms over her face.

"I – I didn't want it to happen this way. I wanted to tell you. So many times I wanted to …" Her breath catches in her throat.

I have so many questions, ones I'd ask no matter what. Others I have to know the answers to. I hardly know where to start. She said there were so many times she wanted to tell me. How long has she known? How long has she been watching over me? Why jump into my life now?

"Come on." Janette grabs a tissue in one hand and loops her other through my arm. "I've waited so long to talk to you. Let's sit down."

I let her lead me the few steps to the couch where I slept last night, wondering how this will play out. Unsure, still, how I feel. Betrayed? Afraid, for certain. But I can't help but second-guess all my moves. I am with my sister, a sister who found me … who obviously worked very hard to find me. It's hard to piece together all the different feelings, but the one that stands out is uncertainty. If she's my sister, and she loves me, why would she ever put me in this position? I can't help but to stay guarded, no matter what she's about to tell me.

"I'm sure you wonder how I found you." She sits down close to me and pulls her legs up beneath her, getting comfortable, maybe expecting an inquisition. For now, I'll just let her talk. These may be the only moments we'll have this close together.

"I found you years ago," she says, in a whisper, "I was always afraid to introduce myself. But I've watched and waited for my moment. I – I have tried to look out for you since you were a little girl." She smiles and I know her mind is flitting to some distant place. "I've always hoped to be able to be some kind of – I don't know what you'd call it. Maybe a guardian angel."

The certainty in her voice tells me she's knows exactly what she'd call it. She must have thought it a thousand times.

"I see myself as your guardian angel." She repeats it, a lopsided smile stretching across her face.

My skin tingles and I feel the hair on the back of my neck stand straight out. I want to wriggle back a few inches, or run, if I thought I could get away with it. I don't know that I'm ready to hear what she's about to confess. How much of my life is a result of her? How much of her is me? How long has she been the guardian angel lurking in the shadows of my worst moments?

What has she done?

I resist the urge to race for the door or reach for my phone or cry out in panic. After the lengths she's gone to to get me here ... I don't know whether I'd make it out alive. Like my sister is reading my mind, she suddenly reaches a strong arm around my back, unable to contain an exclamation.

"Now that I've found you, Sarah," she says, squeezing my neck against hers so tightly it feels like I might choke, "I'm not ever letting you go."

38

JANETTE NOW

All this time I've been chasing her – and now she's the one who found me. She's figured out that she had a sister, though I'm sure she knew all along that some piece of her was missing. I *know* she felt the connection between us. It might take a while for it to make sense, but it will all come together for her. Sarah, my little sister – the girl who needed me – is right here, beside me, on the couch. We can finally, finally be a family now. It's my dream. It's all I ever wanted my whole life.

I just have to prove it to her.

I hope she'll understand.

There were casualties, and it wasn't easy, but it was all because I love her. Everything I've done is because I love her, and I love our mother. I'll never be alone in that heartache ever again. She's the only one in the world who can understand that part of me.

"You can't imagine how much I've wanted to talk to you," I say, releasing her from my embrace and sinking into the couch. She seems reluctant to let me go. It's such a relief to be able to be who I am, to not have to hide anymore. After years of waiting to act, here we are. Sarah was always the doer, the one to take action instead of watch and wait.

But Sarah doesn't lean back against the cushions. She's tense. I'm sure she doesn't understand yet. I'd have questions, too. Or maybe it's all still sinking in. I'm sure some things from her past are just starting to make more sense. I'll have to help her see it my way.

"When did you find me?" Sarah's eyes are anxious, doe-like and nervous, an expression that reminds me of our mother. It's not typical Sarah, but this is not a typical day. This is everything we've both been waiting for.

"Well," I answer, "It sure wasn't easy. I had to save a bunch of money, sneak out –"

"You were a kid?"

"Yeah, mostly. Or a teenager." I don't really want to remember the time – the life I had before Sarah and Mom – but now I have someone to listen, someone to care. "I had a shit childhood, as you might imagine."

Her eyes are blank.

"My adopted family – they were assholes. Especially the guy who was supposed to be my father. I know it sucks growing up without a dad. I know you know that, but there are worse things. I'll leave it at that. He's lucky I ran away. I don't know how much longer I could handle his ..." I think about calling it *bullshit* but then I remember I'm with someone I can trust, someone who loves me. I don't have to be ashamed. I don't have to dance around what I mean. I can tell the complete truth. "I couldn't take his abuse anymore."

Sarah looks at her hands, shakes her head sorrowfully.

"I'm so sorry." She whispers it. I feel the tears well up again in my eyes.

My sister. My soulmate. I've got someone in my corner now, for life.

"Thanks." I reach for her hand. She waits a second, gives it a squeeze, and then lets go. I wish she hadn't.

"Anyway, so the point is I got away from that. It's in the past. It's over." I breathe in, the whirlwind of those first few days on my own, the realization that I was going to be okay, that I could manage to forge my own way. It was liberation. "I found our mom. I moved to the same town where you two were and found a job."

"You talked to Mom?"

I feel the shame stinging in my cheeks, the regret stirring up in my chest.

"No. I didn't have the balls." Tears threaten to stop me again. I pause a moment, letting it pass. "I wanted to, but I never found the right moment. I lost my chance."

Silence, comforting, settles around us – a moment of understanding. She knows how much I hurt.

"At first, I was mad. I was so pissed. You can imagine, I wanted to know *why*. Why would anyone give up their child? Think of Gracie, the way you feel when you're with her. I've seen you with her. You'd never in a million years just give her up to someone you don't know, someone who won't ever probably love her like you would. You'd never know if she's okay. Even if you went crazy for a while, got scared about whether you could take care of your kid, wouldn't you come looking for her? Wouldn't you miss her?"

Sarah's nodding, listening. She gets where I'm coming from.

"Then, when I found out she had another daughter," I pause, watching her eyes scanning my face and unsure what I'm reading in her eyes, "I was even more mad. She even named you … the same as me."

It's so quiet I can hear Sarah swallow. When she speaks, her voice is small, raw with pain: "I thought the same thing. It's hard to … fathom."

"Yeah. It was like she just replaced me." I stop to stare up at the ceiling. It hurts more than I thought it would to say this all out loud. "But then … you know, I forgave her. A long time ago, I came to terms with it. The love was stronger than the anger. Besides all that, our mom –

she gave me *you*. I can always love her for that. And I can't be jealous of you in that way. You know, she abandoned you too." The last line slips out of my mouth and I instantly wish I could take it back. That maybe came across as cruel. That would hurt. But, the thing is, it's true. Now we can hurt together. I'm not alone in the pain anymore.

Sarah doesn't answer. Her expression dulls, her mouth drops open.

It is a lot to take. I expect her to ask me what next, what happened from there, but she goes somewhere else instead. She fast-forwards right ahead.

"So why are you here now? You waited so long, why step into my life … now?" There's that timid, tentative doe face again. I'm really going to have to piece all of this together for her, spell it all out, line by line. I'd rather just skip to the good parts, start building our new life together now that we've found one another.

She doesn't let me. She wants to dredge up all the dirt. I can feel the rage stirring up inside me. Where's her gratitude? She has no idea what I've been through, all for her. I have to explain everything, I guess.

"Charles. You knew he was a problem for me." She stands up like she's afraid I might hurt her. She knows I'd never do that. She has to.

"He had those pictures," I answer, defensively. "He *embarrassed* you."

"Is he one of the problems you took care of for me? Did you step in as my guardian angel there? Did you kill him?"

"I – I –"

"Lug nuts. He died the same way my mom's boyfriend did." She's accusing me, when she doesn't know anything.

"He was molesting you. I'm not going to stand back and watch someone hurt my sister. He needed to be … out of the way, for good."

"What?" Sarah's face twists. She moves farther back.

"You said he was gross. You said he put his hands all over you. *You* said that. Not me. You know you wanted him gone too."

Sarah's lips pinch together like she's about to ask me when. She utters the smallest sound, then stops herself, shaking her head.

"You told me that yourself."

"When did I say that?" She's shaking her head. "When did you talk to me?"

I can't believe it's not registering. I'm going to have to spell this out for her.

"The girl in the grocery store?" I prod. "You dropped all that cereal on the floor."

Her head is still shaking a moment, then she meets my gaze with a knowing look.

"In Alabama? When I was a kid?"

"Yes." I smile, letting out a breath of relief, waiting to see her reaction. She still looks stunned. "Remember, you told me your mom's boyfriend was gross. That he let his hands go wherever he wanted?"

"On my mom," she says, too loud. She's arguing with me. "He kissed and touched my mom right in front of me. I didn't like that and I didn't really like him, but … I'd never say he was hurting me, or molesting me. He wasn't."

Now I feel like the asshole. Well, forgive a girl for knowing nothing anything about men other than abuse. She can hardly blame me for that. I was trying to help her. I was trying to protect her from going through what I went through.

"Well, I guess it's behind us. I'm sure he wasn't what our mother deserved. She deserved so much better. She could have done so much better." I rationalize it aloud. "If she hadn't given up, things could have been different. But we had to make the best of what we had. You always did. I'm proud of you."

She doesn't smile or relax the way I'd thought she would. I would kill to have someone tell me they are proud of me. She doesn't know how good she's had it. I don't even know that she sees how good she has it right now.

"And Charles," I keep on with my explanation, "he was playing dirty. He was trying to hurt you. And it wasn't the first time."

"What?" Sarah asks through gritted teeth. She's really trying my patience.

"The last campaign where he was on the other side … I know his tactics. I know, once he got started, he wouldn't stop until he'd crushed you completely. I won't let him hurt you. I won't let him take away something you love. I *know* exactly how hard you worked for your career. I know how much it matters to you."

"So you killed him."

I really wish she'd sit back down on the couch, let us talk this out like normal people. Like sisters.

"I did it for you. He'll never hurt you again, Sarah."

Sarah's staring at the carpet, something else gnawing at her.

"It didn't just hurt me."

"You're figuring it out." I try not to insert a note of condescension, but, god, she's slow tonight. "Bill's my biological father."

"You nearly wrecked his campaign … killed two birds …" Sarah really looks like she needs to sit down, or she might fall down. I pat the space beside me, but she doesn't move. She's frozen in place.

"Bill deserves it. You know Mom never recovered."

"What about Enid? Another casualty? She could have gone to jail."

She's making this so hard.

"She's a sycophant. She doesn't care about you. She just likes the perks of being around you. She'd have turned on you in a hot second. You know that. In fact, maybe we can figure out a way to straighten out the parts that came undone. Enid takes the fall. Brad is out of the picture, or will be soon, and your life – our life – can come together neat and tidy."

"What do you have against Brad? Why would you hurt him?"

I can't understand why she's having such a hard time seeing how much I love her.

"Brad was in the way," I explain, trying not to sound condescending. "He kept you from what you really need. I wanted things to be the way they are supposed to be. Brad lived; he'll go on with his life. We'll figure out a way to get Gracie back and start over. Two sisters in this together"

Sarah's face contorts in horror.

"I'll make sure you get Gracie."

"I'm sure you would do everything you could," she says, curt. "I'm certain of that."

She's back to being the snotty teen I remember, treating me the way she talked back to our mother. I guess that's natural. The older sister becomes the mother figure when the mother's not around. This will all work out. She'll simmer down. She'll see things my way. This really, really isn't the way I'd imagined all of this happening, but at least it's happened. This is the hardest part. We got it over with. The rest will snap together, just right. Sarah's in the same place, not moving. Probably shocked to her core. I rise and take a few steps. She meets my eyes. I see love there, sisterly love.

Then I feel it in her embrace. A joy fills my heart, a longing finally answered. A lifetime of waiting and now what I wished for is real.

I let her go, see the tears glistening in her eyes. My sister. *You're here.*

I breathe out and try to straighten my thoughts. There's plenty of work to do.

"I'm always going to look out for you," I promise her. "For now, we just need to get Gracie, find a way to iron out things with the police and your sister-in-law. I don't like her, either, by the way."

I start to hatch a plan, but the sound of sirens stops me dead.

The police are here.

How?

Why?

Sarah avoids my eyes. *No. No. Tell me you didn't.* But she won't look at me. I glance over to the tabletop, see the papers she'd handed me, her phone sitting right next to them. I don't even have to ask. Sarah finally looks up at me, and she knows I know. She called the police. She betrayed me, my own little sister.

"I'm sorry." Her voice is hoarse. Her eyes swim in tears ready to fall.

How could she do this?

Everything I'd hoped for, worked for, lived for … at least I'd had it for a moment. I feel like someone's just knocked all the air out of my lungs or hollowed out my insides, but I manage to tell her what I feel. I know she felt it too; she's just backed into a corner. She did what she thought she had to do to get out of it. I understand her. I'll never not love her. And I don't want her to live with the guilt.

"I love you, Sarah." It's the only thing I know for sure, a sister's love. "It's okay. I-I forgive you."

39

NOW

J anette doesn't flinch when the shouts start.

"Police! Open the door."

I know it's probably our last few seconds together before the madness that will follow: jail time, trial, more jail time. I'll never have this moment again.

"Police! Open up!"

"I mean it," I tell her, panicked suddenly at the lost opportunities, the way it all had exploded in her face. "I'm sorry. Not just about this. About everything. I really am. I wish it had been different." For a split second, I wonder whether it's too late to unravel all the damage. Did I do the wrong thing? What else was I supposed to do?

Bang. Bang. Bang.

They'll crash through if we don't move now.

Janette's head drops, eyes on the floor. She makes the smallest nod and then moves toward the door in surrender. Even though she's completely compliant, Martinez and Adams make quick work of the arrest they've been working so hard to pin on me. Without moving from the doorway, they read Janette her rights, Martinez with the handcuffs, clicking as fast as he can, like she might dash out the door at any second or turn around swinging. Her body is limp, not fighting back in any way at all. She's charged with attempted murder and is a suspect in at least one other case. Martinez adds that last, unnecessary bit with a satisfied smirk.

Adams turns to me with a brief explanation: "Your story checked. Her prints were a match." I wince, wishing he hadn't reinforced the betrayal I know Janette feels right now in every fiber of her being. He didn't have to tell me that right in front of her.

Martinez licks his lips and then scowls in my direction, disappointed, I'm sure, that the lead they'd been chasing for days – me – hadn't quite panned out. His glare is a threat. *I'll be watching you.*

But they can look all they want. I've got nothing to hide anymore. Or, after today, I'll have nothing left to hide. I know exactly what I have to do.

They march Janette outside like a prisoner and I watch them dip her head down to load her into the backseat, willing them to be gentle. The last thing I see of the police cruiser is Janette's face, forlorn, peering out the side window in the back. I try to catch her eye, try to mouth *I'm sorry* once more, but I'm not sure if it registers. Her expression doesn't change. The sirens are off, but the lights are still glowing, casting blue and red in every direction, flashing their victory as they spin through the neighborhood.

I feel like I've lost. An emptiness I can't shake surrounds me in Janette's house. It feels wrong to just abandon it, to walk out now, after what I did. I know I should leave – there's so much left to do, and Martinez would be all too delighted to accuse me of tampering with evidence – but I wander back to Janette's bedroom, to the scrapbook that launched my own investigation just this morning. The collection of evidence that led me to a discovery I'd never thought to look for in all my life. All this time, I had a sister.

The first page is where I stay, the little girl smiling on a porch swing, her two front teeth dominating her grin, her legs bent back in mid-swing, the top half of her craning forward with joyful motion. I hope she had some moments of happiness. Every little girl and boy deserves that, and a loving mother and father, a chance at a childhood full of laughter and play in a healthy family.

It reminds me of what I need to do next. I won't let another little girl live the childhood I did, or the one Janette did. The least I can do is make someone else's life better, and she happens to be someone I love with all my heart. I close the leather cover and let my fingers linger over it. *I love you too, sister.* I have more work to do now, but in my heart, I vow, I'll never forget her. This isn't over.

The female officer who'd stood guard for the policeman who'd ushered me off Tracie's property yesterday is the first to step out of her cruiser when I pull up to her house. She makes a sharp nod of acknowledgement.

"Thank you for coming," I tell her. I'll sure be needing her help explaining what happened. I can hardly believe it myself and Tracie won't be keen on hearing what I have to say, no matter what it is.

As suspected, Tracie is skeptical of every word that comes out of my mouth. She's standing at the door, already in her nightgown, her lips pinched tight, brows knit together in disbelief. But the officer behind me confirms that there has been an arrest in Brad's poisoning – and it wasn't me.

That should have been enough. Tracie uncrosses her arms and starts to protest, but the female officer, maybe a mother herself, steps forward.

"Ma'am, you're under police orders to return the child to her mother," she says, firm. "This has been dragged out long enough."

Tracie shuts her eyes and huffs, not missing her chance at a dramatic display.

"Fine." She's seething, but she complies, leaving the doorway empty for what seems like way too long. When she returns, she's carrying Gracie's carrier, heavy in her arms. Inside, bundled up, is my sweetheart. She's drowsy, her eyes only half-open, her mouth a perfect pout. Tracie extends the handle to me. I grab it, set it down, and unbuckle Gracie right there on the concrete steps.

She wakes, fussing at the disturbance, and then sees who it is.

Momma.

Both her tiny hands open and close contentedly at the loose fabric of my blouse as I hold her over my heart, cupping her head in one hand, letting my thumb brush up and down against the softness of her cheek. I rock her right there, holding her tight.

Mommy's here.

Even the hard-boiled police officer and her partner, the rookie who is working backup this time, can't help but crack a smile. Tears blur my vision. Tracie's dropped a pink diaper bag on the doorstep and shut the door on all of us. Then the front porch light goes out, just in case we didn't get the hint.

But I couldn't care less. I'm with my baby girl again. I know, no matter what happens next, no matter how my next move plays out, I've got her.

And she's got me.

I breathe in the powdery smell of her fuzzy hair and plant a kiss against her forehead. She coos back at me and her fists squeeze tighter.

Mommy's never leaving you again, sweet Gracie girl.

Gracie's fast asleep by the time I pull into the hospital. I keep her in her car seat carrier, stepping quickly. Visiting hours end in a half hour, if he'll even let us in. He hasn't answered any of my texts. Maybe he doesn't have his phone close to him.

Maybe he's not even in the same room.

I have to try.

A tired-looking nurse stops us in the hallway of the sixth floor. *Please don't turn us away.* She huffs and glances up at an oversized clock at the end of the hallway. "Twenty-five minutes until visiting hours are over." She grumbles it; I nod silently and keep moving. On to room 611 before anyone else can stop me, before I can second-guess what I'm about to do.

The light is on, the door cracked. Gracie's seat is heavy in the crook of my arm. I can hear the television running as background noise, but no other sound. I rap against the heavy slab of wood. No answer. At least it's not a no. Slowly, I push against the door, sliding it open inch by inch, finding Brad sitting up, his eyes on the television. A college football game, of course.

"Hey there," I whisper and take two steps forward.

He sits up straighter, a look in his eyes I can't read.

"What are you girls doing here?" The words sound warm, but it comes out flat, like he's either numb or trying to be loving when he just doesn't have it in his heart to welcome me. Maybe it's some kind of medication. Maybe it's not. He knows exactly what we're doing here. I texted him twenty-five times. Maybe the only reason he didn't respond with a command *not* to visit was that I said I had Gracie.

His eyes move down to the baby, eyes shut tight, lashes splayed over the tops of her round cheeks. There's the moment his expression warms up.

My heart sinks a little. He really doesn't want to see me.

Maybe there's still time to change his mind.

I move closer, making baby steps, tentative, and take the square-shaped visitor chair next to the hospital bed. I think of hoisting Gracie up to the mattress, but my arms are already like jelly from carrying her through the seemingly endless hospital corridors.

"I'll wake her up in a second so you can hold her," I say, setting her next to my feet. "I – I want to talk to you for a few minutes first."

Brad arches a brow at me but doesn't say a word. Again, a face I can't read, like he's decided to be unreachable. I could never have even pictured Brad this way, cool toward me.

"I picked Gracie up from your sister's. Tracie and your mom had been watching her." That's not what I came here to talk about. I know it. He knows it too.

"Heard all about that," he says, rubbing his scarred eyebrow. "They talked to me about it."

That stings. Brad wants me to know he was okay with them deciding to keep me away from Gracie. *He's just hurt.* I swallow and lean closer, hoping to make a connection, the right one, hoping he still feels a spark of what he used to for me. I try to lock eyes with him.

There. There it is.

He gazes back, the deep blue eyes you could get lost in for days. There's not a wall there, but a well of genuine feeling. He's trying to hide it, but deep down – past the anger and the frustration – is the tenderness I've missed so much. He looks away from me abruptly, runs fingers through his jet-black hair.

"Brad," I whisper, wanting him back, the real Brad. My Brad.

"You're going to tell me you didn't have anything to do with this?" he accuses.

"I didn't. Honest."

He doesn't answer, just chews his bottom lip and looks at his hands.

"They arrested Janette, tonight."

"I heard that from the police," he says, with a sigh. "I saw that in your messages too."

So he had seen my texts. He'd just chosen not to answer. But he also hadn't told us not to come. He wants this as much as I do. I just have to help him make sense of it. I have to let him into a place I never have before.

"You have to believe I had no idea," I say, my voice cracking no matter how hard I try to control it. I have my own well – or a damn, about to break. "I would never have hurt you like this. I'd never want to hurt you at all. I love you."

I'm crying, but he doesn't reach out to comfort me. He's fighting against looking in my direction at all. I'm too late.

I've lost my chance.

I had the whole world. I had everything I ever could have wanted. And I ruined it. I glance down at Gracie, our amazing little girl, still sleeping peacefully. I dry my face. No matter what, I want things between us to be civil. Maybe that will take time. I'm willing to give Brad that.

But when I look back up at him, tears are glimmering in his eyes too. His face is still angry, but the tears betray him.

"Thing is, I thought I loved you too," he says, his voice scratchy. "But I always knew – I knew there was some part of you that you would always hold back."

The words stop in my throat. A hard lump.

"When this happened … I thought I'd pieced everything together. The missing parts of you – you know I'd never have thought you were capable of something like this. I knew you were hiding something, but …"

"I didn't do it," I protest.

"I know," he says. "But I realized, through all of this, that whatever part of you always held back, always wanted to wait …"

His voice trails off, the thought not complete.

I pull in a deep breath. Now, or never.

I choose now.

"It's time for me to tell you the truth," I say, softly, nodding in acknowledgement to the point he was trying to make. "You may not like what you hear." I add, searching his face, desperately hoping to find love there again. "But you deserve to know. Just – whatever you decide you feel about me, I hope we can get along, for Gracie's sake."

I wait a moment, not getting an answer.

"Okay, that's not at all want I want," I blurt out. "What I want is you, us, the three of us. But I'm so afraid if you know my story … I just don't want to lose you. That's what has always scared me."

The tears well up again as I wait for him. He turns on the bed, to face me. I hold my breath.

"Sarah," he says, clearing his throat, "you can tell me anything."

His expression softens, my first glance at the Brad I've always known, the Brad who loves me, warm and open to what I have to say. My heart skips a beat, I feel the deep flush rise into my cheekbones. I want to just reach up and hold him tight against me – but I go ahead, hopeful and yet so afraid to lose that look, that love, this amazing man. The weight of what I'm risking is almost too much to bear. I can't think of it. I can't stop now.

"I want you to know the real me," I whisper, "every part."

He reaches out a hand, ready to listen. Jesus, I love this man. With all my heart, I love him. I take it, soaking in the familiar feeling of his palm against mine, feeling safer already.

40

ONE YEAR LATER

The shades of dried-up green, brown, and tan meld together in a speedy blur out the window, the landscape opening wider as the city's downtown skyline slips farther out of view, snow-capped peaks rising up behind it.

I've come to like this place, my new home. I thought I was a Southern girl at heart and always would be – but the West is winning me over. I also thought I'd never find a job here. I did – not in politics – but I couldn't stay home all the time. It's just not who I am, and I am, finally, at peace with exactly who I am.

I'm happy to say there's no more mudslinging campaigns, no more Charles Devantes in my life. (Though of course I'll never be okay with what happened to him. He didn't deserve that.) There are no more Bills either, puffed up candidates willing to step over everyone underneath them to climb to the top. Instead, I've found my people. VP of marketing for a sustainable food corporation that supports family farms. I get to travel every once in a while, to see the tight-knit families where our food is sourced, the people we help support. The company is growing like wildfire, with distribution in almost every sizable town from here to the long stretch of Pacific Ocean. That happened because of me. I'm proud; I'm valued. I get to be a change-maker within the company – they actually listen to my suggestions – and with what our company does. And they take care of their people. Fair pay, sane hours, great for families. With this kind of stability, I'd even consider one or two more kids. I grin out at the city behind me. *Salt Lake City, you've been pretty good to me.*

Then I look at the man beside me, the guy I'd follow anywhere. He's lost in thought, looking up ahead for his next turn, but he catches me staring.

"What's up?" He flashes me a smile and extends one hand.

I reach for it and he pulls it up to his lips. A quick kiss.

"You sure you want to do this?" he asks.

"Well, I've already bought the tickets," I say, joking.

"I know. But if you want, we can turn this rig around." He's taken to calling our sleek minivan the rig – maybe to make the idea more palatable. "The next exit would take us back into town. Grab lunch. Spend the day together. Watch a movie, or something."

By *or something*, I know he means a football game. Glass of wine for me, beer for Brad. Sounds like a cozy day for the family.

As much as I'd love to, I know I can't. Gracie and I have somewhere to be, and it's important to me.

"How about when we get home?" I ask, glancing back to see Gracie watching out her window. She's wearing her favorite fuzzy gloves. She turns her head to me and flashes a silly smile that only shows her bottom two teeth, her fine hair in pigtails that swing like puppy ears when she moves.

"Okay, babe," he says, switching on the blinker for the airport exit. "Whatever you think is best is okay with me. Just let me know if you need anything."

At the front of the long airport security line, I give him a deep kiss to let him know just how much I appreciate his support. I don't let go, even though I can feel Gracie starting to wriggle against my hip, until the TSA worker asks me to please keep moving. I step back, a little light-headed. This man still makes me swoon. From the look in his eye, I know he feels the same.

"Buh!" Gracie finally has the appropriate opportunity to use her favorite word: *bye-bye.* "Buh, buh, Da-da," she says, giving him the same eyes-shut, bottom-teeth showing smile and flapping her fingers against her palm.

Brad reaches both his arms around both of us.

The TSA agent gives one more warning.

He smooches Gracie's cheek.

"Love you, little pumpkin."

"Ah joo, Da-da." She does her version of I love you. It makes my heart melt every time. Then I turn my attention to the irritated TSA crew. Next stop: Tennessee.

The front of the first building looks almost like a church, brick and white square columns around the front doors, the Tennessee and American flags waving lazily in a neatly landscaped lawn. But the barbed-wire coils over a twelve-foot-tall chain link fence sort of ruin the illusion. I find an empty visitor's space and park the rental before I look back at Gracie, who was an angel on the plane. Even now, she's staring out the window contentedly, her miniature sneakers tapping against the back seat.

"You ready?"

Her head spins in my direction, pigtails flipping.

I pull in a deep breath, wondering how ready *I* am to do this. But it's time. It's been too long. I unbuckle my sweet pea and slide the straps of a loaded-down tote over my shoulder. Minutes later, bored-looking security guards are dumping out the contents and sifting through them. A couple diapers, a small pack of wipes, a cell phone they'll hold on to for me (because I'd forgotten to put it into a separate plastic bin), and then the one, more peculiar, item. I watch the taller of the two guards lift it up and start flipping through – I guess to make sure I'm not sneaking in any drugs or knives or anything else that could make their lives difficult or break the law. When he's satisfied, he puts it back into my tote with care. I nod at him appreciatively.

Gracie and I step through the metal detector, and Correctional Officer Nancy Herdline is waiting on the other side, a wide-lipped grin on her face.

"Sarah, good to see you again," she says, stepping forward. "Janette will be thrilled."

With my tote bag over my shoulder and Gracie wrapped over my hip, I follow Nancy down the long concrete corridor to the visitor's room.

The narrow wedge of space reminds me of a bathroom stall, white-painted walls to my left and right. There's a small plastic chair waiting for me and a tabletop split between both sides of a wall of glass. The other side, nearly identical, is still empty. Gracie situates herself on my lap and helps me get everything ready, her chubby fingers needing to finger what I set in front of us on the plastic tabletop. Moments later, I catch movement through the narrow window pane in the door on the opposite side. The handle turns and a uniformed guard makes a motion for someone to go ahead.

Janette steps through.

She's fresh faced, her hair pulled back in a tidy ponytail, and she's wearing a tan-colored top and bottom that make me think of nurse scrubs, aside from the letters – I-N-M-A-T-E – stenciled down the leg in heavy block letters.

Before she sits, Janette reaches out to the glass, presses her palm against it. Gracie instinctively reaches out to try to touch through. I lean forward and let her go palm to palm with her aunt for a moment before I take my seat. Janette picks up the receiver on her end, and I do the same. I wonder when all of this will make me feel less anxious. But I know it's worth it. I know I'm doing the right thing.

"You came back." She speaks first.

"Of course I did," I answer. "I promised you I would."

"Well, I know a visit to the Tennessee Prison for Women isn't exactly like a beach vacation for you two," she says, with a nervous chuckle.

"You're my sister." Gracie's swiping at the receiver in my hand, so I have to wriggle just out of her reach. "I want to see you, no matter what," I add, not without a note of sadness.

"Thank you."

I look through the glass into her eyes. I wouldn't say she looks happy, but she does look healthier, like she's learning to make peace with who she is. Her eyes have a softness to them and they absolutely light up when she looks at her niece.

"She's getting bigger and bigger," I hear her voice through the receiver.

"Sure is."

"Love the blonde hair, and the pigtails are adorable."

"I know. I know. I do too. She gets that from our side, you know. I was blonde until about third grade. Brad's had dark hair since the day he was born."

Janette giggles softly. "She's precious."

"Thanks."

I pause a minute and take in one more deep breath. Time to get to it. The guards only give us an hour and we've got a lot of material to cover. I open the scrapbook in front of me and turn to the first few pages.

"Where did we leave off last time?"

Janette leans in closer, peering at the faded photographs of our mother before either of us were born. We didn't get to that part yet – but we will. Baby steps.

"I think," she says, "we were into her first year of college."

"Oh yeah. You're right." I flip to around midpoint and find a snapshot of Mom on a bunk bed in her dorm room. She's wearing a cozy over-sized sweatshirt and a completely ridiculous hat. There's a whole story there, the morning after a birthday celebration for her best friend at the time. I remember Mom telling it to me, laughing until she snorted. Now it's my turn to share and Janette's turn to hear everything I know about the mother she never got to meet.

END OF A MOTHER'S SINS

Do you love gripping psychological thrillers with killer twists? Keep reading to discover exclusive extracts from Jo's *A Perfect Mother* and *A Mother's Lie.*

THANK YOU!

Thank you so much for reading my book. I really hope you enjoyed this psychological thriller. If you did enjoy this book, please remember to leave a review.

You can leave a review on:

a amazon.com/author/jocrow

g goodreads.com/authorjocrow

MAILING LIST

If you enjoyed my book and would like to read more of my work please sign up to my mailing list at:
www.JoCrow.com/MailingList

Not only can I notify you of my next release, but there will be special giveaways and I may even be on the hunt for some pre-release readers to get feedback before I publish my next book!

ABOUT JO

Jo Crow gave ten years of her life to the corporate world of finance, rising to be one of the youngest VPs around. She carved writing time into her commute to the city, but never shared her stories, assuming they were too dark for any publishing house. But when a nosy publishing exec read the initial pages of her latest story over her shoulder, his albeit unsolicited advice made her think twice.

A month later, she took the leap, quit her job, and sat down for weeks with pen to paper. The words for her first manuscript just flew from her. Now she spends her days reading and writing, dreaming up new ideas for domestic noir fans, and drawing from her own experiences in the cut-throat commercial sector.

Not one to look back, Jo is all in, and can't wait for her next book to begin.

You can find Jo on:

f facebook.com/authorjocrow

g goodreads.com/authorjocrow

BB bookbub.com/authors/jo-crow

a amazon.com/author/jocrow

BLURB

A picture is worth a thousand words—and every one is a lie in this gripping psychological suspense thriller.

Laurie Miller is left in utter shock when her husband vanishes without a trace, leaving her with a stack of bills she can't pay. As the lonely days stretch into weeks with no reappearance or body resurfacing, the stay-at-home mom accepts a photography job from a former sorority sister, and current Instagram sensation, and returns to her Milwaukee roots—and the trauma she thought she'd escaped.

Her college days left her with scars no camera can capture, and Laurie's old OCD coping mechanisms creep in as she navigates the frightening new life of single motherhood. But becoming a personal photographer to a popular Instagram-Mom is helping Laurie provide for her daughter like any good mother should. She just never expected her daughter to become the center of so much attention.

As the world of celebrity influencers feed her insecurities, Laurie realizes she's not only lost her husband but now is losing the love of her only child. Arguments ensue. Accidental injuries surface. Allegations of neglect and endangerment are flung her way. But when Laurie's daughter goes missing, a twisted scheme thrusts the past into the glaring light of the present.

And this time, her daughter's life is at stake.

Available 3 March 2020
from www.JoCrow.com

EXCERPT

Chapter one

After what felt like forever, I finally made it to the car and slid in behind the steering wheel, heart jittering, hands clammy, skin prickling with the sensation of being watched. Beside me, on the passenger seat, I set down my purse, my camera, and my car keys.

The darkness outside was pressing up against the windows of the car, bringing with it a chill that made me shiver. The college parking lot was badly lit and although, in the distance, I could see the muted light of the classrooms, the space in between was filled with nothing but darkness. With the tip of my elbow, I pushed the interior lock until it clunked loudly and sealed me in.

Safe. I was safe.

Taking some long, slow breaths – in through the nose, out through the mouth – I reached into the inside zip pocket of my purse and took out a small unlabeled plastic bottle. From it, I shook a quarter-sized dollop of hand sanitizer into my palm. Slowly, I rubbed it into my fingers and then carefully wiped the steering wheel. It was the good stuff, the kind used in hospitals and commercial kitchens. It was unperfumed and left my hands papery, raw, and looking older than they should have done. But it did the job.

After I'd cleaned the steering wheel I started on my camera, carefully wiping the body and the controls then dusting the lens six times counterclockwise with the brush Ben bought me for my birthday. Midway through the seventh swipe, a vicious tap-tap-tap on the window shook my concentration. My breath caught in my throat, my heart thundered, my mouth instantly dried up. But then Jenna's face was pressed up against the glass and she was smiling at me, laughing, gesturing for me to open the door.

I didn't. But I did wind down the window.

"Jenna? Did I leave something behind in class?"

"No, silly. We wondered if you wanted to join us for a drink? Every week you say, 'Maybe next time.' But next week's the last class, so…" She trailed off and shrugged, glancing back at the others who were watching us expectantly.

My fingers tightened around the body of the camera in my lap, my knuckles whitening with the pressure. "I'm so sorry. I can't. Next week, though, I promise."

"Sure," Jenna replied, clearly not buying it. "See you."

I opened my mouth to add an explanation. But I couldn't think of one, and she was already walking away.

Sitting back and trying to steady my breathing, I watched Jenna's silhouette disappear. The interruption meant I had to start my ritual all over again. Hands. Steering wheel. Camera. And by the time I'd finished, everyone else from the evening class had left, mostly on foot.

A couple of times, I'd thought about saying yes when they'd asked me to join them. But then I'd pictured myself in a crowded bar with bodies I didn't know jostling up against me, and too much noise, and floors sticky with who-knows-what, and every time I'd said, "No, thanks. Maybe next time."

The same thing happened when I thought about walking to class and back. It was only a few blocks from home, but now that the evenings were closing in and there were ominous shadows and dark corners to contend with I couldn't make myself do it. Plus, it was the one night of the week I had sole use of the car and I wasn't going to give that up.

More often than not, the class, or the car, or both caused a row between Ben and me, and tonight had been no exception. Ben said he needed to 'take care of something' at work and wanted the Honda, and before I knew it I was waving my arms and raising my voice, even though Fay was right there staring at me with her big watery eyes.

"Ben, you work late every night of the week. This photography class is the only thing I have that's for me. You know how important it is."

"I'm not telling you to stay home. My mom will–"

"I don't want her round here all the time."

"It's not all the time, Laurie. It's one night."

"I need the car."

"Can't you walk?"

"No, Ben. I can't. You're staying home. End of discussion." And with that, I'd grabbed the car keys from the hook, slung my camera over my shoulder and slammed the door triumphantly on my way out.

Now though, my bravado had faded and I was starting to wish I didn't have to return home. Maybe I should have said 'yes' to the drink? At least it would have drawn the evening out a bit, made Ben wonder where I was, given him time to cool down. But I didn't. As usual, I simply couldn't let myself be free. So, I had no choice. I had to go back.

Heading away from the college, I noticed Jenna and the others up ahead. They were laughing. Probably at me. I didn't look at them as I drove past, just stared straight ahead and pretended they weren't there. And soon enough, I was pulling into our neat little street with its neat little houses – the white picket fences, and the porch swings, and the gabled roofs – and I knew I was going to have to apologize to Ben.

I'd overreacted; I shouldn't have yelled, especially not in front of Fay, but lately Ben and I just couldn't seem to be around each other without arguing and it was always me who ended up looking like the irrational one. Somehow, he managed to stay calm even when he was angry. He kept his voice measured and soft, never yelled, never cried or stormed out. Me, on the other hand... my emotions were too quick to escalate and my thoughts too jittery to put into any sensible kind of order. Even if I knew what I wanted to say, it never came out the way I intended it to. And afterwards, no matter how convinced I'd been at the time, I'd start doubting myself and wishing I'd handled things differently.

Walking up the four stone steps that led to our front door, I inhaled deeply through my nose and let the air expand in my chest. I held it there for a moment, counting slowly from ten all the way down to one, then reached into my purse for the house keys. My fingers snaked through its insides – wallet, compact, phone – but couldn't locate the keys so I turned back towards the street and angled myself towards the light coming from next door's porch. Our own porch light went out weeks ago. Ben said it looked like kids had broken it because he'd found shattered glass and a couple of small round stones not far from our welcome mat. But neither of us had gotten around to fixing it.

As I finally found the keys, a car pulled into the street. It had a loud engine, dimmed headlights, and it slowed as it approached me. Something about it made me wrap my arms around myself. I narrowed my eyes but the driver was just a blurry silhouette, obscured by tinted windows.

The car stopped, lingering in the middle of the road. Then, as I turned back towards the house, I felt it start to move again. I glanced over my shoulder. This time it parked right in front of mine and Ben's Honda. Almost directly in front of our house. The headlights went out. The engine stopped. But the door didn't open. And then, just as I was about to run inside to fetch Ben and tell him something weird was going on, it jumped back to life and sped off.

Clutching my purse and my camera close, I tutted at myself. If I mentioned it to Ben he'd tell me it was nothing. I was always suspicious of new cars on the street and nine times out of ten they were simply lost and looking at the house numbers. It was the dark that was making me nervous. I always felt on edge when I was out of the house at night but starting to rant about strange cars watching the house would only cause another argument.

Pull yourself together, Laurie, I breathed, reaching out and unlocking the front door.

Inside, the house was still and dark – quieter than normal. Ben would usually be slumped on the couch with the TV blaring, half-asleep with his laptop open and paperwork all over the floor, but the lounge was empty.

I set my camera down on the kitchen countertop and flicked on the coffee machine. Perhaps Ben was in bed. Sometimes, he crashed out in the basement – his 'creative lair', where he came up with new ideas for the bakery and poured over business plans and cash flow forecasts. But when he did, there was always a telltale sliver of light bleeding out from the gaps around the door frame.

With the absence of any such light, I sighed, scraped my hair back and tied it loosely with the band I kept on my wrist. I hated it when Ben was in bed before me because it meant I had to simply wash, change, and crawl into bed, rather than giving the bathroom a quick once-over with the steam mop and some bleach. Still, at least it would delay any confrontation until morning. Maybe by then I'd have figured out how to say what I wanted to say: *I miss you. I'm lonely. You work too much and you don't share things with me anymore.*

The green light on the coffee machine started blinking, releasing a piping hot stream of extra-strong espresso into a short white cup and nudging me out of my tangle of thoughts. Coffee in hand, I took my camera to the nook under the stairs that had become my workspace and plugged it into the computer. Scrolling through the photographs I'd taken in class, I pinged a few Instagram-worthy shots over to my phone and – not for the first time – wished I'd drummed up enough freelance photography work to pay for one of the models that linked seamlessly with your social media profiles and editing software.

Perhaps I'd ask Ben about it. If he was working all these hours, things at the bakery must be going well. Mustn't they?

I stayed in my nook for a little over an hour, playing with the postproduction lighting effects we'd been learning about and, as always happened when I was engrossed in my photography, I managed to forget everything else and just… be.

Eventually, I glanced at the clock in the corner of the screen. It was getting late and the espresso was wearing off, so I tidied my desk, washed up my coffee cup, tucked my shoes neatly onto the rack in the hall, and padded up the stairs towards mine and Ben's bedroom.

Fay's room was on the left, opposite the family bathroom. She was a light sleeper, so I almost didn't dare nudge her door open to check on her, but something told me I needed to.

The door creaked as I pushed it back far enough for me to stick the upper half of my body into the room. My eyes slowly adjusted to the darkness. I scanned Fay's bed for the familiar bundle of legs and arms cocooned beneath the covers. She had a habit of sliding right down into the middle of the mattress, burying herself so it was almost impossible to tell which bumps were her and which were bundled up blankets. But there was always a foot or an elbow that gave her away.

Available 3 March 2020
from www.JoCrow.com

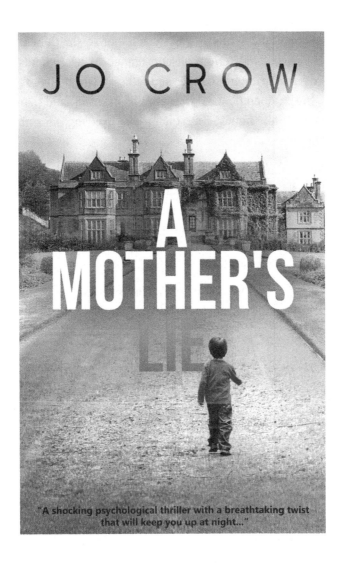

BLURB

When her child's life is at stake, a mother will do anything to save him.

Clara McNair is running out of time to save her son, James. When the two-year-old is diagnosed with a rare form of brain cancer, only an experimental treatment can save his life. She desperately needs money to pay for the surgery, but she'll have to travel back to the site of her darkest memories to get it.

Clara has escaped the demons of her youth—or so she thinks. It's been ten years since the mysterious disappearance of her parents. Widely suspected of murdering her mother and father, Clara fled west to start a new life. Now, a documentary film crew is offering cold, hard cash—enough to pay for James's treatment—in exchange for the sordid secrets of her past.

With no other choice but to delve into a long-ago tragedy, Clara must unravel the lies surrounding that terrible night. Facing hostile gossip, Clara is fighting to clear her name and learn the truth about what really happened. But how far will she go into the dark to save her son—and herself?

Get your copy of **A Mother's Lie**
from www.JoCrow.com

EXCERPT

Chapter One

Dense red clay was pushing between the teeth. Pond mist drifted across the manicured lawns, wisping through the dark eye sockets. Parts of the cranium were shaded a vile yellow-brown, where decomposing leaves clung to its surface like bile expressed from a liver. The jawbone was separated from the skull, its curved row of teeth pointing skyward to greet the rising sun.

Two feet away, closer to the oak tree, other bones were piled haphazardly: a pelvis, high iliac crests and subpubic angle; a femur, caked with dirt, jammed into his empty skull. Sunlight decorated the brittle bones in long, lazy strips and darkened hairline fractures till they blended with the shed behind them.

It was peaceful here, mostly. The pond no longer bubbled, its aerator decayed by time; weed-clogged flowerbeds no longer bloomed—hands that once worked the land long ago dismissed. Fog blanketed the area, as if drawn by silence. Once, a startled shriek woke the mourning doves and set them all into flight.

It was the first time in ten years the mammoth magnificence of the Blue Ridge Mountains had scrutinized these bones; the first song in a decade the mourning doves chorused to them from their high perch.

A clatter split apart the dawn; the skull toppled over as it was struck with another bone.

In a clearing, tucked safely behind the McNair estate, someone was whistling as they worked at the earth. The notes were disjointed and haphazard, like they were an afterthought. They pierced the stillness and, overhead, one of the mourning doves spooked and took flight, rustling leaves as it rose through the mist.

A shovel struck the wet ground, digging up clay and mulch, tossing it onto the growing mound to their left. The whistling stopped, mid note, and a contemplative hum took its place.

Light glinted on the silvery band in the exposed clay—the digger pocketed it—the shovel struck the ground again; this time, it clinked as it hit something solid.

Bone.

A hand dusted off decayed vegetative matter and wrested the bone from its tomb. Launching it into the air, it flew in a smooth arc, and crashed into the skull like a bowling pin, scattering the remains across the grass. With a grunt of satisfaction, the digger rose and started to refill the hole from the clay mound.

When it was filled and smoothed, and the sod was replaced over the disrupted ground, the digger lifted the shovel and strolled into the woods, one hand tucked in a pocket as they whistled a cheery tune lost to the morning fog.

———————

For two days, the bones rested on the grass by the shed, until they were placed, carefully, into forensic evidence bags in a flurry of urgent activity: flashing police cameras, and gawking, small-town rookie officers who'd never seen their like before.

Silence blanketed the McNair estate once more, and the looming, distant mountains stood watch over a town that had seen too little so long ago, and now knew too much.

Get your copy of **A Mother's Lie**
from www.JoCrow.com

Made in the USA
Monee, IL
15 April 2020